# Praise for Ron Faust

"Faust's prose is as smooth and bright as a sunlit mirror."
—*Publishers Weekly*

"Faust's style is laconic, his story engrossing, his
extraordinarily wide variety of characters richly realized."
—Gregory Mcdonald, award-winning author of *Fletch*

"The kind of stunning writer you want to keep
recommending after you discover him."
—David Morrell, author of *Covenant of the Flame*

"Faust is a Homeric storyteller with an eye for the odd
character and a fine gift for Spartan dialogue."
—*Library Journal*

# Dead Men Rise Up NEVER

Ron Faust

A DELL BOOK

DEAD MEN RISE UP NEVER
A Dell Book / May 2004

Published by
Bantam Dell
A Division of Random House, Inc.
New York, New York

ISBN 0-553-58655-6

Manufactured in the United States of America
Published simultaneously in Canada

OPM 10 9 8 7 6 5 4 3 2 1

To Dave and Ellen Hamil

# Dead Men Rise Up NEVER

# Part I
# Spirals

# One

Coils of cigarette smoke hung like spiral nebulae in the dimness.

Near the door, an old man was talking about a cat that he claimed had walked twelve hundred miles to return to its home. Yes sir, from Chicago to Bell Harbor in six months. The cat's name was Bucky.

The yeasty-smelling room was narrow and deep: A black mahogany bar ran two-thirds the length of one wall, with booths and tables opposite, and in the rear section there were pool tables and electronic games and a massive, ticking jukebox.

I walked to the end of the bar and ordered a beer from a fat man in a dirty apron.

"Hot," the man said.

"Very," I said, although it was cool in the bar.

A few stools away, a slattern in pink slacks was loudly saying, "Sure, I believe in fair trials for the innocent. But why waste all that time and money giving fair trials to the guilty?"

On a shelf behind the bar, there were jars containing Polish sausages and jalapeño peppers and hard-boiled eggs. And on the wall were some trophies: lacquered game fish, a marble-eyed deer head, a bearskin, and a dusty raptor—hawk or small eagle, I couldn't tell.

"Burn them in Old Sparky," said the woman who championed fair trials for the innocent.

Two young men were playing pool in the back section. "You hold that cue stick like a nun," one of them said. In this light the speaker's tightly kinked mass of dull red hair looked like a sponge.

I ordered another draft beer and two of the sausages. The bartender removed the sausages with his fingertips and served them on a paper napkin.

The pool players moved in and out of the cone of light, absorbing and losing color and definition; then the straight white thrust of a cue stick and the clicking, swiftly changing geometry of the balls. The patterns reminded me of broken molecular models.

"Where'd you learn to play pool?" the redhead asked his opponent. "In the convent?"

The sausages were too vinegary, but I ordered another and a hard-boiled egg.

"We got pizza," the bartender said.

"Oh, God, don't eat the pizza here," the woman in the pink slacks said.

"Irene," the fat bartender said. "Irene—"

"The pizza here'd gag a vulture." She was drinking shots with beer back. Her lipsticked mouth was twice as big as her natural one.

I walked over to the pool table and put two quarters in the slots. "Play the winner?"

"Sure, Fish," the cocky redhead replied. He was about

twenty-five, not tall but powerfully built. He wore jogging shoes without socks, cutoff jeans, and a fishnet shirt. I could see tattoos beneath the shirt.

"Frank makes his pizza out of cardboard and vomit."

"Shut up, Irene," the bartender said. "Shut up or get out."

"I was only joking the man."

"This is a business."

"Sure, Frank. I'm sorry. I like your pizza."

The redhead called his pocket and sank the eight ball on a fine table-length bank. "Rack 'em, Fish," he told me.

His opponent wandered into the bar section. I racked the balls tightly, hung my suit jacket on a hook, loosened my tie, and selected a reasonably straight stick.

"I break," the redhead said. "Eight ball. Call your shot and pocket." He leaned over the table for a moment and then straightened. "Oh, do you want to play for something?"

"Sure. Let's play for a beer."

"Can you afford it? Look, let's make it for five bucks a game."

"All right."

"Otherwise it's a drag, you know?" He had a redhead's complexion, and his eyebrows and lashes were so pale as to be hardly visible. The membranes rimming his eyes were inflamed.

He sank a solid on the break and then ran three more before deliberately missing an easy shot. I ran five stripes before scratching on the nine.

"Tough," he said. He sank the six, but then blew an easy bank on the ten. "Bitch," he said to the ball.

He let me win the first game. I figured that he had shot about half as well as he was able. He passed me a crumpled five-dollar bill.

I stuffed the five into my shirt pocket and offered my hand. "Daniel Shaw," I said.

He looked skeptically at my hand and then finally clasped it with an I'm-boss power grip. "Gary."

"Nice meeting you, Gary."

"Yeah," he said. "Break, Fish."

I went over to the bar and got another beer. The fat bartender and the few customers at that end of the bar regarded me with the blandly sincere expressions that are meant to conceal pity and contempt.

"You shoot pool real good, honey," Irene said dryly.

I returned to the table and chalked my cue stick. "You a salesman?" Gary asked.

"In a way."

"Yeah? Break."

I won that game fairly easily and he said, "Look, you got ten bucks of mine. What say we play a game for fifty?"

"Fifty dollars?"

"No, fifty matchsticks."

"Well, I don't know."

"You shoot pool lots better than me, but maybe I'll get lucky. The most you can lose is forty bucks." He moved close to me, a not very subtle act of intimidation. I could smell his sour sweat and cheap aftershave. The pupils of his eyes were dilated to half the circumference of the irises. It was dim in the room, but not that dim.

"I guess so," I said.

"Money up front." He withdrew a crisp fifty from his wallet and placed it on the rim of the table. I matched it with two twenties and a ten.

"We'll flip a coin for break."

"It's my break, Gary. I won the last game."

"This here's a new game and it's for fifty dollars. It's only fair. The guy what breaks has got the advantage. We'll flip a coin."

"Put two quarters in the slots and stand back."

I put my weight behind the stick, drove it hard through the cue ball. There was a loud click and the triangle of colored balls burst apart, rebounding off the rails, kissing, deflecting. Three went into pockets, two solids and a stripe. I studied the layout for a while (Gary impatiently tapping his stick on the floor and hissing through his teeth), calculating the order and difficulty of the shots. If I didn't run out, he would.

I chose the solids, ran four of them, had a difficult shot on the ten—a very delicate cut—made that, and left the cue ball in good position for the eight.

"That's a natural scratch," he said, trying for a cheap psych-out.

"Eight in the corner," I said.

Gary moved close to me again, almost touching my right arm, and he bumped me lightly on the stroke, but the ball went in.

I picked up the money, returned my stick to the rack, and put on my suit jacket.

"Where do you think you're going?"

"Your landlady said you might be here, Gary. I have something for you." I withdrew the long envelope from my inside jacket pocket and held it out to him. There was an impressive gold seal on the front.

"What's that?"

"It's a court summons for Gary Tolliver."

"Yeah? Well, you take it and stuff it, pal."

I dropped the envelope on the pool table. "It's yours."

"No, it ain't, man, it's yours. Take it with you when you go."

"The subpoena has been served in front of witnesses. The rest is up to you. But I advise you to make your court date."

"I done nothing wrong."

"Good for you."

"What does that thing *mean*? What did I do?"

"You know that better than I, Gary."

"No, I don't, man."

"Read the subpoena. You can read, can't you?"

"This is unconstitutional," he said.

"It isn't an indictment, you aren't going to trial. Yet. You're just ordered to appear before a grand jury that is investigating certain crimes."

"What crimes?"

"It's about dope, Gary."

"I don't know nothing about dope."

"Then maybe you'll learn something." I started to leave.

"Take that with you. I don't want it. I never saw it."

"Hire a lawyer, kid."

"You son of a bitch," he said softly, furiously. His face was flushed and appeared swollen around the eyes and mouth. He held his arms away from his sides. "Are you a cop?"

"I'm considered an officer of the court while doing this job."

"Does that mean you're a cop?"

I had been warned about Gary Tolliver's background of violence. Assault, assault and battery, assault with a deadly weapon, felonious assault . . .

"Be careful," I said. I thought about hitting him before he hit me; I could lie about it later, through all of my teeth.

But then he seemed to deflate. Probably he thought I was a cop or a lawyer from the prosecutor's office.

"I ought to knock your fucking head off," he said, but the moment had passed and he was only saving face.

On the way out I dropped a twenty-dollar bill on the bar. "Drinks on me, Frank. Take good care of my friends." Behind me I could hear Irene crow, "Who was that masked man?" And then she burst into siren wails of laughter.

The swampy heat was brutal after I'd spent forty-five minutes in the air-conditioned bar. Sour beer rose and stung my throat. Palm fronds hung limply, sunlight flared on store and automobile windows and ignited specks of mica in the sidewalk. Down the street the marquee of a porn movie theater advertised a sleazy twin bill: *Schoolgirl's Holiday* and *Bottoms Up*.

My van had been reasonably clean when I'd parked it at the curb, but a Jamaican kid had smeared it front to back with a greasy rag.

"I watched your car," he said. "I cleaned your car, man."

I gave him a dollar. "Thanks, son."

He stared at the bill, spat twice on the van's door, said, "Shithead," and stalked away.

There was a public telephone stand on the corner. Graffiti had been scrawled over the acoustic panels: grossly exaggerated genitalia, a misspelled dirty limerick, and, whimsically, the words *Oedipus loves Mom* enclosed in a valentine heart. And in a feminine hand, *Call Rachel for a real good time.* I wondered if Rachel herself had composed the advertisement.

My office telephone rang six times before my time-share secretary answered with a chirpy "Hi!"

"Is that how you answer a business telephone, Candace?"

"What? Oh. I'm sorry, Mr. Shaw. I forgot."

"Have there been any calls?"

"Oh, yes, lots of calls."

When she did not elaborate, I said, "Any for me?"

"No. I don't know. Wait. Yes, Mr. Petrie called. Do you have his number?"

"I do. Thank you, Candace. You've earned your nap."

Thomas Petrie was a hotshot trial lawyer who had a suite of offices on the top floor of the Dunwoody Building. He was a nationally ranked fencer with the foil; a wine-and-cheese snob; the city's most eligible bachelor, according to a society columnist; and a brilliant defender of the lost and despised, as long as they were also rich. I'd heard that he was a buzzsaw during cross-examinations; hostile witnesses left the courtroom in small quivering pieces.

"Shaw, you runaway dog," Petrie said when his secretary put him on the line. "Where are you?"

"Southside."

"Good. That's on the way."

"On the way to where, Tom?"

"Key Largo. I have a job for you. You aren't working, are you?"

"I am, in fact."

"Glad to hear it. Now you can afford a haircut. But you have time to locate a man named Peter Falconer, got that? Age twenty-nine, thirty in a day and a half, Friday, last known address in care of West Bight Marina, Key Largo. He lived on a houseboat there until about two weeks ago. Present whereabouts unknown, but he's got to be somewhere down in the keys. How far can you go in a houseboat? He's an oddball, but a well-bred and most fortunate oddball."

"What do I tell him when I find him?"

"Tell the son of a bitch that there are important papers he must sign. In thirty-three hours his inheritance kicks in."

"A substantial inheritance?"

"You'd drool. He's going to be stinking rich. He knows it. I don't know why he hasn't got in touch with me. Tell him to phone Thomas Petrie, no other. Be discreet. Are you wearing your one good suit? Tell him to phone me or, better yet, drive up here to see me. Or, Christ, I'll take the papers down there. The mountain will go to Mohammed. Find him."

"All right. I'll do it tomorrow."

"Did you say you're immediately driving down to Largo?"

"Tomorrow."

"That's what I like most about you, Shaw; you've got fire, you've got thrust. That's why I recommend you to all the lawyers around here. 'Daniel Shaw,' I say, 'he isn't just a penny-ante process server, a paralegal drudge—you can trust the man with important jobs.' "

"Tom, I've got a class at night school this evening."

"On what?"

"Torts."

"Torts. I can't believe it. Torts."

"All right," I said. "I'm on my way."

"Great. Don't stiff me on the bill, Shaw. I mean, you can cheat fifteen percent on the expenses, everyone does that, but I refuse to pay for champagne and whores. Keep in touch. Call me at my home if you must. And be nice to Falconer, maybe a touch servile. He isn't a bum anymore. He's a fantastically rich man now. Powerful. An aristocrat."

"I'll tug at my forelock," I said, and I hung up.

I put more coins in the telephone, punched in Rachel's number, and listened to the electronic twitter. No answer. Maybe she was off somewhere having a real good time.

Gary Tolliver was out on the sidewalk, inspecting my van. He checked the license plates—they were not issued by any agency of government—glanced in a window, and saw that the rear had been rigged as a camper and was littered with fishing and sailing gear. There were no police or legal association stickers on the windshield. So, a dented, rusting, five-year-old Dodge van.

Clearly—I could see the conclusion on his face—clearly,

the owner of this vehicle could not be an important or dangerous man.

He smiled when he looked up and saw me walking down the sidewalk; a mean, mirthless smile, a bully's leer. I was five or six inches taller but our weights were about the same, one-ninety or so. He was a thug, a brawler, a head-butter, an eye-gouger, a testicle-ripper. Stupid pride made me continue walking toward him.

I had been briefed on his criminal record; why hadn't I worn my gun? I was authorized to carry a gun while doing this job. Somewhere nearby, a door slammed and a woman screamed abuse in Spanish. Two black women, holding bags of groceries, were chatting on the far corner.

"Hi, Gary," I said, and I tried to kick off his kneecap, but I missed, striking his thigh. It hardly moved him. He put all of his weight and strength into the kind of punch that can kill a man if it lands square. I partly blocked it with my left forearm, absorbing most of the power, but the remaining force snapped my head back. Panicky, I hit him with a left jab, hooked off the jab, threw a straight right that hit his forehead. The impact traveled up my wrist and forearm like an electrical shock. My right hand was prickly numb.

We both hesitated for an instant, a little confused by this sudden violence, our ferocity. I could taste blood. His mouth was bleeding too.

He advanced cautiously. He respected me now; he had learned that I could throw a punch. He saw that I was acquainted with violence.

I backed down the sidewalk. When he came too close I jabbed him stiffly once or twice and then slipped away before he could counter. Some teenagers had appeared and were watching us from the street, jeering, whistling. Gary aimed a kick at my groin, missed, but recovered his balance before I could move in. A lump had risen on his forehead. His nose was bleeding. Our blood splashed on the sidewalk—red coins. The suit jacket constricted my movements. My leather shoe soles did not give me good traction on the cement. And I worried about my tie; if he managed to grab my tie I was as good as hanged. Sweat burned my eyes. We both were breathing hard. He was a dozen years younger, though. He lunged; I jabbed twice, hooked off the jab, then he grabbed me and we were wrestling, each trying to trip and throw the other (*Don't go down,* I commanded myself, *for Christ's sake, don't go down*), and then I lifted my knee once, twice, driving it into his groin, and it was all over. He doubled up on the sidewalk. He could not breathe. Veins on his neck swelled. He finally caught his breath, sobbed, sobbed again, and then crooned through a froth of saliva and blood.

A crowd had gathered, adults as well as children. They were silent. They watched me speculatively. I walked past them to my van, unlocked the door, got in, started the engine, and drove slowly down the street. In the rearview mirror I could see that most members of the crowd were still watching the van as I turned the corner.

I parked a few blocks away. My lower lip was split, my tongue had been cut, but no teeth had been broken. I removed my torn jacket and threw it in the back, and took off my bloody shirt. There were some casual clothes in a locker. My right hand was swollen and numb. Worse than the pain was my disgust. I had become as much the savage as Gary Tolliver, and it didn't help much to realize that there hadn't been a very good alternative. It might have been me lying on that filthy sidewalk, except that he would still be kicking me in the liver and spleen. Gary Tolliver was in serious trouble. He had, in effect, assaulted an officer of the court. But then, sociopaths like Gary were always in serious trouble, and so too were those innocents who had the misfortune to cross their paths at the wrong time.

I drove to Interstate 75, turned right, and drove south toward the Florida Keys, wondering if maybe this Peter Falconer might be another form of trouble.

# TWO

"Falconer," the dockmaster said, flipping through a tray of index cards. He was a wiry ex-Navy man of about sixty. The tattoo of a mythic serpent coiled around his left forearm. His shack was on the end of the main pier of the Coral Village Yacht Club. Webbed reflections of the water were projected onto the walls and ceiling. Halyards tapped Morse-like signals against aluminum masts, and from somewhere out near the cut I could hear the remote insect buzz of an outboard.

"Falconer, Falconer, Falconer . . ."

Yesterday afternoon and evening I had visited the marinas on Largo, Long, and Islamorada Keys. Starting early this morning, I had worked my way down to Marathon.

"Here it is, Falconer, Peter J-for-Jason. He owns a houseboat named *Deep Six*. Some name. It's an old tub, not much more seaworthy than a stone. Is he your man?"

"Yes."

"I remember him now. So many people come in and out

that it's hard to remember all the names. I mostly remember faces and boats."

"Is he still registered here?"

"Yeah, he keeps his tub over on C-dock. C-Nine. But he's not at the marina now. Do you know the waters hereabout?"

"Some."

"He went out to the Mosquito Keys for a few days. I remember he asked me what he could expect in the way of weather, and he stocked up on supplies at the store."

"Did he leave alone or did he have guests?"

"I don't know. He left a few days ago, on my day off."

"I guess I'll run out to the Mosquito Keys and see if I can find him. Do you have a boat I can rent?"

"A dandy little inboard fishing boat. I'll have one of the guys get it ready for you and bring it around. That's seventy dollars per hour, two-hour minimum. We take all major credit cards."

"What kind of guy is Falconer?"

"You don't know him?"

"I'm just a messenger."

He studied my split, puffy lip for a time, and then said, "Women are getting bigger, stronger, faster . . ."

"What did you think of Falconer?"

"Or maybe you hit yourself in the face with your swollen right hand."

"Falconer?"

"He seemed all right, what I saw of him. He's been here only a couple of weeks. I found him civil, but not friendly, if you know what I mean. Cool, standoffish. But the girls liked him. Jesus, did the girls like him. Girls coming here at all hours of the day and night."

I thanked him, waited for him to process my credit card, and went outside onto the dock. The water was smooth, hardly wrinkled, but the array of yachts lifted and gently heaved on the incoming tide. Insolent seagulls preened on posts, a cormorant perched on a buoy hung out his wings to dry, and a pair of brown pelicans beat slowly toward the gulf. Nearby, four deckhands dressed in nautical livery—white bell-bottom trousers and horizontally striped T-shirts— mopped the teak deck and polished the bronze of a ten-million-dollar motor yacht named *Fortitude.*

I grinned at them as I passed, and one said, "Up yours too, pal."

I walked to the parking area, climbed into the back of my van, and changed into sneakers and cutoff jeans. It was hot now and would be an inferno later in the day. I collected my mask, fins, and snorkel—I intended to paddle around the reef for an hour or so if I failed to find Falconer.

The fishing boat was ready when I returned to the dock. I cruised out of the yacht basin and then turned into the channel that would take me northwest to the Mosquito Keys. It was a luminous morning, painted in garish neon colors, the sort of day that increases both your love of life and your fear of death. Beauty always hurts a little. The water was clear and varied in color according to the depth and composition of the bottom; there were lime greens and yellow-greens, pastel blues, indigo, ultramarine, purple. It was like that: glowing sea and towering cumulus clouds stained by reflections off the water and a nuclear sun that burned a hole in the smooth fabric of sky.

I'd bought a six-pack of Bass Ale at the marina store, and I cruised slowly, sipping ale and looking over the side. The water was not deep, maybe twenty feet, and as clear as I'd ever seen. Scattered over the sandy bottom were sponges, sea fans, clumps of staghorn, elkhorn, and star coral, and the debris left by humans too: old lobster traps, an automobile tire, a half-buried anchor with its frayed twist of cable. And I saw fish: snappers, grunts, small rays, and silver barracuda poised like drawn arrows. Then I passed over an enormous turtle that had somehow, for perhaps a century, eluded the soup pot.

After thirty minutes I saw smears of dark green on the horizon. Vegetal green seemed an alien color here among the infinity of blues.

The *Deep Six* was anchored on the lee side of the largest of the five mangrove islands. She was about fifty feet long and fifteen wide, with a rooftop sundeck and a rear deck space shaded by a canvas awning. A chrome railing enclosed the walkway around the cabin, and a ladder led up to the roof deck. *Deep Six* was built of aluminum on steel pontoons. She appeared derelict.

I cut my engine and drifted in. "Hello," I called. "Is anybody aboard?" I tied my bow line to one of the houseboat's cleats. "Falconer?" The curtains were drawn. I hadn't seen any other boats in the vicinity. It was a little after ten-thirty. Maybe he was ashore on one of the islands.

I opened a bottle of oil. The sun was hot on my back and shoulders. A mosquito found me. The sound of impacting wavelets resonated inside the pontoons; in choppy seas they would bang like kettle drums.

"Peter?"

*Deep six* was sailor's slang for burial at sea, and a strange and unlucky name for a boat—what sort of man would choose it?

I climbed over the flaky chrome railing to the houseboat's deck. Maybe Falconer was ill; maybe there had been an accident. The cabin door was unlocked.

The bed was a fold-down attached to the opposite wall and directly across from the doorway. At first, because I was half expecting something unpleasant, and because of the interior dimness, I thought it was a slain child on the bed. For an instant it looked human, though grotesquely so, freakish. I could smell blood and a funky animal reek. I approached, and gradually my eyes adjusted to the light. The thing's throat had been slashed to the vertebrae. It was naked and pink, with long ears, a stringy beard, four-inch horns, and deformed legs ending in shiny black cloven hooves. All of its body hair had been shaved except for the chin tuft, a patch on the crown of its head, and more around the genitals. The eyes were gelid. Teeth were exposed in a mocking goat sneer.

It occurred to me that I had been careless. There were two inside doors; one led into a cabin packed with expensive diving and photographic gear, the other opened into the head. I checked a couple of lockers big enough to conceal a man, then went outside and ascended to the rooftop deck.

All five of the Mosquito Keys were visible from that height. Here and there a palm arched above the dense mangrove thickets. This was a wildlife refuge, and there were many birds about; I saw herons, egrets, cranes, terns, kites, an osprey, and several vultures, and none seemed agitated. Probably no human was ashore—at least not a living one.

There was a white sail far to the west and, beyond it, halfway below the horizon, a tanker.

I remained for ten minutes, inhaling the clean salt and iodine odors of the sea, then descended.

The layout below was simple. The wheel and control panel were forward, beneath a long windshield that could be cranked open for ventilation. There was a dinette table with benches on both sides, a sofa that could be opened into a double bed, a wicker divan with matching chairs, stereo and television units, some shelves of books and videos, cabinets, and lockers.

A counter, lined with stools, separated the galley from the living space. There were a few dirty dishes and glasses in the sink. On a shelf I found a pair of rubber gloves of the kind you wear to protect your hands while washing dishes. I put them on. Inside the refrigerator I found beer, soft drinks, salami, cheese, bacon, eggs, steak, and a gutted four-pound sea bass wrapped in wax paper. Everything was still cool even though the electrical system had apparently been running off the batteries for some time. I opened the drawers and overhead cabinets: canned foods, plates, utensils, kitchen odds and ends, a wine rack with half a dozen bottles lying horizontally.

I returned to the main cabin. It was clean and orderly except for the carcass. There was no blood spattered around; the ram had been killed elsewhere, perhaps on one of the keys. The goat was decomposing in the heat. Peter Falconer kept a tidy ship except for the odd sacrificial goat.

The television, mounted on a shelf so that it could be viewed from the bed, was connected to a VCR. I got it working and the screen filled with writhing flesh, coupled bodies—an orgy in full color and performed to the *1812 Overture.* Bells were ringing and cannons exploding and bodies convulsing. Crescendo, climax, silence. The camera panned over what seemed like an acre of human flesh. Motionless now, exhausted, the orgiasts looked like corpses strewn over a battlefield. I turned off the machine.

The charts were kept in a drawer beneath the control panel. They covered all of the waters around the Florida Keys as well as the Marquesas and Dry Tortugas. I found a large-scale chart of the Mosquito Keys and unfolded it. The depths were given in feet, and all the numbers were moderate except for a circular area about fifty yards in diameter. There, the depth reached sixty feet.

It was a sinkhole, a cylindrical pit in the limestone bottom. They were fairly common on the Florida peninsula and in the surrounding waters. I had seen it (an indigo blur among the pale blues and greens) from the roof deck. In the Yucatán such sinkholes were called *cenotes*. The ancient Mayans had thrown sacrificial victims into the Sacred Cenote at Chichén-Itzá.

I went outside, started the fishing boat's engine, and headed toward the channel between Big Mosquito and Palm Key. The reef was clearly visible for about one hundred yards and then abruptly vanished beneath me. I cut the engine and let the boat drift. It was silent and very hot. The tanker had slipped below the horizon; the sail was now just a speck of white. I opened a can of warm ale and lost most of the contents in an eruption of foam.

I was not eager to go over the side. The goat had spooked me. My former jobs had taught me something about criminal violence. Men like Gary Tolliver were not a mystery. Most of the men on death row were not mysteries, not really. I half understood murders for profit and revenge, sleazy passion and cheap honor, the murders of careful planning and sudden rage, domestic killings and barroom stabbings, dope murders, even the ideological assassinations. But I did not understand the kind of thinking that the goat represented. I could not fathom the thrill killings, the torture murders committed by cultists and sexual psychopaths, the mystical nihilists. They were crimes of absolute negation and absolute pride. So far I had found only a ritually slain goat, shaved and almost comically obscene, but I was sure—very much afraid—that I would find human victims. And maybe the goat people were still around.

I pulled on my fins, rubbed spit on the inside of the mask's lens to reduce fogging, rinsed it, and went over the side. The sea was lukewarm here. It would be cooler below the thermocline. I bit down on the rubber mouthpiece of my snorkel and finned out over the hole. The water was as clear as the air for five or six feet and then gradually acquired color: the palest of golds, a green-gold, jade green, and then the progression of blues to purple. I could not clearly see the bottom, just the variations in color, obscure pale shapes, a confused abstraction. A school of small fish, flashing silver bellies when they panicked at my shadow, passed below.

I sucked air in through the snorkel and then dived, kicking hard, arrowing down into the deepening shades of blue. I halted at about forty feet, my free-dive limit, and swam laterally over the bottom.

There, a pale form, obscure but recognizably human, female, rounded breasts and the curve of hip and waist, and long black hair coiling and uncoiling like smoke in the current. She appeared to be anchored to the bottom. Anchored but erect and straining desperately toward the surface, toward light, air, life. For an instant I irrationally believed that she might still be alive. And just before turning and finning upward toward the blurry lens of light, I saw another one, another woman, a twin of the first.

I returned to the houseboat. The goat gleamed moistly, as if it were perspiring, and I imagined that the odor of decay was stronger now. There was a liter of scotch whiskey in a cupboard. I put on the rubber gloves, poured a few ounces of whiskey into a glass, and went to the radio. I radioed the Coast Guard, gave my location, told them some of what I had discovered, and advised them to notify the appropriate police agencies. And to bring divers.

I took the whiskey up the ladder and drank it while pacing the perimeter of the sundeck. The *Deep Six* dipped slightly beneath my weight. There were no boats in sight now, no movement on or among the islands. For a moment I felt centered in a vacant blue desert, impaled by silence, invaded by light, the legatee of the murdered women's dread and anguish.

# Three

Within half an hour the boats began arriving—cabin cruisers, sail yachts, outboards, a rusty shrimper, a howling pack of jet-ski boats. It was silent, the sea was empty, and then suddenly I saw them coming like scavengers to carrion. No doubt some boaters had monitored my radio conversation with the Coast Guard. Word had spread. Some of the boats had probably been at sea, fishing or cruising; others had come out from Marathon and the other keys. They circled the houseboat, gawking at it and me. A few passengers took photographs. I ignored their shouted demands for information. I cursed and threatened those who attempted to board the *Deep Six*.

The Coast Guard arrived in a forty-foot cutter, followed by police from the Monroe County Sheriff's Department, the Marathon municipal police, and finally investigators and crime-lab people from the Florida State Police. By that time there were at least two dozen vessels gathered around the Mosquito Keys. One late-arriving cabin cruiser had been chartered by a video news unit from a Miami television station.

The police were suspicious of my split lip and swollen hand. How did that happen? When? Who? They relaxed a bit when I told them that I had been assaulted while serving a subpoena; relaxed further when they learned of my background as an officer, for ten years, in the U.S. Army's CID—Criminal Investigation Division. There were some scowls when I mentioned that I now worked as a paralegal and was studying law at night school. They did not like lawyers much. But I qualified as a provisional member of the club, cop emeritus, maybe not wholly reliable but still one of the boys. The reeking, cryptic goat was the source of crude wit. When one of the technicians emerged from the houseboat, he was accused of enjoying sexual congress with the carcass. There was talk of a barbecue later.

"Hey, *cabrito* is good food," a sheriff's deputy named Ted Arranga said.

We stood on the deck of the Coast Guard cutter and stared out at the dark circle of water. Police divers, late to arrive and slow to prepare, had been down five or ten minutes. The sea was smooth except for the periodic eruption of bubbles. We all waited. The mob on the pleasure boats was quiet now, tensely expectant, greedy.

And then we saw a pale shape rising toward the surface, a blur at first, accelerating as it rose and beginning to spiral. Flesh tones, female form, growing larger and spiraling faster as it ascended, and then it broke through the surface, lifting clear out of the water, falling and buoyantly floating faceup. There was complete silence for perhaps ten seconds, and then the gawkers cheered derisively.

"Mildred," Arranga said. "I thought she was home in the closet."

It was one of those life-size, anatomically correct inflatable mannequins that, in magazine advertisements, were called "The Lonely Man's Companion."

The boat chartered by the TV station eased in closer to photograph the mannequin. Spectators cheered and shouted vulgarities. None of the cops would look at me.

"Wait," Arranga said. "Here comes Mildred's sister."

Another had appeared below in the depths; pale flesh tones, large round breasts, blond wig-hair streaming. The interior air pressure expanded as the mannequin ascended through layers of blue and green and crystal, impelling it faster and initiating a twisty spiral. It too launched itself into the air before falling back and floating serenely near its brunette sister.

"They don't talk sass," Arranga said, "they never have bad headaches, you don't have to pretend to like their cooking."

One by one the rubber mannequins spiraled up out of the sinkhole until there were seven of them placidly bobbing on the surface. Most smiled at the sky; a couple gazed downward into the abyss.

The policemen competed to think up witty names for the collection of "girls." Arranga's were best: the "feminoid flotilla" and "pneumatic nymphs."

And then two divers appeared with a corpse, a woman, pale and naked like the sex mannequins but real, piteously real. The dolls did not seem funny now; they were obscene, unforgivable insults to life.

"Aw, hell," Arranga said.

# Four

I arrived back in Bell Harbor late in the afternoon. My patio apartment was stuffy and smelled of bananas that had gone bad in the heat, and the angled sunlight illuminated dust motes that swarmed like gnats. There were no messages on the telephone recorder. I showered away my sweat and sticky saltwater residue, changed into tennis shorts, sneakers, a polo shirt, picked up my packages, and left the apartment.

The Bell Harbor Marina was a quarter mile from my place. I kept my sailboat there and an old wooden rowboat that Herman, the dockmaster, called "a primitive exercise machine."

He was standing at the end of the central pier, smoking a cigar and hefting a boat hook as if it were a javelin. Herman was a former NFL defensive tackle, now fat and bald, and a blow to his throat in the old days had reduced his voice to a strained croaking.

"What happened to your lip?" he asked.

"I got curious and a guy hit me."

"Yeah?" He grinned. "What's this I hear, Daniel?"

"About what?"

"About you becoming an actor."

"It's a small part at that little theater over on Sunset," I said. "I play a burglar."

"Yeah?" Herman said, grinning on both sides of his cigar. "I bet you play it good."

He helped me launch the skiff and stood watching as I fitted the oars into the locks and began rowing out toward the lighthouse. My swollen right hand ached with every stroke. The bay was calm. Each anchored boat cast a ghost replica of itself on the water's surface. Seagulls mewed like lost kittens.

The lighthouse was four hundred yards from shore. Over my left shoulder I could see the stone blockhouse and the conical tower, whose circle of glass blazed with the late-afternoon sunlight. It was ninety-five years old but hadn't been used as a lighthouse for the last fifty, and was now more a navigational hazard than aid.

Martina Karras had bought it cheap at an auction of state property and spent three times the purchase price in restoring it. It was a pretty little lighthouse that now appeared on postcards and calendars and in travel-magazine layouts. The Bell Harbor town council had recently initiated legal action to seize the lighthouse by right of eminent domain; it had become a precious community totem since Marty restored it. Before, it had been regarded as a derelict stone heap that required prompt demolition.

I rowed into the shallow water in the lee of the reef. The lighthouse was a stone heap, though no longer derelict. There once had been a small cay here, with palms and wild-flowers and a perfect beach, but a hurricane had scoured the cay in the early sixties, and all that remained was the bare slab of limestone reef, piles of smooth ballast rocks, the blockhouse, and the peppermint-striped tower.

Marty's little cabin cruiser, *Puck*, was tied alongside the stone quay. Notices had been painted on the rock, hand-lettered by Martina: KEEP OFF and NO DOCKING and PRIVATE PROPERTY. The problem, of course, was that there were many men in the world—men like Gary Tolliver—who regarded all such warnings as invitations. I secured my skiff behind *Puck*, collected the packages, and climbed the mossy steps to the level reef top.

Martina was standing in the doorway of the house, leaning against the frame, her arms folded. She wore jeans and a bright tie-dyed shirt knotted at the waist. Her feet were bare. Her long foxy hair needed combing.

" 'Home is the sailor,' " she said, " 'home from the sea . . .' "

" 'And the hunter home from the hill," I said, completing the Robert Louis Stevenson epitaph.

"What's in the boxes?" she asked.

"You'll see."

"Not more guns, I hope."

I followed her into what had once been the quarters of the lighthouse keeper and was now Marty's home, studio, and sanctuary.

"I've got to fillet a fish," she said, heading for the kitchen space. "Make yourself a drink. Make me one—gin, tonic, and lime."

The compact kitchen was at the south end of the rectangular room, enclosed by a crescent-shaped marquetry counter and its five stools. On the other side of the counter there was a round dining table, which she rarely used, and then the living space with its old, comfortable furniture, mostly rattan, a sofa that converted into a double bed, a coffee table fashioned from a teak hatch cover, bookshelves, and a smoke-blackened fireplace. Reed mats were scattered over the floor. The bar was the empty cabinet shell of a massive old stereo–television console. A bowl of ice and a plate of limes lay on a tarnished silver tray.

"Do you like *huachinango Veracruzano*?" Marty called.

"I like the *huach*—the *huachinango*, but *Veracruzano* gives me gas."

She laughed.

On the north wall was a heavy oak door with iron hinges and banded by iron strips to prevent warping. It opened into an arched stone passageway that led to the tower. Marty had talked about installing a big picture window on the west, seaward side of the house, but had instead opted for authenticity. The place received light—dimly at most hours of the day—from spaced rows of bronze-rimmed ship's portholes on both leeward and seaward walls.

Martina joined me at an open porthole. We clicked our glasses.

"What happened to your lip?"

"Short story."

"It needs stitches, Dan."

"I served a summons, and the man resented it."

"I was in town last night," she said. "You weren't home."

"I was down in the keys."

"A job?"

"Right. I'll tell you about it after dinner."

"Another short story?"

"No, a long one."

"And an ugly one?"

"Very."

*Huachinango Veracruzano* turned out to be red snapper served with a spicy sauce of tomatoes, garlic, onions, and a variety of peppers. Marty described herself as an apostate vegetarian: She wouldn't eat beef, pork, lamb, or poultry, but she was a savage predator of the fish and shellfish that lived around the reef.

After dinner, we carried mugs of coffee down the arched passageway and into the lighthouse. The tower was large at the base, with a diameter that narrowed proportionately as it rose sixty feet to the platform. A helical iron stairway twisted up the center of the cone.

Marty's paraphernalia was arranged around the circular wall: a computer station; file cabinets; a pair of trestle tables whose surface were arrayed with jars of pencils and brushes, tubes of paint, sheaves of watercolor paper, gooseneck lamps, and a six-foot easel containing a pine drawing board. Taped to the board was a color drawing of an insouciant alligator named Ollie. Marty wrote and illustrated books that were loved by children for their subversive content and despised by censors for the same reason.

I followed her up the tightly coiled stairway to the railed platform on top. A door led to a circular outside walkway. The light mechanism had long ago been removed, though the original wraparound glass—flawed and bubbled in spots—remained in place. It was almost night now. The lights of stars and buoys and boats were beginning to ignite out in the vast gray-blue expanse.

"All right," Marty said. "Tell me your story."

I told her about my phone conversation with Petrie; my trip down through the keys, stopping at marinas along the way; Marathon, where I rented the boat, and my arrival at the Mosquito Keys, where I found the derelict houseboat *Deep Six;* my dive, and the sighting of what I believed to be women tethered to the bottom; the coming of the police and gawkers, the release of the mannequins, and, finally, divers surfacing with the girl.

"Maybe you did see the woman on your dive," Marty said.

"Maybe. One of them—I saw two."

"Ghastly."

"The mannequins looked real at a distance. They were well formed, flesh colored, and had facial features and glued-on hair. Strange."

"Spiraling up out of the dark water."

"I figure the mannequins were taken to the bottom, tied to the rock, and then inflated with compressed air. I don't think they were down very long. They deflated some in the cool water, but the air quickly expanded as they shot up to the surface. It was funny, then not so funny."

"Who was the woman?"

"She hadn't been identified by the time I left Marathon."

"And this Falconer?"

"Dead, I suppose, or a hostage. Or a fugitive."

"So what now?"

"Petrie wants to see me tomorrow."

"To hire you?"

"Maybe."

"Who is he representing?"

"Peter Falconer."

"Falconer the corpse, the hostage, or the fugitive?"

"His estate, maybe. I don't know, Marty, but maybe I can earn good money."

"Baby, how many times have I told you that I'll loan you as much money as you need to finish your studies?"

"I'd rather pay as I go."

"What about your exams in December?"

"That's five months away. I'll be ready."

"No, you won't. You'll fail. Daniel, listen, you're attending night school at a community college that can hardly keep its accreditation. You won't be prepared for the examinations, not without a lot of study, cramming. This thing with Petrie might turn into a long-term job that will consume most of your time."

"Slow down. I'll know more tomorrow."

"You've got to get your degree, and then you must pass the bar exams. Otherwise you're a paralegal who's paid like a paralegal. You do lawyer's work now, cheap. You write briefs, interview witnesses, take depositions, sit at the damned defense table in court sometimes—and you're paid like a clerk."

"You couldn't love a clerk?"

She smiled. "A stud clerk, sure."

"Well . . . ?"

"I'm not certain. You'll have to audition."

"Again?"

"Until you get it right."

We awakened at sunrise, made a pot of coffee, and walked out on the reef. There was a little plateau at the south end; you could dive fifteen feet into deep water, swim around, then climb the rocks for another dive. Marty fished there, sunbathed, and collected mussels from the tideline rocks. Sometimes, at night, we swam nude in the silky water and teased each other with talk of ravenous sharks and giant eels.

We swam for twenty minutes, dried in the low morning sunlight—it was going to be another brutally hot day—and returned to the blockhouse. Marty cooked eggs and fried potatoes for breakfast.

"What about the packages?" she said as I prepared to leave.

"I forgot. Open them up."

The first package contained a lightweight pair of sandals; Marty occasionally cut her feet on the reef. She was pleased, she liked them, but I doubted she would wear them often. She removed a compact cellular telephone from the second package.

"It's ready to use," I said.

"Dan, thanks, it's thoughtful of you. But I don't want a telephone. I like my solitude."

"You don't have to take incoming calls. Turn it off, stick it in a drawer, and take it out only if there's an emergency."

"Haven't we had this discussion before?"

We had discussed it: I worried about her living alone at the lighthouse. Marty was an attractive woman, well-known in the area, and, because of her isolation, an inviting target for any psychopath who owned or could steal a boat. I had tried to give her a gun, but she had refused it; she hated firearms.

"What if you get very sick?" I said. "What if you break a leg on this slippery rock? If you have a phone . . ."

"All right," she said reluctantly. "I'll keep it around. But it will be turned off until I break a leg."

The third box contained a nickel-plated flare pistol and six shotgun-size parachute-flare cartridges. She touched the pistol as if it were a small but highly venomous reptile.

I said, "In an emergency, you can fire off a couple of distress flares that'll be seen for miles."

"It's a gun, isn't it?"

"A flare gun, not a weapon."

"Take it with you."

Martina, wearing her new sandals, walked with me down to the quay. Bell Harbor looked close in the sharp early-morning light, a cubical city now in shadow except for the roofs of the higher buildings and the tops of the royal palms that lined the esplanade. I went down the steps, got into my rowboat, fitted the oars, and untied the bow and stern lines. The boat slowly drifted out. I could see small bright fish nibbling at beards of moss growing from the quay's vertical stone wall and, farther down, sinister twin shadows—a pair of barracudas.

"The *huachinango* was delicious," I said.

"I'm glad you enjoyed it."

"The sex—transcendent."

She smiled.

"Tonight? Here?"

"We have rehearsal tonight. Remember?"

"I do now. See you at the theater, then."

Marty remained standing on the quay for a few minutes, watching me row away, then she waved, turned, and climbed the steps.

I watched her cross the reef and enter the blockhouse. She would go into her studio now and resume writing and illustrating the adventures of her animal characters, the alligators and foxes and raccoons and possums and herons and deer and snakes. In her books and cartoon strip, beasts could be devious, rascally, but never cruel. Adult humans (never pictured or given names) were the villains: faceless men evident only by their works—polluted air and water, drained marshes, burning grasslands, leveled forests. But it was all done in bright colors and clever verses. The pill was sugar-coated. Marty regarded herself as a propagandist for the planet.

# Five

An archaeologist can fairly accurately recon-
struct the history of ancient cities by his
vertical excavations. There is not one Troy, but nine, each of
them a mass of rubble lying beneath a subsequent Troy. In a
similar way one might horizontally survey a modern city.

Start at the core of Bell Harbor—the harbor area itself
and the seafront esplanade—and proceed east through its
various incarnations. First there is the bayside village once
populated by fishermen and Greek sponge divers and the
merchants who served them. That area was strictly func-
tional then; now it is "quaint," it is "uniquely charming,"
with fashionable boutiques and art galleries and ethnic
restaurants and a small theater group housed in an old brick
church.

Pass through its business district and residential section
of tall, narrow frame houses, and you'll come to a second
Bell Harbor, a crosshatch of shady streets lined with board-
inghouses and small tourist hotels. It's shabby in a genteel
way, occupied by old pensioners and young transients. It

seems that no one between the ages of thirty and sixty lives here now.

Continue east and you'll arrive at the third Bell Harbor. Here you'll see a different kind of architecture: split-level and ranch-style houses, pseudoclassical banks, and filling stations disguised as Spanish missions. Coconut palms line the streets. It is lushly green and buzzes with the sound of lawn mowers, and there are swimming pools concealed behind high cedar fences. Swimming pools, tennis courts, flowering tropical trees.

Keep going east. Now you have entered the fourth Bell Harbor, boom town, strip city, which lies on both sides of the coastal highway. Here are the hamburger and pizza and fried-chicken joints, used-car lots, the U-Drive-It and U-Store-It places, gas stations, tire shops, truck yards, warehouses, and motels—the Flamingo, the Sunshine, the Paradise, the Happy Trails, the motel chains. There are cinder-block apartment buildings and boxy duplexes. You'll see few lawns, few palms, and the air is blue with exhaust smoke.

The fifth Bell Harbor begins a couple miles beyond the highway in the palmetto wastes; scattered mobile-home parks, little homesteads with the carapaces of dead cars lying in sandy yards, hillbilly saloons, barren land waiting for the next RV campground or—if the gods smiled—theme park.

The sixth Bell Harbor is yet to be constructed, though it exists in the minds of developers and in the hearts of millions of northerners who dream of someday retiring to the Sunshine State. But at the moment the cattle ranches are not yet golf courses, the orange and grapefruit groves are not yet shopping-center parking lots, and the marshes have not yet been converted into small muddy lakes ringed by condominiums. It is a phantom community now. It may be fifteen years before the first alligator crawls out of the first muddy lake to snatch the first yapping poodle.

The state attorney's offices occupy the fourth floor of the county courthouse building. Craig Christensen, the SA, was more politician than lawyer, a calculating man who had calculated that I could provide no service to his ambition. I got along better with his number two, a career prosecutor who took care of business while Christensen attended to politics.

Nestor Naranjo's office door was open. He was seated behind his cluttered desk, and there was a look of excruciating pain on his face as he read a sheaf of papers. Nestor was a perfectionist, and any imperfection, no matter how small, caused him suffering. He was about forty, square-built, with curly black hair and one of those beards that make a man look as if he had forgotten to shave for a few days.

He sensed my presence, glanced up to see me centered in the door frame, and his pained expression dissolved into amusement. He beckoned me forward, pointed to a leather chair in front of his desk.

"Danny," he said. "I intended to call you." He glanced around conspiratorially, lowered his voice, and said, "Can you fix me up with one of your voluptuous dolls?"

"I think so," I said. "Do you own a bicycle pump?"

He linked his hands behind his head and leaned back in the swivel chair. "Do you know the story of Pygmalion and Galatea?"

"Refresh my memory."

"In the ancient version, Pygmalion sculpted a perfect statue of the most beautiful woman imaginable. Of course, he fell in love with his statue. The goddess Venus answered his prayers and brought the statue to life. He named her Galatea. They married, had a son, and presumably lived happily ever after."

"Is this story somehow related to the mannequins?"

"May I call you Pyg?"

"If I may call you Horse's Ass. Those weren't *my* Galateas."

He grinned. "What's in the briefcase?"

"Three subpoenas that I wasn't able to serve. The villains skipped."

"Gary Tolliver skipped too, but maybe not far. The cops couldn't find him at his usual haunts. But before he ran, he talked to people, said he was going after you. Said you'd hurt him bad, and he intended to kill you."

"He can get in line."

"This is serious. Tolliver is a very bad guy, and he has very bad friends. Incidentally, he complained that *you* attacked *him*."

"I kicked him," I said. "It was a tactical preemptive strike."

"I've got more subpoenas for you."

"Keep them. The job isn't worth it. I don't get paid unless I serve the papers, and when I do serve them I get abused verbally or physically. I'll give you these three back."

"Did you see yourself on TV last night?"

"No."

"You have a noble profile except for that fat lip."

"Has the girl been identified yet?"

"Not our jurisdiction. I've heard nothing. But this Peter Falconer is a nasty piece of work. Two rape charges in five years, one dropped, the other resulting in an acquittal at trial."

"Who represented him?"

"Who else? Thomas Petrie. Falconer has a juve record too."

"Yeah? What is it?"

"Can't tell you. Juvenile records are sealed by the court, as you know or should know."

I fished the unserved subpoenas out of my briefcase and dropped them on Nestor's desk.

"Lunch?" he said.

"Can't. I'm meeting someone."

"Who?"

"Tom Petrie."

"Really? Are you going to work for him on this weird Falconer mess?"

"I haven't yet been offered a job."

"Petrie. I can't believe it. Thomas Petrie—you're going over to the dark side."

"Listen, Nestor," I said, "when I graduate, and when I pass the bar exam and get my ticket—will you hire me for this office?"

"I'll probably be retired then."

"I'd make a good prosecutor."

"I don't think you have a future in this office."

"Then I'm going over to the dark side."

"Even if I recommended you, Craig would veto it. He regards you as a loose cannon."

I got up and started for the door.

"Dan? Tell Petrie that I said he's a swamp rat."

"I will tell him that. And he will be pleased."


The Bell Harbor Fencing Club occupied the former quarters of a dance studio on the top floor of a seaside building. The room was about the size of a racquetball court, with strips of canvas matting spread over the hardwood floor, a section of bleachers erected against the east wall, and big double doors that led to the locker and shower rooms. Blocks of light, looking as solid as crystal, slanted down through windows placed high on the seaside wall. Every now and then a seagull glided past a window and its shadow was projected onto the floor.

There were several pairs of fencers working out. They wore masks, white canvas jackets, trousers, and gauntlets, and their swords rang like chimes in the big room.

Petrie was practicing with the club's fencing master, an old Hungarian who many years ago had won international competitions in both the foil and épée. He wore a black patch over his right eye. They met in violent flurries, blades ringing, then the Hungarian paused to comment on the exchange. Thomas opened each engagement in the same position—"low invitation," his teacher called it—and then Petrie would meet his opponent's attack, fight defensively for a time, retreat, then counterattack. Their feet thumped on the canvas mat. I saw that you needed good legs for the sport. Good legs and a good wrist. "I've got a great wrist," Petrie had once told me. I hadn't understood at the time. The ringing of the blades seemed to hover in the air moments after the action ceased. The combat was too swift and furious for me to follow; it looked rehearsed, elaborately choreographed, though I knew that was not the case.

Later, Petrie tucked the mask under his left arm and approached the bleachers. He was sweating. He breathed slowly and deeply. There was something in his stride and posture that I had never noticed: style, a dancer's elegance in movement and repose. "I'll shower and we'll go to lunch," he said.

"Fine. What happened to the instructor's eye?"

"An accident years ago. His opponent's blade broke off just below the button. It ended his career."

"Naturally."

"Twenty minutes," he said, and he pivoted and walked toward the locker room.

# Six

We ate at a fancy seaside restaurant named La Terrasse. Beyond the terrace there were yards of beach and a thousand miles of the Gulf of Mexico. Sea and sky merged far away in a thin seam. There were palm and fig trees just beyond the low patio walls. The tables were shaded by red and white umbrellas, and sparrows pecked the flagstones for crumbs.

"The food isn't first-rate here," Petrie said, "but they have a fine, eclectic wine list."

We both ordered the Dover sole and split a bottle of crisp Alsatian wine. We talked, mostly about Thomas: his wine cellar, his fencing, his new Porsche Boxster, his flying lessons and the Lear jet he expected to buy in a year or two.

Tom Petrie was about my age. His teeth had been expertly capped, his hair styled weekly, and he wore contact lenses that turned his eyes dark blue. Tom liked to say that he was the seventh son of a family distinguished by seven generations of sloth and failure. But he was born very

bright, ambitious, born, apparently, possessing a fierce purpose and will that was denied to all but a few. He, by God,
was not going to be another Petrie cracker. He had come a
long way and his trajectory was still rising.

He had worked hard and earned a series of important
scholarships: the University of Florida, Northwestern University, and Harvard Law School. You usually heard a trace
of backwoods drawl in his accent, but he could speak fluent
Harvard when he chose. Petrie was still a work in progress.
Day by day he was creating his ideal self. In ten years I
would not know him. And he probably wouldn't know me.

Now he told me that someday he would like to fight a
real duel—"Buttons off"—no mask or protective jacket.
Just the two principals, their seconds, and perhaps a doctor.
Outdoors, preferably, in the spring when life seems most
precious. Such encounters actually took place on occasion,
mostly in Europe, but he knew of one duel that had been
fought in California. Rarely was rancor involved, a grudge:
No, sportsmen met to compete in the logical extreme of
their sport. Duels were a self-testing, a way of inventorying
one's skill and courage and, yes, why not, one's manhood.
The duels did not often end in death, but there were injuries, some serious.

"I don't get it," I said. "What's the point?"

He smiled at my unintentional pun. "The point is, Shaw,
that risking your life in ritual combat is a fast means of ac-
quiring self-knowledge. Better than twenty years of depth
analysis."

I said, "I've been in situations where it seemed that I
might be killed or seriously injured. I can't say that I bene-
fited in any way. I probably know less about myself now
than before. I don't sleep as well."

After lunch we strolled along the seawall. The walk was splashed with seagull droppings. It was bright and very hot. There were not many bathers on the beach: some wives with their young children, schoolkids, old people, regulars whose skin had been baked to the color and nearly the texture of beef jerky. Offshore, surfers were making do with three-foot-high waves.

"I want you to work for me," he said. "I need a full-time investigator, one who knows something about the law."

"I'm here to listen," I said.

"If you accept, you'll have to drop everything else."

"I don't have much going right now."

"I'll pay you forty percent above your usual fee, all expenses, naturally, with a six-month guarantee and an option for an additional six months. We can stick a clause in the contract calling for its termination upon mutual agreement. Also, there will be money available for you to hire other investigators, money for bribes and gratuities, lots of money."

"What, precisely, is my job?"

"First, find Peter Falconer."

"What if he's dead?"

"Find the corpse. But I believe that he's alive."

"Why do you think that?"

"Intuition."

"What if he's guilty of the murder, Tom?"

"What do I care? I'd defend Hitler if he could afford my fee. Maybe I'd defend him pro bono, for the publicity."

"Do you think Falconer might be guilty?"

"I have no opinion. It doesn't matter. If he is, it's my job to have him declared not guilty by twelve jurors good and true. I'll use the evidence you gather in the way most beneficial to my case. I hope Peter is innocent, but that's another thing. Let's keep our minds open. The cops and TV and newspapers have already tried and convicted the man on the basis of rumor and speculation and, Christ knows, mystical divination. We're his advocates. Didn't they teach you about advocacy at your night school?"

"What about your fee if he's dead?"

"I'm screwed. Or maybe not. I might be able to collect from the estate."

"But you know that he's alive, don't you?"

"I have a feeling in my bones."

"Has he been in touch with you?"

"Do you really expect me to answer that question?"

"It's going to be a big trial, isn't it?"

"If there's a trial, it will be big. With luck, it will be televised into half the homes in America. It will be bigger than the Simpson trial, the von Bulow trials, the trial of Jesus."

"I don't think Jesus had an actual trial."

"No. More like a Star Chamber proceeding."

We moved aside to allow a couple of kids on skateboards to pass. A small dog, tongue out, was trying to keep up with them.

Petrie said, "I would have got Jesus off with probation and six months community service."

"This trial, if there is one, will make you nationally famous, won't it?"

"And richer," he said.

We started back toward the restaurant. I could feel the stored heat of the concrete through the soles of my shoes. The wine I had drunk at lunch was sour in my throat.

I said, "Does Peter Falconer have a criminal record?"

He glanced slantwise at me. "Why do I think you already know the answer to that?"

"Nestor Naranjo mentioned a couple of rapes."

"Rape *charges*. The first was dropped, the second went to trial in Dade County—it shouldn't have, but it did. I got Peter an acquittal."

"Did Falconer rape the girl in that case?"

"No. She was a neurotic bitch. It was a vengeance thing, vengeance and money. She wanted Peter to marry her—handsome, charming scion of a fabulously rich family. The rich are targets for this sort of thing. You know that. It's extortion. The woman wanted a payoff. I blew the state's case apart during my cross of the plaintiff. No, Peter didn't rape her."

"The rape charges will look bad at trial."

"They won't come out unless I put him on the stand."

"Can you get an unbiased jury?"

"I can get a stupid jury."

"Anything else in Falconer's record?"

"A few misdemeanors."

"Nestor told me that Falconer has a juvenile file."

"Nestor has a big mouth. Nestor knows that juvenile files are sealed by the court. Nestor might find himself in front of a judge or disciplinary committee."

"He wasn't specific," I said.

Petrie halted. "Do you have reservations about working on this case?"

"Reservations, sure. But they wouldn't affect how I do my job."

"Good."

He shot his cuff so that both he and I could see his gold Rolex. "Look, I've got to be in court in thirty minutes. I'll give you a complete briefing this afternoon at, say, five o'clock. It's going to be fun, Shaw. A good murder trial is more fun than anything you can think of, including *that*. It's a duel. Us against the State. Peter Falconer versus the People. It's a long adrenaline rush."

"Nestor wanted me to tell you that he thinks you're a swamp rat."

Tom was amused; he nodded and smiled. "The devil appears in many forms. Swamp rat is his comic mode."

He offered his hand. I shouldn't have been surprised by the strength of his grip; I had seen him fencing with the one-eyed Hungarian ninety minutes before.

"Ciao," he said.


Candace was sitting at her desk in the outer office, eating chocolate-covered cherries and reading *People* magazine.

"Hey, Mr. Shaw," she said. "Did you know that Burt Reynolds is from Florida?"

"No, I didn't know that."

"It's printed right here."

"Who says the world is a boring place?"

At the back of the room were two doors; one led into my office, the other into Levi Samuelson's. We shared the rent and Candace's salary. She could file, pick up the telephone, type slowly and erratically, and she attracted the building's horny lawyers, who sometimes threw paralegal work my way.

"Oh, Mr. Shaw," Candace said with a sly smile. "Want a cherry?"

"Not on an empty libido, Candace," I said, and I went into my office and shut the door. It was a narrow room filled with fire-sale furniture: desk and chairs, green file cabinets, a spavined sofa, a cedar cabinet, and a temperamental television set. One door led into a small bathroom, the other into Levi's office. I sat down at my desk and got out a virgin legal pad. I wrote:

**Peter Falconer**
1)
2)
3)


After a while I turned on the TV and watched an Andre Agassi–Lleyton Hewitt tennis match. Agassi won 6–4, 4–6, 7–6 (7–3). I closed my eyes and hit a dozen devastating top-spin shots to the Agassi backhand. His shoulders slumped, he shook his head, he smashed a racket. Hey, Andre, did you think you were going against some green kid this afternoon? *En garde*, buddy.

# Seven

It's a beautiful brief, Daniel, as much art as law. There's a harmony between all its parts—rhetoric, precedent, state and constitutional law. I've never written a more compelling appeal. Never seen a better one, in fact."

"That's fine, Judge," I said.

"And now I must—in my mind, naturally—argue before the 1927 United States Supreme Court. A daunting prospect."

"No doubt," I said.

We were in Levi's office. He paced back and forth behind his desk while I sat like a witness in the high-backed chair he reserved for the rare client.

"Bartolomeo was certainly innocent of the crime, you know."

Levi had once been a massive man, a giant, but age and a recent illness had pared him down to mortal dimensions. He was in his mid-seventies, tall and slightly stooped, but there was vigor in his movements and, when he became angry, a ferocious glitter in his eyes. He had white hair and wiry eyebrows and a ruddy complexion—apple cheeks and lips so pink they appeared rouged.

"Sacco was innocent as well. It was a political farce. Have you ever read Vanzetti's letters from prison?"

"No."

"Do it."

"Okay, Judge."

Levi had formerly been a lawyer in private practice, a district attorney, a criminal-court judge, and a justice on a Michigan state appeals court. Ten years ago he had retired to Bell Harbor, but, bored with inactivity, he'd joined the Florida bar. He kept busy by teaching a class at night school, representing an occasional client pro bono, assisting other lawyers in writing death-sentence appeals, and by refighting celebrated lost causes. During the last year he had "represented" the convicted spies Ethel and Julius Rosenberg; Bruno Hauptmann, the kidnapper and probable killer of the Lindbergh baby; and the framed Wobbly leader Big Bill Hayward. He was presently "defending" the alleged (and executed) anarchist Bartolomeo Vanzetti.

"Am I boring you, Daniel?"

"Not at all, Judge."

"Well. And how is the lovely Martina?"

"Fine."

"You really ought to marry her, Daniel."

"I know. But she won't be hurried."

"Martina is what the British call a one-off. Unique, a distinct individual."

"Some people take that to mean eccentric."

"Marry her. *Carpe diem.* Seize the day."

Levi himself was a one-off. He was from a prominent Michigan family named Crowcroft and had been baptized Arnold Elsworth Crowcroft. While he'd served in the Korean

War, a Pennsylvania soldier by the name of Levi Samuelson, a man he hardly knew, a recent replacement, had saved his life by one of those impulsive, selfless acts that seem contrary to the deepest instincts of human and animal—he had died so that a stranger might live. Levi had never disclosed the nature of the man's heroism but, in a quixotic gesture of his own, after the war had changed his name to Levi Samuelson and assumed financial support of the dead soldier's widow and infant daughter. He had not converted to Judaism; he remained a WASP and an Episcopalian.

"More coffee?" he asked.

"No thanks," I said. "Actually, I came here as a client."

"A client." He sat down behind his desk. "Well, fine. I am now your cunning, rapacious legal advocate, and you are my soon-to-be-fleeced sheep." There was a gilded clock on his desk. He slammed the start button with the palm of his hand and said, "Proceed."

"How much do you charge, Levi?"

"Nothing to you, my boy. Professional courtesy."

"I'm not a lawyer, Levi, as you know. Not yet."

"To the point, Daniel."

"What do you think of Thomas Petrie?"

"My colleague on the top floor? Thomas Petrie, as a lawyer?"

"As a lawyer and a man."

"Are you working for him?"

"Yes."

"I'm not sure that the ethical standards of my profession allow me to respond."

"Come on, Judge. Forget for a moment that he's a member of the sacred fraternity."

"I've watched Thomas in the courtroom a few times, and

I would say that he's a good trial lawyer, first-rate. He knows the law. He's always prepared."

"Go on."

"This is a peculiar consultation. The client is interrogating counsel. Well, all right. Petrie is really brilliant in cross-examining the State's witnesses. Sometimes he's sarcastic, other times butter wouldn't melt in his mouth. He lays traps early and springs them late. He can make anyone look like a fool or perjurer—a policeman, an expert witness, an eyewitness, the victim. It's both fascinating and disgusting to see—like watching a large snake slowly swallow a small snake."

"Is Petrie honest?"

"How can I say? Not dishonest, probably. But I suspect he cuts corners now and then, skirts close to the edge, colors the truth with lawyerly casuistry."

"Are you familiar with this Peter Falconer business?"

"I read the newspapers, Daniel, and I watch—I'm ashamed to admit it—television. It's bizarre, isn't it? Shrouded in mystery, as the headline writers say. Those mannequins. That goat . . ."

I said, "I believe that Petrie is in touch with Falconer."

"Whom he represents. What makes you think they are in contact?"

"It's just a feeling, a sense."

"Say it. Your conversation here today is privileged."

"My talks with Petrie are privileged too. I'm working for him."

"Is this Falconer fellow an official suspect in the murder of that young woman?"

"You know how it goes—the police very much want to interview him."

"But he hasn't formally been declared a suspect or fugitive?"

"Not yet."

"Then I suppose Tom Petrie will produce Falconer at the right and dramatic moment."

"In a week or two, probably," I said.

"Why in a week or two?"

"The girl's fingernails were broken. There was a struggle. Whoever killed her is scratched, lacerated. He needs time to heal."

"You think Falconer killed her?"

"It looks that way. But Petrie has hired me to find evidence that will indicate Falconer is innocent of any crime."

"There's nothing *a priori* wrong with that. But of course you must be very careful. You can't put yourself in a position where you're accused of suppressing inculpatory evidence or committing perjury. However, even if Falconer is guilty, your investigation may well assist Petrie in preparing a solid defense."

"Maybe I won't have to testify at the trial."

"You're not thinking. I'll grade you F on that. Even if Thomas Petrie doesn't call you to the stand, the State must. Remember, you were first at the crime scene. And once you begin testifying, the line between privileged and nonprivileged information is very thin."

"Of course. Christ, it's a tangle."

"Then leave Petrie's employ. Now."

"I want this job, Judge. I've become involved and I'd like to follow through. It isn't only the money. I'd poke around for nothing, like you pursue your ghost cases here. I don't care to become just another bit player dragged down by another sharp lawyer."

"Sharp lawyers are the glory of white-collar crime. All right. First, keep a diary. Start with the day Petrie hired you to find Falconer. Carry on from there. Keep this diary or journal religiously; enter everything that seems remotely pertinent."

"Okay," I said.

"I've kept a journal for fifty years. I still make entries daily. Many lawyers keep journals, smart policemen keep journals, even some crooks keep them; all sea captains keep journals called logs. Why?"

"I can figure it out."

"Because, Daniel, when a man is sitting up on the witness stand as a plaintiff, defendant, or witness, with his fortune or reputation or freedom at stake, and Daniel, he can consult his notebook and say, 'No, sir, on the ninth of June, 1998, I was escorting my virgin daughter to Sunday school . . .' You do understand, don't you, son?"

"It's clear."

"Or, if the prosecutor asks you if you said such and such while dining with so and so at the Ticky-Tacky Polynesian restaurant, you can righteously glare down from the witness stand and say, 'No, I said this and he said that.' Enter dates, times, the gist of conversations, the actual words if they're significant. Put it all down. And consult with me every now and then, let me know what you are up to. The law is a labyrinth. Even the most timid citizen breaks a dozen laws per day. I, for example, am about to select from my humidor an illicit Cuban cigar. And you are wearing a criminally garish tie. And let's remember this: In our great Republic, a man can be as pure and innocent as a newborn lamb and wake up one day in the penitentiary."

I said, "Falconer will be denied his inheritance if he's convicted of murder, won't he?"

"Maybe not. As far as we know now, the murder isn't connected to the inheritance—that is, he didn't kill in order to inherit. There might be years of litigation, but I suspect that eventually he'd receive something, perhaps all. We can presume that he won't go to the electric chair, since he's rich, well-connected, and competently represented. Just how big is his inheritance?"

"Twenty-five million dollars, according to Tom."

"My lord."

"That's just part of a huge estate. Falconer's money is held in a trust. Twenty-five million when he turns thirty—that's today. And more millions, control of the bulk of the fortune, when he turns forty."

"Tell me this: How did Petrie, a man practicing criminal law, get mixed up with this inheritance? How did he happen to become Falconer's civil attorney?"

"Petrie defended him on a couple of rape charges. One charge was dropped; maybe settled out of court. The other was tried down in Dade County eighteen months ago, and Falconer was acquitted."

"Oh, my," Levi said. "A record of violent crime."

I stood up. "Thanks for the coffee and counsel, Judge."

He instantly slammed down the stop button on his desk clock. "That's six minutes and forty seconds. Say seven minutes. Tom Petrie would bill you around eighty dollars for that time."

"But since you're not Petrie . . . ?"

He leaned back in his swivel chair and hooked his thumbs through his red suspender straps. "Lunch at Mario's. Soon."

# Eight

Thomas Petrie's suite of offices was furnished like the executive headquarters of a small but prosperous chain of banks. There were puzzling avant garde paintings and sculpture scattered about, the kind of modern chairs and settees that appear graceful but are hell to sit on, and floor-to-ceiling tinted windows overlooking the sea. Petrie employed two criminal defense attorneys, two legal secretaries, and a full-time paralegal. Everyone knew that the firm earned a lot of money, though not enough, some said, to cover the overhead.

Tom's office, naturally, was the largest and plushest in the suite. One wall was stacked with leather-bound law books, just for show, since the information was now more conveniently stored in computers. A large oil painting, perhaps six feet wide and five feet tall, was centered on the opposite wall and bathed in a soft glow from a ceiling light. Unprimed canvas had been violently, thickly smeared with muddy brown and burnt umber and yellow ochre.

"That painting, Tom," I said. "I've seen similar compositions on jail-cell and nuthouse walls. The smeared-feces genre, isn't it?"

His smile was condescending. "That's a Murdoch. If you can borrow eighty-five thousand dollars somewhere, it's yours." Then, referring to Martina, he said, "Murdoch is a painter, not a cartoonist."

He sat behind a walnut desk shaped like an artist's palette, playing with a slab of amber, a paperweight, which contained an ancient insect that resembled a praying mantis. The window behind his desk framed the entire bay and the sea beyond; in the center, toylike in the distance, was the peppermint-striped lighthouse. Surf creamed around the reef.

Petrie removed a thick cardboard portfolio from a desk drawer and pushed it toward me.

"A complete copy of the Falconer file. Confidential and no crap. I'm having a safe moved into your office. It should be installed by the time we finish. Read the file, lock it up. Shaw? Lock it up. You set the combination. Tell me, no other, the numbers. Do I have to warn you not to write the numbers down anywhere?"

He dipped into a drawer and tossed a manila envelope on the desk. "These are bearer bonds to the amount of seven hundred fifty thousand dollars. They're negotiable for whoever possesses them. Good as cash."

"Slow down," I said.

"You could, of course, transfer the money to an offshore bank of your choice and in your name. I thought about it, bud, and you're the only man I know who can be trusted with three-quarters of a million dollars. Does that reflect badly on me or you?"

"You."

He smiled wearily, held up the slab of amber so that it

was ignited by sunlight coming over his shoulder. Inside the honey-yellow glow, encysted for perhaps fifty million years, the praying mantis looked alive, resurrected, and prepared to strike. Tom's display of the trapped insect was his way of emphasizing his next words.

"Peter Falconer is being held hostage. He's going to be— he is worth some twenty-five million dollars, so why shouldn't we buy him for three-quarters of a mil? He's undervalued. Yes? Hardly damaged, price slashed."

"Whose seven hundred fifty thousand are you using?"

"Let's just say we have an investor."

"A gambler."

"Do you like the Bahamas, Shaw?"

"Those islands I've seen."

"It's time to see another one. A chartered Cessna will be waiting at the airport at six tomorrow morning. The pilot will fly you to an out-island called Big Sandy Cay. There isn't much there now, but in a year or two the place will be wretchedly overcrowded. They're building a new hotel and casino and dredging the harbor so that cruise ships can squeeze in. But for now the only decent place to stay is a fishing resort called the Meridian Club. I've booked you a cottage there."

"Is that where Falconer is being held? Big Sandy Cay?"

"Presumably. You shouldn't have a problem smuggling in the bearer bonds. A gun too, if you think you'll need one."

"Do *you* think I'll need a gun?"

He shrugged and showed me his palms. "You know more about this sort of thing than I do."

"Actually, I don't. This is the first time I've tried to ransom anybody."

"Regard it as a career opportunity. Put it on your résumé."

"Who do I see when I arrive there?"

"I don't know. They'll contact you."

"Are there any more surprises in those desk drawers?"

"Oddly enough . . ." He again delved into the top drawer and removed a Polaroid snapshot. It had been taken with a flash in poor light. In the foreground was a metal table, metal chair, and a man who had been severely beaten. His face was bruised and swollen, one eye closed, his upper lip split, and his hair and features were shadowed with blood. You could not read his expression. Swelling and the effects of shock had erased any sign of pain or fear. If anything, he looked quizzical, as if waiting for someone to explain why his right index finger was missing. His right hand, and the severed finger, lay in a puddle of blood on the table. The finger had been amputated close to the big knuckle, and you could see some shreds of webbing.

"Falconer?" I asked.

"Who else?"

"I suppose they sent you the finger."

He removed a glass jar from the drawer. It was the sort of cylindrical tube that holds cocktail olives, and in it, floating nail-up in blood-clouded fluid, was the finger.

I said, "How were the finger and photo delivered?"

"FedEx from Nassau."

"There must have been a note, ransom demand, instructions."

"There was. Written by Peter, in his hand, begging for help."

"Let me see it."

"I can't do that. Some of the information conveyed is highly confidential."

"Confidential how? Related to the murder of the girl?"

He shook his head. "Move on."

"I assume that you haven't informed any police authority. The FBI, the Bahamian police."

"You assume correctly."

"I don't know, Tom. This could be very dangerous."

"Yes." And then, improvising, he said, "That's why I'm adding a seventy-five-hundred-dollar bonus—one percent of the ransom—to our contract, payable immediately if you wish. I'll write you a check now."

"All right. And I hope I live to spend the money."

"Then you'll go? Arrange the ransom of our boy Falconer?"

"If I can do it my way."

"Certainly. There aren't any protocols for this sort of business."

"Let's talk."

"Why don't we play a couple sets of tennis first. A court will be open in twenty minutes."

I had played tennis with Petrie a few times. His game was smooth, accurate, conventional—the product of a thousand hours of instruction by a good tennis pro. He liked to stay back on the baseline, and he played the game as precisely as he fenced. I had learned tennis in public courts and so was not very polished: I had a hard though erratic serve, hard ground strokes, and I charged the net at every opportunity. I had occasionally won a set from Tom, but never a match.

"I'll change," I said. I kept tennis gear in my office.

"Meet me up on the deck. Afterward we'll eat something and talk this out. I'll order a pizza."

"Isn't pizza too working-class for your refined tastes?"

"Gourmet pizza, special order from Rafe's with imported cheeses, morel mushrooms, and a sprinkle of truffle dust. And always with a decent bottle of wine."

• • •

I returned to my office and found Candace busy painting her nails a glossy crimson. She spread her fingers and held her hand aloft to dry the polish (reminding me of the photo of Falconer's bloody hand), and said, "Mr. Shaw, some burly men moved a big old ugly safe into your office."

"Really?"

"They were rude to me." She searched for the *mot juste*. "They were suggestive."

"What did they suggest?"

"You know." She paused. "They had tattoos."

"My God."

"Lots of them. I have only one tattoo, Mr. Shaw," she said coquettishly. "A little red hourglass on my belly. Like, you know, a black widow spider. It freaks out my boyfriend."

"It freaks me out too, Candace."

The safe was, as Candace had said, big and old and ugly. There was an instruction booklet. I selected five numbers at random, set the combination, placed the thick Falconer file inside, and closed the door.

Petrie won both sets, 6–3, 6–4, and afterward we returned to his office in our tennis clothes. He had not been joking about the gourmet pizza and bottle of wine.

The telephone rang while we ate. Petrie picked up the receiver, listened for half a minute, said, "All right. Thanks."

Thomas Petrie was a strong-willed man and a good trial lawyer; by nature and training he concealed his emotions, or allowed one emotion to show in his expression and posture while feeling its exact opposite. But I could see that the telephone call had hit him hard, and for an instant he had the look of a defeated man. But he quickly regained his composure and was once again Tom Petrie, the smartest and toughest kid on the block.

"They found another body," he said.

I waited.

"A young woman. Police divers went back out to the Mosquito Keys early this morning to search the sinkhole for evidence. They found the girl. Apparently the body had come loose from its tether, drifted with the current, and became concealed among some rocks."

"Who phoned you?"

"A friend with the state police."

"A paid informant?"

"Let's say he won't be surprised when a handsome gift arrives in the mail."

"The girls haven't been identified?"

"Not yet."

I helped myself to another slice of pizza.

"That's a forty-five-dollar pizza," he said. "Like it?"

"I prefer pepperoni," I said to needle him. "Tom, is living well the best revenge?"

"No, kid," he said. "Revenge is the best revenge."

# Nine

Leroy Karpe took the Cessna up to three thousand feet and then slanted southeast across the Florida peninsula. A brownish haze of smoke and pollution fogged the landscape below; scattered fires burned in the Everglades, and an onshore wind blew the Miami–Lauderdale filth inland. You could see how far Lake Okeechobee had shrunk back from its original shoreline and the half dozen long canals that channeled water to the coast. They drained the lakes, drained the wetlands, and then complained of drought and fire.

We passed over the strip city that extended from above Palm Beach to well below Miami, and then the Atlantic was below us. The air cleared and I could see Grand Bahama Island to the north and a piece of Andros to the south. The sea was scythed with whitecaps. Boats sailed the coastal waters and the deep blue Gulf Stream beyond: yachts, freighters, tankers, fishing boats, and a cruise ship that to my eye looked like an elongated wedding cake.

Leroy Karpe was a lean, taciturn man about thirty-five,

with stiff black hair and dark eyes. He looked as though he might be part Indian. He didn't talk much during the flight; he seemed a yes–no–maybe sort of man, and all I learned before giving up on the idea of conversation was that he was Thomas Petrie's flight instructor and that Petrie was half owner of his air-charter business.

The Bahama Islands begin not far off the Florida coast and extend some four hundred nautical miles southeast, ending north of Haiti. A few islands are big, others are miles long but narrow, and hundreds more range from a score of acres to sandpits that are half awash at high tide. They are a lovely green when viewed from a height, ringed by white sand, ringed again by foaming surf, shadowed by underwater reefs, and scattered over a vast expanse of brilliant multihued waters that range from champagne to emerald to amethyst.

It was a ninety-minute flight to Big Sandy Cay. Karpe circled the island twice before preparing to land. It was isolated except for a few nearby small cays and dry shoals that supported a few stunted palms. The island was nine miles long, two miles wide, and shaped like a fishhook at the north end. Inside the hook lay a protected harbor with a stone jetty and quay, marker buoys, moored yachts, and a crosshatch of marina piers. A barge at the hook's opening was dredging a deep-water channel through the coral bottom, and onshore a sprawling resort hotel and casino were under construction. The "native" village of pastel-colored shops and houses lay behind the construction site. A crushed-seashell road, dazzling in the sunlight, bisected the island lengthwise, and feeder roads angled off to beaches, small settlements, a church and soccer field, and, on the quiet side of the island, the Meridian Resort—eight seaside cottages set among palms and fruit trees and gaudy flowering shrubs.

The runway was a concrete strip no wider than a two-lane road, ending in a cluster of steel Quonset huts, one of which flew the Bahamian flag. Karpe taxied the plane off the runway and onto a grassy apron. He switched off the engine.

"I'll take care of the customs guys," he said.

"You mean bribe them?"

"Just smile."

Two armed policemen, who also served as customs agents, were sullen at first, rude, but promptly became cordial when Karpe gave each of them a fifty-dollar bill and asked that they ensure that no vandals or thieves molested his Cessna. They vowed that the aircraft would remain inviolate. They declined to search our bags. They offered to exchange our American money for Bahamian dollars at little personal profit.

It was hot in the corrugated steel hut, even hotter outside in the late-morning sunlight. An open jeep-style VW with MERIDIAN RESORT printed on the door panels was parked beneath a palm.

The driver hustled our bags aboard, pulled out of the lot, and drove north along the crushed-seashell road. We passed corn and bean fields, parched in the summer heat; bleached scrap-wood shacks; a ravine filled with trash; and then the driver turned off onto a rutted dirt road that slanted toward the island's east shore.

"We'll bunk together," Karpe said.

I shook my head.

"There's plenty of room in these cottages."

"I'm here on business," I said. "My business requires privacy."

"The cottages aren't cheap, even in the off-season."

"Tom Petrie can afford to pay for two of them."

"Shaw, I don't know what this is all about—"

"Good."

"But Tom suggested that I watch out for you."

"That was foolish of Tom, and contrary to our deal."

"I've got"—Karpe glanced at the driver—"I have a pair of tools in my duffel."

Guns, he meant.

"Tom Petrie has done me some very big favors. I owe him. So when he said you'll probably need backup—"

"What qualifies you for the job?"

"I've been around."

"Around where?"

"I flew a chopper in the Gulf War. I got my stake of the charter service flying product in from the islands and Mexico. I came across bad people, very bad people, in the trade, and I'm still alive."

"Christ," I said.

"I'll stay out of the way until you need me."

"Look, Karpe," I said slowly. "I don't care what Petrie told you. You're just the hired hand who got me here. If you interfere just once, even a little, I'm leaving this island if I have to swim. But before I go, I'll tell these particular bad guys that you're a problem that has to be solved. Do you understand? I figure human life is worth about five cents a kilo to the people I'll be dealing with, worth less than fish chum, cheaper than crab bait. Stay out."

"It's your call," he said mildly.


The cottages were strung out along the waterfront above the beach and pier, four on either side of a frame building that contained a small bar and restaurant, a variety store, and a tackle shop. The cottages were square with long eaves and screened verandas. Trellised vines of pink bougainvillea climbed the outside walls. Behind the complex there was a patio with umbrellaed tables, a swimming pool, and a couple of clay tennis courts. Everything was shaded by palms, and there were hibiscus and jacaranda and lemon trees, and banks of flowers in the gaudy primary colors.

I was assigned cottage number four, next to the main building; Karpe was given a place farther down the line. Some fishermen from Georgia occupied cottage number one, but they were scheduled to leave the island tomorrow morning, according to the receptionist.

I tipped the boy who carried my bag into the cottage and instructed him to return with a couple bottles of cold beer and a sandwich—any kind of sandwich—and then I walked around switching on overhead fans and opening the louvered windows. The place was big and airy, with tile floors and whitewashed plaster walls hung with watercolors in the style of Winslow Homer. There were two bedrooms, a dining alcove, and a small kitchen. This clearly was not a luxury tourist resort. Big-game fishing was available but not a feature. Serious fishermen came here, sportsmen who worked the flats for bonefish with fly rods or light spinning gear, fanatics obsessed by the task of catching swift, wary, inedible fish.

I tipped the boy again when he returned with the beer and a ham and cheese sandwich. There were some skiffs pulled up on the sand and, out on the rickety pier, more skiffs, a day sailer, and a cabin cruiser rigged for blue-water fishing. An old man was working on the cabin cruiser's engines.

The boy who had served my food reappeared and began

combing the beach with a rake. He paused now and then to toss a fallen coconut up onto the grass fringe.

It was very hot. The sun was almost directly overhead now, and glare ignited the shallows into shivering white fire. Gulls perched on the pier posts with the vanity of eagles. The sea smelled tart, iodine, contrasting with the perfumed fragrance of the many flowers.

The boy teed up an empty Coke can and removed it from the beach with an excellent soccer-style kick. He threw up his hands, signaling a goal, and then danced in a circle, acknowledging the delirious cheers of the crowd.

Leroy Karpe appeared, wearing shorts, a T-shirt, a Florida Marlins baseball cap, and jogging shoes. He paused in front of the cottage and began performing stretching exercises.

Petrie—the son of a bitch. Conveniently, the pilot he'd hired, a former drug smuggler, could serve as watchdog, spy, "backup." Karpe was present to watch me and watch the seven hundred fifty thousand dollars in bearer bonds. As I would, naturally, watch him. To Tom's way of thinking, we canceled each other out. Double security; two reports.

Karpe said something to the boy, who grinned, and then he turned and started jogging down the path. He was about five-nine and weighed one hundred sixty pounds. He didn't look hard. He didn't look hard or talk hard or move like a hard man. He spoke softly, drawling, and his eyes were mild. There was no bluster, no macho posturing. I concluded that he probably was as hard as he needed to be.

I showered briefly in cool water, shaved, and dressed in tennis shorts, a polo shirt, and worn deck shoes. Beneath the shorts I wore a money belt whose pocket ran nearly from hip to hip; inside that I placed the sheaf of bearer bonds.

The kitchen shelves were lined with newspaper; I removed some pages and tore them into sheets, and those I placed in the manila envelope that had originally contained the bonds.

I stepped outside into the humid heat. The kid was pushing a wheelbarrow filled with beach debris toward the hotel. Gulls protested, squalling, as I walked out onto the pier, then erupted and flew low over the water.

The cabin cruiser's engine compartment was open, and the old man had spread carburetor parts over the deck. I smelled gasoline and oil and sun-heated teak. It was a wooden boat at least forty years old but well-maintained—polished varnish, gleaming bronze, fresh paint, and shiny railings. The twin engines were clean; there was no grime or caked oil, no frayed wires.

I said, "I've got fifty dollars that claims you can't get this wreck running by sundown."

He leisurely wiped his hands on a cloth, glanced at his watch, then cocked his head to look up at me.

"Done," he said.

"My name is Daniel Shaw."

"They call me Pop."

Pop's hair was like a thick mass of uncombed cotton. And he had skin the color of old leather, deeply scored with wrinkles that looked like healed knife scars and bristling with white beard stubble. His few remaining teeth were long and yellow. Pop was very old, but his eyes were clear and cynical.

I said, "I've got another hundred that says you won't be anchored outside the port's breakwater tonight after dark."

"This American dollar or Bahama dollar?"

"American."

"Done."

"I might want to take a cruise tonight. Maybe. Probably not, but maybe. A fairly long cruise, to an island where there's an airport. Can you navigate these shoal waters at night?"

That question was not worthy of a reply; he turned his head to spit over the side, turned back.

"You get the one hundred and fifty whether or not I show up tonight."

"Another five hundred dollar," he said, "if I take you to Whisper Cay. That's four hours from here. Four hours there with you, four hours back alone. Five hundred dollar. Six-fifty in all."

"All right."

"I need a hundred now. Fuel and such."

I removed five twenties from my wallet and passed them to the old man.

He rubbed them between his spit-wetted thumb and forefinger, and when the ink didn't come off he risked a small smile.

"This a secret?" he asked.

"You bet."

"Shooting going on?"

"No." No, I hoped.

"How long I stay?"

"Outside the breakwater? Until, say, two o'clock."

He nodded. "Plan to fish some?" he asked slyly, knowing very well that, if I came, I would have no time for fishing.

"How can I get into town?" I asked him.

"Melvin drive you, or you can rent one of them bicycles."

# Ten

Boys between the ages of ten and thirteen make excellent spies. They are natural snoops and provocateurs. They roam freely. A pack of roving kids is not worthy of much attention, particularly in third-world countries. Feral boys know adults far better than they are known in return, and they observe strangers with the wary calculation of small predators. They are boys and do what boys do: They wander, they play games, they hustle for coins, they indulge in obscure mischief, they live in the moment, existentially, and like all proper mercenaries they will give fair value for your dollar. After the age of thirteen they become interested in girls and are lost to clandestine work. You'll find your little spies in their natural habitats: in streets and parks, along the waterfront, high in trees, near abandoned buildings, and around dangerous bridges and piers.

The port village was just a crosshatch of narrow streets—most of them dirt—lined with frame buildings painted in bright pastels, blues and greens, pale yellow, lavender. The houses, shops, offices, small hotels, churches, cafés, and taverns were all mixed together helter-skelter, and a small open market, drowsy now in the afternoon heat, was located beneath a grove of dusty trees on the edge of town.

It was quiet now; shutters were closed, curtains drawn, accordion steel doors lowered. Emaciated dogs lay panting in wedges of shade. A variety shop remained open. I went inside and bought one of those disposable cameras with a fixed-focus lens and an integral twenty-exposure roll of color film. Back outside, I walked down the nearly deserted streets to the center of town, where there was a small park with crushed-seashell walks and iron benches and shade trees that dangled pods resembling chili peppers. I sat on one of the benches and waited. The village itself was quiet, but I could hear the noises of men and machinery from the construction site.

The first kid appeared after a few minutes. He was eight or nine, a scrawny barefoot urchin who carried a shoe-shine kit. His face wrinkled in dismay and disgust when he saw my canvas shoes. Then there was another boy, about the same age, who wanted to sell me seashells. He had a box of them, and some were beautiful. I bought three small shells, paid him, and gave a few coins to the disappointed shoe-shine boy.

Then a few more kids appeared out of nowhere and drifted across the park. They were older, twelve or thirteen, and had the half-bold, half-furtive aspect of dishonest merchants. One wanted to sell me marijuana; another offered to take me snorkeling out on the reef in his uncle's skiff; a third knew the exact location of buried treasure. I joked with them and they teased me a little in return. The fourth one, a lanky kid with big hands and feet and a watchful eye, remained aloof. The others deferred to him. They now and then glanced his way, alert for signs of approval or disapproval. His name was Henry.

"Boys," I said, "I'm a detective from the United States, here looking for some very bad men. Killers, maybe. I'll pay you for information and some careful spying. Any strangers on the island?"

Of course there were strangers: Most of the construction crew were from other places, and so were the yachtsmen; some of the yachts had come from as far away as South Africa and Europe.

I nodded, waited.

There was a freighter . . .

"Tell me about that," I said.

An ancient junk freighter had arrived in port two days ago and was presently tied up at the quay. It had delivered no cargo. No cargo was taken aboard. The ship was leaky; you could hear its bilge pumps working at intervals during the day and night. The crew—they had seen five crew members, though there might be more—behaved queerly. They stayed to themselves. Only one had come into the village to buy supplies; the others remained aboard the ship. The older boys had offered to work—chipping rust, cleaning and painting, running errands, anything—but they had been refused. Two Jamaicans—you could tell by their accents and ways. Two whites—one young and the other with very long hair—and a big Mexican who amused himself by playing with a yo-yo. He could do amazing tricks with his yo-yo.

"Bad men?" I asked the boys. "Cruel men, maybe killers?"

The boys looked at Henry, who half closed his eyes and considered. We all waited while he formulated his answer.

"I don't go out on the quay at night," he said slowly.

There are always men of dubious backgrounds and intentions wandering around any archipelago. Vagabonds, smugglers, treasure hunters, adventurers, fugitives, the crews of tramp freighters hustling to score a living from the sea and islands. Many were harmless enough; others, as vicious as rabid dogs. Henry, only thirteen, had seen many such types come and go, and I trusted his instincts.

"Boys," I said, "I'm going to get up from this bench in a minute. I'll leave behind three twenty-dollar bills. Henry, you divide it among the older boys. And buy the little ones some ice cream. Okay?"

Henry solemnly nodded.

"And I'll leave behind this little camera. Just point and shoot. Maybe you can get some snaps of the men aboard the ship. The crewmen, anyone who goes aboard. But be careful—sneaky. All right? And you other boys, just wander around, look and listen. Be cool. You'll get more money tonight. Don't talk. This is just between us."

I got up, leaving money and camera behind on the bench, and walked out of the park.

The bank was a narrow, deep, single-story building with a counter running the length of one wall, a couple of side offices, a vault room at the rear, and some chest-high Formica tables where you might fill out your deposit slip or compose a holdup note. I observed no security personnel or devices. The place looked ridiculously easy to rob. Easy, but then where would you go? It was a little bank associated with a rich and powerful Bahamian bank corporation. I could have opened a numbered account for the sum of seven hundred fifty thousand dollars. I thought about it. Instead, I rented a safety-deposit box and inserted the manila envelope stuffed with torn newspaper.

I filled out the application forms, produced identification, paid the yearly fee, and a pretty young woman named Jasmine led me back to an alcove off the vault room. She fitted the bank's key into the lockbox, waited as I turned the key I had been issued, and then discreetly waited out of sight for a minute, until I called her, and she returned to relock the drawer. I kept my key; she kept the bank's.

I said, "Can anyone who possesses my key gain access to the box?"

"Unless you stipulate otherwise, yes."

"That's fine. I might send someone to collect my deposit." And then I said, "What time do you get off work?"

"Five."

"Will you have dinner with me tonight?"

She smiled. "Why, yes, I think so. May I bring my dear husband?"

"Does your husband have a big appetite?"

"He's a big man."

I said, "Why does love mean zero in tennis?"

"I don't know anything about tennis. Is it hard to score?"

We smiled at our brief flirtation.

I left the air-conditioned bank and stepped into a wall of humid heat and sunblast. There was a bar called Lucky's across the street. All four accordion steel doors had been lifted to admit whatever breeze might be stirring. Fans slowly revolved overhead. A square bar penned in the bartender and his collection of bottles and the humming coolers. Half a dozen men on the opposite side of the bar stopped talking when I entered.

"Beer," I told the bartender. "Any kind, as long as it's cold."

The men on the other side of the bar covertly watched me. I was a stranger. Strangers, especially white strangers, had to be evaluated. Was this stranger a yachtsman, fisherman, diver? Was he associated with the construction company or the corporation that was financing the construction of the hotel and casino? An architect, engineer, investor, or government snoop?

The bartender brought me a plate of tiny cold shrimp with the bottle of beer.

They had seen me enter and leave the bank. I assumed that I was also being watched by one of Falconer's kidnappers; they would know when I arrived on the island, reached the Meridian Club, wandered the streets of the village, and entered the bank with a manila envelope and exited without it.

"You with TransBahama?" the bartender asked.

TransBahama was the name of the corporation that was building the resort complex.

"No," I said.

"The Atlantic Consortium?"

"No. I'm just here for a couple of days. I thought I'd try the flats for bonefish. Some of the best bonefishing in the world here, I've heard."

"Used to be," the bartender said, and he moved away.

They evidently rated me harmless; the men on the far side of the bar resumed their conversation. It was angry talk. They were complaining about TransBahama and its dictatorial ways. One of the men, older than his companions, defended the corporation: There would be jobs, he said, work for all the islanders, male and female, regular paychecks. Real jobs that didn't drain the life out of you. He held up his gnarled, scarred, deformed hands. They were, he said, the arthritic hands of a fellow who had been laboring as a commercial fisherman since the age of ten. All of his joints were arthritic, nothing but aches, even his spine was deformed.

A young man with big shoulders and an angry scowl was sarcastic. "Jobs, yes," he said. "We can be waiters, bellboys, pool boys, caddies, janitors. And our women—room maids, laundresses, cocktail waitresses, whores. Yes, jobs, very good."

I signaled the bartender for another beer.

Big Sandy Cay was a small, poor, isolated island that probably relied as much on barter as money. The present tourist trade had not much affected the economy. It was a self-sufficient and no doubt close community, the people cousins in spirit if not in blood; but that would change in a year or two, was changing now. Everything would change with the coming of mass tourism and cruise ships and gamblers. The local population was going to be overwhelmed.

They talked about friends and relatives who had been cheated by the corporation and government. Apparently much of the harborfront had been privately owned until a year ago. There had been a dance hall and open-air cafés strung out along a stretch of beach. The corporation had bought much of that land through intermediaries, and those locals who refused to sell lost their property through taxation. The government had raised taxes several thousand percent and, when the owners were unable to pay, had confiscated the land and then immediately sold it cheap to the corporation.

"But what can we do?" the old man said. "What can we do?"

"We can fight," the young hothead replied.

The old man shook his head. "Fight the corporation? Fight the government? They're the same. They're one."

A man entered the bar and took a seat three stools down from me. He wore the sort of outfit you saw on weekend golfers: a pink short-sleeved shirt, a visored cap, and pleated peach-colored slacks with a white belt. He was tall, maybe six-four or -five, and very lean, though his arms were well-muscled. He had a long bony face and skin as black and shiny as hot tar, and he wore his hair in a pageboy cut.

He ordered rum and tonic with a squeeze of lime, and when the bartender served him, he asked, "What's to do in this place?"

The bartender shrugged. He had not given the man a courtesy plate of shrimp.

"Sweat? Is that what you do, man? Sweat, I guess." His accent sounded Jamaican.

The man lit a cheroot whose smoke smelled like licorice and, half smiling, he gazed at the men across the bar, stared at the bartender, but ignored me.

"The women, they sweat?"

The Jamaican wore a diamond earring, two gold rings on his right hand and two more on his left, and a gold chain-link necklace. He sipped his rum, tapped a coin in a shave-and-a-haircut-two-bits tempo, sighed, then yawned and stretched out his long arms.

"I am a slave of love," he said. "Love and music." He paused, looking around, and said, "Where is the music? There is no music in this place."

"Tonight there will be music," the bartender said.

"Yeah? Shit music, I guess."

The man was not overtly menacing, but there was something intimidating in his aspect and his words. You sensed that he was unpredictable, perhaps a little crazy. The bartender was uneasy. Experienced bartenders can identify a troublemaker long before the trouble erupts.

Four of the men finished their drinks, paid up, and left

the bar. Only the old man and the angry young man remained.

"There is no happiness here," the Jamaican complained. "This is one unhappy hole, man."

Then he abruptly turned and stared at me. It was a fierce, critical look, and in lilting tones he demanded, "Are you happy, my friend? If you are happy, then you will drink with me."

I said, "I'm happy as the day is long. Beer, thanks."

"They call me Bully."

"Shaw."

"My soul needs the music," Bully said. "Where is the music on this miserable island? Without music we are sad people. I myself, man, am a musician. Reggae. You like the reggae, Mr. Shaw?" He sang a few phrases of the Bob Marley song "I Shot the Sheriff." "But no one likes the reggae no more."

"I like it," I said.

He glared at the two men on the other side of the bar. "You don't like the reggae? Yes or no."

Without answering, the two men paid up, nodded at the bartender, and went outside.

"The bank come and take away my drums," Bully said. "My band split up, man. My brother, he goes to jail. What is this world without music? Dirty, filthy, ugly place that hurt you all the time. 'Fool,' the world says, and it hits you. 'Coward,' the world says, and it kicks you. 'Pay your debts, man,' the world says, and it kills you. There has got to be music. Without music it is all hurt."

I drank half of my beer. "What are you doing now, Bully?"

"I am a sailor."

"Sailing must be profitable this year," I said, nodding in the direction of his rings and necklaces.

"I do another thing too."

"What's that?"

He directed his baleful glare at me, held it for ten or fifteen seconds, shrugged then, as if conceding a point, and said, "I hurt people."

"Just like the world."

"I am an instrument of the hateful world."

"You need music, Bully."

"The music is gone, Mr. Shaw. Gone. Alas."

I finished my beer, dropped a twenty on the bar, and told the bartender to give the Jamaican a drink and keep the rest.

"Where are you going, man?"

"I have errands."

"Go away, then. I don't care. But I'll see you. This is a small place, eh, Mr. Shaw? Tonight we find some music together. Music and sweaty women. We do that?"

"Sure," I said. "See you later, then."

I walked through the empty streets to a curved, palm-lined street. The construction site lay beyond. Work had been halted. There were no sounds of jackhammers or the whine of chain saws. All of the engines were silent now, the diesels of backhoes and front loaders, the huge crane, and groups of workers sat resting in whatever shade they could find. It looked like any big construction site: mud, mounds of dirt, trenches, a confusion of equipment and materials.

The two main buildings were about half completed: a ten-story hotel, angled and concave in front so that every room's balcony had an unobstructed view of the harbor; and the cylindrical casino building, three stories, three layers, with each layer separated by circles of tinted glass. The casino looked like a stack of giant vanilla Oreo cookies.

I wound my way through the construction litter to the waterfront. Ahead there was a small marina with about half of its few dozen berths occupied by native fishing boats, houseboats—wood shacks mounted on aluminum pontoons—and yachts, sail and motor. A few more yachts lay anchored in a bay sheltered by a stone breakwater. Also moored in the bay, riding lightly on the smooth water, was a big silver seaplane with the TransBahama logo scripted on the fuselage. A stubby old freighter, a floating wreck, lay alongside the quay.

I walked along the sandy beach, up some steps, and out onto the quay. On my right there were spaced steel bollards and big steel mooring cleats. I passed a corrugated-steel building that surprisingly leaked breaths of cool fog. ICE, a blue-lettered sign stated. It was an ice-manufacturing plant, and its cool air condensed and turned to vapor where it leaked through cracks into the humid outside air.

There was no one on the freighter's deck, no sign of crew or cargo. A cormorant perched on a ventilator hood. The ship flew the Panamanian flag—a notorious flag of convenience. Maybe only Panama or Liberia would register such an unseaworthy old vessel. It was short, maybe one hundred ten feet long, but high and beamy, squat, out of proportion, as if an ordinary freighter had been cut in two and the blunt stern welded to the prow half.

She was dirty, neglected, smelly. Her hull beneath the waterline was foul with colonies of barnacles and submarine prairies of weed. Paint had chipped and peeled away to reveal four colors: a red primer, a mustard-yellow, a marine gray, and, the most recent coat, black. She was paint-mottled, rust-mottled, and impressed me as both comic and sinister.

Her deck bristled with stubby masts and winches and guy wires and crooked antennae. There was a sizable deckhouse with the bridge mounted on its forward section. Two cargo holds, one forward and the other aft. She was named *Mako*, after the man-eating shark.

I continued on past the freighter to the end of the quay. From there I could see beyond the breakwater to the deeper, darker blue sea beyond. The waves turned concave and crested with foam as they reached shoal water.

Henry, holding a whippy cane fishing pole, sat at the end of the quay. Two fish, queerly flattened and with their eyes seemingly misplaced, lay on the concrete. They were a species of flounder, and very good eating. The throwaway camera lay lens-up near the fish.

"I got some pictures," Henry said.

"Good pictures?"

"Prolly not."

"See anything interesting?"

"No." Then, "They took on ice. That interesting?"

"How much ice?"

"A lot. And they had a visitor."

"Did you get a picture?"

"Sure I did."

"Any of the other boys report to you yet?"

"Floyd; he saw one of them Jamaicans in town. Sitting in a bar with you." The boy grinned.

"Is there anyone aboard the freighter now?"

"I guess. One man I see. He's on the deck I pass by, he says, 'Hey, kid, want to see the ship? Want some cake and soda pop? Look at pictures?' I say, 'No, sir, thank you very much.'"

"Be careful, Henry. Stay away from them."

"You think I don't know that? A boy go down into the dark of that ship, he never be seen again."

"Maybe you should come with me back to town," I said.

"They's one more fish down there. I catch him and then I go. They don't snatch Henry."

I said, "If you wanted to take a little boat ride at night, what would you do?"

He knew what I meant. "Row or motor?"

"A rowboat is all right."

"The yacht people pull their dinghies up on shore when they come in from where they anchored. Leave them while they party. Other boats there most times too."

I dropped a twenty-dollar bill on the quay as I picked up the camera.

"Take care."

"Yeah," Henry said. "Oh, yeah!"

I had spent more than two hours in and around the village and hadn't been contacted by the men holding Peter Falconer, unless my encounter with Bully could be considered contact, and so I thought, to hell with it, and hired a taxi to return me to the Meridian Club.

The resort was silent, crushed-looking, beneath the oppressive heat and the pulsing sun. Palms drooped, seagulls and pelicans appeared half plucked and morose. Pop's cabin cruiser was still tied to the end of the pier, but the old man was gone. I stepped aboard. The cabin door was not locked. Inside I found the usual layout: the controls forward (duplicated above on the flying bridge); a compact galley with a two-burner propane stove, icebox, and food lockers; a dinette that could be converted into a double bunk; a small cabin below in the bows; and a variety of drawers and lockers. I removed my money belt and placed it and the camera in a deep drawer, beneath stacks of old charts.

I had been prepared to deal with the kidnappers, but there had not been a real approach, no honest move to negotiate. Maybe we could conclude the exchange tomorrow.

My visit to the bank might protect me from any outright robbery attempts. I certainly was not going to carry around the seven hundred fifty thousand dollars in bearer bonds at night.

My cottage was hot and stuffy. I closed all the windows and switched on the air conditioner.

There seemed something dreamlike about the day, this island, and my mission. It was similar to one of those dreams that are ordinary, even a little boring, but conceal an obscure menace behind the dull details.

I stripped off my sweat-soaked clothes, showered, and slept for several hours, dreaming of women who spiraled up out of the inky depths and who, though dead, beckoned to me with a forefinger when they surfaced.

It was dark when I awakened. I still felt submerged in dreams, both the actual dream and my surreal dream afternoon, except that it was night now and the menace was emerging, taking shape.

# Eleven

There were only a few customers in the Meridian Club's patio restaurant: the four sun-burned fishermen from Georgia, two well-dressed black couples, and a solitary fair-haired man who glanced at me and smiled in a way that suggested we were acquainted.

The tables were scattered among lemon and hibiscus trees and trellised bougainvillea, and Japanese lanterns—orange and green and yellow—glowed from wires strung overhead. You could smell flowers and an insect spray that was perfumed to smell like flowers but which carried a whiff of chemical astringency.

I was served sea bass, freshly caught, with a salad, french fries, peas, and a half bottle of white wine. Speakers concealed in the trees issued soft music. Waiters hovered.

The Georgians, tired from their long day in the sun, ate silently and soon left their table. The fair-haired man finished his meal, lit a cigarette, and idly blew smoke rings toward an overhead lantern. I noticed that Jasmine, the bank employee, was among the island couples; she caught my glance, wriggled her fingers in greeting, and flashed an amused smile.

Karpe appeared on the flagstone walk as I was finishing my coffee. He wore pressed slacks and a baggy Hawaiian shirt. Karpe hesitated, scanned the crowd, saw me, and approached my table with an aggressive stride. He was not the same man tonight; his calm ways, his deferential manner, were absent, and his gaze was hard.

He snatched at a chair and sat down across from me. "Where the fuck have you been?" he said.

"Care for a drink, Leroy?" I asked.

"I've been aboard the *Mako*. I saw Falconer."

"Keep your voice down."

Karpe looked around the patio, staring hard at the black couples and the fair-haired man.

"That guy," he said. "He's one of them."

The languid fair-haired man nodded to us. I guessed his age at about thirty, though he might have been younger. He wore his hair long in a schoolboy cut, and there was a boyish candor in his gaze and smile.

"His name is Charles," Karpe said.

He wore tasseled loafers, beige trousers, an off-white shirt with a paisley scarf loosely tied at his throat, and a double-breasted blue blazer. The clothes were expensively tailored, and Charles wore them in a way that suggested that he had never owned anything but the best.

"Let's go to town, Leroy," I said. "I feel like dancing."

He gazed at me, his mouth twisted in scorn, and he said, "I don't know what Tom thought he was doing, picking you for this job."

"Tom sent you along, didn't he? I'm just your batboy. Let's go."

It was Saturday night, relatively cool now, and the village

was brightly lighted and swarming with people of all ages. Smoke drifted through the streets. The air smelled of wood smoke and beer and fried fish and pit-barbecued pig. All of the cafés and bars were busy, and a five-piece band played a sort of Caribbean rock in an open-sided dance hall at the edge of town.

I led Karpe to a table near the center of the dance hall and ordered a pitcher of beer. We had to talk loudly to be heard over the noise and commotion. Karpe was still angry.

"Christ," he said. "Where were you? Do I have to do it all myself?"

"Do what, Leroy?"

"You know why we're here."

"I know why *I'm* here."

"Where's the money?"

"Why do you want to know?"

"I told them on the ship I'd make the exchange."

"You misinformed them."

The waitress brought a pitcher of beer, two frosted mugs, and a bowl of salted peanuts.

"Tell me about it," I said.

"In this noise? Let's get out of here."

"Never mind the noise. Tell me about it, Leroy."

After his jog and a swim in the pool, Karpe had gone to his cottage to wait for me; this job was far too dangerous for one man to handle alone, backup was essential, and he figured that I would soon realize that. We had to work as a team. "You know," he said, "you must know, that what they really want is you, me, and Falconer dead—no witnesses— and them sailing away with the money."

Karpe had waited for a couple of hours, finally gone to my cottage, and found that I had left without him. So he had gone into town then, wandered around, asking questions, cursing me, and at last he had been approached by a tall Jamaican with a Prince Valiant haircut and a goofy way of talking. "Do you wish to visit Mr. Falconer?" the Jamaican asked. Karpe replied that first he had to find his partner. "Oh," the Jamaican said, "do not worry about Mr. Shaw. He is at this minute aboard the ship, sharing a drink and a chat with my captain." And so Karpe and the Jamaican had gone to the *Mako*.

"That was risky," I said. "Foolish."

"The Jamaican said you were aboard the ship."

"You weren't obliged to believe him."

"I couldn't find you. Why shouldn't you be aboard the ship? We're here to get Falconer, aren't we?"

"It was stupid."

"I told you, Shaw. I owe Tom Petrie big time."

"Owe him your life?"

"Owe him my freedom."

The band took a break; dancers drifted back to their tables, and Karpe and I were able to talk in normal tones.

"You saw Falconer?" I asked.

"I saw him. The poor bastard."

He and the Jamaican, Bully, had walked out onto the quay. The gangplank was winched down and they had gone aboard the old ship, a junkpile held together by paint and rust, kept afloat by bilge pumps. There were two men on deck: a Mexican built like a gorilla, and another Jamaican, who they called Oxtail. Two white men were in the deckhouse: the snotty Charles, and the captain—an American, about fifty, with a face like a hatchet and a frequent but mirthless smile. You tensed up every time you saw that smile. He was the coldest and hardest son of a bitch that

Karpe had ever seen, and he had seen some cold and hard ones during his days in the drug trade.

Karpe, the two whites, and Bully gathered in a big cabin that, on an ordinary ship, would be called the saloon—this was a rectangular steel pigsty. The captain poured four glasses of a dark, syrupy rum. He lifted his glass and toasted Death: "A friend who looks like an enemy until you need him." Then he demanded the money. Karpe demanded to see Falconer.

"And you saw him," I said.

"They keep him locked in an empty storage room below deck, in darkness. It's worse than solitary confinement in prison, a filthy hole. He's in bad shape. He took a terrible beating. They hurt him, really hurt him. His face is cut and swollen and bruised, and most of his front teeth are broken. He couldn't talk clearly because of his teeth. And he said his hand was infected. He begged me. 'Give them the money,' he said. 'Give them anything they want. Please. Please get me out of here. Please.' And he cried. He cried like a baby."

"Did you know Falconer before?"

"I met him during his rape trial. I flew Tom Petrie back and forth between Bell Harbor and Miami for a week. Peter was free on bail. Yeah, I met him."

"Did you like him?"

"No, and I still don't, but I sure pity the bastard."

"Then what?"

"They took me back to the saloon. I told the captain that I didn't have control of the money, you did. That we would make the exchange. That we were playing it straight, all we wanted was Falconer. The captain said that we had until midnight tonight to bring the money. No bargaining, no negotiating, no quibbling. Bring the money. No money, and he'd chop off Falconer's thumbs. He said, 'The world's a hard place for a thumbless man.' "

I looked at my watch. It was a little after eleven o'clock. "What do you think?" I asked Karpe.

"Take them the money."

"Think again."

"You have to. Christ, Shaw, isn't that why we're here? To buy Falconer?"

"Sure. And I'll deal with them in daylight, in a public place. I'm not going aboard that ship."

"Petrie didn't tell me you were a coward."

"You should have inquired."

"Where's the money? Give it to me. I'll go back there."

"The money is in a safety-deposit box. The bank doesn't open until Monday morning."

"You put the money in a bank!"

"They had all afternoon to contact me. They didn't. Why not?"

"I'll go back."

"And do what?"

"Exchange the safety-deposit-box key for Falconer."

"You believe they'll accept a *key*?"

"I can try."

I removed the lockbox key from my pocket and placed it on the table.

Karpe said, "You really are quitting on this? Turning it all over to me?"

"You're a take-charge kind of guy, Leroy."

The musicians returned to the bandstand. The amplified music was loud and insistent, and the sweating dancers looked lost in a happy group delirium. A couple danced over to our table. The man looked down and grinned at me.

"Hello, Bully," I said.

"Good evening, Mr. Shaw. Good evening, Mr. Karpe. We do have music now, Mr. Shaw, and everybody happy. You see how happy the music make all the people?"

"Indeed I do, Bully. I myself can hardly keep from laughing."

Grinning, he clutched his partner, and together they whirled away across the floor.

Karpe gave me a sour look. "Are you trying to turn them into pets?"

The waitress came to our table, and I ordered another pitcher of beer.

"I'll pass my gun to you under the table," Karpe said. "They took my other pistol. I don't want to lose this one. Hold it for me."

I shook my head. "Hide it somewhere. Bury it on the beach. I don't want your gun."

"You're as close to useless as I've ever seen," he said.

"It's true that I've never done anything as useful as running drugs."

He picked the key up from the table, and tacked through the crowd. Bully followed him.

A girl of seventeen or eighteen came to my table and invited me to dance. We danced two numbers in the heat and flashing lights, and when I escorted her to her table I saw that she was with two other single girls. I danced with one, then the other.

Karpe was sitting at our table when I returned. He had drunk most of the new pitcher of beer. He regarded me with contempt as I pulled out a chair and sat down.

"Enjoying yourself?" he asked.

I wiped my sweaty face with a handkerchief. "Yes. I fell in love three times. You weren't gone long. How did it go?"

"They kept the key but didn't give me Falconer."

"Surprise, surprise."

"They want to see you. Right now."

"I told you, I'm not going aboard that ship. They can cut off Falconer's thumbs, cut off his head for all I care. No."

His smile was tight and malicious. "They told me to tell you that they've got the kid."

"What kid?"

"Some kid—Harry, Homer . . ."

"Henry," I said. "Goddamn it."

"What are you going to do? Abandon this kid the way you've abandoned Falconer?"

"What are *you* going to do? If I were you, Leroy, I'd get out to the airport damned quick and fly out of here."

"I've never run in my life," he said, "and I'm not going to run now."

I stood up.

"Order another pitcher of beer on your way out," Karpe said with a mean grin. "Are those girls good dancers?"

"They dance like angels."

I made my way through the joyful dancing crowd to the street.

# Twelve

The quay was silent except for the throb of *Mako*'s bilge pumps and the splash of expelled water, and a low humming that came from the ice-manufacturing plant. A late-rising orange half-moon was cocked on the eastern horizon. The mast and rigging lights of the yachts anchored out in the basin glittered like stars and planets and, like the stars, were reflected on the cobalt water.

*Mako* was an ugly silhouette against the star-sprayed sky. The gangplank was down. Lights glowed dimly behind the bridge's windows.

"That you, Mr. Shaw?" a voice called.

"It is."

"You want the boy?"

"Send him down, Bully."

"We escort little Henry," Bully said, and four shadows detached from the deeper shadows and drifted down the gangplank to the quay. Three men, one boy.

"Are you all right, Henry?" I asked. I could not clearly see his features, but his posture was rigid and his voice shaky.

"Yeah," he said. "But Bully took all my money."

"Pirates will do that."

"Go away," Bully told the boy. "Keep your mouth shut. Hear? Shut. Or you know what."

Henry walked a few yards up the quay and then broke into a run.

I was carefully searched, then Bully preceded me up the gangplank, with the Mexican and the other Jamaican following. I was not exactly a guest, not precisely a prisoner. *Mako* reeked of filthy bilgewater and rust, diesel fuel and lubricating oil. I was led forward to a steel ladder. Again Bully led the way; the other two men remained below on deck. The ladder led up fifteen feet to a railed walkway. We went through an open door into the bridgehouse, a dimly lighted semioval space that contained the wheel and compass, controls, navigational equipment, and a console lined with dials and switches. Windows curved around the half oval, and I could look down to the foredeck or out toward the village lights. Behind us was a bulkhead with two doors, one of which opened to the captain's quarters, the other to an inside stairway that led down into the deckhouse.

"This is the nerve center," a voice ironically drawled. "This is *Mako's* cerebral cortex. From this place we rule the world."

The fair-haired man, Charles, whom I had seen at the patio restaurant this evening, was slouched in a canvas deck chair.

"You're Shaw," he said.

"Right."

"Call me Ishmael. Care for a drink?"

"A small one."

"Bully? A rum for Shaw, and a tipple for me, if you please."

There was a tray containing bottles, glasses, and a bucket of ice on the chart table. The Jamaican poured two rums over ice, one for me and one for himself, then carried the bottle to the languid Charles.

"Cheers," he said.

A door quietly opened and a man was framed against the cabin's light. Someone moved within the cabin—a nude woman, black, with heavy breasts and bleached yellow hair.

"Behold," Charles said. "Behold Captain Mephisto."

"Captain Raven Ahriman," the man said quietly, watching me.

"Captain Blight," Charles said. "Captain Necro."

Ahriman wore only a pair of khaki shorts. He was a powerfully built man, very fit for his age, which I guessed at about fifty; thick-boned and broad through the shoulders and chest. He had the look of a fair-skinned man who had over the years acquired a permanent blue-water suntan. His body hair—arms, chest, legs—had been shaved to better display the definition of muscle, and he wore his oiled black hair twisted into a single long braid.

"Why are you playing games?" he asked.

"Why are *you* playing games?" I replied.

The woman behind him closed the cabin door.

He advanced into the bridgehouse. Ahriman had been marked by prison as, similarly, a career soldier is marked by the army; it was there, you could see it.

"You don't have the money," he said.

"No."

"Where is it?"

"In the village bank."

"The bank. Naturally. That's where one keeps money. A bank."

"It's in a safety-deposit box."

"Yes, yes, certainly."

"Karpe told you that."

"Did he?"

"You have the key."

"The key to your safety-deposit box? No."

He spoke softly, with deadpan mockery, and the intensity of his stare compelled your attention. Karpe had called him hatchet-faced. There was an acute angle to the planes of his cheeks and the angle of his jaw. His features seemed gathered along a vertical center line, from his widow's peak down a long bony nose to a wide mouth that slanted from middle to corners to a jutting chin. His eyes were a sort of gray, sort of blue, and set close together.

"When does the bank open?" he asked.

"Monday morning at nine."

"Monday at nine. Do you expect me to wait until then?"

"That's your choice."

"No, it was yours. And your bad luck. Falconer's very bad luck."

His malevolence was part theater, of course, the deadly persona some convicts assume when confined with other dangerous men, but Ahriman did project a primitive power and skewed intelligence. He surely had done time behind bars. I had met many criminal psychopaths during my years in the Army's CID and after, interrogated some of them, read the files on others, discussed the nature of the type with psychiatrists, and I knew that Raven Ahriman—not his real name, I suspected—would have been a boss in any prison yard, a petty and violent monarch.

"So," he said, "you intend to keep the money and let Falconer die."

"I can get the money out of the bank on Monday morning. We'll make the exchange then."

He again stepped forward. He remained very still, which made you relax; but then he moved and it was like suddenly noticing that there was no barrier between you and a dangerous zoo animal.

"Look," I said, "I was in the village for more than two hours this afternoon. I had a drink with your man Bully. Before and after those hours I was available at the Meridian Club. At any time you could have produced Falconer and taken the money."

"Are you saying that I'm stupid?"

"Or you could have brought Falconer to the airport this morning. Surely you knew we were coming. Falconer gets into the plane, I toss out the bearer bonds, and we fly away. Clean and simple."

"Do you think I am stupid?" Ahriman asked, as if he really wanted to know.

I cautiously said, "I think it's strange that you would more or less openly conduct a criminal enterprise from aboard this easily recognizable, easily traced ship. You must be very confident that Petrie wouldn't report the kidnapping to the police."

"Your man Petrie only wants Falconer. Isn't that so?"

"Now, yes. But once he has him? Afterward?"

He feigned surprise. "But aren't we all honorable men?"

"That isn't something," I said, picking my words, "that one can count on."

"Where is the film?"

"Film?"

"Don't provoke me any further. The boy said that you had taken back the camera."

"The camera and film are in my cottage at the Meridian."

He moved forward two more steps. He had a distinctly unpleasant smell. It wasn't sweat or uncleanliness, but rather a natural odor, musky and glandular, like the reek of a rutting animal.

"A moment ago you mentioned bearer bonds," he said.

"The bonds are easily negotiable," I said. "As good as cash."

Now I saw the mirthless smile that Karpe had mentioned. It was not a smile at all, but a display of gritted teeth, a reflexive show of aggression.

Charles did not taunt Ahriman now. He and Bully were silent. They did not move. They knew Ahriman, recognized his mood—he was cocked like a gun.

I figured I had nothing to lose; it was going to happen. "Since you asked—yes, you're stupid."

He lifted his two fists and held them before my eyes; the knuckles were covered with lacerations, some raw and others half scabbed, and I saw the commas and crescents of older, healed scars.

He quickly slapped my face, backhanded the other cheek, cuffed me again.

I threw a punch, but he was expecting it, and he easily grabbed my wrist, twisted, and increased the pressure. I felt my wristbones compress. Any more force and he would break them.

He hooked his right fist into my abdomen. The blow knocked me unconscious for a time. I had never experienced such an explosion of pain. Nothing like this. Then I was lying on my side on the floor, curled up tightly, clutching my belly, desperately trying to inhale. I could not breathe. The ache in my guts was forgotten at that moment; all I could think of was air, get a lungful of air. I heard Charles, as if from a remote place, another dimension, say, "You're a fucking brute, Raven. That was not necessary." Then I heard a long rasping sound, like a file on metal, and that too seemed distant, but it was me, and I was breathing again.

"Put him down in the hold," Ahriman said, and turned, entered the cabin, and shut the door.

I needed time to recover. Bully helped me to my feet. Charles gave me a few ounces of water in a dirty glass. My insides felt knotted. Every inhalation hurt.

Bully said, "Got to go now, Mr. Shaw."

"I'll intercede with Raven on your behalf," Charles said. "I'll help you if I can."

Bully assisted me down the inside companionway ladder, and he and the two men waiting below escorted me toward the prow. Music still played in the village. The half-moon was well above the horizon now, and its light etched the bay waters and illuminated the anchored yachts and the seaplane. I looked at my watch: twelve-ten.

There were two teak hatch covers midway down the foredeck. Each provided access to the same cargo hold. The Mexican attached a hooked cable to the forward cover and lifted it with a hand-cranked winch. There was a blast of humid, foul air from the darkness below. I was too weak, too much in pain, to fight them or sprint for the railing.

"Bully . . ." I said.

"I am sorry, man. Go down."

"Lock me up with Peter Falconer."

"Go down, Mr. Shaw, or we throw you down."

I started down the ladder. Bully shined a flashlight into the hold as I descended. It was very hot. The stench seemed to thicken in my nose and throat. I kept going. The ladder and the steel-plated walls were slimy. Water droplets formed crooked worm tracks through a fog of condensation on the plates. Bully flicked his flashlight's beam around the hold, revealing the dimensions of my prison. There was no cargo, but I glimpsed objects that I couldn't identify, debris of some sort, and the reflected yellow glow of a pair of eyes—a rat? Other pinpoint lights sparked red when the passing flashlight beam ignited them.

"Be of strong heart, Mr. Shaw," Bully called. "Strong heart."

I reached the floor. The flashlight was turned off. I saw the starry moon-washed sky through the square opening above, then the hatch cover was maneuvered into place, my view of the outside world was reduced to a thin slice, and finally I was immersed in utter darkness. It was like watching from your coffin as the lid is fitted shut.

Since childhood I had suffered a mild form of claustrophobia. It wasn't debilitating; I had never lost control. It was simply that enclosed places, especially if they were also dark, caused me extreme discomfort. I did not fear heights. Crowds didn't disturb me. I was as much at ease around water as a seal. And I had no more than a normal aversion to snakes and venomous insects and rats except—and this was key—except when they were associated with my claustrophobic anxieties. Hell was a steel cave like the *Mako*'s cargo hold.

# Thirteen

Claustrophobia.

I leaned back against the ladder. My heartbeat and respiration were very fast, as if I had been running for miles, and I was drenched with a greasy fear sweat. I knew I must not panic. I could not allow my imagination to seize control of mind and body. It was a matter of either rationality or dementia. I commanded myself to evaluate the situation: there was plenty of air, I would not suffocate; it was pure delusion to think that the walls were closing in, that water would soon gush into the hold and drown me; rat bites, insect bites would not be fatal; Ahriman would eventually have me released from the hold. He wanted the money. I was being softened up.

The stench was sickening, an evil compound of stagnant water and slime and rust and something else—urine and excrement.

"Is there anyone here?" I called. My voice dully echoed and re-echoed in the queer acoustics of the hold. It was a stranger's voice. Then silence, marred only by a low humming sound and a faint ringing.

It was absolutely black. The only light I saw was self-created—brief retinal flashes that eventually faded. This hot, humming blackness seemed more than the mere absence of light; I vaguely felt that it possessed qualities of its own, substance, and a sort of mystical consciousness. I knew I had to suppress that thought and others like it.

"Is there anyone in here with me?" I called again, and again was surrounded by slurred echoes.

I tried to envision my glimpses of the hold as I'd descended the ladder. Bully's flashlight had exposed the dimensions well enough. The cargo hold was longer than wide, perhaps twenty feet deep, and asymmetrical, with the hull curving down toward the keel and narrowing toward the bows. I had seen yellow eyes, probably a rat, and pinpoint eyes like jewels, and a disorderly scatter of debris. I coaxed my mind to return to that particular view, bring it back and study it as if it were a snapshot.

Many patches of a dull yellow. Straw. I smelled moldy straw as the thought came to me. Straw pallets—dozens of them—and blankets like rags, more rags, which might have been items of clothing, a bucket, a pair of sandals, broken glass glittering in Bully's flashlight beam, empty plastic water jugs, scraps of paper and plastic, strewn rubbish. Was I imagining that I had seen all this? No, the hold did stink of urine and human excrement. People had been confined in this abysmal place, and not long ago. Men, perhaps women and children too. *Mako* was an alien smuggler. I wondered if the poor souls who had suffered here were safely ashore in Florida or decomposing on the bottom of the sea.

I heard, or imagined that I heard, new sounds: the scratch of tiny nails, a scuttling, the hushed beating of wings—not bats, surely. Still, I pictured bat-winged things and big rats and even reptiles, all converging on me.

"Falconer?" I said.

I was alone. Karpe had said that Peter Falconer was confined in a storeroom that was bare except for a metal table and chair, the same room in which the Polaroid photo had been taken.

*Mako* moved gently with the change of tide, and more sounds fractured the general silence: the slosh of water below in the bilges, a creaking as steel plates strained against rivets, and the muted systole and diastole of the pumps.

The intense heat was stifling, but my sweat was cool and I shivered. My guts ached. My abdomen hurt from just below the ribs to the pelvis. I feared that I might be bleeding inside; a blow like the one Ahriman had inflicted can lacerate the liver, rupture the spleen. Sick, a little dizzy, I sat on the wet floor with my back against a bulkhead.

I couldn't read the dial of my watch in the blackness. How much time had passed? It seemed like many hours. Perhaps the sun had risen. Did time appear to run faster or slower when one was isolated in darkness, deprived of all stimuli other than an awful stench and stray noises? The tide was changing. That would tell me the approximate time if I were in Bell Harbor, but I was not familiar with the local tide tables.

There were gaps in time, stretches when no thought or event measured time's passage. It was like sleep, though I didn't lose consciousness. My mind simply experienced periods of emptiness that were preceded and followed by periods of normal perceptions of time.

Later, I actually did sleep, for minutes or hours, and was abruptly awakened by noise, a heavy throbbing that transmitted a tremor throughout the ship. The engines. The cargo hold was converted into a sort of amplifier. Pistons pounded, loose hull plates vibrated.

The noise and vibration increased when the propellers were engaged. Drops of condensation were shaken loose from the underside of the deck above and fell all around like rain. We began moving. My body reacted to the new angles and pressures. *Mako* made a big looping turn to starboard, away from the quay and into the harbor. She later turned again, to port, and I supposed that we were heading out through the channel. The ship began to pitch and roll as it entered the open sea.

We were not under way long when the hatch cover above was lifted and swung aside. I was surprised to see the moon. Its misty light slanted in from the port, the east side. My sense of time had been scrambled; no more than a couple of hours had passed. There were stars visible too, and streams of herringbone clouds. A rectangular shaft of light angled down into the cargo hold, gleaming on the wet metal floor and illuminating the straw pallets and debris. I had not been wrong. *Mako* was an alien smuggler.

A flashlight beam stabbed down, blinding me, and Bully called, "Would you like to come up on deck, Mr. Shaw? We are serving tea and scones."

"Get the light out of my eyes."

He shifted the flashlight beam.

I stalled for time, until my night vision partially returned, and then I slowly started up the ladder. It seemed likely that they intended to kill me. Kill me and toss my weighted corpse into the sea. By leaving port now they implicitly confessed that I was of no value to them. They had made a separate deal.

I paused halfway up the ladder. "I'll get the money," I said.

"What money is that, Mr. Shaw?"

"The seven hundred fifty thousand."

"Oh, that's all right, Mr. Shaw. Mr. Karpe is going to arrange that."

"You people trust Karpe?"

"Come along now, Mr. Shaw. Don't be difficult."

I resumed climbing. Bully grinned down at me. When I reached the top, he grasped my forearm and hauled me up on deck. The Mexican who operated the winch grinned too; they knew how awful even a couple of hours alone in the cargo hold were, and how it could damage a man.

"Jesus," I said.

"See that?" Bully said, grinning. "Jesus did help you, Mr. Shaw, made you free again."

The ship, without cargo or ballast, was riding high in the water and rolling more than normal in these moderate seas. I risked a glance astern, past the deckhouse and bridge; the village lights appeared no more than three or four miles away, and there were other lights sprinkled over the water nearby, native boats probably, fishers of squid and shark. The ship's wake was a seething phosphorescent swath carved into the moon-scalloped sea.

The Mexican moved closer to me. He carried the steel winch handle. Both men were still grinning, but they were tense too, leaning forward a little, their feet set firmly on the deck. Bully held his six-cell flashlight casually, resting the barrel on his right shoulder, but it was positioned so that he could quickly strike.

"I want to talk to the captain," I said.

Bully glanced up toward the bridge. I followed his gaze: Ahriman, a pale figure in the moonlight, was standing behind the railing, looking down at us. He held either a rifle or shotgun.

"I want to talk to you," I called.

Ahriman did not reply.

Bully almost gently, perhaps even sadly, placed his left hand on my shoulder. The Mexican sidled closer. But even violent men sometimes hesitate before committing murder. Killing without anger, without fear, as the execution of another's command, is not easy. It is especially hard when one is not shielded by the efficient impersonality of a gun. It's hard to stab and slash, to strangle, especially hard to beat a man to death with a winch handle and flashlight. At the same time it can be difficult for the chosen victim of murder to act; one is betrayed by hope, paralyzed by fear.

"Doesn't Ahriman trust you with a gun, Bully?" I said.

"Bully?" Ahriman called.

The Jamaican's grip tightened on my shoulder. I pulled back, throwing him off balance, then grasped his wrist with both my hands and, using the initial momentum, swung him past my body and into the open cargo hold. He did not cry out. We heard his body strike the floor twenty feet down. There was the original sound of the impact, a reverberate metallic *bang* like the noise of a distant car wreck, followed by a series of dull echoes.

The Mexican was frozen for an instant. I ran. I sprinted toward the stern, past a tall ventilator hood, past a power winch, past a coil of wire cable, and then I was running along the narrow passageway between the deckhouse and rail. The Mexican was close behind. I had that feeling of running in a nightmare, as if you are moving through a medium much thicker than air, filled with dread, pursued by Death. I cleared the passageway and ran over the broad aft deck. *"Hijo de puta!"* the Mexican shouted. There was a sharp crack and at the same instant something whispered past my ear. Another crack, and then I leaped over the stern rail and into space. Out of control, turning, I glimpsed the boiling neon-green water below and then, turning again, saw a similar bright band arched across the sky—the dense, starry Milky Way.

It was like falling out of a third-story window. I hit hard and sank deep. The sea blazed with phosphorescence. I was submerged within a cloud of millions of flashing green bubbles, pummeled and spun by the jetlike turbulence churned up by the spinning screws. I looked up. The surface, a silvery moonlit lens seen through the glowing, ascending bubbles, seemed very high above me—too high. My lungs burned. My abdomen ached. Gradually the force of the slipstream diminished, became no more than a confusion of currents, and I swam hard, hard, up through the magic green light toward the distorting lens through which I imagined I could see stars, and up, dying, and finally I broke through to that other world. Air, life, hope.

I rested, treading water. Eventually I was able to breathe normally. The swells were no more than three or four feet high. They burned green along the crests, sizzled like electrical fires. I was buoyed up by the swells, poised on top for a moment, and then began a smooth slide into the troughs. *Mako* was half a mile away now, a sinister black hulk trailing a comet of light.

I could see village lights when lifted atop a swell. It was a long swim. I knew that I could swim several miles if I had to, but the currents and tide might be against me, might sweep me away from land. Still, I felt lucky. This was my lucky night.

I was about to begin removing my shoes and clothes when I saw the lights of a boat. It was not far off. Both the red starboard and green port lights were visible, so I knew it was coming directly toward me. The lights vanished when I descended into a trough, reappeared as I glided up the face of the succeeding wave. It was a little closer each time I saw it. I heard the engines, recognized its silhouette—a boxy old cabin cruiser with a narrow flying bridge and long, whiplike outriggers set at a distinctive angle.

Pop had shifted the engines into neutral and put out the accommodation ladder by the time the boat drifted down to me. I hauled myself aboard.

"Thought you told me there wasn't going to be no shooting," the old man said.

I collapsed into one of the fishing chairs. *Mako* was now just a dim shape fading into darkness. "Was there shooting?" I asked.

"Plenty. I seen the flashes. They was shooting bullets at you, at me, at my boat. Put a hole topsides."

"There'll be a big bonus for you, Captain."

"I don't mind hearing that. You still want to go to Whisper Cay?"

"I do."

"Get yourself something to eat and drink," Pop said. "Squeeze the water out of them clothes."

He climbed the ladder to the flying bridge, switched the engines to forward, and the cabin cruiser headed off toward the southeast.

Pop had prepared the boat as if for an ordinary charter; there were soft drinks and cold beer in the icebox, fresh fruits, salad makings, and fillet of beef sandwiches wrapped in foil. My money belt and the camera had not been disturbed.

I ate a sandwich with two Cokes. My body felt ruined but my spirits were high. It is not often that a man is embraced by Death and yet manages to escape. You are dead, and then, by a combination of action and luck, you find yourself alive. Another chance at life, by God, and one that you vow not to waste.

I left the cabin, climbed the ladder to the flying bridge, and sat in the chair next to Pop. How had he managed to find me? He had followed the freighter. He knew right off that I was a man up to no good, and if there was no good happening tonight it would happen around that *Mako* ship. Still, he had been startled to see a man fly off the stern of the ship, surprised too to see the flashes of gunfire and hear one bullet rip into his boat's topsides.

The engines rumbled. The control dials glowed green, the same green as the phosphorescence of the sea, and Pop, while speaking rarely, was as good company as a man could ask for. Together we cruised through the night into a gaudy sunrise.

# Fourteen

Whisper Cay was mostly asleep when we docked at a marina. I gave Pop the money I owed him plus a thousand dollars that I withdrew from an ATM machine—expense money, Tom Petrie's money.

It took a couple of hours to arrange a charter flight to Florida. I ate a big breakfast at a seaside café, then placed a telephone call to Petrie's home. He picked up the receiver after half a dozen rings.

"Am I disturbing you, Tom, on this pleasant Sunday morning?" I said. "Are you on your way to church, maybe? Off to do good work?"

"Shaw? Are you all right? Do you have Falconer?"

"Falconer is off on a Caribbean cruise."

"Goddamn it, man, what the hell do you think you're doing?"

"I thought I had a free hand in ransoming Falconer. Did I misunderstand? Listen, get in touch with Karpe on Big Sandy Cay. Bring him back."

"He is back. In fact, he's with me right now. We're having breakfast by the pool."

"Lovely. When did he leave the island?"

"Last night, just after you went aboard that freighter. He phoned me, and I pulled him out. It was too dangerous the way things were going."

"Yes," I said.

"You really fucked up," Petrie said.

"Did I? Well, it *was* dangerous. Karpe and his freelancing made it dangerous, the arrogant son of a bitch; and you made it dangerous, Tom, you duplicitous son of a bitch."

"Wait! Don't hang up. Do you still have the bearer bonds?"

"I'm sorry, Tom," I said. "Really, truly sorry." I broke the connection.

# Fifteen

Tom Petrie lived among the rich and almost rich in an area a few miles north of Bell Harbor. There, over many years, people had created an artificial paradise by converting drab Florida wetlands into a jungly enclave that the inhabitants fondly called "Venetia." It was an "exclusive" community, with no more than a couple dozen houses on big lots. Each house fronted one of a network of canals. At least one yacht was docked near each house. There were live oaks that trailed great shawls of Spanish moss, exotic tropical trees and shrubs imported from around the world, and, early on Sundays, a quiet in which you might hear the *pop* of a cleanly hit tennis shot or the *clack* of a mallet striking a croquet ball.

A servant led me through the house and out patio doors to the lawn. Tom had guests, maybe thirty people, some casually dressed, others in swimming suits or tennis whites. I recognized some of them: a banker, a real estate developer, a state senator, a sugar-cane tycoon named Pelletier.

Petrie was standing down by the swimming pool, talking

to a beautiful young woman who listened to him with a cocked hip and a skeptical smile. He ratcheted up the charm, and she laughed. I caught his eye. He frowned, nodded, then made an abrupt gesture toward a bar that had been set up beneath a giant oak. He was again smiling when he turned back to the girl.

People were gathered in small groups around the pool and lawn. Four duffers were playing mixed-doubles pitty-pat tennis on the court. I did not see Leroy Karpe.

The bar stocked only imported beers. I got a Paulaner from the bartender and carried it out of the shade to a wrought-iron bench. The lawn looked more blue than green. I wondered where you bought blue grass and how much it cost. Blue grass, blue sky, a blue heron that stalked through the grass fringing the canal, stabbing at insects. The muddy water of the canal gleamed a metallic brown in the sunlight. Tom's forty-eight-foot Bertram cruiser was tied to his dock. Some teenage girls were playing badminton on the lawn across the canal. A woman on her way to the bar smiled at me as she passed. It was a nice party, though maybe a bit too genteel for my blood. Still, it was early, and not much alcohol had been consumed. I was glad that I had stopped off at my apartment to shave and change out of my *Mako*-soiled clothes. I might look like an aloof guest, or at least a tastefully dressed security man hired for the occasion. The sunlight was warm; a breeze whispered in the treetops; flies buzzed. I fell asleep.

"Some people look like idiots when they're asleep."

I opened my eyes. Petrie and the woman were standing a few feet from the bench, looking down at me.

"Try sleeping on a hard bench," I said.

"Try sleeping at home."

I stood up. "I had a hard night, Tom."

"Drinking and dancing, according to what I heard."

"I danced my heart out," I said.

The woman smiled at me. She had supermodel looks, with the shade of light brown hair that streaks blond in the sun, and the bone structure and well-defined features that are often called classical. She was tall, in her late twenties, and she looked familiar though I was sure we had never met.

"This is Shaw," Petrie said. "Our failed go-between."

The woman held out her hand.

"Shaw, meet Susan Falconer."

Her hand was softly padded but the grip firmer than one expects from a woman.

"You're Peter's sister?" I asked.

"Yes."

"God, she's a beauty, isn't she, Shaw?"

I released her hand. She did not closely resemble her brother in the photographs of him I'd seen.

"Beautiful, yes," I said. "But can she cook a meat loaf?"

"Forgive him," Petrie said. "He's addled."

"You saw my brother last night, Mr. Shaw?"

"Dan, please, or Shaw. No, I didn't see him."

She looked at Petrie.

"I made an assumption," he said.

She turned back to me. "They didn't let you see him?"

"No."

"Why not?"

"I don't know." But I thought I knew.

"Mr. Karpe was allowed to see Peter and talk to him."

"Was he?"

"Karpe saw Peter," Tom said firmly. "He told me all about it."

I said, "And where is our Leroy, Tom?"

"He should be here in an hour or two. He flew back to Big Sandy Cay."

"Why?"

"I'm not sure. But he should be back soon."

Susan Falconer brushed some stray wisps of hair away from her eyes. "I don't understand why they wouldn't make the exchange. They have Peter, you have the money. Don't you?"

"You do still have the bearer bonds, don't you, Shaw?" Petrie asked. "Dan?"

"Now, that's a funny story," I said.

"It better not be too funny. That's seven hundred fifty thousand dollars we're talking about. Susan's money, all she could raise."

"If," I said, "*if* there was any chance of making the exchange yesterday, Karpe fouled it up. *You* fouled it up by getting him involved. He's a bad-news cowboy, Tom."

"Yeah, well, you'll have a chance to say that to his face. The four of us are going to have a powwow later. But right now I've got to go circulate and play the oily host. I've got to punch my guests' tickets, so to speak. You two get to know each other. But not too well."

Petrie gave each of us the sort of forbidding look that dog owners employ to warn their pets to behave, and then he turned and sauntered off down the lawn.

Susan Falconer and I watched him go—a shark in the disguise of a suburbanite—and then we sat together on the bench. She crossed her legs. She folded her arms. She closed her eyes and lifted her faced to the sun. Her profile was lovely. She looked perfect: perfect skin and perfect hair and perfect teeth and a perfect figure and a perfectly modulated voice—she did not seem quite real. But I assumed that, like every other person on the planet, she had an imperfect psyche.

A power yacht slowly cruised up the canal, shearing off bow waves and spinning a wake that turned the water a color like root-beer foam. The blue heron turned a cold reptilian eye on a guest who had ventured too close. A light breeze eased the heat a little. The party was gaining pace: The voices were louder, the laughter freer, the small groups of people were breaking up and reforming into different units. One of the caterer's men was firing up a pair of charcoal grills.

"Susan," I said. "Tom mentioned that the seven hundred fifty thousand dollars was everything you could raise. Won't you share in the estate?"

She did not open her eyes; she spoke to the sun. "I have a trust that issues me a few thousand dollars each month. That's all, except for the ransom money. My family believes in primogeniture. Do you know what that is?"

"The eldest son gets it all."

"Almost all, in my case. I received a lump sum when I turned twenty-one. And there's the trust."

"Where do you live?"

She opened her eyes and looked at me. "New York. I came here as soon as I heard of Peter's trouble."

"Do you work in New York?"

"I was an editor with a fashion magazine called *Très Chic*. I did a little of everything. A little writing, a little editing, a little of this and that. I posed for picture layouts."

"Are you going back when this is settled?"

"The magazine is failing. I doubt if there'll be another issue."

"What's next for you, then?"

"I'm not sure. And you," she said, "you're a cop."

"I was, in the Army and for a while after. Now I'm becoming a lawyer. Slowly."

"I make exceptions," she said, "but generally speaking, I don't much like cops."

"Maybe you've never needed one."

"I can't help remembering that the Gestapo were policemen. And the KGB, SAVAC, all the others. And it seems that every time I read a newspaper or turn on the television and terrible things are being done to people—in Africa, Asia, the Middle East, Latin America, everywhere—they are usually being done by police, civilian and military. Cops are the ruling class's iron fist."

"It's nice to hear a member of the ruling class stand up for the poor and oppressed."

She laughed. "Phony me and my noblesse oblige."

"Are you close to Peter?" I asked.

"I was, very close. But he went away to school when I was fifteen. I didn't often see him after that."

"He seems . . ." I said, trying to provoke her, crack her poise, "brother Peter seems like a nasty shit."

"Are you referring to his alleged rapes?"

"He has a juvenile record too."

She was quiet for a time, and then slowly she said, "Peter is a solipsist."

"Which is a fancy word for . . . ?"

"On some level, deep down, in an inaccessible place, Peter believes that only he is truly real and that others are just bit actors, dream people, in his private drama."

"That might be bad news for the dream people."

"The present trouble isn't of his making."

"Maybe not. What did he do? I mean, besides waiting for his thirtieth birthday."

"He searched. He tried poetry, painting, the theater. He

wrote a thin, precious book of philosophy and published it at his own expense. We didn't correspond often, but in his last letter to me he said he was going to be a filmmaker in the style of the surrealist Luis Buñuel. He was very excited, he believed that at last he had found his vocation. *Vocation*—a word he used almost in its religious sense."

"Was filmmaking going to be another passing fancy?"

"I don't know. It always seemed to me that Peter had a powerful creative drive but not much talent. That can be destructive. He's convinced that he possesses genius. He thinks he's great and will someday be recognized by the world as great. Which is a pity, really, because he is gifted in other ways. He's bright, funny, generous, very charming when he chooses to be. He could be successful in many fields. People love him. But then eventually his dark side emerges, this—I don't know—this small-boy arrogance and cruelty. And then they don't love him as much."

"And you? You don't love him as much?"

"He's my brother."

"Are you a dream person?"

"Everyone is at a certain level, for Peter."

"Would Peter ransom you if positions were reversed?"

"Of course."

"Are you sure? You mentioned his selfishness."

"I don't think I used that word."

"You make him sound pathetic."

"Then I haven't explained him at all well."

I said, "I picture him as the sort of small boy who pulled off butterfly wings because they were so delicate and pretty."

"For God's sake," she said with her first flash of anger at my rude probing, "Peter isn't an idiot, a degenerate. He's a complicated, sensitive man—and he's a troubled man. You're clearly too vulgar to understand someone like Peter."

"Tell me more about him."

"I've said enough."

"What you tell me might help in getting him back."

"I doubt that."

"Is he mentally ill, then?"

She smiled tiredly. "No. Did it sound that way? It's impossible to accurately describe a person by focusing on a few flaws—which is what you want to do. Explain Peter Falconer in five hundred words or less."

"I'm sorry," I said. "I've been rough. But not a fraction as rough as Ahriman has been and is going to be."

"Ahriman?"

"Raven Ahriman is what the boss kidnapper calls himself."

"How does he spell Ahriman?"

"I don't know."

"Ahriman—A-h-r-i-m-a-n—is the spirit of evil in the Zoroastrian religion. Sort of the equivalent of the devil as Ormazd—or Ahura Mazda—might correspond to God."

"How do you know that?"

"My college roommate took comparative religion."

"So the man took the name of a spirit of evil."

"And Raven—ravens are considered messengers of evil by some."

"Was another roommate studying ornithology?"

"Wait. Peter considered himself a Zoroastrian when he was young. He read all of Nietzsche's books and especially loved *Thus Spake Zarathustra*. Zarathustra is an alternate spelling of Zoroaster."

"Nietzsche. Did Peter regard himself as a superman?"

She smiled wanly. "I suppose. *Übermensch*. Overman."

"I don't know. Nietzsche, Overman, Zoroaster, Ahriman."

"I'm awfully tired," she said. "This has all been exhausting. I'm going to my room."

"Your room?"

"Tom has been kind enough to give me his guest room."

"Tom," I said, "has a heart of gold."

I watched her walk across the lawn and through the patio doors into the house. Now, maybe, Susan Falconer would go to her room and weep for her brother.

Later, Tom Petrie stopped by the bench on his way to the bar. "What do you think of Susan?" he asked me.

"Beautiful," I said, "and smart."

"I'm in love, Shaw."

"Naturally."

"This is the real thing. It hurts. Love hurts like angina when it's new and true. I'm going to marry her."

"Congratulations."

"She doesn't know it yet."

"Don't spoil it by telling her."

"I am deeply in love," he said, and there was more than a hint of self-mockery in his tone. "It's like dengue fever. You know dengue fever? It's also called breakbone fever. Love aches."

He was halfway to the bar when he stopped and turned. "Are you going to sit there all day like a fucking garden gnome?"

# Sixteen

We gathered in the library after all the guests had gone. Two of the walls were lined floor to ceiling with books. Tom once admitted that he had bought a truckload of used books through his interior decorator—instant intellectual credibility.

Petrie stood behind his desk, no longer the genial host. He was irritably efficient now, in his executive mode.

"Where the hell is Leroy?" he demanded.

"He's eating," Susan Falconer said. "Your Leroy is outside, eating quarts of leftover lobster salad."

Susan lounged on a leather sofa, her back against a bolster and her knees drawn up. She wore shorts and a sleeveless blouse. Her feet were bare. She did not paint her toes or fingernails; she used little makeup and displayed no jewelry. Her lack of artifice was perhaps in itself an effective artifice.

I sat in one of the two swivel chairs across from the desk. On the wall above Petrie's head was another painting by the maestro of mud. Twilight turned to night as we waited for Karpe. The window louvers were open, and a breeze ruffled the gauzy curtains and brought us the buzz and whir and tick of insects down by the canal.

"Tom," I said, "how did you happen to go into business with Karpe?"

"The charter service? It was a good opportunity."

"He said you kept him out of jail."

"I *got* him out of jail, then kept him out."

"He smuggled drugs?"

"At that time," Petrie said, "Leroy was a dashing, reckless youth who temporarily went wrong."

"I didn't know you defended drug dealers."

"Drug dealers," he said, "have many grievous faults and but one virtue: They pay their legal bills."

"Like Mafia capos."

"Like Mafia capos and corrupt politicians and murderers who happen to live in Palm Beach."

"Susan," I said, "did you ever know a friend of your brother's named Charles?"

"Charles what?"

"I don't know the last name."

"There was a friend of Peter's in prep school named Charles Sinclair."

"Light hair, thin, good features, amiable?"

"Yes. I knew Charles Sinclair. He stayed with us in Maine for part of a summer. He and Peter were close friends for a couple of years. I used to wonder if there was something more than friendship between them."

Petrie was alert. "Homosexuality? Not Peter."

"A prep-school infatuation."

"Not Peter."

"Why not Peter?"

"Not Peter, not the love that dares not speak its name."

"It probably wasn't physical." Susan looked at me. "Why did you ask about a Charles?"

"Wild conjecture."

"Was there a Charles on the ship that Karpe told us about?"

I nodded. "About the right age, thirty or so."

"That's all? That is wild conjecture, linking that Charles with Peter."

"Well, they are linked, though maybe not from the past."

"Where is that son of a bitch?" Petrie said.

There was a hard rapping on the door.

"The son of a bitch is here," I said.

Karpe, carrying an attaché case, entered the library briskly, resolute, like a salesman who is confident of his product and his pitch. He nodded toward Susan, said, "Sorry, Tom," to Petrie, and then, without glancing at me, sat down in the other chair. He laid the attaché case flat across his thighs.

"I found something," he said.

"Are you going to show it to us, Leroy?" Petrie said.

Karpe opened the case, withdrew the manila envelope, which had been unsealed, and placed it on the desk.

Petrie removed the sheaf of torn yellow newspaper. "My," he said. He stared hard at me and, when I didn't speak, said, "The floor is yours, Shaw."

I said, "Did you know about the safety-deposit box, Tom?"

"No, and I still don't."

"Did Leroy tell you about the safety-deposit box when he said he was flying back to Big Sandy Cay?"

"Why don't you just tell me about it."

"You'd never have seen that envelope if it was filled with the bonds. Leroy was going to steal them."

To Tom, Leroy said, "You owe me an extra hundred in expenses. I bribed a bank officer to let me in the bank on a Sunday." He turned to me. "A friend of yours—Jasmine."

I told Petrie about my placing the newspaper-stuffed envelope in a safety-deposit box, letting the kidnappers believe that the money was secure in a bank until it was time to make the exchange. That was a ruse designed both to keep me alive and protect the bonds. That night, I told Petrie, Karpe had demanded the key, claiming that he would make the exchange for Falconer. Then, later, he said that Ahriman had confiscated the key. Ahriman denied that. And so, one, Karpe had lied, he had kept the key. Two, without mentioning his true intent, he'd returned to Big Sandy Cay today and withdrawn the envelope. And three, though I couldn't prove it, I was certain that Karpe had been dealing privately with the kidnappers and had, in fact, contrived to have me killed.

Karpe denied all of it. He asserted that it was I, Shaw, who intended to steal the bonds: Why else deposit the worthless envelope in a bank? Yes, he had kept the key. Why not? He thought he was protecting the ransom money. He was trying to fulfill his commission, his obligation to Tom Petrie and Susan and, most importantly, to Peter Falconer. He wasn't trying to steal the bonds; he was ensuring that they were not stolen by me. And as for his trip to Big Sandy Cay this morning? Simple: He had returned there—not aware that the *Mako* had left port during the night—in order to renew negotiations. He would, by God, do what I couldn't or wouldn't do: exchange poor beat-up Peter Falconer for the money. And as for arranging to have me killed by Ahriman?

"I don't need help."

"What a balls-up," Petrie said.

"I went to the bank," Karpe said slowly, playing his hole card now. "And I received something besides the envelope."

"Save that for a minute," Petrie said. "Shaw?"

Without rising from my chair, I uncinched my belt, lowered my trousers a few inches, fished into my money belt, and removed the bearer bonds.

"Hallelujah," Petrie said disgustedly. "What was the mystery and delay about?"

I rearranged my clothes, got up, and carried the bonds over to Susan. She accepted them casually, glanced at the face of the top one, then tossed them on a side table.

"I told you he was going to steal them," Leroy said.

"Don't be silly, Leroy," Petrie said. "If Shaw wanted to steal them they would be stolen, and there's nothing we could do about it."

"I could do something," Karpe said.

I said, "All right, now it's time we give up our misty fantasy. Peter Falconer is dead."

The three of them looked at me as if I had just announced that I was the carrier of a highly contagious, always fatal disease.

"They killed him—accidentally, probably—at the Mosquito Keys. They're keeping the body on ice. That murky Polaroid photo, the severed finger for print ID—that was to convince us that he was alive. Why do you think they refused to make the exchange when it would have been relatively easy? Because no one would exchange three-quarters of a million dollars for a corpse. They only intended to lure someone to the Bahamas and seize the money. Take the money, kill the go-between, and sail off into the sunset. And now we'll probably receive more photos, another of Peter's fingers—maybe his thumbs. Ahriman won't quit. He's just reloading."

"No," Petrie said.

I thought that Falconer was probably dead. Maybe not, but it was something we had to consider before going ahead with further ransom preparations.

"No," Petrie said again. "Leroy saw Peter and talked with him on the ship last night."

"That's what Leroy says."

Karpe sat quietly in the chair next to mine. He was relaxed. His ace was still in the attaché case.

"Leroy described Falconer, described the storeroom," Petrie insisted.

"Both of which were visible in the Polaroid. Did he see that picture?"

"A dead man looks dead, bad picture or not. You really don't think they propped a frozen Falconer in a chair and shot his portrait?"

"Maybe. Or maybe he wasn't frozen at that time."

"Nah."

I looked at Susan. "Sorry," I said.

"He's alive," she said. "Peter is alive."

"What else have you got, Leroy?" Petrie said.

Karpe reached into the attaché case. "When Jasmine and I went to the bank today, a man was waiting outside with this." He held up a tape cassette.

"Well, let's have it."

Petrie accepted the cassette, inserted it into the machine, and punched the play button. There was a quiet hissing for half a minute, and then we heard a voice.

"Christ Christ Christ Suzy-cat, baby, you've got to help me. You're the only one. I can't take this. You know how I am about pain. Please, for God's sake, give them whatever they want, anything, please, I'll pay you back, you know I will."

The voice was somewhat distorted by the room's acoustics, dulled and deepened. Susan nodded to us: It was her brother's voice and diction.

"Suzy-cat? Remember when we were kids and I wouldn't let anyone hurt you? I protected you, didn't I? If—whatever you asked me—I would try. I did try, didn't I? You remember. Why is it taking so long? You know I'm not blaming you, baby, but please . . . You don't know. They—at the Mosquito Keys—it was horrible, I can't say how bad. One of them, one of the men here—"

A voice in the background interrupted with a harsh command. His words were unclear but the intonation left no doubt about meaning. It sounded like Ahriman's voice.

We could hear the sound of Falconer crying and then, in a thick voice, he went on.

"The captain is going to talk to you now, Suzy-cat. Please do what he says. Please! Don't stall, don't go to the police, don't—" And then he screamed in agony.

Susan closed her eyes. Her entire body was trembling as if from an arctic cold.

We listened to thirty seconds of tape, Falconer sobbing in the background, and then Ahriman spoke.

"The price is now two million dollars. Cash. You have ten days."

There was another thirty seconds of hissing as the blank tape unwound. Ahriman, in mocking tones, said, "Suzy-cat? I will skin Peter-cat alive."

More empty tape, and Petrie turned off the machine. Susan covered her face with her palms. She was still shaking violently.

Karpe looked like a smug choirboy.

I stood up. "Tom, am I still working for you?"

"We have a contract."

"Same brief?"

"Proceed as before."

I started to leave.

"Hold it. Aren't you going to tell us what happened on that ship last night?"

"I'll turn in a written report."

I walked out of the house into the swampy night air and drove back to Bell Harbor.

My apartment had been burglarized and trashed. Nothing remained as it was. Mirrors were broken, clothing strewn about and soiled with urine, carpets and mattresses slashed, the toilet plugged with towels, furniture broken, glassware shattered, the walls defaced with graffiti. Obscenities, lewd drawings, semiliterate messages: *This is juss the beggining. How do you liked it? Die! Fuck you.* Marty's oil self-portrait had been removed from its frame and a vile drawing superimposed over her smile.

I did a rough inventory of my possessions. Beretta pistol, gone. Nikon camera and attachments, gone. A compact Sony tape recorder, gone. Some cash, a laptop computer, VCR, binoculars, a few bottles of whiskey, a fine wristwatch given to me by my late father, all gone.

I tried to function coldly and logically even in my rage. There were things that must be done. I would:

Call the police. Report the stolen objects, particularly the pistol, with its serial number. They would dust the place for prints, but I knew who had done this.

Phone my landlord. Tell him what had happened and ask him to hire a contractor to restore the apartment to its original condition. I would pay, of course.

Rent a hotel room for tonight. I could probably stay nights out at the lighthouse with Martina until the repairs were completed.

And tomorrow I would employ a private detective agency to help me with details of the Falconer investigation. Tom wanted to proceed. I would also direct the agency to locate Gary Tolliver. I hoped that they would require at least a couple of days to find Tolliver. Any sooner and I might kill him.

I was about to leave the apartment when Petrie phoned. "They found another one," he said.

"Another girl?"

"A man by the name of Stewart Dahl. He was known around the keys as Falconer's assistant. They were making a film out there."

"Wouldn't it be nice if the police did a thorough search and turned up all the bodies at a single go."

"He was found on one of the keys—Little Mosquito—tangled up in mangrove roots. Badly decomposed, mutilated by crabs and such, but there was ID on the body. Family from Gainesville. Photographer."

"Have the two girls been identified yet?"

"No."

"Approximate times of death established?"

"Not that I know of."

"Okay. If you need to get in touch with me, use my cellphone number."

"Listen, Shaw, you're wrong. Falconer is alive."

"How do you know?"

"Susan phoned her apartment in New York to check her answering machine just after you left. There was a message from Peter."

"Saying what?"

"He said, 'Save me, Suzy-cat. Save me.' "

"That's all?"

"You're being perverse. Peter Falconer is alive—not well, maybe, but alive. Karpe saw him yesterday. Tonight we heard the tape of Falconer and Ahriman. Susan received a message on her answering machine. We have the photo, the finger."

"Is all that evidence you'd take to court?"

"I've gone to court with less."

"And lost. Tom, you're Falconer's civil as well as his criminal defense attorney. Does Peter have a will?"

"Yeah."

"Who is the beneficiary?"

"That's privileged."

"Tom . . ."

"Susan. She gets it all."

"But if Peter was killed *before* his thirtieth birthday, before he inherited?"

There was a long humming silence. He said, "Then everything goes directly into a black hole— the Falconer family foundation."

"When exactly was his birthday?"

"A few minutes after eight A.M., Friday."

"Friday. The day after I found the abandoned houseboat. A day—more likely two days—after he was abducted. If Ahriman got too rough . . ."

"Shaw, make your choice now; either remain aboard or jump ship. Peter Falconer is alive."

"He has to be alive, doesn't he?" I said. "Either that, or we have to prove that he died *after* his birthday."

"There," he said. "See? It only requires faith and logic."

I laughed. It was surprising to hear Thomas Petrie unite words like *faith* and *logic* in the same sentence.


My hotel room was one of those uniform sterile cubes that are everywhere these days; I might just as easily have been staying in Istanbul or Tokyo or Malaga. The windows could not be opened and the stuffy room, with its heavy drapes closed and the lights off, was dark except for the dim yellow glow of some electrical switches. Silent too, aside from the whisper of air-conditioning. I again felt my fatigue and the abdominal pain from Ahriman's bolo punch. Sleep came incrementally.

# Part II
# Questions

# Seventeen

On my way to work I stopped off at a photography shop and turned in the little disposable camera. I asked the clerk to rush the developing and to provide five-by-seven prints of each negative.

Philip Robles, M.D., had an office on the third floor of the Dunwoody Building, a thing considered by other Bell Harbor physicians to be a foolhardy provocation—why would a doctor establish his practice in a building full of lawyers, the same villains who might eventually file malpractice suits against you? Dr. Robles, with a sharkish grin, usually replied that it was within his discretion to "neutralize" any attorney who dared consider such an outrage. For several years, early in his career, he had worked as a physician at the state prison at Raiford, and his experiences there had eroded the objective, sober doctor's mien taught in medical schools. I was his first patient that Monday morning.

"Come in for your prostate violation?" he asked.

"You're thinking of one of your geriatric patients, Doc."

"How did you get that lip?"

"I was punched."

Dr. Robles examined my split lip, said it seemed to be healing well and would not require stitches. He puffed out his cheeks when I removed my shirt to exposed the big purplish bruise below my rib cage, and ordered me to lie on the examining table.

"This contusion is going to be lovely as it heals," he said. "Like a tropical sunset—violet, green, yellow, orange. Same guy do this?"

"No. A different one."

"And they call me pugnacious. It looks like you were kicked by a mule." He palpated my abdomen while watching my face for flinches of pain. "Hurts, doesn't it?"

"Of course it hurts."

"When did this happen?"

"Saturday night."

"Any blood in your stools or urine?"

"No."

"Vomiting?"

"No."

"Does this hurt?"

"Hell yes, it hurts."

He probed with his fingers. "Where am I now, anatomically speaking?"

"Liver?" I said.

"And now?"

"Spleen?"

"Bzzzt," he said. "Wrong answer. Large liver lobe on your right side, spleen left. Or wait—is it the other way around?" He grinned at me. "Put on your shirt. I can't bear to look at that bruise any longer. It makes me feel faint."

"I'm reassured," I said, buttoning my shirt.

"Playing any tennis?"

"Petrie beat me on Friday."

"Petrie. I'd like to get him in here. First stuff a rag into his mouth, muffle his screams."

I laughed, picked up my tie, and began tying the knot.

Robles was a member of the Bell Harbor Racquet Club, where I sometimes played as a guest. He was known as bad-tempered, a complainer, and possibly a cheat. He had experienced difficulty arranging matches until one hot afternoon he had saved the life of an opponent who had collapsed from cardiac arrest. After that Dr. Robles had no trouble finding partners, usually stiff, elderly men who accepted his bullying as the cost of remaining alive.

"Call me or proceed to the emergency room if you have any internal problems. Pain, blood, nausea. That stuff."

"All right."

"Stay home on Saturday nights."

I put on my suit jacket. "Thanks, Doc."

"Don't thank me, just pay my assistant in the outer office. And tell all your friends and acquaintances to come in—I'm buying a new boat."

"You're a howl, Doc."

"Yeah? But I've got a medical license, which enables me to discern the differences between a human female and a vinyl dolly."

I walked up the stairs to my office on the fourth floor. Candace greeted me with a distracted smile. A wire ran from a Walkman on her desk to her ear, and the music, inaudible to me, seemed to be causing her anguish. I waited until the music ended, until she experienced what appeared to be a mild seizure, then she snatched the plug from her ear and breathlessly said, "Elvis."

"Candace, I want you to run a couple errands for me. First, take this check to the bank for deposit in my account. On your way back, pick up some film at the photo shop. Got that?"

"Sure."

"Is Mr. Samuelson in?"

"I don't know," she said.

I went into my office, shut the door, opened the safe, and removed the Falconer file.

Five minutes later Levi knocked on the interior door, opened it, and stood hesitantly on the threshold.

"Where is Candace?" he asked.

"She's running errands for me."

"I want her to transcribe a tape."

"The Vanzetti case?"

"Yes. Do you want to hear it? Brilliant oratory on my part, I must say, during my appearance before the Supreme Court."

"Later, Judge. I have to read this file, make some photocopies, and then drive up to Tampa."

"How long will Candace be gone?"

"It's a half-hour job, so she should be back in ninety minutes."

"Very well." He closed the door.

Peter Falconer, after his acquittal on the rape charge, told a Miami reporter that he was grateful for the jury's just verdict; now he intended to resume work on a movie that he expected would "revolutionize world cinema." It was an exploration of the dark underside of the American dream—the American nightmare.


Morgan Lloyd was a former FBI agent who had retired early to set up a firm named SureSecure. They sometimes did

ordinary investigative work along with providing general security (personal, computer, industrial antiespionage, etc.)
for a variety of state and Caribbean clients. He had a staff of
nine at his Tampa office, plus a number of on-call men and
women around the state who worked on a contract basis.

I was early for my appointment. A woman around forty
sat with me in the waiting room. She was a former Tampa
policewoman who was applying for a job and was nervous
about it. She had worked for a private detective agency during the last year but had done little except sit at bars—many
bars—watching bartenders to see if they stole money from
the till or the customers.

"Do they?" I asked.

"Not nearly as many as bar owners think."

When she was summoned for her interview, I picked up
a copy of the Tampa newspaper. An item on the front page
reported that three bodies, two male and one female, had
been recovered from the sea in Florida Bay. Fishermen had
sighted the corpses among the wild cluster of mangrove islands scattered between the southern tip of the state and the
arc of keys curving down to Marathon. The bodies were
badly decomposed, and a Coast Guard spokesman stated
that the deaths had probably occurred five or six days ago.
Identification indicated that the three victims, of Asian ancestry, were citizens of China. It was believed that they
might have been part of a large group of illegal aliens who
had callously been put ashore in that isolated and hostile en-
vironment. The Coast Guard was presently searching for
other victims and, it was hoped, survivors.

The receptionist informed me that Mr. Lloyd apologized
for the delay; he would see me now.

When Morgan was with the FBI and I with Army CID,
we had worked together investigating a murder that had

taken place on a Pueblo Indian reservation in New Mexico. He was there because the federal government had authority over Indian affairs; I was called in because the victim, Billy Luhan, was a sergeant in the U.S. Army. We had, with the tribal police, solved the case in a few days. (Sergeant Luhan had been murdered by his brother-in-law in a dispute over ownership of a horse.) At that time Morgan was thinking about retiring early from the FBI. He was from North Dakota, hated cold and snow, and had listened carefully when I'd talked about the west coast of Florida.

His office was large but sparsely furnished: a desk, file cabinets, potted plants, a long trestle table lined with chairs, and a corkboard pinned with maps and wanted posters and newspaper clippings.

Morgan rose and advanced halfway across the room to greet me. He was a lean, vigorous man who looked a dozen years younger than his fifty years.

He said that his wife, Marian, was fine. His kids were fine; Earl was getting married in December, and Judith had given birth to another son, that's three grandsons now. Business was very good. You could hardly fail in the security business these days. His golf handicap had increased to twelve strokes; there was not enough time to get out on the course and keep his edge. One's short game was the first to suffer from neglect. We each brought the other up to date, and then he buzzed the outer office and asked for McKinley and Fineman to be sent in.

"You said it was a big job," Morgan said.

"Several small jobs, actually."

Robert McKinley and Jake Fineman were both in their middle fifties. I assumed that they too were former FBI agents. McKinley had big shoulders, a squarish head, and a bristly mustache. Fineman was thinner and bald except for a fringe around his ears and the back of his head. He wore frameless octagonal glasses. He looked like the clichéd image of an accountant. Perhaps he was one: For a long time the FBI had favored recruiting accountants as well as lawyers.

We sat at one end of the trestle table. The receptionist brought in a pot of coffee and a platter of donuts. The calm attentiveness of the three men prompted me to pause a moment to organize my presentation. They would become impatient if I rambled.

"Morgan has probably briefed you on a general idea of what I want. Let's save the questions for later. Now, I have a thick file on Peter Falconer. Much of that information is confidential; other material I've photocopied and will give to you. But his background—excepting the past few months, including the incident at the Mosquito Keys—is pretty well known. I'm more interested in the Falconer Foundation: who sits on the board, who is the chairman, how they dispense the money and to whom, details of the charter, how they are likely to react if—when—Peter claims his inheritance. And what are the present assets of the foundation."

Fineman nodded. This was his special territory.

"Peter Falconer attended an exclusive private boys' school in New Hampshire, the Camden Preparatory School. You've probably heard of it. While there, Peter had a very close friend named Charles Sinclair. I'll show you a photograph of him in a minute. I haven't yet had the chance to show Susan Falconer a print, but she can tell us if Peter's boyhood chum, Charles Sinclair, is the same Charles who is now involved with Raven Ahriman. I'm sure it's the same guy. It fits. Find out all you can about him, his background, history, the source of his income. Any encounters with the law? What has our Charlie been doing since prep school?"

McKinley scratched a few words on his notepad.

"Susan Falconer, Peter's sister. We don't need an all-out investigation of her past and personal life, but I'd like to know more than I know now, which is virtually zero."

I consulted my notes. "All right, the prime villain, Raven Ahriman. That's certainly not his real name. An ex-con for sure, a cold and tough and cruel son of a bitch. He sails a small tramp freighter throughout the Caribbean basin. Legitimate cargo from time to time, but mostly he smuggles— guns, dope, illegal aliens. In today's newspaper there's an article about the discovery of three bodies in Florida Bay, illegal Chinese immigrants. They might have simply been put ashore in the swamps to survive or perish, or maybe a bunch were murdered and dumped over the side. Ahriman's capable of that. And this puts him in the vicinity of the Mosquito Keys around the time the two women were killed and Peter Falconer disappeared."

Morgan brushed donut crumbs off his palms. "You're suggesting that this Ahriman is responsible for what happened at the Mosquito Keys?"

"Something like that."

"Do you believe that Peter Falconer was abducted?"

"It's a possibility."

" 'Something like that.' 'A possibility.' "

"I am bound by confidentiality in certain matters."

All three men smiled.

"Anything else before we grill you?"

"Yeah. The police investigating the murders at the Mosquito Keys are being unusually cagey about releasing any information. That, or they haven't learned much. Falconer was making a movie there. The body of the photographer was found there. We know who he is. But the murdered girls haven't been publicly identified. What do the police have? What can you find out?"

"Is Falconer a suspect in the Mosquito Keys murders?" Fineman asked.

"Probably, but not officially named as such."

"Did he do it?"

"I don't know."

"Is he alive?"

"That's uncertain."

"Was he abducted by this Ahriman?"

"In some quarters it is feared that Peter might have been abducted."

Morgan covered his eyes with a palm, Fineman placed a hand over his mouth, and McKinley shielded his ears.

"Funny routine," I said. "Look, Falconer's closest relative, his sister, has decided against bringing in any police authority. It's her decision. Don't call any of your pals in the Bureau."

"I infer," McKinley said, "that the young millionaire has been kidnapped and is being held for ransom. Do you want us to find him?"

"Find the ship, the *Mako*. She'll be in foreign waters, either at sea or in port. She shouldn't be too hard to locate."

"And then?"

"We'll take it from there."

"Pay the ransom?"

I removed the envelope containing the photo enlargements from my briefcase. Henry had not carried out his mission very conscientiously. There were pictures of his pals, shots of the harbor area half blocked by his fingers, a couple of blurry arm's-length self-portraits, a gathering of people in a dirt yard—his family, perhaps. And last on the roll, a photo of the flounder he had caught at the end of the quay.

But mixed in among the useless pictures was one of Leroy Karpe walking down the quay toward the freighter; another as he walked up the gangplank; and a final shot as he was greeted by Charles and Ahriman. I passed out the relevant prints.

"Karpe is the visitor," I said. "He works for Petrie. Charles is the thin, light-haired one, and the third man is Raven Ahriman. The pictures were shot from a distance, but I brought the negatives, and if they're blown up more you can get a better look."

Morgan got up, went to his desk, where he rummaged around in the top desk drawer, and returned with a magnifying glass. He briefly looked at the faces of Karpe and Charles before concentrating on Ahriman. We watched while he tilted the print to catch the light and adjusted the lens's focus.

"I've seen him. Or pictures of him. Christ, I know him, but . . ."

"He's the dark-alley guy," Fineman said.

"The one you wouldn't want to meet there," McKinley said.

Morgan lowered the magnifying glass. "The name will come to me."

They questioned me for twenty minutes, bringing out all the specific details I had omitted in my general outline. Except for the matters that Petrie considered confidential, I told them all I knew and half of what I guessed. When McKinley and Fineman were satisfied, we shook hands and they left the room.

"More coffee?" Morgan offered. "A drink?"

"No thanks. I've got to get back to Bell Harbor. I'll write you a check for your retainer. Does five thousand dollars sound right?"

"That's plenty."

"One more thing, Morgan. You'll probably want to assign someone else to this. It's personal, so bill me separately."

I told him about Gary Tolliver, our fight outside the bar after I'd served him the subpoena, and my conviction that it had been Gary who trashed and burglarized my apartment.

"Nestor Naranjo in the SA's office told me that the cops couldn't find Tolliver but that he'd threatened my life. See if you can locate him. Where is he living? Who is he hanging around with? Address, license plate, you know."

"I know."

Morgan escorted me to the door. "Come up one of these days. We'll play a round of golf."

"I don't golf, Morg."

"Poor soul," he said.


On the drive back to Bell Harbor I thought about when Morgan and I had worked together on the Billy Luhan investigation. That was three years before I left the Army. I had enlisted after college, thinking to see a bit of the world at government expense before entering the "real" world. I hadn't intended to remain for ten years.

After I had received my commission as a second lieutenant, the Army sent me to the "spy school" at Fort Holabird, Maryland, to train for work in the CIC—Counter Intelligence Corps. Someone thought I had the makings of a spook. I completed training and was waiting for assignment when, mysteriously, the same person or another concluded that I was better fitted to join the CID, the Criminal Investigation Division. I apparently had the makings of a detective.

I liked the job and I was good at it. Eventually I became

part of a special unit that was assigned to unusually difficult or sensitive cases of crimes committed by or to Army personnel. We traveled the world: I worked in Japan, Okinawa, the Philippines, Germany, England, and Saudi Arabia, as well as many locations in the U.S. We investigated large-scale thefts, violations of security, incidents of racism, rape, and murder. I made captain. It seemed logical that I would be promoted to colonel before retiring with full pension and benefits.

But I began to weary of all the travel, the often petty military discipline, mediocre food and quarters, the narrow society. I decided that I wanted stability, a new career, a wife and kids, a home. Bell Harbor. Bell Harbor was not then actually my home—my family was from Ohio, though we had annually vacationed in Florida—but that was where I wanted to go. I regretted neither my years in the Army nor my decision to resign, despite the so-far sluggish progress in my civilian life.

North of Bell Harbor I passed a housing development called Falcon Heights. It was built on property formerly owned by the Falconer family, one of their many possessions. They still owned places in New York City, New Hampshire, the south of France, and half an island off the coast of Maine. Falcon Heights was just a few feet above sea level and as flat as a parking lot.

Candace had a copy of *Playboy* spread out on her desk and was studiously examining the centerfold layout. A bottle blonde with silicone breasts and lips puffed full of collagen was bawdily sprawled out on a tiger-skin rug.

"All she needs is a merkin," I said.

"What's a merkin?"

"A sort of beard—false pubic hair."

"Oh, Mr. Shaw, there can't be such a thing."

"Why not?"

"Do you know Mr. Kelleher?" she asked.

"Isn't he one of Tom Petrie's young lawyers?"

"Mr. Kelleher is a photographer too, and he says he can get me into *Playboy* as Playmate of the Month. What do you think about that?"

"Lawyers don't lie, Candace," I said, and I went into my office.

# Eighteen

The Bell Harbor Community Theater was situated in an old brick building, formerly a church, which had been renovated over the years as funds permitted. It still looked like a church from the street, with an intact bell tower and conical steeple and an oval stained-glass window above the double doors, but inside it was all theater, with a spacious lobby, a good-size stage, and two hundred comfortable seats set on an incline.

I arrived early for rehearsal, took a seat in the front row, and watched the painters and carpenters work. The set, according to the playwright's instructions, was *the well-appointed living room of an upper-middle-class home.* There was a door stage left, a stairway stage right, and French doors on the backdrop through which I, the Burglar, would enter midway in the second and final act. The play, *Temptation,* was a fast-paced, not very witty comedy with a cast of seven. My part was small; the Burglar was merely a plot device. Martina played the female lead.

I was thinking about Martina when she came down the aisle and slipped into the seat next to me.

"Hi." She arranged a leather portfolio flat across her thighs.

"What have you got there?"

"I did illustrations for the program and advertisements."

"Featuring the beautiful and haughty Gloria?" Gloria was the name of the character she played, Gloria Dupree.

"Hardly."

"I've been thinking about my part."

"Yes?"

"I've been plumbing my emotional depths so that I might add a true and searing dimension to my role."

She smiled. "Yes?"

"I have been revisiting painful episodes of my childhood. In me, deep down, is a burglar; what does he think, what does he feel, what is his motivation?"

"I think his motivation is to steal the silverware."

"I've decided to play the part wearing a mask."

"Good idea. Maybe all the cast should wear masks. The author too, wherever he is."

The air-conditioning was set too low and it was chilly in the theater. Marty showed me the goose pimples on her arms. At five o'clock the carpenters gathered their tools and materials and wandered off the stage.

"Crew exits stage left," I said.

"To a thunderous silence."

"Marty, can I stay at the lighthouse for a week or so? My apartment is being redone."

"Why? It's a perfectly fine apartment as it is."

"We were talking about burglars a moment ago. My place was burglarized over the weekend, vandalized—it's a mess."

"Did you notify the police?"

"Sure."

"And they . . . ?"

"They're working on it."

"Dan, I know you, baby, and I know when you're withholding something."

"I'll tell you about it later. Can I stay nights at the lighthouse?"

"Of course."

"I'll rent a boat at the marina and follow you out there tonight."

"Is this—the burglary and vandalism—related to the Peter Falconer business?"

"No. This is something else."

She shook her head. "All I ever wanted was a safe, quiet life."

"I'm sorry, Marty. But these are unquiet times. It's hard to remain cloistered, even if one lives in a lighthouse."

"Cloistered? As in cloistered nun?"

"Well, is there a feminine noun for hermit? Hermitess? Hermitelle? Hermitoid?"

"Reclusée?" she suggested. "We'll shop after rehearsal. What would you like for dinner?"

"A big steak, medium rare, baked potato, and a salad, with a decent cabernet."

"Pasta primavera it is, then."

Harold Guderian, a teacher of English at the community college and the director of the play, came wheezing down the aisle. He was a stout man with a spade beard, a black eye patch, and a home-cultivated British accent.

"Well, well," he said. "Beauty and the Beast."

I said, "How dare you call my girl a beast."

"Harold," Martina said, "we've decided that each member of the cast should wear a mask during the performance."

"Brilliant, darlings. And why shouldn't you all be nude as well? Raving naked, but wearing masks."

"Masks and merkins," I said.

• • •

We reached the island just before sunset. I tied the rental skiff behind Martina's little cabin cruiser, *Puck,* and followed her up the mossy stone steps. Trespassers had strewn rubbish over the rock plateau and the little crescent beach: beer cans, french fry and Big Mac cartons, a silvery condom that reminded me of a jellyfish. And someone had tried to smash open the blockhouse door with a rock; the wood around the lock was gouged and splintered. There were old pale scars on the wood where others had tried to force entry. But the door was thick and sturdy and secured by a pair of dead-bolt locks.

I carried the groceries inside, emptied the bags, and took one bag outside to hold the trash. I kicked the condom off into the sea. Intrusions like this were not uncommon when Martina left the island. We might or might not talk about it during dinner. She knew how I felt about her staying alone here; I knew how determined she was to preserve her independence, live her life as she wished despite the occasional ugly and potentially dangerous invasion.

She was slicing vegetables when I returned to the block-house. The place was hot and stuffy after being closed all afternoon. I walked around, opening portlights and interior doors.

"A drink?" I asked.

"Gin and tonic. A big one."

I got limes and a tray of ice cubes from the refrigerator, two twelve-ounce glasses from a cupboard, and made a pair of tall gin and tonics. I was aware of the muted throbbing of the generator and, behind that, the sob and sigh of waves washing up along the windward side of the reef.

"The sun is going down," I said.

"All right."

We carried our drinks down the tunnellike passageway to

Martina's studio and then climbed the spiral stairway to the platform. It was very hot in the upper level of the lighthouse; the circle of thick glass intensified the sun's rays and was fogged with condensation. We went through the door and outside onto the circular balcony. The sun was half submerged below the horizon now.

" 'You're early,' " Martina said. " 'The invitations said eight. Did you RSVP? Who the hell are you, anyway?' "

They were lines from the play, spoken by Gloria to the Burglar, whom she has just surprised taking a pair of heavy silver candlesticks from the mantel. The Burglar spins around, holding the burning candles aloft.

" 'Oh,' " I said. " 'Hello. Early? I'm here . . . I'm here to read the meter.' "

Martina smiled. "It ain't Noel Coward."

"It ain't Neil Simon."

"It's a sitcom. Harold has been talking for years about doing Shakespeare. Maybe we'll do *King Lear* someday. I've always wanted to play Cordelia." She waited, looking at me.

"I've always wanted to play the Fool."

My words echoed and re-echoed during the ensuing silence. Finally, both grinning, we turned and went back through the door and down the stairway.

While Marty cooked, I told her about the burglary of my apartment; it had been, I was sure, the work of Gary Tolliver, the hoodlum I'd had a fight with the previous week. No doubt he would soon be arrested. He was wanted on several charges, including failure to respond to a grand-jury subpoena. The police were looking for him, and so was a private detective agency that I had today contacted on another matter.

"He's dangerous, isn't he?"

"While he's free. He won't be free long unless he leaves the state, and even then—"

"I think I'll adopt a dog from the animal shelter. A big dog. Maybe two big dogs."

"Good idea."

"So. And how was your trip to the Bahamas? What was that all about?"

I told her an abridged version of the events on Big Sandy Cay, omitting my imprisonment in the *Mako*'s cargo hold and my desperate dive into the sea. She was a worrier. We each, perhaps, worried too much about the other, but neither of us would abandon the life that generated the worry.

"So you didn't pay the ransom, then," she said.

"No. They didn't produce Peter Falconer."

"Why didn't they?"

"I'm not sure."

"He's dead, isn't he?"

"I think so. Petrie and Falconer's sister think not."

"What is she like—the Falconer girl?"

"Beautiful and smart."

"Should I be jealous?"

"And spoiled. I think both she and her brother were badly spoiled."

"What a funny word to use in describing people. Spoiled. Spoiled rotten. What does it mean exactly?"

"Maybe it means that they've won and won and won, since they were in diapers, they've won so frequently and for so long that it seems a violation of natural law for them to lose, and they don't take it very well."

"But you really don't know them, Dan. People are never that simple."

"You're right. I shouldn't be so quick to judge."

"Am I spoiled?"

"Like an overripe peach or melon."

"I can tell you're hungry. Set the table."

After dinner, Marty went to her studio; she had a deadline to meet. I went outside and walked along the rock slab to the southernmost tip of the reef. Dark waves broke against the tumbled boulders with a dull crack and carbonated fizz. It was full night now, hot and still, oppressive. We had endured day after day of sultry heat. Each day was pretty much like the one before and the one to follow, and the weather prophets daily forecast more of the same. Unless, until . . . They pointed to graphic symbols on their maps, little vortexes; a tropical depression over there, a tropical storm down here, the birthing of a hurricane southeast of Jamaica. Eventually one of those systems would provide relief. Provide, maybe, a hell of a blow first.

A sport-fishing boat, sprinkled with lights, rumbled through the opening in the breakwater and cruised slowly toward Bell Harbor. They were flying a "caught fish" pennant. Figures moved on the aft deck, and hearty voices carried clearly over the water.

I was startled by the abrupt beeping of my cell phone. I'd forgotten it was in my pocket.

"My place tomorrow night at seven," Petrie said. "I'm going to receive a print of the movie that Falconer was making down in the keys. It was found by police aboard the *Deep Six*. The negative was developed at a commercial lab, and a friend in the state police had them run off an extra print. Don't ever repeat that. It's, ah, probably a prosecutable offense for both my friend and me."

"All right. Anything else?"

"Yeah. An audiotape arrived from Ahriman this morning. It was posted from Kingston."

"And?"

"Three minutes of Peter talking incoherently. Weeping, rambling. He sounds *non compos mentis*. Poor bastard."

"Any indication of whether it was taped BD or AD?"

"What's that?"

"Before death or after death."

"Very funny."

"Have you raised the one million two hundred fifty thousand?"

"Don't concern yourself with that."

"Speaking of money, Candace took your check to the bank this morning. They refused to honor it."

"What check?"

"My seventy-five-hundred-dollar bonus check."

"Can't be. My accountant has strict instructions to maintain that account at no less than twenty thousand dollars."

"Well, the check didn't clear."

"Send it through tomorrow."

"And I wrote a five-thousand-dollar check to SureSecure this morning on the same account. Their retainer. Keep that check in mind too."

"Who told you that you could write checks on my accounts?"

"You did. You gave me checks and informed the bank."

"Son of a bitch," he said.

"Tom—you aren't going to use your own money for the ransom, are you?"

"Your voice is breaking up," he said, and the phone went dead.

Marty finished working a little after ten. We went out on the reef, stripped off our clothes, and dove from the high shelf of rock. The water seemed to possess a special warmth and silkiness at night. A gentle mix of conflicting currents caressed our skin. We swam fifty yards out from the reef, challenging monsters of the deep.

# Nineteen

I drove up to Venetia the next night and arrived at Petrie's house at seven. He met me at the door. He said that he had rented a projector and screen and set them up in the living room and all we had to do was dim the lights and hit the switch. But first a bite to eat.

He led me into the kitchen, where Susan, just in from the swimming pool and still wearing her bikini, sat at the table. She smiled and wriggled her fingers at me.

I said, "She's lovely, this Falconer woman."

"Careful," Petrie said. "I generally blind men who look at her like that."

Petrie set about preparing a light meal while Susan went off to change. A ten-foot-long chopping block occupied the center of the kitchen. He got a slab of pastrami from the refrigerator and placed it in the microwave oven; shaved a red onion so thin the slices were transparent; got the pastrami from the microwave and carved slices against the grain. He placed bread, mustard, horseradish, glasses, utensils, and plates on the table.

Finally he poured glasses of wine for himself and Susan and opened a bottle of beer for me.

"Voilà!" he said. "Bachelor efficiency."

Susan, wearing jeans and a T-shirt, returned to the kitchen. She was still barefoot and her hair was spiky-wet.

"Bless me for this grub," Petrie said.

While we ate he told us that he had been perplexed by Peter's film being referred to as surrealistic. What did that mean? He was familiar with the word and, vaguely, the concept, but he wanted to know more and so this afternoon he had done a little research.

*Surrealisme,* he told us, was a word coined by the French poet Guillaume Apollinaire in 1917; literally translated it meant *superrealism.* Surrealism was closely related to the earlier Dada movement, which was antiart, antichurch, antimilitary and antigovernment, antisense, antieverything. It was anarchy, chaos, calculated insult. One might translate the word *dada* as baby talk. Some of the original Dadaists, like Tristan Tzara and Andre Breton, later became leaders of the surrealism movement, which had officially been proclaimed by Breton in 1924. Its goal was the "liberation of the unconscious."

Surrealism envolved and became focused on dream states and shocking juxtapositions—a maimed hand swarming with ants, a razor-slashed eyeball, a bloody cow sprawled over a piano. Those images were from *Un Chien Andalou,* a film by two Spaniards, Luis Buñuel and Salvador Dali. That film, probably, was the prototype for what followed. You had the films of Buñuel and Jean Cocteau, the paintings of Chirico and Duchamp and Dali, Man Ray's photographs, etc.

Susan had heard all of this before; she got up and walked into the other room.

So, Tom continued, what had commenced as a quirky, somewhat vicious avant garde movement developed into one of the dominant art forms of the century. Today you found its descendants in museums and galleries (shock art was an example, with its exhibitions of decaying animals and dung madonnas) and in Hollywood movies and Internet porn and TV advertisements and pop-music videos. Dada–*surrealisme* was everywhere, and what a joke—a Dada–*surrealisme* joke—on the founders, since their contemptuous view of mainstream culture had been adopted by mainstream culture itself.

I occasionally nodded and made sounds that could be misinterpreted as murmurs of interest.

When he'd finished, I said, "Fascinating stuff, Tom. Now, where is your stooge tonight?"

"Leroy? Leroy is hunting down the *Mako*."

"How is he going about that?"

"Checking with the mariner's union, shipping agents, ship's chandlers, the Coast Guard. This afternoon he flew down to Jamaica."

"Because the last tape was sent from Jamaica?"

"He'll look around the ports down there, see if *Mako*'s around. He thinks he can persuade Ahriman to stick to the old deal. He can't, but he thinks so. He wanted to take the bearer bonds along just in case."

"Which made you laugh."

"I smiled politely."

"Tom, I figured out why I couldn't make the exchange down at Big Sandy Cay."

"Really? And why was that?"

"Because when I showed up with the seven hundred fifty thousand, Ahriman realized that he could squeeze out a lot more. Like two million dollars."

"Brilliant. It's humbling to find myself in the company of genius. And you just recently figured that out?"

"I was on the wrong track. I believed Peter was dead."

"You don't think so now?"

"I'm leaving it open. Maybe he's dead, maybe not."

"You can listen to the new audiotape later."

"The tapes don't prove much."

Petrie drank his wine, reached across the table for Susan's glass, and finished that. His gaze was long and steady, as if he might be making a new appraisal of me or revising the old one.

"I read your report," he said. "Ahriman, Charles, Bully, all of them. The cargo hold. The cargo hold that not long before was swarming with crazed, pigtailed Chinks. Then your swan dive over the stern rail and miraculous rescue by—what's his name? Pop? Yes, old Pop. Romance on the high seas. Like something out of Conrad."

"You don't believe it?"

"I do, I do believe it. In fact, I think it might have been a lot worse than you reported. It all probably made you a bit shaky, bud. Spooked, maybe, a little."

"I'm all right."

"Can you imagine how it is for that poor bastard Falconer?"

"No, I can't imagine it."

"Can't imagine what?" Susan said, entering the kitchen.

"Life without you," Petrie said.

She smiled faintly. "I'd like to see Peter's movie," she said, "if the old boys have finished swapping lies."

Earlier Tom had moved the furniture to clear a path down the center of the long living room; the projector was on a table at one end, reel-threaded, and the screen erected against the opposite wall. Petrie sat at the table; Susan and I moved to a nearby sofa.

"I don't know what we've got here," Petrie said. "All the different strips of film were spliced and wound on three reels. It's probably out of order, mixed up. Hit that light switch, Shaw."

The screen was illuminated with a bright glowing blob of greens and browns and yellows. Petrie adjusted the focus and we were immersed in what looked like a jungle clearing. It was circular, cylindrical if you considered the green walls of vegetation rising all around, and about thirty-five feet in diameter. A black man wearing a loincloth was hacking at the brush with a machete. He was tall, leanly muscled, and his machete strokes exerted a powerful leverage. But he had not cleared the forest with a machete; most of the limbs had not been chopped but cut clean through, probably with a chainsaw. You sensed too that he was not alone, that there were others with the cameraman outside the frame.

There was no soundtrack. It was silent in the room except for the blower on the projector and the ticking of running film. The man paused in his labor, straightened, and half turned toward the camera with a quizzical smile.

"Stop it there," I said.

Petrie halted the advance of film.

"Back it up a few frames."

The man was frozen in mid-action, his smile still forming, the machete at his side.

"That's Bully," I said, "on one of the Mosquito Keys. Okay, go ahead."

Bully clowned for the camera for a few seconds, and then there was a blank flickering of light followed by several short vignettes: views, both short-range and telephoto, of vultures circling above the mangrove island; a dead barracuda on a sandy beach, swarmed over by flies and small crabs; an extreme close-up of a female mouth, writhing lips, which eventually produced a blue-irised glass eye; the same staring glass eye inserted between a woman's genital labia.

Next there was a casually shot section of several persons

relaxing on the stern deck of the *Deep Six*. The angle indicated that the cameraman was on the cabin roof.

"Stop it there, Tom," I said.

He halted the film.

"The slender blond man sitting on the railing," I said. "That's Charles. Susan? Charles Sinclair?"

"Maybe," she said. "He looks like Peter's friend from prep school. I think so, yes. Yes."

With Charles were two nude women. One sat in a canvas chair; the other lay supine, sunbathing, on a patch of deck. Both were young, probably no more than nineteen or twenty, small, and pretty in a pink and glossy doll-like way. One was a brunette; the other had frizzy bleached-blond hair. Bully was there, deftly rolling a marijuana cigarette. Also present, at the edge of the frame, stood a man with sparse graying hair and a goatee. He had to be Stewart Dahl, the Hollywood exile, the professional photographer that Peter had hired. And it had to be Peter up on the roof deck, filming the gathering—cast and crew relaxing after a hard day's shoot.

There was considerable silent merriment: the girls laughed and gestured, Bully clowned, Charles drank directly from a gin bottle, Stewart Dahl shaded his eyes and said something to Peter on the roof, then leaned over and lightly pinched the brunette's breast (she indignantly slapped his hand). It was a forced jollity, a silly dumb show, the sort of awkward show-off behavior you saw when drunk or drugged people reacted to the presence of a camera.

Stewart Dahl and the two girls were dead now, of course, murdered. Bully might be dead as well; he had plummeted headfirst down into the *Mako*'s cargo hold. And I was not convinced that Peter remained alive despite the tape cassettes and Karpe's story of seeing him at Big Sandy Cay. It was likely that only Charles, of the five, still lived.

The last few inches of film fluttered through the threading brackets and the screen turned white. Petrie switched off the machine.

"Amateur hour," he said.

"Is that all?" Susan asked.

"Two more reels. Maybe twenty-five minutes of film."

Susan turned on the lights. "It seems harmless," she said. "Silly and harmless."

We watched Petrie thread the new reel onto the projector. It was a task I might have fumbled at, but he was very deft and precise. I could imagine those white, long-fingered hands suturing heart tissue or defusing a bomb. Tom always surprised me with his physical grace. It seemed contrary to the blunt, abrasive thrust of his personality.

He said, "I didn't see the freighter anywhere in the background."

"You wouldn't. *Mako* draws eight or ten feet even without ballast. She couldn't navigate the waters around the Mosquito Keys."

Susan hit the light switch. The screen was abruptly converted to many shades of green, from green-black fading toward the yellow end of the spectrum, as we returned to the forest clearing. A day or two had passed since the original sequence with Bully had been filmed; leaves of the hacked and sawed shrubbery had withered, curled, and turned crisp around the edges, and now a goat was tethered to a stake in the center of the clearing.

"I never really believed in the goat," Petrie said.

The ram had been closely shaved (you could see razor cuts on its skin) except for the chin beard and patch of genital fur. It was much as I remembered it, though now it seemed pathetic rather than sinister—just a goat, a frightened and bleating goat. This piece of film contained a soundtrack, scratchy and indistinct and not quite synchronized with the visual. The shorn animal, tormented by insects, tugged at the rope and bleated. It was an oppressive scene beyond the strangeness and cruelty; you could sense the heat and humidity, smell decaying vegetation, hear the whine of mosquitoes and flies on the soundtrack. At the far end of the clearing there was a glimmer of blue—the sea, obscured by brush and mangrove roots as thick as pythons.

Now Bully, naked except for sandals and a chain of shark teeth looped around his neck, emerged from the forest and slowly advanced toward the goat. He carried a bowie knife that flashed blurs of sunlight off into the brush. There were old welted scars on Bully's torso—evidence, perhaps, that he knew knives from the sharp end as well as the blunt. The ram bleated and leaped against its tether, leaped toward Bully. Did the beast think it was being rescued?

"This Bully seems to enjoy playing the savage," Petrie said.

The camera began to slowly zoom in, excluding almost everything except Bully and the goat, and it recorded the "sacrifice" in vile detail. Bully grasped the animal beneath its jaw with his left hand, twisted and lifted so that its front hooves left the ground, and then, blade flashing, he cut its throat. The goat fell, tried to rise and failed, and then bucked and kicked on the ground for a time before lying still. Bully dipped a forefinger in the blood and tasted it, dipped again and drew blood chevrons on his cheeks. He grinned.

The screen went dark for a moment. A sign, printed in gothic script, appeared:

JUNGLE CONQUEST

Another fade-out and fade-in, and then we saw Bully and one of the girls—the bleached blonde—copulating in the center of the clearing. It looked more like an act of violence than sex. The girl, her head back and eyes closed, arms spread cruciform, might be presumed dead except for her harsh expulsions of breath.

The cameraman walked a 360-degree circle around the figures, the goat and the copulating pair. A microphone recorded the sounds: the slap of flesh, rapid breathing, Bully's grunts, and, at the end, the girl's catlike mewing.

The screen turned white, the film end rattled through the brackets, and Petrie switched off the projector.

"Charming," Susan said. "Edifying."

"What it ain't," Petrie said, "it ain't going to sell no popcorn."

"It ain't my brother. I can't imagine Peter involved in this wretched thing. Not the Peter I know."

I said, "It ain't a snuff flick. Not a human snuff flick, anyway. Just a goat snuffed so far."

The final reel opened with a view of Peter standing in the center of the clearing. He was alone. Bully and the girl were not visible. The goat had been removed, but the vertical wooden stake remained, casting a short shadow, which indicated that the time was close to noon.

"Something happened here," Peter said. His voice was not quite synchronized with lip movement, a bit delayed, but the sound was good. "Not long ago, something happened. You see—the blood is still fresh. Something strange, something mysterious, happened in this place."

I had seen still photos of Peter in the file—snapshots, newspaper pictures taken during his rape trial, a studio portrait from his college days—but the film animated him, brought him to life. Peter was no longer an abstraction to me. He was real at last.

"Wait," he said. "Did it happen? I mean, did it happen in

your mind as well as on film? Think about that. Is it all in your brain now, chemically stored, ready to be recreated by faint electrical charges?"

His voice had a rich timbre and was carefully modulated. You could see that he enjoyed speaking. He might be proud of that voice. It could be that he had often practiced speaking in those rich, confidential tones. Perhaps he sang beautifully. It was not the strained, high-pitched voice I had heard on the audio cassettes.

"In the mind's more remote precincts, imagination and experience merge, become indistinguishable one from the other. And so, if I have engaged your imagination, these film experiences become your own. You have sacrificed a goat and tasted its blood, you have raped a lovely girl, you have . . . There is more."

He paced to the fringe of trees and stood there back-to-camera for a while, as if looking to see what might lay hidden in the thickets, what might emerge; and then he returned to the center of the clearing. He casually placed his left palm on top of the stake.

"There is more," he said, and he smiled.

Documents in Peter's file had given his height as six foot even and his weight at one hundred seventy pounds. Eyes blue; hair brown. But in the film his hair was nearly auburn, feathery and grown fairly long. He moved well. He moved well and spoke well and did both with complete assurance.

"I'll reveal some of your secret dreams," he said. "Dreams you didn't know you dared to dream."

You could see his resemblance to Susan around the mouth and eyes, but whereas she was beautiful, Peter was not far from ugly. His was a long, asymmetrical face, planes and angles, with sharply defined brow, cheek, and jawbones, and taut, unlined skin. Still, women would be attracted to him, drawn by his voice, his casual charm, his complete assurance. His smile.

He smiled at the camera and said, "Follow me."

We were immediately plunged deep into the sinkhole. It was all blackness on the periphery. Particles of matter swarmed through a cone of bright light. The light ignited flecks of color in the chalky rock, bits of red and orange and yellow, and the sandy bottom glowed. A fish passed, another, something scuttled across the bottom and buried itself in a puff of sand. The camera-mounted light moved through a tumble of coral-encrusted rock and suddenly exposed a figure—one of the mannequins. Painted lips, wig-hair floating free in the current, an inflated dummy tied to a slab of rock and straining toward the surface. There were more, seven in all. The cameraman—Peter, surely—swam in a slow wide arc around the circumference of the sinkhole, exposing one after another of the mannequins. Particle-swarming light, blackness on the periphery, and then a pale figure that gradually acquired detail. Then another, another. Blond dolls, brunettes, redheads, all writhing in the currents.

We tensed. We were expecting it, but the sight of the first girl was a shock. She emerged slowly out of the blackness. She was naked. The camera light gave her an eerie, luminous shine. It was the blond. A rope tied to one ankle was tethered to a chunk of rock. She floated four or five feet above the bottom, swaying, flexing, her yellow hair flickering in the current like a candle flame. Her eyes and mouth were open as if in surprise. Dead eyes, dead mouth, but her body was still lithe, appeared alive. She should not have been buoyant. Submerged bodies do not become buoyant until the gases of decomposition lift them. Perhaps her lungs or chest cavity had been filled with compressed air so that she might float prettily during Peter's filming. The girl waved a sad good-bye as the camera moved past her and through darkness to the brunette.

The currents were strong and conflicting there, and the girl appeared to be dancing an improvised, ghastly, corpse ballet. Some of her movements were abrupt, others graceful. She danced on point; she half pirouetted, her face and arms lifted, and she appeared to leap, she curtsied, she bowed. It was like blundering into a room where a solitary girl was dancing and dreaming, and you tried to retreat unseen. But the camera persisted in its brutal intrusion, obscenely lingered, until at last the film ran out.

We were quiet. Images of the two girls had vanished from the screen but would not be so easily expelled from our minds. Susan got up and turned on the lights. She had been silently weeping, was weeping now.

I said, "I probably arrived at the Mosquito Keys soon after they left."

"How so?" Petrie asked.

"The condition of the goat—it hadn't decayed much. The mannequins hadn't deflated in the cool water. I had the feeling, when I went aboard the houseboat, that it had recently been abandoned. Say they were interrupted or feared an interruption. Christ, there were three fresh corpses; they couldn't hang around. Say *Mako* is out in deep water. Bully and Charles grab Peter, get in the *Deep Six*'s Zodiac, and motor out to rejoin Ahriman."

"Maybe," Petrie said.

"Go back further. Sometime during the last few months Charles looked up Peter. Old chum from prep school. Great pals. They talked about the old days, got along well, decided to team up for a while. Charles joined the film project, maybe contributed some money toward it, brought Bully in. Charles knew about Peter's inheritance. Been thinking about it for years. Timed the abduction for around Peter's thirtieth birthday. Yes? Ahriman and the rest of the crew had gone north to dump off the Chinese immigrants in Florida Bay, returned, radioed Charles aboard the *Deep Six*. . . ."

"Killed the girls and the cameraman to eliminate witnesses?"

"That seems extreme, even for Ahriman. It could be that with all the dope and booze and bloody games, things got out of hand. One was killed, and the others had to die."

Petrie was skeptical. "And so Peter says, 'Bad luck, but as long as it happened I'll incorporate the bodies into my masterpiece.'"

"I don't know, Tom. I'm only speculating."

"Right. Well, shit, let's get out of here, go somewhere for a drink."

"My brother is sick," Susan said. "He is sick and he needs help."

"What he doesn't need," Petrie said, "he doesn't need a jury to see his movie."

# Twenty

Early Wednesday morning a courier delivered a package to my office. It had been sent down from Tampa by Morgan. Inside the package were several nine-by-twelve manila envelopes, the flaps glued shut by red sealing wax stamped with the SureSecure logo. The motorcycle courier and the sealing wax were nice touches that almost made up for the paucity of information. Most of the reports were written in that stilted prose peculiar to law-enforcement officers; one had to read between the lines.

The present location of the freighter *Mako* was unknown. No port had reported its arrival or departure. No maritime agency had recently indemnified a cargo. There had been no sightings by the U.S. Coast Guard (the ship was on the Coast Guard's "Watch" list). *Mako* was not represented by any known shipping agent. The Panamanian Ship Registry Office could not provide an address for the company (Raven, S.A.) that owned the vessel. Raven, S.A., was not a member of the international maritime organization that provides satellite tracking of merchant vessels. There had been no intercepted or monitored radio messages to or from the *Mako*. The ship was presumably at sea or had called at a small port that did not disseminate information to the various concerned agencies, law enforcement or commercial. It was possible, considering the age and disrepair of the vessel, that the *Mako* had been lost at sea; there were presently two tropical depressions moving out of the Atlantic into the Caribbean basin, though no local heavy weather had been reported since the ship's last known sighting at Big Sandy Cay in the Bahamas.

The freighter had been constructed during 1958 and 1959 in a shipyard at Piraeus, Greece, and in late 1959 was commissioned and christened *Arete*, Greek for *virtue, excellence*. For fourteen years she sailed the waters of the Mediterranean and Red Seas from Marseilles to Aden, and in 1974 was sold to a corporation based in Monrovia, Liberia. A Turkish shipyard performed extensive repairs on the vessel, including removing her coal-burning engines and replacing them with diesels. The new owners renamed her *Southern Cross*. For almost twenty-five years the *Southern Cross* was engaged in the legitimate transport of cargo and passengers along the West Coast of Africa. In 1998 the ship, considered unseaworthy even by lenient African maritime standards, was sold to the company known as Raven, S.A., sailed across the Atlantic, registered in Panama, and renamed *Mako*.

For several years the *Mako* had been suspected of involvement in the smuggling of arms and narcotics and, more recently, illegal immigrants. The U.S. Coast Guard had circulated advisories to all American ports requesting that the ship and its master be detained and the Coast Guard notified.

The major part of the Falconer fortune originated with Joseph Joshua Falconer, a second-generation American whose grandparents had emigrated from Surrey, in England. He inherited, while young, a small New Hampshire textile mill from his parents and gradually expanded the business. He was prominent in the Republican Party, a supporter of Lincoln, and though he himself was not then rich, he counted many rich and powerful men among his friends. He prospered but did not accumulate a large fortune until the Civil War, when he received contracts for the provision of uniforms to the Union Army. And at that time he opened an arms-manufacturing plant, which, despite its unproven status, also received lucrative contracts.

There were many bitter accusations during and after the Civil War. Some of the arms and ammunition he provided to the Union Army proved defective and, it was alleged, cost the lives of soldiers. The uniforms, his enemies charged, were of very poor quality and very high price. Joseph Falconer was also long criticized for brutally exploiting child labor at his textile mills (he then owned three) during a period when child labor was a national scandal. It required generations of image-building to redeem the Falconer name.

Joseph Falconer and his heirs greatly expanded the family's holdings, investing in railroads, manufacturing plants, and timber holdings in Maine and oil in Texas. In 1926 Randall, Joseph's grandson, formed the Falconer Foundation with an initial endowment of eight million dollars. There were later grants of money, stocks, and valuable real estate.

The foundation's current wealth was considered to be in excess of two billion dollars, presently controlled by a "maverick board" chaired by Jeffrey Desseaux, nephew of Louis Falconer, and a cousin to Peter and Susan Falconer. *The Wall Street Journal* described the seizure of control of the foundation's board by Desseaux and his allies as a *bloodless coup*.

Louis, the father of Peter and Susan Falconer, died in

1996 of pancreatic cancer. Their mother, Evelyn, now lived in isolation in a family summer home on an island off the coast of Maine. Their younger brother, Randolph, who was afflicted with Down's syndrome, was institutionalized soon after his birth.

Peter Falconer attended Yale University for four years, majoring in theater arts, though he did not receive a degree. He was variously described as "indolent," a "dilettante," and a "rogue." He had twice been charged with rape. Charges were dropped in one case, and he was acquitted in the other.

Susan Falconer graduated with honors (French lit.) from Bennington College in 1996. Immediately after college she moved to Europe, where she remained for almost four years, residing for periods in Paris, Florence, and Milan. She did some modeling for the couturier Versace while in Milan. She returned to the United States in May 2000 and took employment with the fashion magazine *Très Chic,* now defunct. A former colleague at the magazine described Susan as "rich, beautiful, and sad." Susan Falconer had no known encounters with police in either the United States or Europe.


Charles Arthur Sinclair was from a good family, a prominent family long resident in Boston. His father, grandfather, and two paternal uncles were successful physicians, highly regarded in the Boston community as well as the medical community at large. His mother was a Kendle—another respected family—and an accomplished musician. Naturally it was assumed that Charles would enter the medical profession and distinguish himself and further honor the family. He was very bright, though perhaps a bit lazy; socially adept, though maybe not always as discriminating as he ought to be (he occasionally fell in with bad companions);

and he was spirited almost to the point of rebellion. It often seemed that with Charles, his virtues, carried to extremes, became inverted into faults. But everyone believed that he would soon settle down and fulfill his family's expectations.

After prep school he entered Dartmouth College, where he excelled academically during his first year; his grades fell off during the second year, and there were rumors of too much drinking and sexual outrages and pranks that skirted close to criminality. He was expelled from college midway through his sophomore year. Failing grades were the official explanation, but there was an ugly scandal, only partly hushed up, involving Charles's relationship with the fourteen-year-old son of a college dean.

The following autumn Charles entered a small private college in Vermont. He lasted only a few months before again being expelled. This time the rumors were about the importation and selling of drugs, the theft of money and objects from fellow students and faculty, even an attempted extortion.

He returned home contrite. He deeply regretted the shame he had brought to his family, the Sinclairs and Kendles, and he vowed to put his life back on the path of honor. He just needed a little time to reflect. He had begun to think that perhaps he had a religious vocation. Within the month he was stealing valuable objects from the house and forging checks on his father's and mother's personal accounts. Charles was again expelled, this time from the family.

He next appeared in Santa Fe, New Mexico, and was soon established as a dealer in fine art. He had a motto that he repeated frequently: "I will not sell an object I love to a person I do not respect." He sold few pieces, none regarded as major, but each was rare and special in its own category: a small oil painting by Camille Pissarro, a Cartier brooch, a drawing by Tiepolo, a John Singer Sargent portrait of a remote

Sinclair ancestor. All of those were genuine, stolen from the family's collection, but Charles also presented works, mostly drawings—Picasso, Matisse, Grosz, Blake—that were forged by a Romanian artist then living in Avignon.

His clients were the celebrated rich—movie and TV and pop-music people—and the merely rich, noted only for their money. For a time Charles was one of Santa Fe's darlings: young, rich himself it was presumed, and from an old Boston family (his expulsion from the family was confidential); a witty and cultured homosexual, not at all campy; and a man who was always off to Paris or New York or Athens to obtain the exquisite antiquity or work of art you deserved.

Most of his clients were ignorant about art. A painting or fine drawing on the wall symbolized prestige, a financial coup, a score or arrival, not much different than the Ferrari in the garage or the racehorse in the stable.

The rumors started after eighteen months: talk about provenance, authentication, a Dallas museum scandal that damaged reputations. It became clear that most of the artworks sold by Charles were either stolen (and not all from his family) or forged.

There were angry threats of prosecution and lawsuits, but eventually most of the legal actions were halted. Celebrity millionaires do not care for the kind of publicity that casts them as gullible parvenus, and museum curators and art dealers thrive on their knowledge and discrimination and might be ruined if it became known that they had been so easily duped. But one woman, purchaser of a fake Millet, persisted, and the district attorney filed charges. Charles was tried and convicted of fraud, fined, ordered to pay restitution, and given a two-year prison sentence, which was suspended in favor of probation. Charles vanished two days after the trial.

He fled to San Francisco, circulated among the higher social and economic levels of the gay community, and soon formed a relationship with a wealthy businessman three times his age. He moved into the man's house. His patron was generous, but Charles almost immediately began stealing and forging checks.

Charges were filed. His violation of the New Mexico probation became known. He was tried and convicted on several counts of theft and forgery and was sentenced to serve two to five years in the penitentiary. His lawyer pleaded with the judge to direct that his client be held in a minimum-security facility: Charles was very young, nonviolent, and surely would be brutally victimized by the hardened inmates of a medium- or maximum-security institution. The judge was not swayed. He sent Charles to San Quentin.

Charles Arthur Sinclair, according to the report, was a *model inmate.* He was assigned to work in the prison hospital, first as a nurse and then, after study and training, as a paramedic. He was highly praised by the professional medical staff for his skill, compassion, and devotion to the patients in his care, as they testified at the parole hearing. Charles was paroled after serving two and a half years in the penitentiary. He afterward paid one visit to his parole officer and then immediately vanished.

I telephoned Morgan at his office in Tampa. A sexy computer voice advised me to wait. I listened to tinkle-tinkle music for a while and then Morgan came on the line.

"I received the reports," I said. "Thanks."

"Interim reports," he said. "We're still working. I was just about to call you. We've just received information on the location of the *Mako.* She's anchored in Chetumal Bay. Know where that is?"

"Mexico? Just north of Belize?"

"Right."

"Any information on Ahriman?"

"Sorry. Nothing. I don't understand it. Any shipping company or ship's captain has a long paper trail. Manifests, invoices, port and pilot's fees, medical clearances, union records, licenses—but this Ahriman's a ghost. It's killing me. I know the guy, I've seen him or his photo, but I can't dig out the name."

"Morg, it occurred to me that maybe Ahriman and Charles met at San Quentin. Maybe we can trace him to there."

"Occurred to me too. I'm looking into that."

"Anything else?"

"Falconer's two rape victims—reputed rape victims—refused to talk to our man in Miami."

"I'm not surprised."

"The cops IDed the girls killed down in the Mosquito Keys. Sally Baker and Kristen Leroux, both eighteen, from Valdosta, Georgia. After getting out of high school last spring they decided to move to South Florida and lead the glamorous beach life. They kept in touch with their parents until a few weeks ago."

"Well, hell, what can you say? 'Poor kids.' That hardly does it. Anything on Gary Tolliver?"

"Nothing yet. But that Stewart Dahl? He was a cameraman in Los Angeles, all right, strictly porn. And I'm going to pin down that Ahriman identity quick, I promise. Wait—one more thing. Seen the newspapers today?"

"No."

"Last night eleven illegal Chinese immigrants were found hiding in the big mangrove swamp northeast of Flamingo. Half dead of thirst and hunger and dysentery. They'd been dumped on a tiny island that's mostly submerged at high tide and somehow made it to shore. Three of them drowned, two are still missing. The authorities talked to the survivors. There's no doubt that Ahriman and *Mako* were involved."

"Keep digging, Morg."

I had just hung up when the phone rang.

"Get your lazy butt up here."

"Ask me nice."

Petrie hung up.

I rode the elevator to the top floor. Petrie obliged me to sit in the waiting room with a pair of felons for five minutes before I was summoned into his imperial presence. He sat behind his desk, slouched back in the swivel chair with his hands folded behind his neck.

"I'm paying you a lot of money, am I not?"

"Yes. Thanks."

"Where's the *Mako*? Where's Peter Falconer?"

"Ahriman gave us a week to raise the money. We'll be hearing from him soon."

"I'm paying Leroy a third of what I'm paying you, and guess what?"

"Wait," I said. I tore a sheet of paper from his memo pad, wrote *Chetumal, Quintana Roo, Mexico* on it, folded the sheet, and slipped it beneath the slab of amber on his desk. The ancient, encysted praying mantis was still patiently waiting for his next meal.

"Leroy," said Petrie, "found the ship, found Ahriman and the others, found Peter."

"Well, of course Karpe knows where they are. He's in with them."

"Crap. You've got this paranoid obsession with Leroy. He's working hard while you're frolicking around with your hammy theater pals."

He snatched the sheet of paper from beneath the paper-weight, read it, and let it drift down into the wastepaper basket.

"Why didn't you tell me, for Christ's sake."

"I just found out."

"Leroy's down there. He's made contact with Ahriman."

"Why am I not surprised?"

"Pack a bag," he said. "We go tomorrow morning. I'll fly us to Miami in the Cessna. I've made reservations, Miami to Merida, then we'll try to charter a plane to fly us down to Chetumal, or hire a car. This is it."

"Have you raised the other million two-fifty?"

"Of course."

"How?"

"None of your business."

"That's a lot of money."

"I can count."

"Tom, have you thought this all the way through?"

"Duh. Me tink so."

"What did you do? Mortgage your house, sell out your portfolio, borrow your limit from the banks?"

He looked at his watch. "Tick tick tick," he said.

"How are you going to get the money into Mexico?"

"Wire transfer. Susan will carry her bearer bonds." He suddenly grinned at me. He was cheerful now, excited. "This is a big-time blood-bubbling adrenaline rush. It's buttons off, kid. We're putting our lives on the line. This Ahriman creature will devour us if we're not careful and lucky. Are you scared?"

"You bet."

"Me too."

I went down the stairwell, into the office, and past Candace, who was foaming at the mouth—brushing her teeth above an empty coffee cup—and over to Levi's door. I knocked several times, heard him call out, and went inside.

"I haven't seen much of you," he said. "Why no consultations?"

I sat down across from his desk. "I've been busy, Judge."

"I may be busy myself soon. I have a client, Daniel. A petty criminal, a thug, a liar, and a thief, but nevertheless a client. After all, I style myself these days as a criminal-defense lawyer. Why shouldn't I then defend a criminal?"

"No reason at all, Judge."

"No appointment, he walked in off the street. An odious fellow. Candace loathed him. He tried to chat her up, procure her phone number and such, but Candace turned to ice."

"It isn't very often that our Candy turns to ice around males."

"No indeed."

"Why does this guy need a criminal-defense lawyer?"

"Oh, a plethora of reasons. I'll be busy until spring. Defying a grand jury subpoena, charges of assault, outstanding warrants, parole violation, drug dealing, car theft, boat theft—he's a one-man crime wave."

"What is this character's name?"

"George Tell."

"What did he look like, Judge?"

"He's one of those blotchy-skinned redheads, you know, with pale eyelashes and greenish eyes. Powerfully built, walks with a swagger. Why? Do you know him?"

"When was he here?"

"Monday morning, while you were in Tampa."

"He must have known I was out of town. His real name is Gary Tolliver. I don't think you'll be seeing him again. He just came here as a way of threatening me."

"Not a genuine client? It's back to Sacco and Vanzetti,

then. Well? Are you going to inform me about Mr. Tolliver aka George Tell?"

"If you'll pour me a tot of your rare old single-malt scotch whiskey."

He got up and walked to the walnut cabinet. "The red-haired son of a bitch," Judge Levi Samuelson said.

# Part III
# Hurricane
# Lorraine

# Twenty-One

The light airplane that Petrie had chartered was ready to fly as soon as we cleared customs at Merida. Both the aircraft and the pilot were old and tired-looking. The left side of Juan Morales's face and his left arm showed crepy scar tissue from old skin grafts, and he walked with a distinct limp. Petrie was not concerned: He said that nothing was more encouraging to see than an *old* bush pilot; it was the young bravos who landed you in the trees. Clearly, Morales had learned his lesson. But I noticed that Tom was savagely chewing his lower lip as we taxied down the runway.

We flew southeast over scrubby forest patched with cultivated fields and dotted with the huts of smoky little villages. And we could see Mayan ruins from two thousand feet: Uxmal to our right, Chichén-Itzá on the left, and more ruins ahead, some completely excavated and others little more than dirt hills thickly grown with shrubbery.

The country became wilder, the forest thicker, when we crossed from Yucatán State into Quintana Roo. Jaguars down there, I thought, crocodiles, and Maya Indians who still practiced many of the old ways. There were fewer roads, fewer villages, and heat and humidity glazed the air—it was like looking at the world through another's eyeglasses. And even at altitude you could smell the forest, rank, sour-sweet, ancient.

Petrie sat forward with the pilot; Susan and I were behind them. She slept. From time to time I glanced at her, noting the dark curve of her eyelashes, the gentle flex of her nostrils, the damp wisps of hair at her temples. Sleep erased a certain tenseness around her eyes and mouth, and she looked years younger, like a college girl exhausted after a big outing. Susan had become rather remote after seeing Peter's film, alone among friends. Her expression lately reminded me of the fashion photos of her in *Très Chic*—it was a frozen beauty, ideal and sterile.

The sky was beginning to cloud over. This was the rainy season in tropical Mexico; we could expect furious storms every afternoon. Now the Caribbean, a milky emerald in this light, appeared in the east. Offshore islands, like beads on a string, dotted the sea. Soon we were approaching Chetumal Bay. It was a large, roughly triangular body of water that thrust up into the lower Yucatán. Outside, a peninsular wedge of land, extended by a long island, created a bay protected on all sides. The city of Chetumal, tucked at the southwest corner of the bay, was just above the border of Belize.

Petrie instructed the pilot to fly the length of the bay before turning toward the airport. There were a few ships anchored offshore and a few more tied up at the quay. Chetumal was a small, shabby-looking port city, squeezed between forest and sea.

*Mako* was anchored a mile or so offshore. She pointed prow-to-land in the ebbing tide. Black, squat, riding high without cargo or sufficient ballast, she impressed me as being an evil entity. I knew that was foolish; the ship was just a mass of steel shaped a certain way, designed to fulfill a certain function; even so, the freighter aroused in me something like dread. Maybe there was truth in Petrie's suggestion that I had been spooked—damaged—by my experiences aboard that ship.

Leroy Karpe met us at the airport. He wore an embroidered *guayabera* shirt outside white trousers of coarsely woven cotton, huaraches, and a straw field-worker's hat.

"Gone native, Leroy?" Petrie asked mildly.

Karpe was all jittery energy and cocky swagger. He did not think to help Susan with her bags. He led us out into the steambath heat and across the parking lot, talking all the while and gesturing expansively. A taxi was waiting for us. He issued commands in crisp idiomatic Spanish. Leroy was full of surprises.

He sat in the front seat with the driver. Petrie, Susan, and I were in the rear. Leroy half turned and regarded us one by one.

"I've talked to them," he said.

"Have you seen Peter?" Susan asked.

"No."

"Why not?"

"Raven said no more free looks."

"Did he," Petrie said.

"It's all set, but Raven has to confirm. We'll meet with him tomorrow night."

"Why not today?"

"Raven said tomorrow night, Tom. He's calling the shots."

"I thought you were calling the shots, Leroy."

Karpe either missed or ignored Petrie's irony. "I hope you raised the whole amount," he said. "Raven won't settle for a short count or excuses."

"Raven, Raven, Raven," I said. "You sound like you've signed on as Ahriman's spokesman. Spokesman, lackey, gofer."

"Did you have to bring along the big mouth?" Karpe said to Petrie.

"Yes, I did."

"Miss Falconer—I can see that. She's in the way, maybe, but it's her brother. But him"—he hooked a thumb toward me—"we don't need Shaw. He'll just fuck it all up like he did the last time."

"Turn around, Leroy," Petrie said. "I want to look at the back of your head for a while."

Chetumal had a population of about seventy thousand, but it looked smaller. Few of the buildings were more than four or five stories high. Hunchbacked vultures perched on rooftops and along the steel arm of a giant crane parked near the docks. Chetumal had that decrepit paint-peeling, plaster-crumbling look of many tropical cities.

We drove along the Malecón—the seaside boulevard—to the northern edge of the city. The Hotel Presidio was a boxy modern building with a checkerboard facade patterned with rows of balconies and set among acres of lawn and flowering trees. You went through the doors into a forty-foot-high atrium. There were polished parquet floors and pre-Columbian statuary and, on two of the walls, big frescoes done by an artist who admired Diego Rivera too much. Leroy, according to instructions, had reserved a two-bedroom suite for Petrie and Susan on the top floor. We each had a single room on the floor below.

My room was spacious, with tile floors scattered with throw rugs, heavy furniture crafted out of dark tropical woods, and French doors that opened out onto a balcony. It was only a little after two o'clock, but dark outside. I could see the Malecón below, a strip of beach, and beyond that the gray expanse of Chetumal Bay. And I could see the *Mako*, a black silhouette that was rapidly blending into the darkening sea and sky.

The rain came suddenly. There was no spatter of rain-drops, no preliminary drizzle, just a hard downpour that frothed over the sea and rattled like popping corn against the glass doors. There was not much of a wind. The rain came down straight and hard, steamed on the hot pave-ment, ripped through the palms, and obscured the sea and sky. *Mako* vanished.

What was I doing here? This affair had somehow turned into a shared obsession. Peter Falconer was at the center, and around him the rest of us orbited: Tom Petrie and Susan and Karpe and me, and on the other side, as much collaborators as enemies, were Ahriman and Charles and the rest. A great deal of money was involved, but now it almost seemed as if money were no longer the point; the two million dollars served as counters in a complicated and dangerous game.

The rain halted as abruptly as it had arrived. The sky be-gan to clear in long, lateral blue streaks. *Mako* reappeared se-quentially, as if it were being constructed from stem to stern out of mist.

I rode an elevator down to the lobby, walked outside, and got into the first of a line of taxis. I asked the driver if there was something like a pawnshop in the city. He nodded and pulled out onto the Malecón. There are pawn or resale shops in every port city; seamen, desperate for a woman or another drink, will sell whatever they own for whatever they can get.

The sun was out now, and the wet streets smoked with vapor. We drove to the city center, then turned off to a busi-ness section a couple of streets behind the Malecón. There were shops and offices, a bank, hotels, a movie theater, and on the corner a brick store with a window full of the kind of merchandise that interested me.

It was a big, cluttered place, with warped wooden floors and a dozen glass-topped counters spaced around the perimeter. More objects were hanging from wall pegs or spread on wooden tables.

The proprietor, a middle-aged man with a big belly and a thin mustache, nodded and gestured with his hand held palm-up—*look around*.

Most of the seaman's gear was located along the south wall, inside glass counters or displayed on tables. Navigational equipment, sextants and chronometers, tools, a ship's compass probably salvaged from some wreck. An entire case was filled with knives: clasp knives and sheath knives, blades that hooked at the tip, double-edged knives, daggers. I picked out a clasp knife with a wooden handle and a five-inch blade of Solingen carbon steel. A third of the blade's width had been sharpened away over the years. The proprietor removed it from the case. There was another counter nearby that contained binoculars and telescopes. I picked out a pair of Zeiss binoculars; some of the stitching had come loose from the leather case, and there were scratches and dents on the frame, but the optics were good. I carried the knife and binoculars over to the cash register.

"Are you the owner?" I asked the man.

"Me, yes. And my brothers."

"Would it be possible to buy a pistol?"

"Impossible."

It is difficult to buy a handgun, any sort of gun, in Mexico. There are strict laws and stricter penalties.

"I'm willing to pay twice the normal price," I said.

His stare lasted ten or fifteen seconds. He was a middle-aged man, but his eyes were young, large, and cocoa-brown, fringed by lashes so black and shiny they appeared lacquered. It was not a hostile stare; he was appraising me, my look, my stance, my return gaze, and making the many small calculations necessary for him to make a decision.

"Come back in three days."

"No sooner?"

"Three days."

"If I'm still in town."

"I had a pistol, a Beretta, but I sold it yesterday. To an American."

I asked him to describe the American. It was Leroy Karpe.


Air-conditioning had cooled my room. Chill inside air met the hot, humid outside air at the French doors, and condensation fogged the glass. I opened the doors and carried a chair and my binoculars out onto the balcony. The Zeiss lenses were even more powerful than I'd thought; I turned the focus wheel and the *Mako* leaped toward me—rust- and paint-mottled steel-plated hull, deckhouse and bridge, an ugly ship bristling with masts and antennae and winches. She flew the Panama flag.

A man was working on the foredeck. He half turned and I recognized the big Mexican, Yoyo. He fussed with a tangle of ropes and pulleys. Yoyo had a smooth, glossy brown face that looked like it had been carved out of some hard jungle wood. His eyes were slitted, his mouth broad and mobile even as he worked. He was singing to himself.

Half an hour later Ahriman and Leroy Karpe emerged from the deckhouse. They walked toward the lifeboat. Leroy still had on his Mexican outfit; Raven wore only a pair of tight shorts. He was barefoot. His braided black hair, oiled and glossy, fell to his waist. He moved with a slow, don't-fuck-with-me jail-yard strut. Karpe was a fit, well-built man, but he looked small next to Ahriman.

They reached the ladder. Ahriman said something. Karpe laughed. Ahriman spoke again. The glasses brought them close; if I had been a lip-reader I might have been able to follow their conversation.

I studied Ahriman. A big man, even bigger than I had perceived in the dimness of the *Mako*'s bridge that night. He had pumped a lot of iron in prison and continued pumping it after getting out. He was vain about his physique. You could tell that by the way he moved, held his head, flexed an arm or knee.

Karpe and the Mexican, Yoyo, descended the ladder and climbed aboard the Zodiac. Ahriman, leaning over the rail, watched them. The Mexican cast off the line, started the engine, and pointed the prow toward Chetumal. The boat rolled a little in the chop, leaving a haze of blue engine smoke behind. Its wake arced to the south, toward the docks that harbored the city's fleet of commercial fishing boats.

Leroy would meet with Petrie and Susan tonight. Together, they would resume plotting and conniving, spinning and weaving. I didn't mind being excluded. I knew my way to the airport.

I turned the binoculars back to *Mako*. There was no one on deck now. I looked at the forward hatch cover. It was disturbing to recall my night in the cargo hold. Had Bully survived his fall?

I again scanned the length of the freighter. I missed him on the first sweep, but on the second Ahriman came into view. He was standing on the railed walkway that circled the bridge, looking at me through a telescope mounted on a rifle. He was grinning. We looked at each other for half a minute, he through the telescope, me through the binoculars. A rifle bullet will easily carry more than a mile.

I got up from my chair and, trying not to hurry or fumble, opened the French doors, went inside, and closed the drapes.

# Twenty-Two

Early the next morning I ate breakfast in my room, then took a chair and the binoculars out onto the balcony. It was hot even at that hour, six-thirty, bright and hot and still. The bay was glassy, and *Mako's* reflection, laying flat on the water, was nearly as sharply defined as the upright ship itself. Gulls and pelicans appeared to be working harder than usual this morning; there was no breeze, no lift, to assist their flight. It was the sort of oppressive day that often precedes heavy weather—the quiet before the storm—though, according to weather reports, Tropical Storm Lorraine still lay far east of Grand Cayman Island.

There was one person on *Mako's* deck, a tall black woman, the same woman I had glimpsed naked in Ahriman's cabin that night at Big Sandy Cay. She was hanging clothing on a cat's cradle of rope strung from rail to rail on the foredeck. She was at least six feet tall, wide through the shoulders and hips, and her skin shone a dark brown-gold in the sunlight.

A man emerged from the deckhouse carrying a wicker basket full of more wet clothing. I had not seen him before.

He was thin, bony, and his hair was cut and formed to fit like a helmet. A black fringe fell to his eyebrows. He looked like the forest Indians you saw in television documentaries about the Amazonian peoples. He carried his basket to the foredeck and set it down. He and the woman did not speak. The Indian stood at the rail for a while, looking south, and then he returned to the deckhouse.

Tom Petrie and Susan Falconer appeared below in the hotel's gardens. They were holding hands. Tom was dressed in a dark suit with a white shirt and tie; Susan wore high heels, a pleated white skirt, and a navy blue sleeveless top. They were a handsome couple, absorbed in each other, and for the first time I wondered if they actually were in love. They got into a hired Mercedes.

Five minutes later Leroy Karpe appeared below. Today he wore khaki shorts patched with many pockets and a tight red T-shirt. Leroy climbed into the backseat of a taxi, which headed south down the boulevard.

A trawler, painted black like the *Mako*, had motored out from the docks and was approaching the freighter. It was about sixty feet long, old, but appeared to be in good repair. It was not rigged for fishing. I saw no identifying flag, name, or number. The trawler sounded its horn when it was about a hundred yards from *Mako*.

Charles, eating what looked like a rolled tortilla, came out of the deckhouse. He waved at the woman, who smiled, then he went to the ladder and began descending. The Jamaican friend of Bully's appeared on the trawler's deck to help Charles board. Another man, perhaps Yoyo, was at the controls inside the wheelhouse.

I waited until I was sure they were heading back to the commercial fishing docks, then left the hotel and caught a taxi.

A seafood restaurant overlooked the maze of piers. Most

of the berths were empty, the boats at sea, but a few remained—shrimpers, purse seiners, trawlers, in for repairs or
to deliver their catches or take on ice. Gulls flew mewing
above the boats, begging for handouts. The air smelled of
fish and tar and fuel oil. I sat out on the wooden deck with
a cup of coffee and a split bolillo smeared with butter.

I was beginning to think they were headed elsewhere when
the trawler appeared and pulled into a berth midway down the
main pier. Charles tossed his scrap of tortilla over the side, adjusted his clothes, spoke briefly to the Jamaican, then stepped
off onto the pier. His stride was jaunty, chin up and eyes directed straight forward. He wore a lightweight pale blue blazer
and tan trousers, loafers without socks, and a lavender scarf
was loosely tied at his neck. Suave Charles, insouciant Charles.

I waited a few minutes and then followed him. He proceeded along the palm-lined bayside walk. He looked neither left nor right. He was a man on a mission.

But his pace slowed after a while, and he paused several times
to mop the sweat from his face. I followed him to the city's business center. Charles waited for a traffic light to change, crossed
the street, and walked up a flight of concrete steps on a corner
building that looked like it might have been converted from a
small hotel to another use. There was a tile mosaic on the wall
that showed brave seamen weathering a storm, and a sign above
the entrance read *Unión de los Marineros*.

I sat on a bench in the little park across the street. A pack
of kids drifted toward me. I had my shoes shined, bought a
packet of chewing gum, two Swiss chocolate candy bars,
and a morning newspaper. The kids told me that the top
two floors of the corner building were occupied by a medical facility for the benefit of indigent seamen.

After twenty-five minutes Charles emerged from the
building. He stood blinking in the angled sunlight. He did

not appear so jaunty now; the heat and exercise had tired him. He was pale and sweaty, and he glanced vaguely up and down the street before starting off down an alley.

The ground floor was mostly taken up by offices. I walked up the stairs. Half of the second floor was occupied by a large barracks-type room strung with hammocks. Men were sleeping back in the dimness. Seamen could rent hammock space and the use of a lounge and shower room for a few pesos.

The hospital admissions desk was on the third floor. A stout woman was hunting and pecking at a computer keyboard. I told her that I had missed my appointment with a young American; we were to visit a friend here this morning. Yes, the American had left not more than five minutes ago. I asked her if I could see the patient. Yes, that would be all right. Would she be kind enough to brief me on the patient's condition? She was not as zealously protective of information as American hospital workers. Room 416. Mr. Kingsley Kincaid, thirty-six, a citizen of Jamaica, had been very seriously injured in a shipboard accident. His left ankle had been shattered, and both the tibia and fibula of his left leg were broken. There were other, less serious injuries.

"Your friends made a contribution. It would be most welcome if . . ." Surgery was scheduled for three o'clock this afternoon.

"Would five hundred dollars help?"

"Oh, yes. Very much."

I wrote her a check, then went up the stairway to the fourth floor. Most of the rooms on either side of the hallway were empty. I passed a pair of chatting nurses, a custodial worker, and an aluminum food cart with a cat on top picking at the leftovers.

There were three beds in the room, but only one was occupied: Bully lay on his back on an iron-framed bed next to the far wall. A tented sheet covered his legs and hips. His face and bare torso shined with sweat, and his eyes, when he opened them to look at me, were mucoid and dull. A slow-turning ceiling fan revolved overhead.

I pulled a chair to the bed. "How are you doing, Bully?"

"Did you bring me anything?"

"Candy," I said. I placed the candy bars and the gum on the bedside table.

"No rum?"

"Sorry, no rum. They're going to operate on you this afternoon."

He stared at me.

"Shaw," I said. "Don't you remember me?"

"Now I do. Please go get me a bottle of rum, Mr. Shaw. I hurt so bad. I been hurting for days and days. I never hurt like this ever."

"You've got the reflexes of a cat. Last time I saw you, Bully, you were flying headfirst down into the cargo hold."

"You shouldn't done that to me."

"You were going to kill me."

He was quiet for a moment as he thought back. He nodded. "They was orders."

"Your orders to kill, not my orders to die."

"Go buy me some rum, Mr. Shaw. Please do that. I can't take this hurt. I ain't slept since I busted my leg all to pieces. Please."

"When did they last give you a painkiller?"

"Painkiller, huh! They give me aspirins, when they think of it."

A pair of sash windows were open, and I could hear noises from the street below—a swish of tires on pavement, a policeman's whistle, the fluty voices of some passing children.

"What happened at the Mosquito Keys, Bully?"

"Why tell you?"

"I'm your friend."

"Bully's got no friends."

"Who took care of you on the ship? Who brought you to this hospital?"

"Charles, he did."

"Well, he's your friend. So am I."

Bully was stabbed by a sudden rush of pain. It went through his body like an electrical current. His limbs stiffened and he arched his back. All of the muscles on his chest turned rigid. Tendons and veins on his neck bulged. He looked as though he were being electrocuted. The pain that caused this seizure created even more pain. Finally he shuddered, relaxed a little, and began weeping.

Bully had no resources left. The sleepless days, the incessant pain, had broken him. His face wrinkled, he sobbed, and you could see little Kingsley Kincaid, the boy who had grown up to be Bully, a fellow who believed himself an instrument of the world's meanness and punishment.

I left the hospital. There are usually pharmacies in the vicinity of any hospital. The Farmacía Yucatec was located on a street around the corner. One doesn't need a prescription to obtain most drugs in Mexico. I asked the pharmacist for a strong painkiller, and he gave me twelve Percodan pills in a plastic bottle.

There was a jug of *agua pura* in the fourth-floor hallway; I filled a paper cup and carried it to the room. Bully washed down a Percodan with the water, then said, "One more, Mr. Shaw."

"Later, maybe."

He closed his eyes.

"Bully, what happened at the Mosquito Keys?"

"I hurt so much. So much."

"All right, I'll give you another pill."

He took the pill with the rest of the water. "I don't know about no Mosquito Keys."

"I saw the film. Peter's movie."

He turned his head to the wall.

"It was stupid to leave the negative aboard the *Deep Six*. It's evidence enough to fry the lot of you. You must have been in a rush to leave."

"I didn't kill them girls," he said. He turned his head and opened his eyes: He wanted to be able to read belief or disbelief in my expression.

"Who did kill them?"

"I killed the man, the camera fella. But Bully don't kill women."

"Who killed them?"

"Peter killed the one."

"Which one?"

"The blond one, the Kristen girl. They was on the island together and something go wrong, man, mean sex. Peter strangles the girl. Then, you know, the camera fella and the Sally girl got to die. I only kill the man."

"Who killed Sally?"

"I don't know."

"Bully?"

"I want to sleep so bad. I don't sleep, Mr. Shaw."

"Aren't the pills helping now?"

"Some, I guess."

"You said Peter killed one of the women. Who killed the other?"

"Charles, he did."

"No. Charles didn't kill anyone. Who, Bully?"

"Raven."

"No. Raven wasn't there. Who killed her?"

"Peter, Peter kill them both."

"No. You killed Sally."

"No more. Don't talk no more. Go away."

"All right." I stood up.

"Leave me them pills."

"I'll give them to the nurse. Good luck, Bully. This afternoon the surgeon will operate on your leg. You'll be walking in six months."

I was lying to him. This very small, poor hospital probably could not call on the services of a first-rate orthopedic surgeon. Smashed ankle, broken tibia and fibula, and maybe other injuries that hadn't yet been diagnosed. No doubt Bully would spend the rest of his days crippled.

"Go buy Bully some rum, Mr. Shaw."

"Is Peter Falconer alive?"

"He's dead."

"Sure?"

"Last time I look, he's dead."

"Good-bye," I said.

"This is a mean world," Bully said.

I left the remaining Percodan pills with a young nurse, informed her that the patient had taken two of them fifteen minutes before, and walked down the stairs to the ground floor.

# Twenty-Three

Charles was sitting on a bench in the little park. He smiled at me and lifted a hand. I crossed the street and sat down next to him. The ground was littered with flower petals, and not far away a bronze military hero, sword half unsheathed, sat nobly astride a rearing stallion.

"I noticed you following me this morning," he said.

He had regained his high spirits. Additional spirits remained in the silver flask that lay on the bench between us, along with a quartered lime and a pinch of salt in a twist of paper napkin.

"Drink?" he asked.

"No."

"Smoke?" He offered a pack of anise-scented cheroots.

I accepted one, and we sat together smoking in silence for a time. Charles had polished manners in these rude times. He was casually attentive. He looked me in the eyes and smiled easily. He seemed pleased to see me. Perhaps he was.

I said, "Bully told me everything."

"I don't think so. Bully doesn't know everything."

"I understand a lot of what took place at the Mosquito Keys."

"God, what a horrible mess that was. You have no idea, Shaw. Absolute nihilism, a bloody nightmare."

"Didn't you expect a mess when you thought up the abduction?"

"No, actually. I never expect a mess, though a mess usually results."

"I learned something about your past, your family, your criminal record."

"Did you? It's very strange. Can you believe that I hate violence, detest crime, have always wanted to live decently? It's true. But somehow I can't. There seems to be a fuse out somewhere in my brain, broken connections. I'm like a fat man who solemnly vows to diet and immediately after orders a pizza and a six-pack. I want to be honorable. My intentions are often good, but there is a definite kink in my soul and things turn out messy. There it is. I like you well enough, Shaw, but I'm afraid I'd steal your eyes if I had the impulse and opportunity."

"I'm sure you would."

He smiled and shrugged boyishly, a little shy, someone you might trust even though he had just talked about stealing your eyes.

"I'm unable to visualize consequences," he said. "I make perfect plans. Even honest plans at first. I plan immaculately. But I always forget that plans are static and people are not. People never behave as I think they should. Fate plays droll little jokes on my immaculate plans. You understand, don't you?"

"Life isn't a board game."

"Well, it is and it isn't."

"So Peter Falconer is dead."

"No."

"Bully told me he was dead."

"I saw Peter just before leaving the ship this morning. He was unequivocally alive."

"Bully told me that the last time *he* saw him, Peter was dead."

"Bully has been delirious for days. By now he doesn't know what is dream and what's reality."

"He told me that Peter killed one of the girls."

"Yes. It all got out of hand. Peter . . . Peter is a bit twisted, you know. He likes very rough sex, violent sex. He obviously went too far."

"Bully said you killed the other girl."

Charles smiled. "No. Bully himself killed her with a drug overdose. I think it was intentional—maybe not. Then he killed Stewart Dahl. As I told you, it was a bloody fucking awful mess. I was there to oversee things, but it got out of my control, anyone's control. It just blew up."

"Susan believes her brother is alive."

"Susan. Isn't she beautiful? Stunning. And maybe very rich soon. She's the sort of girl I would have married if I hadn't been what they used to call polymorphous perverse. Maybe they still call it that. Peter and I were very good friends in prep school. I met Susan a few times back then, once at the family's summer place in Maine. Truly, Shaw, with a different roll of the genes I might today be an exemplary citizen and bound to Susan in holy matrimony. A couple of little nippers running about. Alas."

"Have Petrie and Susan met with Ahriman yet?"

"No, that's set for tonight."

"Where?"

"At your hotel, Petrie's suite. Raven and I have been invited for dinner. You weren't informed? Well, perhaps you'll receive an invitation today."

"Who is the black woman who lives aboard the ship?"

"Mirium? Mirium is Raven's wife."

"That's a surprise."

"You're surprised that he's married or surprised he married a black? Shaw, you really ought to concede that Raven is at least half human."

"I saw an Indian on deck this morning too."

"Guyana. Cook, steward, cabin boy. Is your interrogation nearly over?"

"Charles, aren't you afraid of Ahriman?"

"No. Why should I be? Raven is an old friend of mine."

"Peter Falconer is an old friend of yours too."

He nodded. "A point," he said, staring off toward the equestrian statue. An artist might render his profile, I thought, with a single clean stroke of the pen.

"When did Peter die? Was it that first day on the *Mako*?"

"I told you, Peter is still alive."

"I saw the photo. Ahriman beat him to death, didn't he?"

"It was awful—broken nose and teeth, lacerations, a bad concussion. But Raven didn't do that. Peter was being winched aboard ship, in a harness, when the winch chain slipped. The ship was rolling. He fell five or six feet and smashed hard into the hull. Broke his face. We used his injuries in that photo to elicit sympathy and horror. Did they?"

"Why didn't you just bring him up the ladder?"

"The sea was too rough. I was waiting below in the Zodiac when it happened. It didn't look serious, half a dozen feet of slack chain, a quick arc—it was like cracking a whip, though. One of his fingers got caught in a chain link and was nearly torn off. It was held by a tiny strip of skin."

"The finger sent to Petrie."

"We've taken good care of Peter. Really. I'm a well-qualified and experienced paramedic. Are you sure you won't have a drink?"

"What about the tape cassettes that were sent to Petrie and Susan? The weeping, the begging, the sheer terror in his voice."

"I told you Raven didn't hurt Peter, I didn't say Raven didn't terrorize him enough so that the tapes would sound authentic."

I stood up. "At first," I said, "chatting with you is like chatting with a bright kid, a delinquent kid but basically good at heart—candid, playful, charming . . ."

He laughed. "Ah, but then!"

"Then one senses in you a deep and advanced rot."

"Metaphysical decay?"

"But I suppose you saved Bully. You got him off the ship and into that hospital across the street. So maybe you have a decent instinct or two left."

"Dear boy, don't bet your eyes on it."


There was not a message for me at the hotel desk. Nothing had come over the fax machine. No one answered the phone in the suite shared by Petrie and Susan. I tried Karpe's room, but he was gone.

I went out onto the balcony. There was no breeze. A filmy membrane of haze filtered much of the blue from the sky, and now both sea and sky had a silvery, molten look. I studied *Mako* through the binoculars. No one. The ship appeared derelict, a wreck slowly sinking into its own watery reflection.

I became aware of a vaguely familiar sound, a remote snap and hiss. The sound had been there all morning but I hadn't been conscious of it. A muted snap and hiss followed by a silence of seven or eight seconds. I cocked my head. Snap and hiss, silence, another snap and hiss. Then I recognized it. Heard close by, that barely audible snap and hiss would become a thunderous crack and roar. Big surf was breaking on the ocean side of the peninsula. Although the storm was still hundreds of miles to the east, it had churned up big seas, which were now breaking all along the coast.

It rained hard in midafternoon, a furious downpour that obscured the *Mako* and turned the boulevard into a shallow, rushing river.

Tom Petrie phoned my room at five-thirty. "Cocktails in our suite at eight," he said. "Dinner at nine. Raven Ahriman will be joining us."

"Sounds genteel. Will he be bringing Falconer?"

"Heads up—this is the nexus."

"What exactly is a nexus, Tom?"

"Think of it as the coming together, the connection, of diverse people and objectives."

"Like a traffic accident," I said.

I had informed SureSecure of my whereabouts. Half an hour after Petrie's call, a bellman delivered a long fax that had been sent to me in care of the hotel. Morgan had done his job. It was an exhaustive report, filled with names, dates, numbers, copies of documents, cold facts, all of which I distilled into the life and times of Alexander Lermontev, aka Raven Ahriman.

# Twenty-Four

Raven Ahriman was born in Soldotna, Alaska, a small town near Anchorage, in 1958. He was baptized Alexander Ivanovitch Lermontev in the Russian Orthodox Church in Anchorage. His name was Russian, but he was a fifth-generation Alaskan of mixed ancestry: Russian, Swedish, German, and Inuit—a maternal grandmother was an Eskimo from Inuvik in the Canadian Northwest Territory. The first Alaskan Lermontevs, Ivan and Serge, and their wives settled in the territory in 1848, years before it was sold by Russia to the United States in the purchase known as Seward's Folly.

For generations the Lermontevs earned their living from the sea, as fur-seal hunters under sail until that trade was no longer profitable, and then as fishermen. There were good years and bad years, but on the whole both sides of the family did well. By the time Alexander was born, they owned five fishing boats and part interest in a cannery. Some of the children attended college in Washington or Oregon; Alexander's older brother, Leonid, became an executive with

Boeing in Seattle, while his sister, Anna, fluent in Russian, went to work for the U.S. State Department.

But Alexander, though obviously bright, hated school, was often truant, and got into the kind of scrapes typical of a bold, energetic boy who was impelled to test the limits of freedom. At fifteen he dropped out of school to work as a fisherman; at eighteen he earned his master's ticket and command of one of the family's boats, the *Polaris*.

He fished for salmon, king crab, pollack, whatever was in season (and out of season—he was accused of poaching). He was a born seaman, they said, but reckless. It was dangerous enough to fish those icy northern seas, particularly the Bering Sea, without crewing for a skipper who took unnecessary chances. Soon the older men, the family men, refused to sail with him, and he assembled a crew of bravos his own age. Alexander and his gang went out fishing when prudent men remained in port. He was good, and he was lucky, but more-experienced fishermen knew that both skill and luck were often negated by the power of wind and sea and ice.

Alexander Lermontev also had a reputation as a barroom brawler. He enjoyed fighting—clean or dirty, you choose. He even fought in the ring down in Seattle a dozen times. He usually won his fights, in the barroom or prize ring, but accepted the occasional beating cheerfully, no hard feelings, shake hands until the next time. There was about him an aura of danger, a devil-may-care indifference to consequences, that appealed to women. Women liked Alexander, and he liked women. But he wasn't a ladies' man. Men liked him, even those who refused to crew on his boat, even men who lost teeth and facial symmetry to his fists.

He got married, was soon divorced, but remained on good terms with his ex-wife, a high-school teacher who said that Alex had been born in the wrong time and place: He was really a sixteenth-century man, a mercenary *condottiere*, perhaps, or a pirate ruthlessly preying on the Spanish fleet and raiding Caribbean ports. He didn't belong in the here and now.

When Alexander was twenty-three he lost his boat, five members of his crew, and his captain's license. He and the only other survivor were rescued from the Bering Sea by a Coast Guard helicopter. Some people said that Alexander was never the same after that. Others scoffed, declared that he remained exactly the same, that the sun and moon would change before young Lermontev did.

He drifted down to San Francisco, where he worked on the docks for a year before being admitted to the merchant seaman's union. Then, for six years, he shipped as a deck-hand on freighters that sailed all over the Pacific, calling at ports from Yokohama in the north to Christchurch in the south, and most of the countries and islands between. Family and friends rarely heard from him. They assumed that he was a first-rate sailor while at sea and a first-rate drinker, brawler, and fornicator while in port. It was rumored that, in his last year at sea, he virtually commanded a big cargo ship whose skipper was a drunk.

He killed a man with his fists in a barroom brawl in a San Francisco sailors' dive. He was tried and convicted of homicide in the second degree and sentenced to twenty years in prison. It was a harsh charge, a tough verdict, and a hard sentence. His lawyer protested that a charge of manslaughter, voluntary or involuntary, would have been appropriate. There might have been a plea bargain or prosecution on a lesser charge if the man killed hadn't been an off-duty policeman.

He served the first seven years of his sentence among the general inmate population at San Quentin. He was soon tested, as all new convicts are tested: There were two fights, two men seriously injured, two disciplinary actions that put him into isolation for six months. He was rarely challenged after returning to the general population. There was something about him, his walk, his eyes, his smile, that aroused caution in other men. He was "crazy." That is, he hardly seemed to respect his own life, let alone the life of another.

He remained separate. There were a number of groups and subgroups in prison—biker gang members, black and Hispanic and Asian gangs, the Aryan Brotherhood—and it was rare for an unaffiliated prisoner to be regarded as a "boss."

During his fifth year at San Quentin, the twenty-year-old Charles Sinclair arrived to begin serving his time on a forgery conviction. A man like Charles—nonviolent, gentle in his ways, a young and "pretty" homosexual—could easily survive prison physically, but not without being psychically destroyed. Charles knew that he needed a powerful ally; he would be unable to endure otherwise. He went to Alexander Lermontev and asked for protection. It was granted, and he was soon transferred to Lermontev's cell. Inmate bosses could usually arrange such things with the corrections staff.

Charles received parole after serving two and a half years. Months later Anton killed an inmate with his shank in a quarrel over an unpaid wager. The prison authorities knew that Anton was guilty of the murder but were unable to prove it: There were witnesses, but none who would testify in court, and no scientific evidence.

Anton Lermontev was transferred to the Soledad State Penitentiary, where he was isolated in a maximum-security, level-4 "adjustment unit." He was confined to a six-foot-by-nine-foot cell for twenty-three hours per day for almost a year.

In 1996 the California courts ruled that overcrowding in

the state prison system amounted to cruel and unusual punishment and ordered that the inmate population promptly be reduced to acceptable levels. Lermontev was released a few months later. He was not the only violent criminal to receive an early release.

Alexander Ivanovitch Lermontev vanished in June 1997. Raven Ahriman appeared in October of 1998, in Monrovia, Liberia, where he purchased the old vessel then named the *Southern Cross*.

# Twenty-Five

A man came out of Petrie's suite as I was walking down the hall. He was short, with straight black hair, and he wore a chalk-striped suit that had been tailored when he was twenty pounds lighter. Gold-rimmed, amber-tinted eyeglasses, a thin mustache, the undeviating stride of a man who expected others to move aside.

*"Buenas tardes,"* I said.

He passed on without a glance.

I figured that he was a professional man, doctor, lawyer, banker, maybe a politician.

Petrie answered my knock wearing boxer shorts and a sleeveless undershirt, and I followed him through the foyer into a living room that had the look of the VIP lounge in a Latin American airport. It had a high-beamed ceiling, parquet floor, heavy furniture that looked as though it had been designed for a race of seven-footers.

"You're early," Petrie said.

"Who was your visitor?" I asked.

"None of your business."

"Banker? Politician?"

"Nah. Mexican politicians are tall."

"A mortician?"

He deflected my questioning by giving me a prolonged critical stare and saying, "Is that the best you could do? Chinos and your rural grandfather's wrinkled old suit jacket? The thing looks like it's made out of mattress ticking."

"It's seersucker, Tom. It's supposed to be wrinkled and look like mattress ticking. Anyway, you don't look very elegant."

"Wait half an hour," he said. Then, "The drink cart's over there. Go easy. Let Leroy in when he gets here."

"Leroy's still involved?"

"Leroy's still in all the way. I'm counting on Leroy in the crunch. No offense, buddy, but I don't think you're up to speed on this."

"No offense taken. I sleep better knowing that Leroy is watching over us."

He started to reply, shook his head over the futility of employing reason with me, then crossed the room and went through a bedroom door.

I poured white Italian vermouth over ice, added a twist of lemon peel, and strolled around the room. All of the paintings, pots, and faux Mayan ceramic figures were interesting but nothing that a guest would be tempted to steal. The dinner table was set on an elevated section next to a bank of windows that looked out over the bay. A long buffet table had been erected nearby.

I sat on one of the two couches placed on either side of a massive stone table. The table was round, maybe six feet in diameter and three feet thick, all rough stone except for the polished surface. It reminded me of the Aztec sacrificial stone in the Museum of Anthropology in Mexico City, though it hadn't a hollow in the center or blood channels running off to the sides.

Susan emerged through the same bedroom door that Petrie had entered a few minutes before, approached, and handed me a string of pearls.

"Tom's showering," she said. "Will you fasten this for me?"

I seized the opportunity to lightly caress her neck as I fixed the clasp. She gave me a quizzical look over her shoulder, smiling tentatively, and then moved away.

"Thank you."

"My pleasure."

Her hair was up, and she wore a black dress with spaghetti straps and a hem that fell just below her knees. Susan did not normally use makeup, but tonight she wore lipstick, mascara, and a touch of eyeshadow.

"Care for a drink?" I asked.

"Not right now." She walked to a chair, sat down, and crossed her legs.

"Is the exchange going to be made tonight?"

She ignored the question. "Tom told me that Leroy has a gun."

"Yes."

"Do you think it will be needed?"

"Not tonight."

"When?"

"Never, if Ahriman plays it straight."

"And will he, do you think?"

"No."

"Why not?"

"He can't. It isn't in him."

"Do you fear Ahriman?"

"Men like him have the advantage. They aren't constrained by any civilized codes. They act, we react."

"And he's not a romantic figure? The outlaw, the rebel, the man standing alone against society, the man who's strong enough to take what he wants?"

"Ahriman probably sees himself in that light."

"I suppose he's attractive to women—some women."

"I suppose."

We heard a hard rapping on the door.

"That must be Karpe. Would you get it?"

I walked through the foyer and opened the door. Leroy was wearing slacks and a new *guayabera*, this one sky-blue with raspberry embroidery. It was baggy; I couldn't see where he was carrying his gun.

"What do you want?" I asked.

"Get out of my way."

"Certainly, Leroy."

Karpe's gait changed when he entered the big room and saw Susan. His walk, his posture, his expression changed; he turned boyish. He too was at least half in love with Susan Falconer. She recognized it. She had been dealing with male fevers since puberty.

"Good evening, ma'am."

"Good evening, Leroy."

"You look great."

"Thank you."

"I was going to bring flowers . . ." Leroy waited for a reply, then walked over to the drink cart, poured a glass of tonic over ice, and added a slice of lime.

"Leroy," Susan said. "You know this brute Ahriman, don't you?"

"I've talked to him a few times."

"The Zoroastrian devil. Will he eat with his fingers? Blow his nose on the tablecloth? Stuff food in his pockets for later?"

"He isn't an animal," Karpe said.

"Will he undress me with his eyes?"

Karpe was uncomfortable. He looked down into his drink.

I said, "Of course he'll undress you with his eyes. He'd consider it unmanly not to undress you with his eyes."

Karpe shook his head. "I don't advise anyone to treat Raven Ahriman like an animal."

"And why is that?" Susan asked.

"He was caged like an animal for years. Raven won't take it."

A phone on a table next to Susan's chair rang. She lifted the receiver. "Yes? Yes. Is he muzzled? I said—never mind."

She covered the mouthpiece with her palm. "Mr. Ahriman is at the desk. Shall we invite him up?"

"By all means," I said.

"By all means," Susan told the desk clerk. "Tell Mr. Ahriman that cocktails are now being served."

We waited. Karpe rattled the ice cubes in his glass. Susan looked at me with her eyebrows lifted.

Petrie, knotting his tie, came through the bedroom door. He was freshly shaved, his wet hair was comb-tracked, and he wore one of his conservative lawyer suits.

"Jesus, Leroy," he said. "First Shaw comes in looking like the referee of some arcane Middle European sport, and now you arrive wearing a shirt that you won at the carnival."

There was a knock at the door, one sharp rap. I beat Leroy into the foyer.

Ahriman was wearing his hair center-parted and pulled back into a long braid. There was a turquoise earring in his left earlobe. His black suit was old, frayed around the cuffs, and shiny with wear, and beneath the jacket he wore a black T-shirt.

"Bad guys wear black," I said.

He waited for me to step aside, smiling a little but otherwise motionless. His derisive smile and hard gaze informed me that the situation tonight required tolerance on his part but that he was also keeping score and I should not push too hard. I recalled the night he had slapped my face and hooked his fist into my belly. I could tell from his eyes he was remembering the same thing.

"This way, Crow," I said.

He gave a short nod—that's two—and preceded me into the room. The end of his braid fell to his waist. His hair, unbraided, would probably reach the back of his thighs. It was black, shiny, and as thick as a ship's hawser.

Petrie surprised me by offering to shake Ahriman's hand, but then, Tom was a criminal-defense lawyer and he had shaken hands with a multitude of devils. Petrie was civil, Susan cold, and Ahriman sardonic, mocking us all with his watchful eyes and private smile.

After an awkward introduction and awkward silence, Susan said, "And how many men have you killed . . . Raven?"

"Personally? Seven."

"Is that all? How many women?"

"Only one," he said, and he grinned at her.

"You're very tough," Susan said. "A few years ago I knew a man who was nearly as tough as you. I caught him wearing my panties."

Ahriman laughed. "Maybe you'll let me try them on."

Susan's hostility made Petrie uneasy. In a hearty voice he said, "What will you have to drink, Raven?"

"Anything."

There are individuals who, simply by their presence, can dominate a gathering much larger than this one. Susan could, with her beauty and poise, and the same was true of Raven Ahriman in a contrary way. He advertised danger in his stance, the way he held his head, the contempt in his

gaze and voice, the way he moved slowly and with a choreographed precision. He was self-conscious in the sense that
he calculated the effect he had on others, how they responded to his menace. Ahriman was like an actor playing
himself. Overplaying himself.

Charles arrived, apologized for being late, and presented
Susan with a bouquet of mixed red and white roses. The
mood changed; there was not so much tension. Charles
liked to talk, and he talked well, with a droll wit and a
raconteur's timing.

He reminded Susan of their previous meetings. "You do
remember, don't you? I was Peter's houseguest on the island."

"I do remember you," she said. "Of course."

"August nineteenth, nineteen eighty-eight. We went sailing together. I nearly capsized the boat. I'm not much of a
sailor, as Raven will attest. I'm not deft at any task that requires ropes and pulleys and such."

"You were drinking, as I recall."

"Was I? I probably was. Yes, most certainly I was drinking. I fell in love with you that summer."

"I thought you were in love with Peter."

"Well, yes. But could I not fall in love with both of you?
Love can be qualified, perhaps, but not quantified."

"You loved Peter so much that you waited fifteen years to
conspire in kidnapping him."

"That!" Charles smiled in his charming bad-boy way.
"Well, maybe I was wrong, love *can* be quantified."

Petrie glanced around the circle. "Ah, the carefree, lan-
guorous summers of filthy-rich youth. Sailing, tennis, country-
club dances, spirited horses—everyone had his own horsie,
right? Shaw, how did you spend the halcyon summer days of
your youth?"

"Inventing calculus," I said. "Describing the motions of planetary bodies. Discovering some of the properties of light."

"Leroy?"

"I worked. I worked my ass off."

"Raven?"

"I'm not good at phony cocktail-party chatter," Ahriman said. "Pass me by."

"What are you good at?" Susan asked him.

"Being a man."

"How do you go about that?"

"I can show you."

"That remark was predictable," she said. "You say the same things that the man who wore my underwear would say."

Their mutual antagonism was like an electric pulse running through the room, as if they were positively and negatively charged.

I looked at Petrie. He shrugged, which I took to mean that this grotesque dinner party was Susan's idea.

Four young men in waist-length white jackets arrived with pushcarts of food and supplies. They worked swiftly and silently, and within a few minutes both the buffet and dining tables had been readied. The food was kept warm in chafing dishes. There was shrimp, lobster tails, shellfish, fillets of beef, whole small birds—squab or quail—and vegetables, salad mixings, and a variety of sauces. Candles in ornate silver candelabra burned on the dining table. Two of the young men were prepared to remain behind to serve as waiters, but Petrie dismissed them. Tom had earlier opened the wine—six bottles, three red and three chilled whites—and the young men carried them to the table before leaving.

"Let us now dine in relative tranquillity," Petrie said.

# Twenty-Six

**P**etrie and Susan sat at opposite ends of the table, with Charles and Ahriman on one side—Ahriman at Susan's right—and Karpe and I opposite. We carried our plates to the table; we selected our wines, poured them, and commenced eating.

But Susan was not inclined toward tranquil dining. Her hostility was made even more obvious by her lilting tones and angelic smile.

She leaned toward Ahriman in a confidential way, and said, "Ahriman—isn't that the name of the Zoroastrian spirit of evil?"

"That's right," he said.

"How odd. Raven Ahriman—that's like naming oneself Vulture Satan or Rat Lucifer, isn't it?"

"If you say so."

I said, "He was baptized Alexander Lermontev."

Ahriman shot me a cold glance.

"Are you a follower of Zoroaster?" Susan asked him.

"Zarathustra."

"Yes, properly Zarathustra. The Persian prophet Zarathustra lived in the seventh century B.C. Is that correct? The religion has been in decline for a long time, with the exception of sheep-herders and the stray criminal entrepreneur."

Ahriman poured wine into his glass.

"Zarathustra, in the Avestan, means 'owner of old camels.' Did you know that?" Susan had not learned this Zoroastrian trivia from her college roommate; she had, like Petrie on the subject of surrealism, researched the topic.

"I didn't think I would have to endure so much witless babble tonight," Ahriman said.

"Ormazd is light, Ahriman darkness."

"I think I got a tainted lobster tail," he said, and he grinned at her.

Charles leaned forward. "Our interest, Raven's and mine, isn't so much the owner of old camels and the religion he founded, but Friedrich Nietzsche's work, *Thus Spake Zarathustra*. Great philosophy, great poetry. That book and *The Will to Power* and a few others by Nietzsche have created a revolution in consciousness—for those who are prepared."

I tapped a fork against my wineglass. "I don't like my tax dollars going to stocking prison libraries with subversive literature."

Charles smiled. "Have any of you read the man?"

"A friend of mine," I said, "Levi Samuelson—you know the judge, Tom—knows a little about everything. He told me that Nietzsche was brilliant—brilliant and often misunderstood. Levi can't figure out why, starting with the Nazis, the philosophy has become the favorite of thugs who move their lips when they read."

Charles laughed.

Petrie said, "Wasn't Nietzsche the one who said, 'Whatever doesn't kill me makes me stronger'?"

"Yes," Susan said, "but syphilis didn't make Nietzsche stronger, it made him insane. And I believe he was also the first to say, 'Live dangerously.' "

" 'Live dangerously!' " Ahriman said quietly. " 'Send your ships out into uncharted seas! Live in conflict with your equals and yourselves. Be robbers and ravagers as long as you cannot be rulers and owners. . . .' "

Susan leaned close to him. "Why, you *are* the Superman, the blond beast. Well, you aren't blond, but the other seems to apply."

I got up from the table and went into the bathroom. Doors led left and right into the two bedrooms. I turned on the water tap, flushed the toilet, and entered the bedroom on my left. It hadn't been used. Petrie and Susan occupied the other, larger bedroom. In there I found a leather bag beneath the bed; it was shaped like a doctor's satchel, though considerably larger, scuffed and wrinkled with use and stuffed with packets of currency, worn fifties and hundreds wrapped around with tape stamped with the Banco de Mexico logo. Susan's bearer bonds were on top. I pushed the satchel back beneath the bed, went into the bathroom to turn off the water, and then returned to the big room.

As I sat down, Ahriman was saying, "What you call psychopaths are fascists with dirty faces. There's a bright, clean, shining kind of fascism too: your kind. Your kind rob and plunder, maim and kill, and smile all the while, innocent as lambs while you deplore the dirty-faced fascists."

"You admit to being a fascist?" Susan said.

"If you like. Psychopath, fascist—choose your insult. But I'm not talking about political fascism only, I'm talking about the business of slaves and masters. Power. It's all about power, force. Some wear crowns, some wear ecclesiastical gowns, some wear five-thousand-dollar suits and two-thousand-dollar shoes, others have bloody feet and wear rags. It's about force: subtle force or brute force. But we are all psychopaths"—he grinned at Susan—"under the skin."

"Did someone mention witless babble?" Susan asked.

I said, "Alexander Lermontev himself is from the minor feudal nobility of Alaska."

Ahriman placed his big fists on the table. He needed to show us his fists. His voice was deep, reverberant, and not unpleasant.

"Anthropologists tell us that our entire species is descended from a few dozen early humans. How could they have endured and survived if they hadn't been what you call psychopaths? A few dozen, maybe, and now we're billions. Do you think nature is kind to the weak and the meek? Is that what they taught you at your elite schools? Liberal humanism? I learned about the world and human nature in prison. There, all the lies, the hypocritical masks are dispensed with, as in war or severe repression. Then you see that humanity is all about power. There are slaves and masters. Most men go into prison as slaves and come out slaves. I went in a slave and came out—you judge."

"A different kind of slave," Susan said.

"You see a cat stalking a songbird. You say, that cat is a predator, that is his nature. You see, maybe, a television film of hyenas pulling down an antelope and eating it alive. You say, hyenas are predators and scavengers, that's hyena nature. But you'll live your entire life aware of wars, destruction, starvation, cruelty, madness, and you say, that is not me, not us, human nature is essentially decent and good. We have saints. Hyenas don't have saints."

Susan started to speak; Ahriman stopped her with a raised hand and a smile.

"Don't think I disapprove," he said. "No one knows how

many were killed in World War Two—sixty million, eighty million, one hundred million? Perhaps as many will die violently during your lifetime. Talk to me of psychopaths." He laughed. "I have personally killed only a few, a few more indirectly. You will probably regard me as a piss-poor sort of psychopath."

"The beast speaks with passion and eloquence," Susan said. "And with odious self-pity and rationalization."

"You talk to me of rationalization, do you?" Ahriman said. "I know a little about you and your people. Charles told me about your family, the history. He told me about the faulty arms and ammunition sold to the Union Army during the Civil War. Shoddy merchandise that cost lives but increased profit. Please don't think I disapprove. And Charles told me about the child labor in your family's textile mills in New Hampshire. How many nine- and ten-year-old boys and girls did your family kill swiftly or gradually? How many died of fatigue and malnutrition and tuberculosis and beatings and despair? Don't think that I disapprove."

He showed her his hungry shark's grin. "Tell me, princess, how many soldiers and kids died to secure the beginning of the Falconer fortune? How many die today because of the foundation's investments in Africa and Asia? I'm just a goddamned amateur at crime. And you talk to me of psychopaths."

"That was a mistake," Susan said coldly. "I should have talked to you about communism."

His eyes rounded, he stared at her for a moment, then with a grin said, "Oh, that hurts. Psychopath, fascist—I can take that. But communist!" He leaned toward her. "Are you going to report me to the Chamber of Commerce?"

Susan flushed. She had lanced Ahriman's vanity all evening, had made him look a fool, but now his mockery and the personal nature of his attack had put her on the defensive. She did what most people do when under attack; she looked around for allies.

I said, "I don't like my tax dollars going to buy communist books for prison libraries."

Charles laughed. He was enjoying the conflict in an impartial way, amused by each point scored, each insult parried.

Ahriman reached over and gently placed his palm over Susan's hand. With anyone else, one might interpret the action as a gesture of amity or even affection; but this was Ahriman, and his intent was to intimidate. The touch lasted only a moment before Susan withdrew her hand from beneath his. I was left with a sense of how slender her hand was, and how fragile her wrist.

Ahriman leaned back in his chair. "All right, you have succeeded in provoking me. Now fuck you all."

Petrie abruptly got to his feet. "Okay, enough of this merry banter. It's time we conducted our business. All right, Raven? Susan? Very well. Karpe and Shaw can go now."

"I'd better stay," Leroy said.

"No, you're going."

"Tom . . ."

"I hope you both enjoyed the chow, the booze, and the spirited repartee. Out."

As we were walking toward the stairwell, Leroy said, "You got anything to drink in your room?"

"Scotch."

"*Escocés*. All right."

There was no ice, no mix. I broke the seal, drew the cork, splashed whiskey into two glasses, and gave one to Karpe.

"Well, shit," he said.

We regarded that as an appropriate toast and sipped the whiskey.

I said, "The money's up there in a bedroom. Under the bed."

"Yeah? What's to stop Raven from just taking it and walking out?"

"I don't know. Sportsmanship?"

"Shit. I've never known Tom to be so dumb."

"Love has addled his brain."

"That Susan Falconer—Jesus, she's suicidal to talk to Raven that way. I thought he was going to smash her in the face."

"Would you have shot him?"

"No. How long do you think they'll be upstairs?"

"I don't know. Coffee, brandy, cigars maybe. Some serious bargaining."

"What they got to bargain about?"

"Search me."

"What a lot of bullshit I had to listen to tonight."

I said, "I saw Bully today. He told me that Falconer was dead."

"Bully. Bully's gone crazy with pain and the drugs Charles gave him aboard ship to stop the pain. Anyway, there's a whole lot of lying going on."

"A whole lot. Charles told me that Peter got his injuries while being winched aboard the ship."

"Yeah, Raven wanted everyone to think he was torturing Falconer. Pressure us."

"Did you really see Peter that afternoon at Big Sandy Cay?"

"One last time," he said. "Don't ask me again."

"Have you seen Falconer since that day in the Bahamas?"

"No. I asked to see him, but Raven wouldn't let me."

"Why not?"

"Don't know. Don't think I care anymore."

Karpe picked up the binoculars from the dresser and looked at me. I nodded, turned off the room lights, and we stepped out onto the balcony. Even without the glasses I could see *Mako*'s night lights and the string of lighted portholes in the deckhouse. A double corona ringed the moon, and each star had a blurred quality. The spaced, dull thud of surf rolling up on the seaward side of the peninsula carried clearly across the bay.

Karpe lowered the binoculars. "Let's go."

I finished my whiskey.

"Unless you're scared."

"How do we get out there?"

"I hired a boat a few days ago. I still got it."

"How do we get onto the ship?"

"The crew will let me board. I've been around enough so they don't worry. They think I'm Raven's pal."

"Are you?"

"Coming or not?"

We returned to the room.

"Bring the bottle," Karpe said. "Have you got a flashlight?"

"No."

"I'll get one from my room."

Karpe lightly punched my shoulder. We were buddies. His grin was anarchistic. Leroy was tired of being a responsible member of the team, and so was I.

"Let's raise hell," he said.

# Twenty-Seven

Karpe's rented boat was a twelve-foot wooden skiff powered by a thirty-horse Yamaha outboard. There were four or five inches of water in the bottom. Leroy began bailing it out with a plastic bucket.

The trawler with no name, no home port, and no registration number lettered on the transom or hull was docked nearby. A pier light gave it definition and dimension. I estimated its length at about sixty feet. It was old, painted black like *Mako*, and had a rather boxy look, but it was no doubt seaworthy—she wouldn't be afloat after all these years if she were not. *Mako, Junior.*

"Ahriman doesn't fish that boat, does he?" I asked.

"Don't know," Leroy said. He finished bailing and moved to the rear of the boat. "Doubt it."

We cruised slowly through the black, oily waters of the dock area, and then Karpe opened the throttle. Our seething wake curved away from the bight toward the freighter's dark silhouette. The bay remained unnaturally smooth, hardly wrinkled, and smelled sharply of the plankton that fired up phosphorescence. A stream of thin, ribbed clouds advanced from east to west, and the moon dimmed and brightened, dimmed and brightened. Cirrocumulus clouds, forerunners of the distant storm.

Leroy cut the engine thirty yards from the middle of the freighter and the skiff slowly drifted in, finally banging lightly against the hull. The deck was only twelve feet above; we were at the lowest point of the sheer between the higher bow and stern.

"Ahoy, *Mako!*" Leroy shouted. He grinned at me. "*Soy Leroy con un amigo y una botella de escocés. Yoyo? Andale, Yoyo!*"

He got a rusty wrench from the bottom of the skiff and hammered against *Mako*'s steel plates.

"*Venga!*" he shouted.

A head and shoulders appeared directly above us. It was the big Mexican they called Yoyo.

"Leroy?" he asked.

"*Otro no. Como sé vas, Yoyo?*" Karpe was acting drunk.

"What do you want?"

"We want to come aboard, *primo. Como no?*"

Yoyo vanished and returned a few minutes later with a ladder. Karpe tied the skiff's line to the lower rung. He glanced at me, I nodded, and we commenced climbing.

The Mexican recognized me immediately and stepped back.

"It's okay," Karpe said.

Yoyo weighed at least two hundred seventy-five pounds, and not much of it was fat. He held his hands away from his sides, and his feet were spread and braced against the deck.

I smiled at him, shrugged, and lifted my palms, telling him by those gestures that I was not hostile, that I remembered his and Bully's attempt to kill me but that was in the past and I held no grudge. He seemed to relax, then surprised me by stepping forward and enfolding me in a powerful *abrazo*.

"Okay?" he said.

"Okay," I replied. *"Está bien."*

Karpe and I walked with him toward the deckhouse. There were lights in the rigging and more small lights, some of them colored, spaced along the ship's length. A white "anchor-out" light burned up in the bows. Beyond I could see the sodium-vapor lights on the Malecón glowing a poisonous sulfur-yellow, and beyond a checkerboard of lights on the hotel facade. All of the windows in Tom Petrie's top-floor suite blazed.

The deckhouse was fogged with marijuana smoke. A portable radio blared Mexican *ranchero* music. Two crewmen sat at the long mess table: the Jamaican, Bully's friend, and the Indian whom Charles had called Guyana. He had coarse, straight black hair, coppery skin, and, like some Indians, his eyes were narrowed by epicanthic folds. A curtain separated the cabin from a bunkhouse and galley.

Karpe greeted them cheerfully, placed the nearly full bottle of whiskey on the table, and handed me his flashlight. Yoyo went to a cabinet for clean glasses while the Indian began rolling a joint. We all sat down at the table.

*"Salud,"* Karpe said.

We echoed the word, and drank. Karpe and Yoyo started a conversation in Spanish.

"How is Bully doing?" I asked the Jamaican.

"Bad, very bad," he said. "They cut off his leg today."

"Cut it off? Why?"

"Gangrene, they say. Cut it off above the knee, man. Bully is going to die, I think."

The fractures, untreated for a week, probably had caused a loss of circulation to Bully's lower leg.

"I'm sorry to hear this," I said.

"That Bully, we're friends a long time. We come from the same hometown. Brighttown, it is called. Wish I never left that place. Bet Bully wish that too now."

The Indian had finished rolling the joint. He ran his tongue along the seam. He too was very sad about Bully. A good man, Bully, *au fond*. A man of humor and *sangfroid*. Guyana's English was limited and so he substituted a French word or phrase when necessary. He lit the joint, inhaled deeply, and passed it to Yoyo on his right.

The three men were already high on marijuana when we arrived, a bit sluggish and dreamy, and alcohol was compounding the effects. The joint reached Karpe; he faked it, taking in just a little smoke but inhaling deeply and holding it a couple of seconds before exhaling. He gave me a warning look: *Don't drink much and be careful of the pot.*

I saw movement out of the corner of my eye. The curtain had parted and Ahriman's wife, Mirium, looked out at us. She had a squarish face with high cheekbones and wide-set eyes. She stared impassively at me for a time, then closed the curtain and returned to the galley.

Guyana was rolling another joint. The bottle of scotch was now half empty.

"Let's drink to Bully," I said.

Karpe and I just sipped the whiskey; the others drank deeply in honor of their comrade Bully.

The cigarette, sticky brown with residue, came to me. I took in a little smoke, exhaled, and passed it on.

"When are you sailing?" Karpe asked Yoyo.

He shrugged. He didn't know. Whenever the captain ordered them to sail. You sit in port for days, weeks, sometimes months, and one day Ahriman gets in a fury and orders the anchor lifted.

"Big seas outside," Karpe said.

Yoyo shrugged again. Yes, a hurricane had formed far to the east. Hurricane Lorraine, they had named it. Fishing boats had been running into port all afternoon and this evening.

The joint came around to me. Again I inhaled only a little smoke, exhaled the thin vapor, and passed the tarry stub to the Jamaican.

I glanced at my watch. We had been sitting at the table for twenty minutes, but it seemed much longer than that, it seemed hours. We were on pot time. I had not inhaled much smoke, but the marijuana was potent and I felt a bit detached, brain-fogged, and inwardly slack.

I deliberately kicked over my chair when standing up. "Air," I said, and I went toward the open hatch with that overly careful walk of the drunk or stoned. There was laughter behind me as I stepped through into the fresh air. I looked across the bay toward the hotel; the lights in Petrie's suite still burned.

I climbed the ladder to the walkway and went through the door into the bridge. Several lights burned dimly. Ahriman had not stinted on navigational equipment: There was a radar screen, depth sounder, radio transceiver, and a compact global satellite positioning device—you could pinpoint your position within ten meters with that. The compass, in the binnacle just forward of the helm, glowed green and shifted fractionally with the slight tidal movements of the ship. There was an entire cabinet full of charts, and a chart pinned to the slanted top showed Chetumal Bay with the soundings in fathoms and the channels and exits to the sea marked by dotted lines.

I heard a burst of laughter from below in the deckhouse. Marijuana smoke drifted up the inside stairway and spread throughout the bridge.

I crossed to the cabin door, opened it, and stepped inside. It was dark, with a medicinal smell and the barely perceptible sound of breathing. I switched on my flashlight and, for a heartbeat, returned to the instant when I had entered the houseboat in the keys, except now I saw not a goat but a man, Peter Falconer, his one eye opened and the other half closed and dully gleaming.

I found a light switch. Peter lay naked on his back in the portside bunk. All of the facial swelling revealed in the Polaroid photo was gone, but some bruises remained, faded now to pastel yellows and greens. His right hand was bandaged. The gauze was clean, there had been no seepage of fluids; the infection had been successfully treated. The left side of his face sagged. Skin, eyelids, mouth—all were slack while the right side remained firm. Two faces, two Peter Falconers.

"Peter?" I said.

He did not stir. His breathing was slow and shallow.

Ahriman's cabin had been converted to a makeshift infirmary. An empty plastic IV bag, its tube and needle dangling free, was fastened to a hook above the bunk. There were drawers full of drugs and medicines, a stethoscope, blood-pressure apparatus, hypodermic syringes, half a dozen medical texts. The starboard bunk was rumpled and sour-smelling. That was where Bully had lain in agony for more than a week. Charles had nursed both men.

I found a clipboard that contained the Peter Falconer medical chart. It listed temperatures in centigrade, respiration, blood pressure, pulse, times of intravenous feeding, times and dosages of various drugs, and some scrawled notes:

*hemiplegia*—half paralyzed?—and *aphasia* and *agnosia* and *blind?*

I had at first assumed that Falconer's brain had been damaged by violent trauma, either from Ahriman's fist blows or, as Bully had told me, an accident when he had pendulumed into *Mako*'s hull; the notes indicated that Peter had suffered a massive stroke when a clot in the carotid artery had cut off blood to the brain. Whatever, it was incredible that he still lived after so long, in such primitive conditions, and while receiving inadequate medical care.

"Peter?"

I had no way of knowing if he was conscious, half conscious, or comatose; whether he heard my voice and understood my words; whether thoughts and images still existed in the man's devastated brain. Perhaps he might someday partly recover. But how could you tell? The charming, the bright, the roguish Peter Falconer had been reduced to a vegetative state.

The cabin door opened. Mirium, carrying a tin basin of soapy water, stood in the door frame for a moment, then stepped aside to allow me to pass. She avoided my eyes. We did not speak.

I went through the bridge, out onto the railed walkway, and down the ladder to the deck. A narrow passageway separated the rear of the deckhouse from a small structure shaped like an outdoor privy. Inside, an iron stairway descended some ten feet to a platform; below was the engine room. A catwalk led from the platform toward the stern. The space smelled of diesel and lubricating oils, and the old twin engines and shiny lengths of propeller shafts reflected the light with an oily gleam. Much of the space was taken up by fuel tanks. Fuel tanks, engines, a workbench, lathe, a rack of tools, a network of cooling pipes and electrical conduits, banks of dials and meters. Except for the bridge, it was the only part of the ship that was clean and well-maintained. Stairs continued down from the platform into the engine room.

There was a steel door on the bulkhead at the end of the catwalk. I could feel the effects of the marijuana, a touch of vertigo, as I walked that way. The door could be secured shut by lowering a steel bar between steel brackets welded to the bulkhead on either side. I ducked my head and entered a boxy steel room whose walls were lined with shelves and lockers. A metal table, chair, and bunk with a thin mattress were bolted to the floor. There were half a dozen candle stubs on the table, and a kerosene lantern hung from a wall hook. This was the storage room where they had taken the photo of Peter, recorded his pleas, terrorized him. The floor, walls, and ceiling radiated heat. Above, a wire-meshed opening ten inches in diameter admitted an occasional breath of air; it led through a shaft to a ventilator hood on deck.

I heard a clanging and stepped to the doorway. The engine-room lights had been turned brighter, and I saw Petrie coming toward me along the catwalk. His face was empty of expression. He did not acknowledge me. Karpe was behind him. Behind Karpe, carrying a sawed-off shotgun, was the grinning Ahriman.

"Mr. Shaw," Ahriman called. "Good of you to drop in."

I backed out of the doorway, retreated across the room until stopped by the wall.

"Inside, lawyer," Ahriman said.

Petrie, looking dazed, entered the room.

"Inside, pilot," Ahriman said cheerfully.

Karpe hesitated an instant at the doorway, as if about to turn and fight, then he entered the room and stood with us at the back wall.

Ahriman hunched his shoulders, lowered his head, and grinned in at us. He held the shotgun casually, now aimed at the floor.

"You have been tried and found guilty of stupidity," he said. "Guilty of *innocence.* Sentenced to life in the hole." He laughed, closed the door, and then we heard the bar clang down between the steel brackets.

I turned on the flashlight.

"You fucking moron," Leroy said.

I had never heard him speak to Petrie with disrespect.

"Jesus Christ. Good Jesus, Tom, why did you and your . . . your fiancée come out here?"

"To pick up Falconer," Petrie said.

"My God. It didn't occur to you to have Raven deliver Falconer to you? You trusted him?"

*"Mea culpa,"* Petrie said. *"Mea maxima culpa."*

Leroy lifted the kerosene lantern down from its hook. It contained half a tankful of fuel, a few inches of wick, and when adjusted burned cleanly with a soft amber light. We looked around the confines of our hot steel box. I was self-ishly glad that this time I was not alone; the claustrophobia would not be so acute.

"You know," I said, "for a guy who hates prison, Ahriman certainly enjoys locking other people up."

# Twenty-Eight

Petrie told us that it didn't make sense. He had dealt with a great many criminals, bad men; Christ, that was how he made his living, and a good living it was. He wasn't one of those green, gullible, just-out-of-law-school dopes over at the public defenders' office. He knew Ahriman was a criminal, dangerous, a sociopath, a killer. But a professional. Now, of course you couldn't trust a professional criminal, but you might reasonably expect a certain logical pattern of behavior. Not honor; intelligent self-interest. Ahriman had what he wanted—the two million dollars. He had the satchel in his hand when they left the hotel. It was then simply a matter of turning over Peter Falconer. All that remained was transferring Peter to the trawler, taking him to the docks, and then on to a hospital. What did Ahriman have to gain by abducting four more people?

"He had nothing to lose," Leroy said.

I said, "He had five things to lose. Witnesses to kidnapping, extortion, and, if Peter dies, murder."

"Ask me," Karpe said to Petrie, "you're just about as green and gullible as those public defenders."

"Leroy," I said. "Twice in the last week Ahriman has taken your gun away from you. I don't think you should be allowed to play with guns until you learn how to hold on to them for more than an hour or two."

"Stare into the bores of a sawed-off twelve-gauge shotgun," Leroy said hotly, "then talk."

"The three stooges," I said.

Petrie told us that he and Susan knew that Falconer had suffered a serious stroke in the Bahamas. His face and head had been battered and he'd lost a finger while being hauled aboard the *Mako*, and Charles said that just when it seemed that he was on the way to recovery from those injuries, the stroke hit. Charles had helped to treat a number of stroke victims while in the penitentiary. Sometimes it was caused by cerebral bleeding; other times when a clot cut off blood flow to the brain. The left side of Peter's body had been paralyzed. Hemiplegia. He was unable to speak or, probably, comprehend. Aphasia. And he was probably unable to recognize familiar objects. Agnosia. Charles also suspected that Peter had been blinded. He was presently comatose.

Naturally Susan and Petrie had decided to pay the ransom. Of course they had. Peter was a man, not goods damaged in transit. And maybe, with the best of medical care, the best specialists, and the best rehabilitative care, Peter might achieve at least a partial recovery.

"Where is Susan?" I asked Petrie.

She was up on the bridge, in the cabin with her brother and Charles. She and Charles were attending the patient.

It was assumed by Ahriman, by all of them, that they would go aboard to ensure that Peter was as comfortable as could be, that he was gently and carefully handled, that no new accident should occur during the transfer. There was never a point about going aboard or not going aboard, it just happened naturally, and why not? The business had been concluded.

Ahriman had ascended the ladder first, followed by Susan and then Petrie. Susan had been eager to see her brother. She was more optimistic than Charles's report justified. You could see that Ahriman was furious when he found his crew and Karpe together in the saloon, bottles on the table and the air hazed with marijuana smoke, but he'd said nothing. He'd led the way up the inside stairway to the bridge, then directed them into the cabin. Susan was shocked by her brother's condition. She had wept, sobbed. Charles, Susan, and Petrie had gone into the cabin. Ahriman had remained outside.

"He took me by surprise," Leroy said.

Ahriman had returned to the deckhouse with a sawed-off shotgun. Karpe had no chance. It didn't matter whether the shells were loaded with bird shot, buckshot, or slugs, you had no chance against a sawed-off shotgun. The crew had scattered when they'd seen it. Leroy expected to die there and then.

"Yoyo came up to get me," Petrie said. "And now here we are."

"Is Susan okay?" I asked.

"She didn't seem to grasp what was happening. She's in shock. Christ, that Ahriman is crazy."

"Really?" I said. "Then you'd use the insanity defense if you were representing him at trial?"

There was a sudden thunder above us. We all flinched. Someone had banged a metal object or his fist against the ventilator hood.

"Crazy, am I?" Ahriman shouted into the ventilator. He had been listening. His voice, normally deep, was deepened further and amplified by the steel room. "Plotting mutiny, are you?" He laughed. "Bilge rats, galley roaches, woodworms!" His laughter was deep and unrestrained. "You've paid well for your passage to hell." He again roared with laughter, and was still laughing as he moved away from the ventilator and out of hearing.

"That Raven is something," Karpe said, and there was admiration in his tone.

A few minutes later we heard a loud rumbling. The bulkhead and hull plates chattered with the vibration. The noise gradually diminished in volume and became smoother as the engines were adjusted.

Petrie looked at me.

"Bon voyage," I said.

"We're leaving port?"

"Listen."

Any loud or unusually pitched noise was transmitted throughout the hull. Tap a wrench against a steel plate up in the bows and the sound would reverberate to the stern. Now we heard the clang and rattle of the anchor chain being drawn aboard and coiling in its below-deck compartment.

"Where the hell is he taking us?"

"No idea, Tom. But there's a hurricane three hundred miles to the east and it's heading this way."

The noise and the fog of diesel fumes increased my sense of confinement: the steel room seemed a bit smaller than before, the walls closer, the ceiling lower, and I thought, *Déjà vu*—fate had ordained that I was to die aboard this old wreck. I had escaped once and, like a panicky rabbit returning to the jaws of the fox, I had come back.

The engines changed pitch, became lower and a bit quieter, and there was a new rhythmic pounding as the pistons commenced turning the propeller shafts.

"The screws have been engaged. We're under way."

A while later I said, "We're heading east across the bay. Soon we'll pick up the ship channel, which turns south and then east again. We'll probably exit into open sea through the cut between the southern tip of the peninsula and Ambergris Cay."

"How do you know this stuff?" Karpe asked.

"I looked at the chart earlier."

"Where the hell is he going?"

I said, "I think there may be a problem getting through the cut, especially at night. It's narrow, and there's bound to be shallow water around there, sandbars maybe. That means steep swells, maybe breaking seas."

"This," Petrie said, "may be defined as surreal. Is there any way out of this fucking sardine can?"

"Only a snake," Karpe said, "could crawl up that ventilator shaft."

The storage room was filling with diesel fumes, and there was a continuous vibration that you could feel on your skin and within the abdomen. The ship proceeded across the calm bay waters without much lateral movement, just a slight rolling. All three of us were sick from the fumes. Petrie's face was gray.

I found myself imagining what it would be like if the ship went down. Would she sink prow first or stern first? Maybe, since *Mako* was insufficiently ballasted, top-heavy, she would roll over before sinking, turn turtle. So our ceiling would become the floor. Great torrents of water would rush into the engine room, killing the diesels, creating great clouds of scalding steam. No, *Mako* was not steam-powered; there were no boilers to explode. So then, engine room flooding, the ship would begin to spiral down into the cold black depths. Screaming? Would we scream? Sure. The door of our steel tomb was tightly fitted, the ventilator shaft narrow; we might still be alive when the ship sank fifty feet below the surface, seventy-five feet, while the hull creaked and groaned from the enormous pressure. Deeper then, still alive, fighting for the remaining pockets of air while the hull was crushed to the noise of demonic music—the shrieks and thunder of rending metal, the machine-gunlike report of rivets popping, a ghostly howling, and then, at last, silence, infinity.

I was aware as the ship changed direction. South first and, later, east. The channel to the sea was intricate, as I recalled from the chart; a short jog north between a tiny island and the tip of Ambergris Cay, a near half circle, and then a course southeast between another tiny island and the cay. The channel was marked by lighted buoys but was still a hazardous passage, particularly by night and with big seas running outside.

"I got to piss," Leroy said. He got up and began rummaging through the lockers for a container of some sort. He found an empty kerosene can, unscrewed the top, and was urinating when the ship suddenly rolled violently. Leroy stumbled across the room, hit the wall, and fell hard. His pants were wet with urine when he stood up. He cursed, cursed again when he saw my smile.

"Damn your eyes," he said.

There were now separate motions that you could sense by the forces exerted on your body: ponderous rolling, at least twenty degrees to starboard and then, after a moment upright, twenty degrees to port; and pitching too now, the prow rising up the face of a swell while the stern dropped, and then the reverse as the ship plunged into the trough, prow diving as the stern rose; and *Mako* seemed to turn on her axis—yawed—as the swell passed its length. The room gyrated. Light and shadow carved the space into continually chang-

ing geometrical shapes. Karpe did not seem affected by the
motion, but both Petrie and I were sick, Tom more than me.

"I'm going to puke," Petrie said. He was sitting on the
floor, clinging tightly to a table leg.

He vomited. "Sorry."

Twice a ground swell broke over the bows, and the ship
shuddered along its entire length, shook free of the tons of
water, and plowed forward. Water dripped down through
the ventilator shaft. The room stank of urine and vomit and
diesel fumes.

The motion moderated after about thirty minutes. We
were now in deeper water, well beyond Chetumal Bay and
the steep ground swells, and the intervals between crests
were longer.

"Puke," Petrie said in disgust. "I puked on myself."

"Piss," Leroy said, grinning. He was wedged into a corner. "I pissed on myself."

"I just don't get it," Petrie said. "We're sailing toward the
hurricane. What can the bastard be thinking of?"

I said, "Ahriman will probably turn south later, run out
of the storm's path. Trouble is, hurricanes can't be trusted to
keep to a particular trajectory."

"They'll come for us eventually," Karpe said. "We'll rush
them. There's not much room to maneuver out on that catwalk."

Not much room to maneuver in this space either, I
thought, nor while framed in the doorway, nor out there on
the catwalk engaging in hand-to-gun combat.

"I'll go through the door first," Karpe said. "The instant
they lift out the lockbar. Shaw, you follow me."

"Sure, Leroy," I said.

"Tom, you're last, okay? Tom?"

"Right, Leroy. I'm all ears."

I said, "There's a lot of shoal water directly south of us, so Ahriman has to take the ship well out to sea before turning south."

"South to where?" Petrie asked.

"There'll probably be two of them," Karpe said. "Someone's got to stay at the wheel, maybe one more down in the engine room. Two—Yoyo and the Jamaican, I figure. They'll have guns. Guns misfire. It's hard to use a gun when someone's just kicked you in the stones. We got a chance if we move fast and together."

"So we're headed east?" Petrie said to me.

"Maybe a little southeast, so that Ahriman can quarter into those big seas."

"You dumb shits," Karpe said. "You're like sheep in a pen waiting to be slaughtered."

"Don't fret," Petrie said. "We'll line up behind you, Leroy."

"And don't think we won't be appreciative, Leroy," I said, "if you have to take a few bullets for the good of the team."

Petrie's laughter was choked off by another spew of vomit.

# Twenty-Nine

The ship continued to pitch and roll and yaw, but in a predictable rhythm; once you adjusted to the sequence it became tolerable. Only rarely did a wave break over the bows. We felt the impact then, and heard water hissing along the canted deck. Water splashed down through the ventilator shaft. The ventilator, like most things aboard the *Mako,* did not work properly. We sat on the wet floor, automatically bracing for the next phase of motion. Leroy talked no more about his proposed breakout when they came for us. Petrie, a couple of times, worried aloud about Susan.

The lantern began to smoke. Karpe turned up the wick, but that didn't help for long; soon the flame turned bluish, wavered, dimmed, and went out. There was no more fuel. The room was black now except for a faint blur of light filtering down the ventilator.

"I've got the flashlight when we need it," I said.

It was natural, in the darkness, to imagine the walls closing in, the floor rising and the ceiling descending, the boxy steel room collapsing like a medieval torture device. The air stank of vomit and urine and diesel fumes. Now and then, when my claustrophobia became acute, I flicked on the flashlight for fifteen or twenty seconds, until the room reacquired its normal dimensions.

At four-thirty, three hours after the anchor had been raised, there was another change; the engines became less noisy and the cadence of driving pistons slowed. I thought, judging by the various sounds and motions, that the propellers were still engaged and turning, but the ship seemed almost stationary now. It was a tactic sometimes used in big storms: the ship heaved to—pointed into the seas under just enough power to maintain control and stability. To a certain extent, the ship was left on its own, permitted to give way to the seas rather than power through them. But the *Mako* was so old and poorly designed, top-heavy now without cargo or sufficient ballast, that it seemed to me a dangerous procedure. The greatest peril was that the underpowered vessel might broach, turn sideways, and wallow helplessly in the troughs. She might then dip her rail under and turn turtle or be overwhelmed by a sea breaking full-length along her hull.

Later we heard voices through the ventilator pipe. Two men, maybe three, speaking in normal tones. They did not sound excited or fearful. One laughed. I was able to discern a few words: *winch* and *leeward* and *hold it!* and then a phrase in Spanish, Yoyo saying, *"Arriba, hombres."*

"What now?" Petrie said wearily.

"They're repairing something, probably," Leroy said.

More voices, laughter, a curse, another voice—Ahriman's—and then all the voices receded and soon were silent. But the ship didn't resume speed; the drumming of the pistons remained slow.

I said, "I think they left the ship. One of them must have been following in the trawler."

"No," Leroy said.

"Susan," Petrie said in a choky voice. "Did they take Susan?"

The darkness and our confinement were even more oppressive now. We were locked in a room below the deck of an unmanned ship that was slowly heading toward a hurricane named Lorraine. Despair silenced us. My perception of time and the time indicated by my watch no longer corresponded.

And then we heard another voice, a woman's voice. Susan. I turned on the flashlight.

Petrie leaped to his feet and shouted up toward the ventilator. "Susan? Susan!"

We heard a faint cry.

"Susan, we're here. Here! Susan, can you hear me?"

Her voice sounded closer. "Where are you?"

Petrie spread his legs and braced himself against the ship's ponderous roll to starboard. "There are ventilator hoods near you. See them? We're below one of them."

"I'm alone," she cried. "There's no one—"

"You're not alone. We're here."

"Where?" She spoke directly into the ventilator. "Help me," she said.

"First you must help us. You've got to let us out of here."

"Out of where? *Where?*"

"We're in a room below you. There's a small structure just behind the deckhouse. See it?"

"Yes."

"There's a door. Steps. Take the steps to a landing halfway down."

"Steps. A landing."

"You'll see a catwalk, a narrow walkway, that leads to a door."

"A door, yes, I'll go."

"Wait. The door is locked by a steel bar. Lift out the bar and we'll be with you."

We heard her cry out as a wave broke over the bows. *Mako*'s prow dipped under and she twisted on her axis. The ship shuddered, seemed to stall or slide back, and we heard a hissing as tons of water rushed along the deck. Water sprayed down out of the ventilator shaft.

Petrie lost his footing on the wet floor, slid halfway across the room, and slammed up against a bulkhead. He got up and, limping, returned to the center of the room.

"Susan? Susan!"

The ship had righted herself, lifted her prow, and begun a counterroll to port.

"Goddamn it!" Petrie shouted hoarsely.

We heard her voice. "I fell down. I'm all right."

"Do you understand what you have to do?"

"Door, steps, catwalk, door, iron bar. Yes."

We waited. It was only about thirty feet from the ventilator hood to the doghouse, eight or ten steps, another twenty feet across the catwalk to the storage room's door. Three or four minutes, considering that she had to take care on the slippery, wildly canting deck.

"Leroy," I said. "When we get out, you go down into the engine room. See if you can get me more power. I'll run up to the bridge."

"Where is she?" Petrie said. "What if they turned off the engine-room lights?"

I said, "There's probably an intercom or a speaking tube between the bridge and engine room, Leroy. But first I need power. Not full power, about three-quarter speed."

"All right," Leroy said.

"Jesus Jesus Jesus," Petrie chanted.

Then we heard the clank of metal against metal outside the door. The bar was lifted, the door opened. Susan stood outside on the catwalk. She was drenched, wide-eyed, and sobbing, and her right wrist and hand were bloody. She thrust her hand toward me, as if seeking sympathy, and her mouth formed words that were not vocalized.

I slipped past her, moved along the catwalk to the platform, and then, pausing a moment for the ship to complete her roll, went up the stairs and out onto the deck.

Light hurt my eyes after the long immersion in darkness. The seas were enormous, thirty feet from crest to trough, maybe higher, but they were not excessively steep and not breaking. It was soon after dawn: Clouds in the east were stained scarlet and crimson and a sulfurous yellow and arced in parabolas away from the sun like the smoke and lava from a volcanic explosion. I could see the sun only when the ship crested a big swell. I had never seen it look so huge, so strange, like an alien star. Swollen, crimson, seething, its nuclear fires burned through the morning mist and incandesced the advancing rows of cirrus.

I ran to the deckhouse, climbed the ladder, and was inside the bridge before the next swell reached us. The helm's spokes had been lashed by two lengths of line that prevented much play. *Mako* was heading almost directly east. I removed the ropes, turned the wheel until our course was roughly southeast, and the ship began quartering into the swells, slowly ascending them at a diagonal. Now we needed more power. I estimated that our speed was not more than two or three knots, less than the pace of a brisk walk.

I glanced over the control console. The radio and the GPS unit had been removed. There was a box that looked as though it might be an intercom. I switched it on and could hear the thudding of pistons.

The huge swells advanced in endless rows. They were a translucent sea green when the sun shined through them, an opaque jade green when the sun dimmed behind one of the ribbed clouds. There was not much wind. Here and there I saw flashes of white; patches of foam, a tumbling crest, but the water, though divided into great hills and valleys, was fairly smooth on the surface.

Petrie and Susan climbed the ladder to the bridge. He held her protectively as they moved toward the cabin. The wildness was gone from Susan's eyes now, the fear and bewilderment, and she appeared sleepy from the effects of shock. She held her bloody hand palm-up. Her black dress was wet and rumpled, she was barefoot, and I noticed that she no longer wore the pearl necklace. Ahriman had probably taken it.

"Tom," I said, "where's Leroy?"

He shot me an accusing look, as if I were responsible for Susan's distraught state and bloody hand, and then he guided her into the cabin and firmly shut the door.

The ship angled up the slope of a wave, paused a moment on top, and then, gaining speed, glissaded down the back side into the trough. There was still a danger that the underpowered ship might fall off the face of a swell and broach.

"Shaw?"

I turned up the volume on the intercom. The engines and pistons created a noisy background racket, but I could hear Leroy well enough.

"I got it figured now," he said. "How much do you want?"

"Can you give me seven or eight knots?"

"Nothing down here about knots."

"Give me three-quarters speed, then."

"No way to control the engines from up there?"

"I don't see anything. No."

A moment later the ship lurched forward, shuddered as the screws bit in, and arching white waves erupted at the bows.

"That's good, Leroy."

"I found something down here," he said. "It's bad."

"Are you going to tell me about it?"

"Eight sticks of dynamite, a detonator, a switch, a battery, and a cheap alarm clock."

For an instant I thought he was joking. Then I believed him and could not speak. Finally I said, "What time is it set to go off?"

"Six o'clock."

"It's six-twenty now, Leroy."

"I know. The clock stopped. It stopped at five forty-three. The bomb is chocked in by the fuel tanks, so they'll blow too if the thing detonates."

"Can you disarm it?"

"Maybe. When I stop being scared. The thing is, I'm afraid that when I cut a wire, either of the two wires, it'll open the circuit."

"Do you want me to come down?"

"You know anything about bombs?"

"Nothing."

"The clock might start again. The thing might just go off—it's an amateurish kind of bomb."

"I'd better come down there."

"No point in that. Stay away. Leave the intercom on. I'll keep a close watch on it, figure out something. I think it'll be okay. If it isn't, you'll hardly know what happened."

"Leroy?"

But he had left the vicinity of the intercom or chose not to talk anymore.

# Thirty

The sun lost its bruised, poisonous hues as it rose, and a parhelion, a sun dog—a bright false sun on a luminous halo—appeared parallel to the sun and to its south. It was caused by the reflection of ice crystals in the atmosphere. It meant nothing in itself but was ominous in relation to other weather signs.

I began to feel more confident at the helm. The compass card did not swing so wildly now. I was not alarmed by the way *Mako* rolled nearly rail to rail. She was quirky, "tender," and slow to respond to the wheel, but after a time I began to anticipate her eccentricities. The broad troughs between seas gave the ship time to recover from my errors.

Petrie came out of the cabin. His face was frozen in the mask that, in some men, tells you more about their emotions than mobile expressions or passionate words. He stood near me, holding tightly to the chrome rail. His clothes smelled of stale vomit.

"How is she?" I asked.

"Not good."

"Peter?"

"Alive. I guess you could call it that—alive."

"What happened to Susan's hand?"

He looked at the veering compass card, then looked at me. "Do you know what you're doing?"

"Sure. I own a sailboat, remember?"

"I can spit the length of your sailboat. Ever been out of sight of land on that sailboat?"

"More than once," I said. Twice, actually, for a total of maybe twenty hours, on a cruise from Bell Harbor to the Dry Tortugas and back. "I've taken Coast Guard courses too."

"So have I. Did your courses include freighter handling?"

"Do you want to take the helm? Get the feel? I've got to go down to the engine room and give Leroy a hand. We've got a problem."

"Really? A problem? Oh, my, a problem." He was quiet a moment, looking forward as the *Mako* lifted her bows toward the crest of a big swell, and then he said, "I don't understand what those bastards are up to."

"They went aboard the trawler," I said. "The trawler is seaworthy and relatively fast. They can run away from the storm."

"I figured that out. But still—why?"

"Ahriman's got two million dollars. He doesn't need this rust bucket anymore. *Mako* vanishes in heavy weather. We vanish with it."

"He raped her," Petrie said. "Ahriman. Twice. Just before they sailed from Chetumal Bay, Ahriman handcuffed one of Susan's wrists to the bunk, and he raped her. And before they abandoned ship he came back to the cabin and sodomized her. He hurt her. She's been bleeding. But she managed to get out of the cuffs. By God, she did that."

"She saved our lives."

"I'm going to kill him, of course."

"Of course."

Petrie slipped in behind the wheel. He owned a big cabin cruiser and soon was more comfortable and steadier with *Mako* than I had been. He adjusted to her sluggish responses in just a few minutes.

"Stick to this course?" he asked.

"Roughly."

"Roughly. Why haven't you turned south? We're still heading directly into the bitching hurricane."

"Bitching Hurricane Lorraine," I said. "There's a lot of shoal water south of us. We've got to make some miles to the east and then angle back southwest. Look at the chart."

"This isn't going to work. Why don't we, for Christ's sake, just radio for help?"

"No radio. They took the radio and the satellite-positioning unit with them. They're portable and worth money."

"Okay, piss off. You and Leroy attend to your problem."

I waited until the ship completed its slide into a trough, timed the roll, and went down the stairs. The saloon's floor was littered with objects; everything that hadn't been secured before sailing had broken loose. I went outside. There was no apparent wind from any quarter, just the breeze caused by the ship's passage. Our wake was straight; Petrie was doing a fine job of steering. It was quiet in the wilderness of seas, except for the throbbing of the engines and the hiss when the prow bit into a rushing swell and peeled avalanches of white water off the bows.

I went through the doghouse door, down the first flight of stairs to the landing, paused a moment, then descended into the engine room. Leroy, holding a long-snouted oilcan as big as a teapot, stood between the engines and the starboard bulkhead. There was not much open space, just a network of narrow walkways that provided access to the machinery. Fuel tanks, many pipes (the hot ones painted red), side-by-side diesels, gear levers, rows of thrusting pistons whose vertical energy was transferred to the circular by a complicated apparatus, and the shiny, spinning pair of propeller shafts that angled down toward the stern before disappearing beneath the floor plates.

"Good engines," Leroy said, shouting above the noise. "Old diesels'll run forever if they're maintained."

"We're lucky to have a man who knows engines," I said.

"My redneck upbringing."

The ship steeply tilted along its axis, prow down, and at the same time started to roll to port. Leroy compensated for the motion by crouching with his legs spread. I grabbed one of the unpainted pipes.

"Don't fall into the engines," he shouted. "Hot. Don't fall onto the pistons—you'll get skinned. Don't fall onto the prop shafts." He grinned, and angled his body to absorb the energy of the counterroll.

"Is the bomb disarmed?"

"It's sleeping."

He led me past the shafts and engines to a pair of fuel tanks that extended the width of the ship. They were separated by a niche just big enough to allow a workman access to the pumps. The bomb, packed tightly in a wooden box, lay on the grimy floor between the fuel tanks. It was as Leroy described it: eight sticks of dynamite wrapped in duct tape; an alarm clock, battery, switch, and detonator; and two wires, both red, that linked the battery terminals to the detonator and clock.

Karpe said something that I didn't understand.

"What?"

He raised his voice. "High-school stuff."

"You attended a different high school, Leroy. Did you disarm it?"

"I left well enough alone."

The clock hands read 5:51. I looked at Leroy.

"Uh-oh," he said. "It's working again. Cheap fucking clock."

I kneeled on the floor and leaned close to the device. There was no second hand. I could not hear ticking in the general noise, but I did see the minute hand jump half a notch.

"Christ, Leroy, why didn't you disarm the thing when the clock was stopped?"

"Scared. Cut a wire and who knows what. Anyway, the clock was stopped."

I got to my feet. "What can we do?"

"Shit our pants, I guess."

"Come on, Leroy, we've only got nine"—the minute hand moved again—"eight minutes."

"Carry it up on deck and throw it over the side."

"Wouldn't the water short it out, blow a hole in the hull at the waterline?"

"Might," Leroy said. "Might not."

My mouth was dry and tasted chalky. Leroy saw me trying to swallow, and he grinned. His grin was sickly around the edges, but it was genuine. You had to take an objective view to find any humor in the situation.

"Flip a coin," I said.

"Odds and evens. Simpler." He put his right hand behind his hip.

"Odds," I said. "Go."

I had extended one finger; Leroy, three.

"Give me time to get away from here," he said. "I'll prop open the door."

The clock now read 5:53. Plenty of time, I thought. I heard the ringing vibration of the metal steps as he pounded up toward the door. I kneeled, slipped the box out of the niche, and slowly rose to my feet. There were clear beads of moisture on the dynamite sticks. Were they sweating nitroglycerine?

I waited until the ship had returned to an upright position and, with mincing steps, left the labyrinth of machinery and crossed over to the stairs. Earlier, accustomed to the pitch and roll, I had moved confidently. Now all that confidence was gone, and I feared falling or lurching off into an obstruction and dropping the box. How sensitive were the blasting caps? Was the dynamite old and unstable?

The ship started to roll. The stairway tilted at a twenty-degree angle to starboard. There was a brief pause before it commenced its reverse roll to port, and I climbed the stairs to the landing. The clock read 5:54. Plenty of time. My hands were sweating. My vision dimmed. There were times on the tennis court when I forgot to breathe during a big point. I felt the same now. The door above was propped open, and I could see a rectangle of dirty gray clouds.

The prow lowered and the stern lifted as *Mako* steeply carved a diagonal down the back side of a big swell. When she reached the trough I went up the top flight of steps, through the doorway, and out onto the tilted wet deck. Karpe was standing at the stern railing.

I took a couple of steps, slipped and fell (cradling the box as if it were a newborn baby), and slid on my back down to the port railing. The air smoked with a fine mist. Leroy gestured wildly and shouted something that I couldn't understand.

The clock read 5:56. Four minutes. The goddamned clock was still ticking.

I cautiously got to my feet, leaned with my belly pressed against the railing, extended my arms, and dropped the box. It made a small splash, submerged for a moment, and then floated back to the surface.

Leroy yelled something. He was grinning and pumping his fist.

The half-submerged box bobbed along close to the hull. Surely, I thought, surely immersion in water had stopped the clock. And the wiring hadn't short-circuited.

Turbulence near the stern trapped the box, and it remained stationary in relation to the ship. It revolved, dipped, and bobbed, but remained captured by a whirlpool of water churned up by the screws. If it exploded now it probably would damage the rudder, and maybe the props.

Karpe leaned over the railing and saw that the box was almost directly below him. He jerked back, turned, and jogged down the deck toward me.

The box remained with the ship for a few more minutes and then, like a satellite freed from its gravitational bondage, drifted off into the boiling wake.

Karpe, grinning wildly, shook my hand. "And I thought you were a fussy old auntie," he said. "Damn! My stones crawled up into my belly."

I caught movement out of the corner of my eye and looked up toward the bridge. Susan's face was centered in one of the cabin's rear portlights. She did not return my wave, didn't smile, but continued staring down at Karpe and me.

We heard a thud, turned, and saw a powerful geyser erupt sixty feet off the stern. The spout rose straight up in a foamy column and collapsed back on itself, leaving behind in the air a haze of droplets that flashed with the colors of the prism.

"What the hell?" Leroy said. "Can't trust an amateur's bomb."

Susan's face was gone from the portlight when I turned.

# Thirty-One

Leroy returned to the engine room. I climbed the outside ladder to the bridge.

"What were you clowns doing?" Petrie asked.

"Getting rid of a bomb."

"That's nice."

"I'm not kidding."

"I didn't think you were kidding."

The sun dog had vanished behind the thickening clouds, and now the burning of the true sun was diffused over half of the sky. I could see deep into the translucent swells, past the surface facets and flecks into luminous and hypnotic green depths.

"The barometer is still falling," he said.

"I see."

"Have you looked at the fuel gauge? It's below half full. Have we got enough fuel to run east for—how long?—and then southwest to land?"

"Easily," I said. "These freighters can run thousands of miles on a full tank."

Petrie was steady at the helm. I stood a few feet away, gripping the rail, watching him. He appeared relaxed, but his eyes never left the sea, and the muscles and cords of his forearms were tensed.

"No radio, no navigation equipment—how are we going to find our way to port?"

"I don't know, Tom. Maybe we'll just have to run her up on the beach."

He shook his head. "We've got to get through this somehow."

"We will."

"I'm going to kill Ahriman."

"Yes."

"Kill him."

"I know, Tom."

"Kill the son of a bitch."

"First we'll have to find him."

"I'm going to kill him."

"Yes."

"But if I fail, then you have to do it."

"Right. But let's just think about survival now."

"You'll see what he's done to her. She'll never be quite the same. Susan was—what?—she was complete. You know? And now she's a collection of fragments like the rest of us."

"Go to her. I'll take over here."

"She's a little crazy at the moment. Quietly. Politely crazy."

"I'll take the helm now, Tom."

"I've known bad men. But this Ahriman is in a different category altogether. He's intelligent, he's aware, he's conscious. He chooses. He elects. He isn't just another blind, mindless, robotic thug—he calculates. He wanted to humiliate Susan, destroy her emotionally before he sent her to the bottom of the sea. What is that? He isn't insane. He's what?"

"We'll get him."

"Oh, yes."

"But bank the fires for now."

"We'll get that son of a bitch. You've got to promise. If something happens to me, if Ahriman kills me, then you've got to do the job."

"I promise. But now, for Christ's sake, go to Susan. I'll take over here."

Leroy Karpe mounted the stairs and joined us at the front of the bridge. He said that he could monitor the diesels by their sound through the intercom and occasionally go below to check.

"How is Miss Falconer?" he asked.

Petrie stepped aside to allow me to slip in behind the wheel.

"How do you think?" he said, and he crossed the bridge and entered the cabin.

"What's wrong with him?" Karpe asked me.

"Long story."

Karpe was an aviator and knew the fundamentals of navigation better than I. He worked out a rough—very rough—dead-reckoning approximation of our position by calculating the time we left Chetumal Bay, the ship's estimated speed and course then, our lower speed—about three knots—during the period between the crew abandoning ship and our escape from the storeroom, then the change of course, the increase of speed to about eight knots, and the total time elapsed.

He wrote an X on the chart. "Here," he said. He drew a circle around the X. "Within fifteen miles."

"Then we probably ought to turn southwest soon," I said.

"Yeah."

"We'll clear Lighthouse Reef?"

"With inches to spare."

"Glover Reef?"

"Easy."

"How far is it to the coast of Honduras?"

He placed one point of the dividers on his X, the other on the Honduran north coast, then measured the spread against the nautical-mile bar. "Say one hundred fifty miles."

"It'll be full night before we get close."

"Yeah."

"The nautical almanacs and large-scale charts will give us the location of the lights, their types and intervals."

Leroy studied the chart. "There'll be lights for sure at Puerto Cortés, Punta Sal, and the Islas de la Bahía. Lights on the reefs too. We probably ought to try for Puerto Cortés."

The north coast of Honduras juts far out into the Caribbean, but the charts indicated that there were few well-protected ports: Puerto Cortés in the west; Limón; the Laguna de Caratasca far to the east, just above Cabo Gracias a Diós; maybe a couple more. We could hardly expect to blunder into one of them along the nearly four-hundred-mile-long coast. Our inability to establish the ship's position was the equivalent of blindness.

"Time," I said, "to turn this wreck and start running away from Lorraine."

"I can go down to the engine room and give you another two or three knots."

"We don't want to shake all the rivets loose. Anyway, the following seas should give us a couple extra knots."

Our turn to a new compass heading was less difficult than

I had feared. I waited until we had crested a larger-than-average swell and then, on a long, gliding descent down the back side, I rapidly turned the wheel until the prow pointed directly south. We ran along the trough, down a moving valley of water, with the oncoming wave to our port and the one receding on the starboard. I continued turning the wheel. *Mako* responded slowly. Leroy had been right; a few more knots would have helped during the maneuver.

We took the next sea on our beam; *Mako* simultaneously lifted and tilted some thirty degrees to port, straightened, hesitated, and then rolled just as wildly to starboard as the sea passed beneath her keel. Objects clattered on the floor. But now the ship had time and space to complete the turn. Our wake carved a white parabola through the next trough. *Mako* completed the turn to the south.

The cabin door flew open, and Petrie shouted, "What the hell is going on?"

"It's all right, Tom," Leroy said.

"A change of course," I said.

"You damned near threw Peter out of his bunk!"

"Tuck him in good," Leroy said quietly.

"Look, give us a call when stuff like that is going to happen," Petrie said, and he closed the cabin door. We heard the bolt snap into place.

Leroy looked at me. "Is he going to help us or baby-sit the Falconer kids?"

*Mako* did not handle as well with following seas. There was great pressure on the rudder, and the ship occasionally skewed off course on the "downhill" run. She rolled, yawed, and once even surfed out of control down the face of a wave. We were moving faster now, carried along by the rushing seas, but our speed relative to the seas had diminished, and that affected control. But after a while I got the hang of it.

You had to be alert every moment, anticipate, and correct any error before it snowballed into a crisis.

Leroy, gripping the rail with both hands, closely observed my actions at the helm, checked the compass, the chart, the barometer, the cloud formations all around.

After forty minutes, he said, "Tired?"

"My back is killing me."

"I'll take over."

"Have you got it figured?"

"Got it locked."

We switched places. Karpe was a little shaky at first, with a tendency to understeer, but he quickly adjusted and got a feel for the ship's tendencies. After years of flying helicopters and other aircraft, the quirky steering of the old freighter was not a serious challenge for Leroy.

I backed down the outside ladder to the deck. From that lower perspective, the waves looked even bigger and faster, and here and there fizzed with comets of foam. I waited, timing the motion, then hurried over the wet deck to the prow. *Mako* accelerated as it angled down the face of a big sea. Cold spray kicked up by the bow waves misted the air. Here you became fully aware of the great forces involved, the weight and speed of the freighter, the vast power of the sea.

The anchor was stored out of sight, chocked in its niche a few feet below on the starboard side, with the chain spooled in an inside compartment. There was not a windlass on deck. The anchor was raised and lowered by a winch in the compartment, which derived its power from the ship engines and a set of gears. I had seen the controls on the bridge console. We would need the anchor later, perhaps need it desperately.

I walked aft to the deckhouse. The saloon section smelled of spilled whiskey and stale tobacco smoke and lamp oil. An unlatched locker door on creaky hinges, timed to *Mako*'s roll, swung wide open and then clattered back against its frame. I slammed the door closed and fixed the latch.

I went through a curtain into the crew's quarters, a rectangular space crowded with bunks and lockers. There was a coffin-size shower stall in the corner. Another curtain opened into the galley. A skinny brown-and-white cat skittered madly across the floor and vanished through a hole cut in the base of a cabinet. The ship's mouser.

The galley was half again as big as the bunkroom and looked clean and well-equipped. Lockers and cabinets, bins, worktables, a big double sink with a hand pump that brought fresh water up from the tanks below, an oven, a stove with the four burners set below gimbals, and a pair of six-foot iceboxes. The iceboxes were empty, but I found a locker containing canned goods—tuna, coffee, corned beef, chili, milk, vegetables; a produce box full of sprouting potatoes and rotten onions; and a case of Chilean red wine.

I opened a can of tuna and carried it to the cat's den. Her fur bristled and she hissed at me when I opened the cabinet door. She lay on a pile of rags, nursing four kittens, each not much bigger than my thumb. I slipped the can of tuna inside and closed the door before she could claw me. There had to be another cat around, a male, or she had been impregnated while whoring on shore leave.

I carried one of the wine bottles through the bunkroom and saloon and climbed the stairs to the bridge.

Leroy, legs spread, shoulders hunched over the wheel, without turning said, "I saw you up forward. Anything wrong?"

"No. Just figuring out the anchor system. How's it going here?"

"The ship pretty much steers itself if you don't interfere. Fight her, and she'll kick your ass."

I uncorked the wine, took a swallow, and passed the bottle to Karpe. "Has Petrie come out?"

"No. I can't figure him. Tom's always prided himself on being a cold son of a bitch. Lately he moons around like a lovesick kid."

"Ahriman raped Susan. He handcuffed her to the bunk."

"That's how she got her wrist and hand all bloody and raw? Pulling out of the cuff?"

"Yes."

"Well, hell, I guess she asked for it last night, twitching her ass around and talking to Raven like he was shit in that snobby, superior way she's got."

"Every time I find myself starting to like you, Leroy, you spoil it by expressing an opinion. I'm going below for a rest. Call me when you need relief."

I picked out the cleanest of the six bunks, a lower that smelled as much of soap as sweat. There was something bulky beneath the blanket: the portable radio that had been playing last night. I sat on the edge of the bunk, extended the aerial, turned up the volume, and twisted the frequency control. Ranchero music, a baseball game in Veracruz, a woman speaking Creole French, a male voice shouting about a product that was *estupendo!*, and finally a Spanish-language news broadcast. I could not be certain—the batteries were weak, my Spanish not quite up to the speed of delivery—but it seemed that Hurricane Lorraine was now eighty miles southeast of Jamaica and moving eastward. Both Jamaica and Grand Cayman Island were being assaulted by strong winds and rains and storm tides. Cuba was making preparations in the event the system turned north. Hurricane Lorraine was classified as a grade three on a scale of five.

I turned off the radio. We might catch hell from the periphery of the storm, but there seemed no chance that we would be enveloped by the worst of it. If the old ship held together, if the engines didn't fail . . .

I did not expect to sleep, just rest my back, but I dozed off almost immediately and awakened three hours later. The motion of the ship seemed no more extreme than it had been when I'd crawled into the bunk. I stripped, turned on the pump, and stepped into the shower. There was a bar of yellow soap on the floor. The water was tepid and did not issue very forcefully from the shower head, but I scrubbed for five minutes and washed my hair, and exited from the shower feeling much better. My clothes stank as bad as Petrie's and Karpe's. I rummaged through the lockers and found a pair of jeans and a denim shirt that fit. The Jamaican, Bully's friend, was about my size. They were clean, evidently among the clothing I had seen Mirium drying on deck a couple days before.

Leroy looked the same as when I'd left him hours earlier, his legs spread, shoulders hunched as he gripped the wheel spokes, but now a two-inch cigar stub fumed between his teeth.

"Why didn't you call me?" I asked, moving next to him.

"Doing fine," he said. Then, "You smell like a flower."

"Petrie? Susan?"

He shook his head.

I recalled that Peter Falconer was with them in the cabin. You had a tendency to forget Peter; he seemed more dead than alive and was no longer a player. The game continued without him.

Visibility remained fairly good despite the heavy dark cloud cover. The seas were no bigger, no steeper, but a wind had risen that tore spray off the crests. The barometer had fallen more, the fuel-gauge needle had not dropped much, and the compass card was steady on the correct course. The night was going to be black, moonless, and starless, maybe foggy as well.

I stepped in behind the wheel. Leroy stood nearby, gripping the handrail and fogging the air with cigar smoke. It took me a few minutes to regain the feel as *Mako* ascended and descended the seas and plowed across the smoother trough waters. The motions, the roll, and the pitching seemed to have a slower rhythm now.

"She seems sluggish," I said.

"Lots of water sloshing around the bilges." He gestured toward the control console. "I switched on the pumps a half hour ago."

"Engines?"

"I've listened over the intercom. They sound okay. I'll go down there in a few minutes."

"Well, hell, Leroy—with a little luck . . ."

"Lotsa luck," he said. "I tried the radar. It doesn't work. I found the RDF; it doesn't work."

Leroy was gone only a few minutes when Petrie emerged from the cabin. His unshaven face was pale and creased, doughy-looking, and his rumpled clothes still smelled of vomit. The suave Thomas Petrie today had the look and smell of a derelict.

"Christ. Who's smoking cigars?"

"Leroy. Are you sick, Tom?"

"A touch of the *mal de mer*."

"Susan?"

"Heartsick."

"And Peter?"

"Still drooling."

*Mako* skewed as she surfed down the face of a big swell.

"Hell ship," Petrie said. "Death ship. Nautical funhouse."

"I'm actually starting to feel affection for this *Mako* beast."

"It looks horrible out there. Do you and Leroy have any idea at all of what you're doing?"

"We're learning on the job, Tom."

He nodded, smiling a little. "Have you found anything to drink?"

I told him about the case of Chilean wine in the galley. "There's food too, and a shower stall in the bunkhouse."

"Can't eat. But the wine and the shower sound good." He went down the stairs to the deckhouse.

The circular motion of the storm brought the wind in on our port side, and the ship leaned nearly to the starboard rail when a roll and wind gust coincided. Both sea and sky were gray-black.

"Tom?"

Susan was standing in the cabin doorway, her hands braced against the frame on either side. Her feet were bare. She had put on a shift of Mirium's that was flower-patterned in bright reds, blues, and yellows. Mirium was tall, at least six feet, and the shift was too big for Susan. Her hair was tangled, her right hand bandaged, and her feverishly bright eyes were ringed by dark hollows. Petrie had reminded me of a derelict; Susan now looked like a sickly child.

"Where's Tom?"

"Below. He'll be back soon."

"Thank you," she said, and she slipped back inside the cabin and closed the door.

# Thirty-Two

We did not see the sunset: By then the distant eastern clouds had formed into dense, dark, towering cumulonimbus, a Himalaya of glaciated peaks and shadowed valleys that were now and then veined by lightning. The seas were a little bigger, a little steeper than they had been a few hours ago. The sky was dark all around but black in the east, and the storm had spun off squalls that smoked on the horizon. We were being chased by huge seas, chased by the advancing hurricane. There was hardly any transition between dusk and night.

The bridge lights were turned to a soft red to preserve our night vision; outside lights defined the ship, separated it from the sky and sea. Rain and wind came after dark. Often, pulsing shivers of lightning illuminated the clouds and, for an instant, revealed the great seas and broad troughs through which we sailed. The water was laterally streaked by foam, and the wind tore spindrift off the wave crests. The waves were steeper now, and occasionally one avalanched blue-white in the vast darkness. Other strange bluish lights appeared and vanished around us. *Mako*'s motion, the rolls and pitches and yaws, the surfing down rushing wave faces, was extreme now; the deck was often awash with water, and spray from the bow curls reached the bridge's oval of windows. Spray, rain—the wipers could not keep the glass clear for long. There was resistance when you turned the helm's spokes. The following seas exerted great pressure on the rudder.

Karpe and I relieved each other at the wheel every two or three hours. Petrie did not come out of the cabin. He was, as Leroy saw it, baby-sitting the Falconer kids. I supposed that he had been rendered nearly helpless by sickness.

Leroy relieved me again after midnight. He steered while I studied the large-scale charts detailing the waters off the northern Honduran coast. I thought that I might be able to determine our position by comparing the soundings on the charts with the glowing numerals on the depth sounder. The charts gave depths in fathoms, the depth sounder in feet; I had to mentally reconcile the different numbers. The depth sounder now showed that *Mako*'s keel was two hundred four feet above the bottom—thirty-four fathoms. I would know when we reached the shallower waters off the coast, maybe even be able to pinpoint our position by a particular series of soundings.

"What do you think?" Karpe asked.

"I don't know. Damn the torpedoes."

I was at the helm when, four hours later, the depth sounder began to tick off lower numbers; it went from more than two hundred feet to ninety feet in just a few minutes. We had passed over the continental shelf. Now, in shallow water, the big seas steepened, turned concave, and broke all around us. I was not able to effectively control the ship; mostly she found her own way, half buried in foam, surfing down the avalanching waves, skewing thirty degrees to port and then starboard. The depth sounder read eighty-four feet, seventy-seven, sixty-eight.

"Is that a light?" Leroy said.

"Where?"

"Ahead and to the left."

There was nothing but darkness, and then a light flashed, vanished, darkness again for a time, and then another flash.

"Time it, Leroy," I said.

The depth soundings held steady at around sixty feet.

"Seven seconds."

"Time it again."

The helm vibrated from the forces exerted on the rudder. All around, the sea flashed blue-white and the roar of breaking seas was indistinguishable from the peals of thunder.

"Seven seconds."

"What does the chart indicate?"

I glanced at the depth sounder: sixty-four feet, sixty, fifty-five, fifty-two, and then back up to sixty.

"Roatán, I think."

"Can't be."

"Occulting light, seven-second interval."

If that was true, then we were far east of our tentative destination, Puerto Cortés. Roatán was the name of the larger of the Islas de la Bahía, and the name too of its major town. There was another, smaller island less than twenty miles to the west.

"Any other lights visible?" I asked.

"No."

I turned the wheel to carry the ship farther to the west, away from the shoal waters around Roatán.

"We're going on the beach," Leroy said.

"Maybe we'll blunder into the channel between islands."

"Shit. Put me in an airplane anytime."

After a while I said, "Where's the Roatán light now?"

"To port and a little behind us."

"How far away, do you think?"

"Too close, if I can see it in these conditions."

The depth sounder's red digits remained between the high forties and the low sixties. There was little I could do to guide the ship in these breaking seas except try to keep her prow pointed toward the coast. I couldn't let her broach. We were passing through a boiling cauldron, whites and phosphorescent greens, the air all around fogged with spindrift.

The seas no longer marched along in orderly rows; waves were deflected off the island, creating powerful cross chops. Twice the screws came out of the water, and we could hear them screaming over the noise of seas and storm, and once *Mako* was knocked down past her starboard rail. She rose slowly, very slowly, when there was no clear reason for her to rise at all.

The depth sounder indicated that there was just thirty-six feet beneath the keel, and then the numbers abruptly began rising. The height of the seas diminished, fewer of them broke, and the wind gusts were not as strong. We were in the lee of the island.

I waited a few more minutes and then spun the wheel hard to port. The ship rolled steeply, burying her starboard rail again, remained in that position for a while, too long, before righting herself and again powering west. The water was still choppy, wind-whitened, but we had reached shelter. We proceeded west between Roatán and the Honduran coast. Within a few miles the water was relatively calm.

"Dumb luck," Leroy said, grinning at me.

*"Suerte estupendo!"* I said. "Leroy, get below quick and shut down the engines. I'll release the anchor from here."

"Goddamn," he said. "Yes!" And he turned and pounded down the steps to the deckhouse.

The anchor was holding firmly when Leroy reappeared. We still could hear wind high in the rigging, the rattle of rain overhead, and the spaced pounding of surf on the windward side of the island, but we were at least free of the diesels' incessant pounding and the teeth-chattering vibrations. The depth sounder showed 29. We had twenty-nine feet between the ship's keel and the coral reef.

Petrie came into the bridge. He still looked like a derelict, though now a sick, fall-down-drunk sort of derelict; there was a bruise on his left cheek and a laceration on his forehead. They apparently had done some bouncing around inside the cabin.

"Have we finally reached it?" he said. "Hell?"

Half an hour later the four of us were sitting at the mess table in the saloon. Susan, with Petrie's help, had prepared a meal of canned chili, canned corned beef, and a loaf of half-stale bread. All of us, except for Susan, were a little giddy from fatigue and relief. She was quiet. She sipped a little wine, ate a few spoonfuls of chili. There was something almost ghostly about Susan now. She seemed less substantial, halfway out of this world—fading away like her brother.

The ship rocked in the sharper wind gusts, and rain swarmed against the portlights and snapped on the roof.

"Tom," I said. "You're the lawyer; you deal with the Honduran port authorities and police in the morning."

He nodded.

"They'll have plenty of questions. Who the hell are we, where our papers, and what are we doing with this ship?"

"We sailed *Mako* from Chetumal as a favor to our friend Raven Ahriman."

"Our friend Raven Ahriman and his ship are on watch-and-seize lists all over the Caribbean. He's a smuggler, most recently wanted for the smuggling of aliens into Florida Bay. At least three of them died. And how do we explain Peter? We went on a recreational cruise through the fringes of a hurricane with a seriously damaged stroke victim on board? He'll have to be treated at a hospital before we fly him home."

"I have a senator who owes me," Petrie said, "and a congressman who owes me more. And if all else fails we can pass out some serious bribes and lies. I'll work out the details."

"When you've worked out the details, tell us so we'll tell the same story."

"What I want to know is—where's Ahriman?"

"South America, I think. One of the Guianas."

"Guyana? Isn't that where the Reverend Jones and his people committed suicide with a soft drink?"

"Right. Guyana, formerly British Guiana. East of there is the former Dutch Guiana, now Surinam, and east of that is French Guiana. I think Ahriman will be there—French Guiana."

"Why there?"

"I found a drawer full of receipts, most of them from Cayenne in French Guiana. Dockage fees, shipyard repairs, receipts for fuel, a cargo manifest, port-authority documents . . ."

"Doesn't sound like much to go on."

Susan placed her palms flat on the table—the bandage on her right hand stained with blood—looked at each of us with a mechanical smile, then got up, crossed the saloon, and climbed the stairs to the bridge and cabin.

I said, "Ahriman has to have a home base somewhere. I'm guessing French Guiana."

Petrie looked skeptical. "We can maybe start down there."

"I'll go," Karpe said. "Scout around."

"There aren't many port cities along that coast," I said. "Georgetown, Paramaribo in Surinam, Cayenne. He'll be around a port."

"I don't know," Petrie said.

"There's another reason I think he'll be in French Guiana. Cayenne is the site of the old French penal colony. I think, I really do think, that it would amuse Ahriman to live near the infamous Devil's Island."

"I want that son of a bitch," Petrie said.

"You want the two mil too, don't you, Tom?" Leroy said with a mocking grin. "Almost as much as you want revenge?"

"Tom?"

We turned to watch Susan descend the stairs. She moved uncertainly, hand on rail, taking the stairs slowly, one by one, like a small girl who is afraid of falling. And she looked waifish too, dressed in Mirium's gypsy-bright, oversize shift. She paused on the bottom step and said something we could not understand.

"What?" Petrie said.

Softly, shyly, like a girl who fears she will be reproached by intolerant adults, she said, "Peter died."

# Part IV
# Dead Men
# Rise Up
# Never

# Thirty-Three

We scattered Peter Falconer's ashes in the Gulf a few miles off Martina's lighthouse.

Peter had been cremated, according to the instructions in his will, but not before Susan hired a respected pathologist to conduct an autopsy. Peter had officially died of asphyxiation, a complication stemming from a massive stroke previously incurred. Susan also had the death certificate and other documents from the Honduran medical examiner's office. She followed Petrie's advice in these matters—the Falconer Foundation was sure to contest the will and question the events surrounding Peter's death.

We had left a lot of confusion and loose ends in Honduras but hadn't been seriously challenged by the authorities. There had been talk of an inquiry. An inquiry, an investigation, an inquest. *Mako* had been seized and impounded. Functionaries, both civilian and military, issued vague threats, promised inconvenient delays. Petrie sorted it all out and we were permitted to leave Honduras after only a day and a half there.

Leroy Karpe had not returned to Florida with us; he'd gone directly from Honduras to South America. Leroy had telephoned Petrie several times during the last few days. No luck so far. He'd been to Georgetown, the capital of Guyana, in the north; to Paramaribo, Surinam; and was next heading for Cayenne in the former French Guiana. If you ever need to hide out, Leroy said, this is the area.

Petrie, Susan, and I went out into the Gulf on Tom's cabin cruiser. It was a hot and humid morning. The sky was hazed over by a yellowish membrane of cloud spun off by Lorraine. The hurricane had hooked north into western Cuba, causing considerable damage, but had stalled over land and been downgraded to a tropical storm. Meteorologists thought that it might again pick up power when it moved back over warm water.

When we were a few miles off Bell Harbor, Susan and I tilted the urn over the transom and let the gritty ashes and bone fragments sift into the sea. Then we released the urn and watched it float away on the wake.

Petrie cut the engines, came down from the flying bridge, and we gathered in the deck well.

*"Requiescat in pace,"* Tom said.

It was awkward. Susan was with us only in a physical sense. It was impossible to guess what she was feeling or thinking. She appeared to have recovered her poise and self-assurance, but there was something in her eyes—fear, hatred, dementia—that disturbed me. Her eyes and skin seemed to glow feverishly. She had lost her brother, had been brutally used by Ahriman, but I thought it was more than that: I believed that she had killed Peter, suffocated him while the rest of us were below in the saloon. It was not about money. She intended to fight for the estate and control of the Falconer Foundation, but if she really had killed him it was not out of self-interest but an act of euthanasia. Peter had been physically and mentally devastated by his stroke. He might, even with the best of care, have remained comatose for years, paralyzed, mute, blind. . . . And I suspected that Susan had, in part, killed her brother out of shame and a sort of familial justice. Peter had, we all were sure, murdered at least one of the women at the Mosquito Keys, maybe both. But if she had killed him, it was while she'd been so emotionally ravaged that the decision and act were now questionable. Her guilt would be profound. Maybe he could have partially recovered from the effects of the stroke. Maybe we were wrong, maybe he hadn't murdered anyone but had all along been a victim of the lies and manipulations of Ahriman and Charles. The mercy killing of one's brother was dreadful. More dreadful still was the conviction that it might not have been the appropriate action.

I didn't confide my thoughts to Petrie. He was fiercely protective of Susan and would not have tolerated a mention of such things, though I wondered if Tom himself might privately question Peter's sudden death.

We drifted for an hour, not speaking much, then Petrie started the engines and we returned to port.


Afterward I met Martina in town. We lunched at a fast-food restaurant and then headed out to the lighthouse. Her new dog was frolicking along the quay when we arrived in *Puck*. He nearly knocked Martina down in greeting, and licked my hand when we were introduced. Then he raced madly around and around the reef, chasing phantom seagulls, as we walked to the blockhouse.

"He's a sweetheart," Martina said.

She had adopted the dog from the town's animal shelter

and named him Cerberus, after the three-headed, dragon-tailed dog that guards Hades in Greek myth. He was a big composite sort of mutt, maybe one hundred twenty pounds, black and tan, with mismatched parts: you might guess his ancestry at a little Lab, a bit of rottweiler, a touch of mala-mute for his eerie bluish eyes, though he had the head and fur of an Airedale. He was three years old, scary to look at, but he had the temperament and sloppy manners of a puppy.

"Does he bark?" I asked Martina.

"I haven't heard him bark, no."

We changed into swimsuits and carried a pair of deck chairs out onto the reef. Cerberus greeted us as if for the first time and then again raced off to chase a memory of seagulls.

"Does he swim?" I asked.

"He hasn't yet. I think he's afraid of the water."

"I may be leaving again soon."

"Where to this time?"

"South America."

"Well, you're racking up the frequent-flyer miles. When is this Falconer nightmare going to end, Dan?"

"Soon."

"Will you be back Saturday for the opening of the play?"

"You bet. It couldn't go on without me."

"Because Harold is the understudy for all the male parts. Imagine Harold playing the Burglar."

I tried to picture it. "I think the play might be improved if the Burglar had a certain queenly manner. Maybe I should do it that way."

She laughed. "Maybe."

Cerberus approached us carrying a large rock in his jaws. He deposited it at Martina's feet and looked up for a sign of gratitude.

"Good boy, Cerberus," Martina said.

• • •

Petrie telephoned me that night. "Leroy's found the son of a bitch. You were right, he's in French Guiana. I've got reservations for tomorrow, Miami to Georgetown, a connecting flight to Cayenne. Pack. We're going to get that bastard."

"Okay," I said.

"Do you remember what you promised me on the boat?"

"No."

"You promised that if I failed to kill Ahriman, if he took me out, that you'd kill him."

"I remember now."

"Meet me at the airport at seven-thirty. We'll fly down to Miami in the Cessna. And, kid? I can guess what you've been thinking about Susan. Susan and Peter, aboard the ship. Forget it. It didn't happen that way."

"How do you know, Tom?"

He hung up.

# Thirty-Four

Raven Ahriman's house was constructed of squared timbers creosoted almost black to protect the wood from insects. It had a steep roof and long eaves, a stone chimney, and a big front deck that extended to within twenty yards of a beach and pier. The house was small, solidly built in a mix of architectural styles—part ranch house, part log cabin, part tropical bungalow. A high green barricade of forest rose up behind the house.

"We'll go in by boat," Leroy said. "Three in the morning. A surprise raid. Take out Raven and whoever else is there, grab the money, get back in the boat. Go to the Cayenne airport, fly to Georgetown, fly to Miami. Bingo. Fast and slick, in and out."

"Slow down, Leroy," Petrie said.

We were at a shabby hotel in St.-Georges, a small town some hundred miles south of Cayenne on a river, the Oiapoque, which separated French Guiana from northeastern Brazil. Raven Ahriman's place was located about halfway between St.-Georges and Cayenne, tucked in a bay that provided shelter from all but northerly winds. The house, Leroy told us, was more easily accessible by sea than land: A dirt track that led through the forest from a paved strip of coastal road was virtually impassable during the rainy season. The house was isolated; the nearest settlement, a small fishing village, was several miles away at the end of the peninsular arm. .Raven liked his privacy. Raven was paranoid. We would not have to worry about Yoyo and that gang—they were living aboard the trawler at the Cayenne docks. Only Ahriman, Charles, a couple of servants, and Ahriman's wife, Mirium, lived at the house. Anyway, those were the only persons Leroy had seen during the time he had reconnoitered the area and shot the videotape.

"You weren't seen?" Petrie asked.

"No."

"Sure?"

"I shot the video from the forest, about two hundred yards away."

"I don't know, Leroy."

"Tonight. We'll do it tonight."

I said, "You really don't expect us to kill Charles and the woman and servants, do you, Leroy?"

He lifted a shoulder in a contemptuous half shrug.

The hotel air-conditioning did not function and it was stifling in the room, at least ten degrees hotter than the outside, and the temperature there was ninety-plus. Petrie and I had arrived in St.-Georges the day before. Tom had broken out in a scarlet heat rash. I had picked up an intestinal bug. Florida, the Bahamas, Mexico, Honduras, now South America—months of humid heat had siphoned my strength and abraded my nerves. But Leroy Karpe, like a reptile, thrived in the cloying heat, and he appeared unaffected by what we were doing, the crimes, the imminent danger and violence.

"Well," Petrie said. "You've done a hell of a job, Leroy."

That was true. Karpe had managed to track down Ahriman in this big, wild region; discovered where the man lived and with whom; reconnoitered the area; and shot thirty minutes of videotape that familiarized Petrie and me with the terrain of our planned nighttime assault. And he had somewhere purchased weapons: a Winchester shotgun and two revolvers so old that almost all of the bluing had worn away. But there were no rust pits, no loose parts, and the barrel rifling grooves were still deeply incised. Mine, a .38 Smith and Wesson, had a cracked grip and bent sight. But it would shoot. It was at least seventy years old, and I figured that it was likely that men had been killed with that revolver, and it might soon kill another. Leroy told us that the guns were the best he could obtain in the circumstances and without arousing attention. Anyway, he said, it wasn't going to be long-range shooting, no cowardly sniping. In close, head or belly shot, if necessary a bullet in the back of the head for the *coup de grâce*.

"Leroy," Petrie said wearily, "Ahriman scares me, but you're beginning to scare me even more. We've got to get a few things settled before we go in."

"But we're going in?"

"Yeah."

"Tonight?"

"Ahriman has one and one-quarter million dollars that belong to me. Without it, I'm just another bum like you and Shaw."

"Not to mention," I said, "your knightly vow to avenge the dishonor done to Susan."

"Run the tape again, Leroy," Petrie said.

Karpe's vantage point was from partway down the peninsula that hooked north from the mainland, forming the bay.

He'd shot the video over water, through a gap in the foliage, through clouds of gnats. The house was far off until he adjusted the zoom lens. You could hardly discern it from the forest background, but then he'd turned the lens and the house expanded to nearly fill the screen. Thick, creosoted timbers, a steep shake-shingle roof with overhanging eaves, a railed deck upon which were placed pieces of furniture— an umbrellaed table, a few chairs, a pair of chaise longues, a dome-lidded barbecue brazier.

Most of the video had been shot in the early morning. The windows were frosted by sunlight and all of the shadows angled west. I had missed it before, but now I noticed part of a building in the brush behind the house: the servants' quarters. Then I picked out an even smaller structure, a shed, that probably held the electrical generator. The T-shaped pier was made of the same kind of creosoted squared-off timbers—mahogany, perhaps—that had been employed to construct the house and outbuildings. An inflatable boat, a pair of outboard engines mounted at the stern, was tied at the end of the pier. It was the same Zodiac I had seen in Chetumal Bay, the same one that had been the property of Peter Falconer and kept aboard the *Deep Six*.

The camcorder had slowly panned down the peninsula, past the house and along the stretch of beach to where it curved around the mainland side of the bay. The little fishing village, a shantytown built of scrap lumber and tar paper, lay near the peninsula's cape. Half a dozen skiffs were pulled up on the sand; nets had been strung out to dry.

"To Ahriman's at three," Leroy said, "out by four. The fishermen'll be headed out before sunrise."

The TV screen went dark, and when it brightened we were again looking over wind-ruffled water to the beach and house. The light and shadows had changed; it was around noon now. Charles emerged from the house. He wore beige slacks and a pale yellow shirt and carried a book. He sat at the table, lit a cigarette, and began reading. A few minutes later a stout black woman, a servant, came out to set the table for lunch.

Charles was joined by Ahriman's wife, Mirium. Charles, ever polite, rose from his chair. She was several inches taller. They sat together at the table without speaking. Then Raven Ahriman came out. He said something, listened to Charles's reply, and laughed. He was barefoot and wore only a pair of white shorts, and his unbound hair fell in a black curtain past his waist. Ahriman didn't walk, he strode. He strode around as though on the deck of a great ship that he commanded. He was Captain Raven Goddamned Ahriman, and he was something.

"That's enough, Leroy," Petrie said. "Turn it off."

I picked up the phone and told the desk to send up six cold beers, *cold,* and some sandwiches.

"How many servants?" Petrie said.

"I told you, just two. The housekeeper–cook and the groundskeeper–handyman."

"All right. You shot this video, what, two days ago. We have no way of knowing how many are there now. Maybe Yoyo and that gang arrived. Ahriman himself is plenty. We don't need any others."

"That place is too small for houseguests," Karpe said. "Anyway, crew is crew—they don't socialize with the boss."

"Leroy," Tom said, "we aren't going to hurt anyone unless we absolutely have to. Ahriman's another matter."

"I'll save him for you."

They were dreaming. Ahriman would not be saved; whoever saw him first would promptly kill him or be killed himself.

"There's something else," Leroy said. "I spent an awful lot of money."

"You know I'll take care of your expenses."

"Travel, living expenses, the camcorder and VCR, the guns . . ."

"Didn't I just say I'll pay all your expenses?"

"Tom, I want a cut of the two million, if we recover it."

"A cut."

"A percentage. Look, I've done most of the work. I've risked my life half a dozen times, and I'll risk it again tonight. You aren't paying me much. A salary, and not a fair one considering the job."

"How much do you want, Leroy?"

"Ten percent of all we recover."

"Two hundred thousand dollars if we recover it all?"

"That's right."

"You're crazed with greed."

I stood by the window while they haggled. The rain had started, just a misty drizzle now, but it would soon become a deluge. The palms and flowering trees down in the court-yard were beginning to writhe in the gusts of wind.

At last it was settled. Leroy would receive two and a half percent of all money recovered: fifty thousand dollars if we got it all.

"How about you?" Petrie said quietly. "How much do you want?"

"I made a deal," I said.

"So did Leroy."

"Express your discontent to Leroy, not me."

I held open the door for the room waiter. He carried in six bottles of beer stuck in a bucket of ice and a tray containing six ham and cheese sandwiches, mustard, and a jar of pickle relish.

"All right," Petrie said when the waiter had gone. "Let's go through your plan, Leroy. Step by step, detail by detail. No speculation, no wishful thinking—earn your fucking bonus."

I stood by the window while Leroy again outlined his strategy. It was dark outside. The rain came down suddenly and hard. Cold flickers of lightning illuminated the court-yard below, and the thunder was long-rolling, the kind that seems to reverberate from horizon to horizon. Palm fronds spun like windmill blades.

"You're not interested in this?" Petrie asked me.

"Not much," I said.

You could not expect an operation like this to go as planned. Strategy was an expression of the ideal; tactics was how you saved your ass when the strategy failed.

# Thirty-Five

Leroy had hired a St.-Georges policeman named Jules Boulanger to serve as our driver through the night. He would use his police car, a ten-year-old Ford, and be available to assist us in the solution of unforeseen legal problems. He had also rented us the boat we were going to use. Leroy said that he'd learned that you could usually halfway trust a corrupt cop, whereas the average criminal was vain, touchy, and as likely to turn on you as your pet rattler. You paid the corrupt cop generously, promised him more, presented him with gifts, and that was that.

Jules got off-duty at twelve. We waited for him on the hotel veranda.

"Does he know what we're going to do?" Petrie asked.

"Nah. I told him we were going fishing. He laughed. He doesn't want to know anything."

Jules Boulanger was a big-chested man who wore sunglasses at midnight and, when he smiled, displayed a mouth full of gold teeth. He had on a sweat-stained khaki uniform, a straw cowboy hat, and cowboy boots, and he wore a wide belt that sagged beneath the weight of a holstered pistol, a truncheon, handcuffs, a sheathed knife, and loops holding cans of Mace.

He got out of the car, helped us with our few bags, and shook hands all around. Leroy loaded the camcorder and VCR in the truck, told Jules they were gifts of friendship, and we engaged in another round of handshaking.

There was not much traffic outside of town, just a few semitrailer trucks whose drivers hogged the road and blasted their air horns as they passed. Insects snapped against the windshield. The air blowing in through the side windows felt thick and syrupy and exhaled a jungle stench that smelled both rotten and spicy.

Jules told us the story of his life, commencing with his great-grandfather, a French escapee from the penal colony at St. Laurent, and his great-grandmother, a free bush Negro. I lost interest when he proceeded on to the next generation of Boulangers.

My anxiety emerged as fatigue. I had rarely felt so tired. Tom Petrie was affected differently: He was full of adrenaline and nervous energy; he could not remain still. Leroy, sitting in front with Jules, appeared relaxed, cheerful. I suspected that he enjoyed all of this, the intrigue and danger, the possibility that someone, one of them or one of us, might be dead within a few hours. Karpe didn't use hard drugs anymore. He got high on risk.

After fifty minutes Jules pulled off onto a side road that slanted into the forest. Branches met overhead, forming a low tunnel, and brush scraped along the sides of the car. The road was graveled for the first half mile, then it deteriorated into a track of orangy clay that glowed like neon in the headlight beams. We reached an impasse, a depression in the road that had filled with rainwater. Jules stopped the car, turned off the engines and lights, and we all got out.

The clay was slippery underfoot. All around us the forest buzzed and clicked and creaked with insect noises. The mosquitoes quickly found us. Petrie and Leroy smeared their arms, faces, and necks with insect repellent that smelled like cheap cologne.

"You know where the boat is," Jules said quietly to Leroy. "Three kilometers, no more. There is a red reflector on a tree there. Here is the key to the padlock."

Leroy put the key in his pocket. "Jules, loan me your handcuffs and a can of Mace."

Jules detached the objects from his belt and gave them to Karpe. *"Bonne chance!"* he said.

We started down the track, Karpe in front with the shotgun and a flashlight, Petrie in the middle, and me following behind with another light.

We walked cautiously on the slimy clay, tormented by mosquitoes and other sucking, pinching, biting insects. Flying beetles zigzagged through the flashlight beams, wings buzzing, and we saw quick bats and moths as big as saucers. There were parasitic vines, fungal growths, toads that had been stained orange by the mud. And we saw night-blooming flowers, maybe orchids, delicately perfumed. We stopped to rest after a half hour.

"Think he'll be there when we get back?" Petrie asked.

"Jules? Sure. He wants the rest of his money."

"I hope you were extravagant, Leroy."

"Five hundred up front, a grand at the airport in Cayenne. That's half a year's salary for the bozo."

We went on. After another hour we could smell the sea and soon after saw the red reflector that Jules had mentioned. A muddy path led us down to the water. The boat had been pulled up from the beach and chained to a tree. It was a sixteen-foot aluminum skiff with a twenty-five-horsepower engine mounted at the stern. A pair of oars lay on the bottom.

It was a dark night. Smoky clouds obscured most of the sky. The bay was smooth except for the twists and ripples of tidal currents. The high-mark waterline on the sand indicated that the tide was well out, perhaps about to turn. I knew the general direction of Ahriman's house from the video, but saw no lights burning. No lights, either, from the fishing village near the cape.

"We'll never find this spot on our way back," Petrie said.

"We won't bother to try," Leroy replied.

I walked back up the beach and, in a hard whisper, warned them to be quiet. I told them that small sounds can carry for miles over open water. Noise sometimes seems to amplify with distance under certain conditions. I became angrier as I hissed at them, "And for Christ's sake, don't kick or bang this tin boat—it's a drum." My anger turned into a kind of choked fury. That was from the adrenaline, the fear and eagerness. It was like being back in the Army. I couldn't see their expressions, but they remained still and listened. My whispers would not carry far, though they were harsh enough to convey my anger to Petrie and Karpe. "And we can't use the motor on a night like this. We'll row. *I'll* row." I told them that I had learned a few simple things during my time in the military. I demanded that they both wash off the stinking insect repellent: Men had died because of the smell of repellent or aftershave or tobacco smoke. Men died because they feared insect bites more than bullets.

Karpe released the skiff from its chain and we dragged it down the beach and into shallow water. I got in, sat on the center seat, lifted an oar, and fitted its bracketed metal pin into the metal shafts on the gunwhale. I did the same with the other oar. Leroy, moving carefully, climbed aboard and sat in the prow seat. Petrie moved to the rear.

At first the rusty oarlocks creaked alarmingly, but I found that I could reduce the noise to a cricket's chirp by shortening my stroke. I rowed a diagonal across the bay, pulling in the general direction of Ahriman's place. It was not much farther than the distance from the Bell Harbor Marina to the lighthouse. I had rowed that route two or three times a week for months and had built up my back and shoulder muscles. This course, despite the weight and the awkward handling of the skiff, was nothing. Soon I knew the boat, knew how to quiet the oarlocks, and I pulled harder.

"Left a little," Leroy whispered. He had seen the house.

We heard faint, hallucinatory music drifting over the water from the peninsula. Jules, the idiot, was listening to his car radio.

My shirt was soaked with sweat, and I paused a moment to wipe sweat from my eyes. We were vulnerable now. Ahriman had the survival instincts of a hunted cat. I thought about Chetumal, when I had been scanning *Mako* with my binoculars and seen Ahriman, on the ship's bridge, aiming a rifle at me.

We reached the beach north of the pier. Leroy got out, moved forward a few yards, kneeled, and aimed his shotgun toward the house. Petrie and I pulled the skiff up on the sand. It was quiet except for the muffled throbbing of the electrical generator in a shed behind the house.

Petrie and I drew our revolvers and moved forward to join Leroy. The three of us hesitated. The assault had been carefully planned, but now that we were on the site everything looked and felt different. This wasn't videotape or bold talk, it was real, and for an instant we doubted.

Leroy and I went up the steps to the deck while Petrie started around the house. Tom would stand watch at the back door, gain entry if he could, and also make sure that no one escaped.

We crossed the deck. The door had three locks: an ordinary one in the knob, useless for security, and two solid dead bolts. We waited to give Petrie time to get into position.

"Ready?" Leroy whispered.

The three locks held the door securely shut. Karpe would blow away the hinges. It is almost always quicker and easier to gain entry by blasting the hinges and then opening the door from that side.

I moved a few yards down the deck and turned away so that my face, my eyes, would be protected from flying wood splinters. After our long immersion in the nighttime hush, the shotgun reports sounded like the detonation of explosives, and echoes dully resonated through the surrounding forest.

Leroy ripped the door away from the frame and went through into the house. I came in behind him, found and hit the wall light switch, and moved a few steps to the side. The living room ran the width of the house. Tile floor, bright throw rugs, cane chairs and sofas, round dining table and chairs, timber walls painted white and hung with nautical prints, bookshelves.

Leroy lifted his shotgun and blew a hole in the ceiling. Intimidation. He dropped a cartridge on the floor while reloading. He was excited. I was excited too. Everything appeared brighter and clearer than normal. Everything seemed to be happening at half speed.

Leroy went through an archway on the right. I heard him shouting. I ran down a short hallway on the other side of the house and through the kitchen to the back door. I unlocked the door, pulled it open while stepping to the side.

"Tom," I yelled. "It's me."

Petrie didn't shoot. He came up a few concrete steps and into the kitchen. His eyes were rounded. He was breathing as if he had just run a hundred-yard sprint.

"One of the servants came out," he said. "I chased him back inside the little house. There's a car—I've got to disable the car."

"Go!" I said.

Leroy and I hadn't been in the house long, maybe twenty seconds, but I felt that things were spinning out of control.

There was a door at the far end of the kitchen. I opened it. A pantry. Leroy was still shouting somewhere in the front of the house. A hallway, another door: bathroom. And another door. I went through with the flashlight in my left hand away from my body, the revolver in my right. I nearly shot Mirium. The room light was on and she was sitting on the edge of a bed, tying the waist cord of her robe. Her expression was more quizzical than frightened. There was a bassinet alongside the bed, and inside lay a boy who looked about a year old.

"Where's Raven?" I said to Mirium.

She cocked her head, looked at me.

I supposed that she didn't know English. French was the first language of this country.

I gestured toward the front room with my gun. *"Allons!"* I said.

She rose, picked up the crying baby, and preceded me down the hall to the living room.

Charles, his mouth bloody, was sitting on the floor with his back against a wall. He was testing the firmness of his upper front teeth with a thumb and forefinger. He wore pink-striped pajamas and a little pillbox nightcap.

"Where is Raven, goddamn you!" Leroy shouted.

Charles removed his fingers from his mouth. "Gone," he said, drooling bloody saliva.

"Gone where, goddamn you!"

I couldn't tell how much of Karpe's fury was genuine and how much theater.

Mirium had opened the top of her robe and was now nursing the baby. She sat on the edge of a rattan chair.

I realized that Charles's pajamas and nightcap were replicas of the outfits worn by convicts in the prison colony many years ago. Whimsical Charles.

"Raven isn't here," Charles said.

Karpe walked over and stood above the woman. "Where is your husband?"

She continued to placidly nurse her baby. He was a husky kid, the color of milky coffee, with straight black hair and a long face. His fists were clenched. Raven Ahriman's son.

"I will ask you one more time," Karpe said.

"She's a deaf mute," Charles said.

We turned to stare at him.

"She can't hear or speak. Don't scare her. Raven's in Trinidad. He left yesterday."

"Son of a bitch!" Leroy said. Then again, "Son of a bitch!"

I said, "Why did Ahriman go to Trinidad?"

Charles pried a bloody top front incisor loose from his gums, held it up to the light, and studied it with interest, as an anthropologist might examine a rare fossil.

"Charles?"

"To look at a boat. A yacht. We're going to sail around the world."

"Where's the money?"

"He took it with him."

"No, he didn't."

Petrie came into the room. "I locked the servants in the generator shed." He looked at the baby. "What's this?"

"Raven's son," I said.

"Yeah? Anyone check the kid for horns and cloven hooves?"

Karpe turned abruptly and went down the hallway toward the kitchen and the outside.

"Ahriman's in Trinidad," I said.

"That's great. Where's the money?"

"Charles is just about to tell us."

"I don't know," Charles said.

"That lisp suits you," Petrie said.

"Raven took the money. It's in the bank."

"Those are cute jammies," Petrie said. "I love them."

Charles's puffy lips parted in a little smile.

The baby was sleeping now. Mirium was gently kissing his eyelids and cheeks.

Leroy returned carrying a five-gallon can of gasoline. He unscrewed the cap.

Petrie grinned maliciously. "Leroy is going to barbecue you, you debonair little turd."

Karpe splashed gasoline over Charles's lap. "Yea, hallelujah," he said. "I'm sending you a Roman candle, Lord."

"The money is buried in the garden," Charles said.

"Precisely where?"

"In the tomato patch. First row at the end."

Petrie left the room.

"You really wouldn't have done it," Charles said.

Karpe grinned at him. "No?"

"Would you?"

"In a flash, so to speak."

"The gas is burning my genitals."

"Pity," Leroy said.

Mirium was hugging her baby. Her cheeks were wet with tears. She did not look at us.

"We thought you all were dead," Charles said.

"You thought wrong."

"Alas."

Petrie was carrying the mud-caked satchel when he returned. "It looks like it's all here. Most of it, anyway. The bonds too. Jesus!" Tom was very happy. "Damn, we did it."

"Charles," I said. I approached him. He looked up. "We're going to lock you and Mirium and the baby in the generator shed with the servants. We'll give you a jug of water to wash with. You'll find a way to get out of there eventually. But—listen to me, Charles—remember how you and Ahriman obtained that money. Charles? You're criminals. Don't be impulsive and run to the police as soon as you get free."

Petrie and I conducted a quick search while Leroy led Charles and Mirium—her baby crying again now—through the house and out the back door. He would close them in the shed with the servants. The shed could be locked from the outside with a padlock, but in addition Karpe intended to nail a few two-by-fours across the door. There were carpenter tools inside as well as gardening implements. They would free themselves in time.

Petrie and I walked down to the beach. He showed me Susan's pearl necklace; he had found it in Mirium's jewel box. I had taken a pint bottle of good dark rum from the liquor cabinet. I uncorked it, drank, and passed the bottle to Tom.

"Can you imagine the bastard? He rapes a woman, then steals her pearls and gives them to his wife. 'Here, my love, an expensive token of my affection.'"

We heard the baby crying and a little later the sound of hammering as Karpe nailed the door shut. Leroy emerged from the shadows, accepted the bottle from Petrie, drank, then walked along the beach and to the end of the pier. He would disable the Zodiac.

"I only wish Raven had been here," Petrie said. "I didn't get to settle the score. He is one lucky shit."

I thought Tom was kidding himself and me: We were both relieved that Ahriman had been gone tonight. Maybe Leroy was truly disappointed that we had failed to "settle the score," but then he had more than once demonstrated that he himself was a little psycho.

Dawn was still an hour away, but there was a buzz of engines out on the bay as fishermen headed out from their village on the cape. The water had a silvery, viscid look, like mercury, and exhaled a pleasant coolness.

Karpe returned. We dragged the boat down the beach. I waded knee-deep, then climbed aboard. Petrie followed.

Leroy started to get in, then said, "Wait. I forgot something."

"What?"

"My shotgun."

"Leave it," I said.

He jogged up toward the house.

"Have you got the flask?" Petrie asked.

"No, Leroy took it with him."

"Any tobacco?"

"No."

"I'm beat," he said. "Really beat. All the adrenaline is burned up. I could sleep for a week."

Leroy came down from the house carrying his shotgun. "Let's go."

Petrie started the outboard, adjusted the throttle, and we

cruised diagonally across the bay toward where Jules had parked his car. The shotgun and the two pistols were dropped over the side. The flask was passed around. We were almost to shore when I noticed that the water had acquired a pinkish hue. For a moment, confused, I thought I had been mistaken about the time and the sun had come up, and then I turned: Ahriman's house was burning. Flames leaped high into the darkness, contracted, leaped again, and a spiral of sparks twisted up in the shape of a tornado funnel. The entire building glowed. The structure itself appeared to be constructed of flame. Fire defined every timber, door, and window frame, the deck and roof. We could not hear anything over the engine noise.

Karpe was defiant. "So what?" he said. "Fuck it."

Neither Tom nor I said much. You could not talk to Leroy.

This was the rainy season. It had rained hard during the past two days. The forest was drenched. Everything was sodden. But Mirium and her baby, Charles, and the two servants were trapped in the solidly built shed. If it was ignited by flames or sparks . . .

I was angry enough to kill Karpe. I might have killed him if I'd still had the revolver. Killed him in that first, awful surge of rage when I'd turned and saw the conflagration. But it was too late. The gun was gone. It was the sort of thing that had to be done without thought, instantly, and the moment had passed.

Jules drove us to the Cayenne airport. He was very pleased with his money and the gifts and rewarded us with hearty embraces and vows of undying friendship.

We flew to Georgetown. Leroy and I waited at the Georgetown airport while Petrie took a taxi to town and deposited the money in the National Bank of Guyana. He would later arrange to have it wire-transferred to his bank in Bell Harbor.

He returned forty minutes before our flight to Miami was scheduled to depart. We waited at a booth in the first-class lounge. The staff and airport security guards watched us suspiciously. We were exhausted, filthy, our clothes stained with sweat and caked with orange mud, our faces and arms spotted with insect bites that looked like boils. One by one we went into the lavatory to shave and wash up and change into clean clothes.

We were surprised at how easily we passed through customs, both at the Georgetown airport and later in Miami. We evidently resembled responsible, decent citizens, though we—at least Tom Petrie and I—felt like terrorists.

# Thirty-Six

The opening performance of *Temptation* went well: doors opened and closed smoothly; none of the scenery collapsed; all of the actors promptly responded to their cues; only a few lines were muffed; and we played to a full house that generously demanded two curtain calls and did not protest when we stole a third. The female cast members were presented with bouquets of flowers, as arranged by Harold. We all held hands, and the men awkwardly bowed while the women gracefully curtsied.

There was a party onstage after the show, after most of the audience had exited the theater. The cast, some members of the crew, and invited guests remained behind. Pizzas were delivered. Spirits, wine, and beer were available.

Levi Samuelson was the only member of the audience who had come to the theater in a tuxedo. "Bravo," he said.

"Did you enjoy the show, Judge?"

"Oh, yes. It was great fun. And you were a stealthy burglar, Daniel, with exquisite comic timing."

"Really?"

"Sitting there in the audience I started thinking about perhaps writing a play about the Sacco–Vanzetti case. It would make stirring courtroom drama. One could appropriate actual dialogue from the trial transcripts and letters. Would you care to play a small part in the play?"

"Possibly. Send a copy of your script to my agent, Judge."

"And who is your agent?" he asked, smiling.

"Candace."

"I escorted Candace to the theater tonight, but between acts she ran off with a shady lawyer."

"Speaking of shady lawyers, excuse me, Judge."

Tom Petrie, looking bored and irritable, was sitting alone on one of the sofas.

"Enjoy the show?" I asked, sitting next to him.

"In the same way I enjoy watching amateur baseball or listening to amateur musicians. That is to say, not at all."

"Where is Susan?"

"New York."

"Maybe you ought to go there."

"Yeah."

"Help her get through this."

"I don't want to discuss Susan now, okay?"

"Fine. I gave Leroy a ticket to the show, but I didn't see him in the audience."

"Live theater isn't Leroy's style. Leroy likes to be in the company of machines."

"Well, anyway, his incendiary lunacy worked out okay."

"Barely."

Leroy had contacted Jules Boulanger in French Guiana and been assured that no one had perished in the fire.

Petrie finished his drink, placed the glass on the floor, and got to his feet. "In fact, I'm on the way to see our bad boy, to give him his percentage."

"Ciao," I said.

He made an angry exit stage left.

"Your buddy appeared vexed." Nestor Naranjo, wearing a three-piece pinstriped suit with a Phi Beta Kappa medal displayed on a vest chain, was looking down at me. There was a smear of makeup on his cheek; he had hugged an actress, maybe his wife, who had played the role of Gloria's neighbor and rival, Camille.

"Your wife was great," I said.

"I don't like the sound of that."

I laughed. "What's new, Nestor?"

"The wheels of justice are sometimes swift," he said, "and grind exceedingly fine. Earlier tonight Gary Tolliver was arrested while holding up a Stop and Rob. He'll be going away for a long time." Stop and Rob was police slang for a convenience store.

I felt as if I had held my breath for weeks and could now finally exhale. Gary Tolliver was in jail. The world was a slightly better place.

"And I think I may have a job for you. There's an opening in the SA's office for a full-time investigator. Fair salary, good benefits, stimulating work. I think I can clear it with Craig."

"Thanks, Nestor, but no. I'm going to hit the books hard to prepare for exams. I've missed a lot of class time."

He nodded. "I do fervently hope that if you ever really become a lawyer—God forbid—that I can at least once oppose you in the courtroom."

"Be careful what you wish for," I said.

I bummed a cigarette from Harold and went out through the theater's back exit. The sky was overcast, and a hot wind blew dust and scraps of paper down the alley. I could hear the dull reverberation of surf striking the distant breakwater.

Lorraine, downgraded to tropical storm when it had stalled over western Cuba, had regained hurricane status—Grade One, the least serious—after returning to warm Gulf waters. It had then moved slowly west, toward Mexico, before hooking north again, and was expected to reach the Alabama–Mississippi coasts sometime tomorrow night. Bell Harbor would not be hit full force by the storm—we were on the periphery—but we could expect high seas, wind, and rain.

I returned to the theater, found Martina, and extracted her from the admiring attention of a young college teacher. Her eyes were bright and she could not stop smiling. Marty was normally reserved, modest, but she was able to show herself off in theater performances. She was excited now by the attention and admiration she'd received.

"We'll stay at my place tonight," I said.

"Why?"

"The storm's arriving."

"Bad?"

"Not really, but bad enough to make passage out to the lighthouse risky if we don't get under way soon. It's probably better to stay in town."

"But I left Cerberus outside."

"He's a dog. He'll just get wet."

"And scared. And he hasn't any food. We might not be able to get out there tomorrow."

"Then we'd better go now. I'm sorry. I know how much you're enjoying yourself."

"It's all right. I've soaked up enough adulation for one night." She smiled. "There will be further triumphs."

# Thirty-Seven

The west wind blew twisting streamers of mist past the light standards lining the esplanade and bent the royal palms nearly double. It was a fine rain now, and just a thirty-five-knot wind, but it would grow progressively worse tonight as the storm passed. Lorraine was getting in her last licks.

I told Martina that I was sick of water in all of its manifestations: in the air or on the ground, fresh or salt, shallow or deep, calm or stormy, water as a fluid, gas, or solid, water coming out of a tap or passively diluting the whiskey in my glass.

"Move to the Sahara," she said.

"Too wet."

I parked the car in the marina lot, and we ran down the pier to where *Puck*, rocking like a hobby horse, was docked. We were soaked. I went into the cabin, ran the blowers for a couple minutes, started the engines, and then Martina untied the lines and jumped aboard. I eased the boat away from the pier. Martina stood beside me. She usually liked to operate the boat herself, but tonight she tacitly turned *Puck* over to me.

Big seas were smashing into the rocky breakwater out-side—we could hear them over the noise of the engine—but it wasn't too rough in the bay. The water was shallow and there was not enough fetch for the wind to kick up big waves. It was choppy, though, confused by contrary wind and tide, an expanse of white-capped three- and four-foot waves erupting and subsiding all around us. Puck's screw came out of the water a couple of times. It was a rough ride, though not really dangerous, and the water calmed when we came into the lee of the reef.

Martina held tight to a railing. "I was good, wasn't I, in the play?"

"My God!" I said. "My God, you were *fantástico! Estu-pendo! Espectaculár!*"

She laughed.

The cell phone in my jacket pocket rang. I was beginning to view telephones as Marty did. I let it ring.

I slowed the engine when we reached the relatively smooth water behind the reef and eased *Puck* in alongside the concrete quay. Martina went out to tie the bow and stern lines to the bollards, and I shut off the lights, the engine, and joined her outside in the cold rain. We went up the steps and across the reef plateau toward the blockhouse.

A great wet hairy yowling beast materialized out of the shadows and repeatedly leaped on Marina, nearly knocking her down. Cerberus. When he finished abusing Marty, he leaned heavily against me, lightly clamped his jaws over my hand in an ambiguous gesture of doggy affection, and then raced off toward the door.

"It's me or that dog," I told Martina.

"Let me think about it."

It was hot in the house, as usual after it had been closed up, and I went around opening portholes and switching on lights. Martina had stripped off her wet clothes by the time I finished. She observed me looking at her, smiled, and said, "Later," and went off to put on dry clothes.

Cerberus shook himself violently, spraying half a gallon of water around the room.

My cell phone rang. I switched it on and extended the aerial.

"I've been trying to reach you," Petrie said. "Leroy's been beaten half to death. He's in a coma."

"What happened?"

"I went out to the airport to give him his money. You know the layout."

There was a small apartment behind the charter company's office; Karpe lived there, saving on rent. The Quonset where they hangared the Cessna 182 was nearby.

"He was in the hangar. A coffee-drinking buddy found him. The cops were there when I arrived."

Martina could probably hear my half of the conversation. "The bird, you think?" I asked.

"Who else? We expected something, but not this quick."

"Yeah. Hold on a second, Tom." I went to the door and shot the bolts. "Did you call Susan in New York?"

"No."

"Call her, warn her."

"She'll be all right. Ahriman's after us, you and me, and the money."

"Call her. The bird is likely to do anything. Are you at home?"

"No. Hell no. I'm going to make myself scarce for a while."

"Good idea. Did you tell the police who you think did it?"

"Of course not. I didn't want to open a can of worms. Can of scorpions. But I wanted to let you know."

"Right, thanks. I think I'll be all right here at the lighthouse, at least tonight and tomorrow. It's blowing hard."

"Oh, yeah," he said. "That sissy Raven Ahriman is afraid of boats and rough water."

"Take care of yourself," I said, but he had broken the connection.

"Who was that?" Martina had changed into white duck pants and a light sweater.

"Petrie," I said.

"What did he want?"

"He's leaving town for a couple of days."

"And he has to inform you?"

"I'm hungry. I didn't get any of that pizza."

"I'll fix something as soon as I feed Cerberus."

I changed into dry clothes, got a flashlight, and went through the door and down the tunnellike passage to the base of the tower. There were lights in Marty's studio, but none above at the top of the spiral stairway. I climbed the stairs to the inside platform. I could not see much out in the darkness: a string of buoy lights, a light at the end of the breakwater, the green-white flashes of breaking waves. The window glass vibrated in the wind gusts and hard-driving rain. I locked the door leading to the outside platform. I could not imagine anyone climbing the tower—it was steep and smooth—but I didn't think I would sleep tonight if this door were not locked. I went down the stairs and returned to the house.

Cerberus was wolfing down a bowl of dog crunchies. It made a noise like cartilage being torn, bones splintering.

There were blackout curtains at each of the portlights. Martina closed them at night; she didn't like the thought of someone prowling the reef, seeing but unseen. I shut all of the portholes, drew the curtains.

Of course, there were no guns in the place. Plenty of knives, though. A speargun. A big dog that indiscriminately loved all humanity.

Martina was cleaning shrimp and slicing vegetables. A pot of rice was simmering on a burner.

"You like curry, don't you?" she asked.

"Are you kidding? I'm so hungry I could eat . . . curry."

"Open a bottle of wine, will you?"

I put a bottle of dry white wine from an obscure vintner in an obscure California county in an ice bucket, spread a cloth over the table, put down plates and utensils, and lit some candles.

"Is anything wrong?" Martina asked.

"What? With whom?"

She pointed a knife at me.

"Do I act like something's wrong?"

"Yes. You become very casual and relaxed and droll when there's something wrong."

"You mean I act like there's nothing wrong when there's something wrong, and vice versa."

She went back to cooking.

Ahriman, naturally, had been enraged by our late-night raid. We had seized the money, endangered his wife and son, abused Charles and the servants, burned down his house. Leroy Karpe had been the first to pay. I had no doubt that he would try to kill me whenever he had the chance, Petrie too, and maybe Susan as well, but I doubted that he would attempt it tonight, during the storm. This place was like a fortress. Tom Petrie was the next target. He had the money. At the same time I knew it wasn't fair to Martina to remain silent; she shared the risk while with me.

I told her a few lies and half lies while we ate. Explaining the entire Ahriman–Falconer affair would take all night, with each fact generating a volley of questions. I could tell her the entire story later. And so I told her that the police had warned me that Gary Tolliver was in the area and vowing revenge.

"You remember," I said. "He's the one I had a fight with, the one who burglarized my place and threatened to kill me. He'll soon be dead or in jail, but in the meantime . . ."

Martina was only mildly concerned. "Listen," she said.

We listened to the wind howling along the reef and thumping against the building, the thunder of big surf coming ashore at the breakwater, and the steady pounding of small waves assaulting the windward side of the reef.

"But, baby," she said, "you are going to extricate yourself from all these mad adventures, aren't you?"

"I'm returning to school Monday night. Torts class. Incidentally, this is a superb curry. You ought to open a restaurant."

"Chez Karras?" she asked. "Maison du Martina?"

"The Lighthouse Café. Dine in or take out."

After coffee I got up to open the curtains and portlights. Cerberus, his snout on his front paws, warily watched me, perhaps thinking, *Is this caninephobe going to throw me outside?* Martina was waiting for me in bed. I turned off the lights.

We made love to a discordant symphony of breaking surf and driving rain and thunder that seemed to shake the house and tower. Trembling flashes of lightning glowed through the line of portholes.

Afterward, Martina said, "That was . . . operatic."

"Thank you," I said.

# Thirty-Eight

Iawakened at false dawn. It was still raining, but the wind had diminished and the cracking of the surf sounded less violent. Lorraine was taking her mischief north. I pulled on a pair of shorts, stepped into old canvas sneakers without laces, and walked out into the main room. Cerberus was sitting in front of the door, scratching it with a paw while looking at me over his shoulder. He was lighthouse-trained.

"Got to pee, Cerb?" I said.

He whined and scratched at the door. Cerberus was just smart enough to know how to eat and sleep and eliminate his wastes and smell crotches.

I went to a porthole. Misty predawn light, slanting rain, heavy air, a salt–iodine–algae smell.

I decided to go out there, leave the fortress, confront the demon. Ahriman, in my imagination, had become more demon than man. He had assumed an independent existence in my mind; it was occupied territory now. I couldn't allow that. He was surely not out on the reef this morning, but in my mind he was, as he would be *out there* (as Gary Tolliver had been) when I was in my office or walking down the street or dancing with Martina. It was like a child's dread: You knew absolutely that no monster was under your bed, in the closet, behind the door, and yet . . .

I got my door keys, a sharp chef's knife, which I stuck in my belt, and the speargun. I fitted a spear into the groove, locked it, and pulled back the powerful rubber ring. Cocked. The spear was a milled aluminum shaft with a wicked barbed point. It did not give me a sense of security.

Cerberus squeezed out the door ahead of me and raced to the north side of the reef. I stood in the doorway for a while, looking around. The rain was steady. The wind had dropped to about twenty-five knots, a little more in the gusts. Big surf still thundered against the breakwater, but the bay had settled down a bit.

I locked the door, walked a few yards, and concealed my keys beneath a slab of rock. It was not a good idea to carry them. Keys could be taken from your body. This way, if something did happen to me, Ahriman could not enter the lighthouse, reach Martina, if she were as cautious as usual. But of course he wasn't here except in my mind: He was pursuing Petrie, who had the money, or he was holed up somewhere, waiting out the storm, preparing for his next move—his next murder. And yet . . .

The rock gleamed black in the rain and was greasy underfoot. There were puddles in every depression. Half a dozen gulls, flushed by Cerberus, whirled overhead and flew off toward the east. I could see a dim sprinkle of town lights through the misty gray, but there was not yet enough ambient light for the buildings to emerge.

There were only a few places where a man could hide: behind the lighthouse complex, among the jumble of stone blocks at both the north and south ends of the reef, down at the dock. But Ahriman was not a man to hide—he acted.

I circled the lighthouse. The bay waters on the windward side were choppy, white-capped, and seething around the fringes of the reef. Cerberus was lying among the pile of rocks, breathing hard and airing out his tongue.

The wind-blown pellets of rain were cold and stinging on my bare legs and torso. I walked north. The footing was very slippery, and I paused a moment to kick off my sneakers. A pair of pelicans, like prehistoric creatures in the mist, flew overhead, not making much progress against the wind. Petrie had once told me that pelicans were not aerodynamically sound and therefore incapable of flight.

He might have been dozing. He was just a few yards away, sitting among the mound of tumbled stone blocks. I had been climbing the small incline, careful of my footing, when the spectral Raven Ahriman of my imagination and the actual Raven Ahriman combined. He opened his eyes.

"Be careful of that harpoon, mate," he said, grinning up at me. He was shivering. Evidently he had been out in the storm for many hours. He was trembling, and his gun wavered, but I didn't think he could miss at that distance.

"Good to see you, friend," he said. "I've been waiting."

There was a three-inch gash on the bulge of forehead just above his left temple. His hair was clotted with blood, and blood trickled between the raw lips of the wound, was diluted by rain, and washed down his cheek and jaw. He had received a terrible blow, one that, an inch lower, would have crushed the thin, brittle temple bone.

"How did you get the cut?" I asked.

"Leroy. He hit me with a wrench."

He had removed the sandal on his right foot. The ankle

was swollen, as big and smooth as a grapefruit, and darkly bruised. It was either broken or very badly sprained.

"Leroy did that too?"

"I fell. Wasn't on the fucking island five minutes when I slipped and busted it. Enough questions. Sit down."

I sat on one of the blocks, resting the speargun across my thighs, pointed away from him. We sat a few yards apart in the stinging cold rain.

He seemed to be having difficulty with his vision. Often he squeezed his eyes shut for an instant and then opened them wide.

"You need medical care, Ahriman," I said.

His lips were bluish and his skin had a sickly gray-white pallor and a coarse texture like oatmeal. Now and then he shook uncontrollably. He tightly gritted his teeth with each small seizure. Ahriman was concussed and hypothermic and had a fractured or badly sprained ankle and probably a fever. Things escalated. One thing led to another. The concussion seriously affected your judgment and physical control. You went out to the reef, seeking revenge, and slipped on the wet rock and injured your ankle; then you were immobilized and forced to remain exposed to the wind and cold rain for hours.

"Why didn't you simply shoot Leroy?"

"I wanted him to pay. I beat him to death with my fists. I wanted him to know. I wanted him to suffer."

"He's not quite dead, the last I heard," I said.

He held the gun casually, resting on his thigh. It was a nickel-plated revolver, probably a .38, with a four-inch barrel. He wore jeans and a bloody khaki shirt that clung to his skin and was soaked to near-transparency. His hair was pulled back into the long braid. He hadn't shaved for three or four days.

"Listen to me," he said. "No more bullshit. We're going into the lighthouse."

"Your ankle?"

"I can walk on it if I have to. Listen. We're going into the lighthouse. You'll lead the way. Slowly. Hear? You will not try to run. I can shoot. Do you hear me?"

I nodded.

"By God, you'd better obey. We will go together to the lighthouse. Then you will go get Charles. Charles will come and set the fracture and stitch up the cut and take care of me until I can get around."

"Where is Charles?"

"At a motel, the Sans Souci."

The Sans Souci—*without a care*—was a crumbling, stuccoed motel out on Highway 41.

"You'll move me into the lighthouse. Your girl will be my hostage. I won't hurt her if you obey. You'll go to Charles, get whatever medical supplies he needs, and come back here. Charles will help me."

He was not so much instructing me as he was trying to convince himself that his plan was logical, it could work, he would, in time, with Charles's care, recuperate and once again be the strong, the indomitable Raven Ahriman.

"We can work it out," I said.

"Don't humor me, you son of a bitch."

Ahriman would surely pass out while trying to walk. He looked as though he might lose consciousness at any moment. He could not control me, control the gun, control his pain, during the time required to move across the reef and into the house.

"All right," I said. "I'll get Charles, bring him back here. He can set the break, splint it, put on a cast, whatever. You'll rest here a week, two weeks. And . . . ?"

And then he would kill Martina and me, grit his teeth, and on crutches go off to kill Petrie and take back the money.

It was still raining hard. I was chilled and yet I had been outside for no more than twenty minutes. Surf cracked like pistol shots out at the breakwater.

His gaze was empty. He was unable to think sequentially. His words were slurred, he sounded drunk, and there was a persistent palsy in his left hand.

"Karpe handcuffed her and sprayed her with Mace."

"Your wife? Mirium?"

Petrie and I had been in the house when Karpe had locked the three of them—Charles, Mirium, and her baby—in the shed with the servants. Leroy must have handcuffed and Maced her in retaliation for Ahriman's treatment of Susan.

"I'm sorry about that," I said. "I didn't know."

His eyes closed, his head tilted to one side, and he passed out for a moment, maybe long enough for me to swing up the speargun and shoot, but I hesitated, and he quickly snapped awake.

"Toss your gun away," I said. "I'll help you." Like hell.

"The baby got some in his eyes. Mace."

He passed out again, this time for four or five seconds, long enough for me to kill him, but I was sure that this time he would not regain consciousness. Then he stiffened and opened his eyes.

"Is she all right? Susan Falconer?"

"No. She isn't all right."

"Too late," he said, "too late to learn regret," and he either grinned at me or another tremor caused him to lock his teeth together in a savage grimace.

"You need medical care, Raven, and soon."

"I won't go back to prison. No. Never. *Never.*"

"We can work it out."

"My boy. You saw my boy?"

"A fine boy."

"Alexander. He's got a grip like an eagle. He can hang three, four minutes from my fingers."

"Strong. I can see both you and Mirium in the boy."

He was faint, again close to losing consciousness, but then he seemed to gather his strength, marshal his rage.

He said, "The money—fair enough. But you burned my house. You humiliated my wife. You put my wife and son at risk. You can't do that. No, by God, that can't be done."

Raven Ahriman—convict, smuggler of human cargo, kidnapper, rapist, and murderer—was choking with fury because we had not shown a decent respect for his family and friend and servants and property.

The rain blew almost horizontally in a gust of wind. The sun was rising now or soon would rise. We would not see it, not in the heavy cloud cover and fog and slanting silver rain.

I wanted him to think about something else, anything else. "Were you surprised that we were able to sail the *Mako* to port?"

He slowly rose. His broken right ankle prevented him from standing fully erect. He crouched a little, with his left knee bent, his left leg supporting his weight. His face twisted with the pain.

"As good a time as any," he said. "As good a place."

I understood. He had seen the futility. He had no future, he had quit, and he intended to kill me and then himself, and I was swinging up the speargun—too late—when Cerberus bounded up onto the pile of stone blocks. Ahriman half turned, and the dog, one hundred twenty pounds of slavering good cheer, hurled his body against Ahriman in greeting. The gun discharged. Cerberus, terrified by the report, bounded aside and scrabbled away over the rocks at the same instant I released the spear. My quickened perceptions had the effect of slowing time. The aluminum shaft appeared to very slowly complete a solid, faintly glowing line through space, connecting me to Raven Ahriman. There was a sound like a baseball hitting a catcher's mitt.

I had aimed for the center of his chest, a heart–lung shot, but the spear flew low and struck him a couple of inches above his belt buckle. There was that sound, and he dropped the revolver. He did not fall. He was strong even now, Raven Ahriman, and he clutched the spear shaft with both hands. Perhaps his reaction was instinctive, like the fox that chews off a foot to escape a trap or the animal that savagely bites at its wound. Ahriman tried to extract the spear. He twisted the shaft and pulled. He groaned, then made a keening noise as the barbs tore his guts. Maybe he was deliberately causing himself this agony, this further injury, in order to speed up dying. Maybe it was simple rage. He half sat and half fell back on the rocks. Blood rapidly seeped through the fabric of his shirt.

Cerberus, out of sight behind the rock pile, bayed like a foghorn. Ahriman was still alive. I approached. He looked into my eyes but I doubt he saw me; his gaze focused inward as he concentrated on the task of dying, of reconciling himself to the void. Then he did see me for an instant, just as death embraced him, and his lips peeled back in that defiant Ahriman grin, and he said, "Fuck . . ." but he didn't have the time and strength to finish with . . . *you*.

The spear had penetrated deeply, maybe to the spine. I left it there. It could not be removed without tearing out his guts. Rain diluted the blood on the rock and carried it away in tiny rivulets. I picked up his revolver.

Light was seeping across the eastern sky, though the sun remained concealed behind heavy cloud cover. The fog was starting to lift.

Cerberus was afraid of me; he stayed his distance while I walked down to the quay. A boat was tied up behind *Puck*. I recognized it from the marina: *Two-Timer*, a fast, open twenty-footer with a big stern-drive engine. The young couple who owned it used it mostly for waterskiing or mindlessly racing around the bay. I returned to the plateau.

Death was molding a new expression on Ahriman's face. There was a slackness now. His half-lidded eyes were gluey. The flesh around his mouth and eyes was bluish, bruised-looking. I could see skull bone between the lips of the wound above his temple.

I studied the corpse of Raven Ahriman/Alexander Lermontev. He was big-boned, slabbed with muscle. I estimated his weight at around two hundred forty pounds. A big man, a heavy man, but adrenaline was still pumping through me. I knelt, wrestled with his dead weight, got him into position for a fireman's lift, and managed—my knee joints and ligaments popping from the strain—to stand erect. It was difficult picking my way through the tumbled blocks. Cerberus, curious now, came over for a closer look. He crept up to sniff the corpse when I dropped it on the slab of reef. The smell of blood alarmed him, and he backed away, his ruff bristling.

It was simplest to drag Ahriman across the reef by his thick rope of hair. That braid finally served a purpose other than vain decoration. I hauled him over the reef and down the steps to the dock, then dumped him into the ski boat. Cerberus watched, prancing, from the quay as I untied the bow and stern lines. He behaved like a dog who fears that he is going to miss some guilty fun. I started the engines, shifted into reverse, and backed out to where there was room to maneuver.

*Two-Timer* had been designed to aquaplane at speed, and she leaped from wave to wave across the bay toward the opening in the breakwater.

Surf was breaking at the harbor's mouth. The Lorraine-spawned seas were still big, and they turned concave and collapsed into white avalanches when arriving at the outside sandbars. Getting out through the surf and returning the same way would be the only serious difficulty. But I had speed, lots of speed, and maneuverability.

A few times the boat bucked completely free of the water, propeller screaming, and once a hissing graybeard nearly swamped the boat, but I was able to hit the throttle and ascend the breaker at a diagonal.

After a few hundred yards I was free of the surf, free from collapsing seas. The water deepened to ninety feet a mile off the breakwater. I went out three miles and shifted the engine to neutral. *Two-Timer* rode the big swells smoothly. There was a package of cigarettes and a butane lighter in a dashboard compartment. I lit a cigarette, leaned back in the driver's seat, and tried to relax. We had sifted Peter's ashes and bone splinters into the water in this general area. He and Ahriman would be neighbors.

The light had not increased much. Visibility remained poor, although I could glimpse some buildings along the boulevard when the boat poised atop a swell.

The boat carried a Danforth-type anchor secured to thirty feet of chain and another hundred feet of nylon rope. I wrapped the chain and rope around and around the corpse and tied it with a lumpy tangle of knots. Then it was only a matter of wrestling Ahriman, anchor, chain, and rope over the side without capsizing the boat.

He lingered on the surface for a moment. Raven Ahriman floated on his back, the spear rising straight up out of his belly, and then the attached weight snatched him away. I watched him sink down through the gray-green layers. A string of tiny bubbles spiraled from his nostrils. And then he lost color, lost contour, and he was gone. The spear flashed, reflected the last of the penetrating light, and then it too vanished.

The anchor flukes would dig into the bottom so that even if the gases of decomposition lifted the corpse and chain, it could not float free or move laterally.

It was easier entering the bay than leaving it. I got in behind a big swell and, maintaining the same speed, followed it in to where it finally broke, and then I accelerated through the eruptions of surf.

Cerberus was waiting for me at the quay. I switched off the engine while twenty yards away and looked around to make sure that nothing of Ahriman's or mine remained aboard. The boat would eventually wash up somewhere around the bay's perimeter. Stolen, set adrift by the storm—it didn't matter. There was some blood in the bottom, but all of the water taken aboard had diluted it to near invisibility. I was bloody too, from carrying the corpse; it all was washed away as I swam to the dock.

Cerberus barked at me and tried to snarl—a noise like water spinning down a faulty drain. He followed me to the plateau, where I retrieved the speargun and boat hook. I had dropped Raven's gun into the sea.

"Come on, Cerb, you son of a bitch," I said, knowing that, for a dog, such a sentence was regarded as factual and evidence of affection.

• • •

Martina was awakened by the smell of coffee. She came out tousle-haired and sleepy-eyed.

"Huh," she said.

"Huh yourself."

She poured a cup of coffee, sipped it, made a face, and placed the cup on its saucer.

"You're trembling," she said.

"I've been outside. That rain is cold."

"See any bogeymen?"

"Just a bogey dog."

"Huh," she said.

"Marty, I think I'd like to buy Cerb a present."

"I thought you didn't like him."

"He's not so bad. I taught him to bark this morning. Tomorrow I may teach him to wag his tail."

I couldn't tell Martina about Ahriman now. I had killed a man on her little island, disposed of his corpse a few miles offshore. If she knew about that, and the police came for me, she might be regarded as an accomplice, or at least culpable of obstruction of justice. There were a lot of loose ends that led to me and Petrie. Charles, now in a Bell Harbor motel. The investigation of the attack on Leroy Karpe. The murders of the two girls and the cameraman down in the keys. Our association with Peter Falconer and Ahriman in the Bahamas, Mexico, Honduras, the raid in French Guiana. And I worried about the chance that a bird-watcher, amateur astronomer, or ordinary voyeur had been observing the reef and the sea outside early this morning.

"What kind of present?" Martina asked.

"Well, since canines are not naturally vegetarian, I thought I'd buy him a five-pound sirloin steak. Bone in."

"Okay. But you'll have to cook it first. I won't have my Cerberus eating raw flesh."

# Thirty-Nine

A week later I was Petrie's guest at the Bell Harbor Racquet Club. Martina had come along and was sitting with a few others in nearby bleachers. Tom, always looking for an edge, had reserved a clay court. I didn't have the right shoes for clay, and that slow surface was not good for my serve-and-volley game. But this was my day. I played a level higher than my usual standard: I got most of my first serves in, well placed, and I managed to volley away many of Petrie's returns. I won the first set 6–4. We went to the bench for a breather.

"I can't concentrate," he said. "I'm worried about Susan."

I faked sympathy. He was playing well. It was just that I was playing better.

"Is she still in New York?"

"Yeah, but thinking about going to Europe. She sent me a check for all my expenses and fees."

"Did you tear it up?"

He gave me one of his long, pitying Petrie gazes, the kind that informed a court witness or an opposing attorney that he was retarded, perhaps deranged, but that he, Thomas Petrie, would not condemn a man simply because he happened to be the victim of an unfortunate genetic defect.

"Do you think that you and Susan will get together?"

"It doesn't look good. I don't think she wants anything to do, ever, with the people who were involved in the recent Falconer epic, including me. Including herself, I think."

"What about the estate?"

"There'll be a long and nasty court fight. It will take years to settle."

"Are you representing Susan?"

"She needs a big firm that specializes in civil law, and that's what she's hired." He stood up. "Let's go. My serve."

"My serve, Tom. You served the last game of the set."

An atmospheric high had moved in from the north and broken the heat wave. Today was bright and relatively cool, about seventy degrees, and the wind was just strong enough to evaporate our sweat without much affecting the flight of the tennis ball.

Petrie worked hard and made a few dubious line calls, but I again beat him 6–4. We went to the bench to towel off and drink from a jug of poisonously hued sports beverage.

He said, "You wouldn't stand a chance if I hadn't torn up my shoulder aboard *Mako*."

This was the first I had heard of an injured shoulder. It hadn't been evident on the court. Tom wanted badly to win, whether on the tennis courts or in the judicial courts or the court of public opinion or when courting a woman like Susan. He had taken a beating in most venues lately.

"You mentioned you had seen Charles," I said.

"I went to the Sans Souci out on 41. The original roach motel. He cried, he actually cried when I told him that Ahriman was dead. Charles was desolate. He perked up a bit when I gave him two thousand cash and told him to get out of town. Well, guess what—he wanted a lot more."

"Sure he did."

"I hit him. It was unpleasant for both of us. I was ashamed. Charles was ashamed for me. We had a drink and he decided that it was his duty to go down to Guiana and tell Mirium and the *Mako*'s crew about Raven's death."

"He'll show up one of these days."

"Right. Charles is like gum on your shoe sole." Petrie screwed the lid on his jar of chartreuse sugar water and stood up. "Your luck is holding. First you have the phenomenal luck to go up against Raven Ahriman and survive. Granted, he was crippled, and you were saved by a mutt that Martina not long ago rescued from execution in the doggy gas chamber, but still . . . And now all your net-cords and mishits are falling in. One more set. My serve."

"My serve, Tom."

Petrie was demoralized, and I beat him 6–1 in the third set.

He cursed me, quickly apologized, and said, "Do you think I'm a bad loser?"

"Sure, Tom. But you're a bad winner too."

"Worse than Doc Robles?"

"No, but the Doc can jump-start a failed heart."

Petrie, Martina, and I went to a table in the club's patio restaurant. He ordered two bottles of Taittinger champagne and a pitcher of freshly squeezed orange juice, asked for menus, then went off to the locker room.

"Don't you think," Martina said, "that you should have let Tom win one of the sets?"

"What?"

"You won the first two. You should have allowed him to win the third."

"I'll lose next time," I said. I probably would.

I had informed Petrie of the events at the lighthouse reef and my disposal of Ahriman's corpse, and he, always the lawyer, advised me not to confide details of any possible criminal activity to Martina. But I intended to tell her the entire story when the time was right, when it was safe, over. The passage of time might blur the ugliness a little. And I thought it important that she maintain her sense of security and independence. She was happy now because she believed that the Gary Tolliver and Peter Falconer crises had been fully resolved.

She said, "Let's give a party at the lighthouse next weekend, invite our friends."

"I don't know about your friends, but all my friends are carnivores."

"You can barbecue a buffalo or something for the carnivores."

Petrie returned to the table. He had changed into slacks and a blue-striped shirt open at the neck. He half filled our glasses with wine and topped them off with pulpy orange juice.

"We're giving a party next weekend," Martina said. "Will you be there?"

"With rings on my fingers and bells on my toes. It will give me the opportunity to steal you away from this bum."

We ordered brunch, and then Martina went off to chat with friends at a distant table.

"I saw Craig Christensen in the locker room," Petrie said.

"And what did our noble SA have to tell you?"

"Well, he *didn't* say a body has washed up."

"Ahriman is down," I said quietly, "and he'll stay down."

"They're seriously investigating the assault on our Leroy."

"Sure they are."

"Leroy's associated with me. With you now, and Susan."

"I know."

"But what the hell, we were both at the theater when Leroy was beaten. And all of the other stuff—to put everything together they'd need cooperation from police in the Bahamas, Mexico, Honduras, French Guiana, and Florida. What are the odds against that?"

"Case closed," I said skeptically.

Our table was set well apart from the others, in the right angle of two brick walls covered with bougainvillea vines, but even Petrie kept his voice soft and, like a convict in an old prison movie, barely moved his lips on crucial words and phrases.

He said, "Did you carefully think it through before you took Ahriman's corpse out to sea and deep-sixed it?"

"Not really. Was it a bad idea?"

"Look," he said, "it isn't illegal to pay a ransom. We paid for Peter Falconer and got what was left of him. *Caveat emptor*. It *is* illegal to burn down a house and terrorize the inhabitants while obtaining a refund, but I don't think we'll be hearing from French Guiana. It isn't illegal to kill a man in self-defense. It *is* illegal to clandestinely dispose of the body, but you say that it will never be recovered. Also, you found the corpses down in the Mosquito Keys and you—we— became involved but not implicated. It's a tangled mess, a Gordian knot. They'll never be able to unravel it. So?"

"So I'll just have to sweat it out."

"Nah. You're forgetting that I'm the best criminal-defense lawyer in the state of Florida, maybe the country. Although," he added with a sly, tilted, up-from-under-the-brows look, "you can't afford my fees."

Martina returned and, in a stage voice, cried, "Darlings, it's going to be a lovely party." *Party* was pronounced *potty*.

Petrie refilled our glasses with equal mixtures of champagne and orange juice. He lifted his glass. "To Leroy," he said.

"Who's Leroy?" Martina asked.

"A hero."

"Is he the one . . . in the newspapers . . . ?"

"Yes. He regained consciousness this morning."

"Hero. That sounds like Petrie irony," Martina said. "Even so . . ."

We drank deeply to Leroy Karpe, hero.

Petrie refilled our glasses again. "And now let's drink to the eternal damnation of the bird."

"I'm not sure about eternal damnation," Martina said. "Who is this bird?"

"The Raven."

"Proceed without me, gentlemen."

Tom and I clinked glasses.

"To the Raven," I said. "Nevermore."

Petrie dashed his empty glass on the flagstones. I hesitated a moment, thought what the hell, and threw my glass down. Martina was embarrassed. This was the Bell Harbor Racquet Club. It was one of those prolonged moments of disapproving silence and frozen faces. And then Martina, choosing solidarity, finished her drink and shattered the glass on the stones.

She looked at Petrie and me for approval.

We approved.

Ron Faust has played professional baseball
and has worked for newspapers in Colorado Springs,
San Diego and Key West.
For several years he resided in Mexico.
He currently lives in Wisconsin.

If you enjoyed

# Dead Men Rise Up Never

turn the page for an exciting preview of
Ron Faust's new Dan Shaw novel,

# Coral Bones, Pearl Eyes

coming from Dell in October 2004

# Coral Bones, Pearl Eyes

## On Sale September 28, 2004

We were slowed by the clotted traffic on highway 54 outside
Bell Harbor, an area known as the Death Zone because of
the frequent automobile accidents. We passed a three mile-
long strip of fast food restaurants and gas stations and used
car lots and sex shops and tourist hustles and motels. You
could rent a room, fetch a pizza, obtain an erotic massage,
buy a handgun, hold up a liquor store, get drunk, get laid,
relaid and parlayed, shoot the punk who cut you off in traffic, and do all of that without putting more than a couple
miles on your car's odometer.

Ahead I saw the scrolled neons of the Motel Sans Souci.
That was the place where Ahriman and Charles had stayed
when they came north to kill us—me, Tom Petrie, and a
man named Leroy Karpe. The Sans Souci was a decrepit di-
nosaur among the newer chain motels, and cheap, a place of
peeling stucco and sheet metal roof patches and a parking
lot that sparkled with broken glass. It advertised accom-
modations by the day, week, month; rooms, kitchenettes,
housekeeping units; senior rates, free coffee and donuts, cable TV.

"You think . . . ?" Petrie said.

"Sure. He wants to be found."

Petrie turned the Porsche into the asphalt parking lot and

halted among a cluster of the old, shock-sprung, smoking Detroit iron favored by that category of the poor which favored big engines and springy rides.

I went into the office and talked to a sour retiree who resentfully informed me that, yes, a Charles Sinclair was registered in Suite 268, second floor corner.

I stepped outside, gestured to Petrie, and together we went up the warped wooden stairs and down a sagging walkway to the last unit, 268. Moth-eaten curtains were drawn across dirty louvered windows. A MAID SERVICE card hung from the door knob. It would read DO NOT DISTURB on the reverse side. I knocked on the door.

"I was here, this same unit, back in September," Petrie said. "I punched Charles."

"I remember. You told me."

"I gave him twenty-five hundred dollars to get out of town."

"I know, Tom. But he's back."

I was about to knock again when the door opened and Charles, peering through the screened door, smiled out at us.

"I expected you sooner," he said in a tone of mild reproach. "Have you lunched?"

"My old friend," Petrie said. "We plan to sup on your flesh, quench our thirst with your blood."

"If I had known, I would have eaten lots of garlic and marinated myself in Grand Marnier."

We went through the screened door and into a boxy living room that smelled of mildew and insecticide. The Sans Souci was the sort of place that had to be sprayed monthly for roaches, termites, fire ants, and maybe body lice. But Charles was far superior to his surroundings; he was always princely.

"How friendly of you to call," Charles said. "You're both looking fit."

"And you as well, you jolly scamp," Petrie said.

The TV, sound off, flashed with images of tanks rolling down a dusty street lined by devastated buildings. The "suite" comprised the living room, two bedrooms—doors shut—a dining alcove, and a kitchen behind a plastic curtain. Petrie went off to search for bogeymen.

"What will you have to drink?" Charles asked.

"Nothing, thanks."

A human skull and some bones—a femur, ribs, a few vertebrae—were displayed on top of the dresser. Stubby candles, set in saucers, flanked the skull, and there were plastic flowers, an incense burner, and a photograph of Raven Ahriman taped to the mirror.

Charles, observing my reaction, smiled, then stepped forward to light the four candles and a pellet of incense that smelled like burning weeds.

"There," he said. "Raven is with us."

Charles was still boyish at thirty-one or -two, slender, with pale skin and dark blond hair that he wore in a preppy style, and which always looked full of static electricity. His eyes were that near-violet that some people counterfeited with contact lenses. Long-lashed blue eyes, a candid gaze. Many had suffered because they had carelessly read innocence in that gaze.

Petrie emerged from a bedroom, halted and, with his head cocked, stared at the display.

"Hey, nice shrine, Charles," he said. "But isn't it a bit . . ."

"De trop?"

"Yeah."

"Honest emotion always appears rather vulgar, don't you think?"

"You've never had an honest emotion in your life."

"Well, I thought it might amuse you."

"Oh, and it does. Doesn't it, Shaw?"

I said, "Very campy, Charles. We're amused."

Charles was the prodigal son of a prominent and rich old Boston family that had, quite rightly, disowned and disinherited him soon after his twenty-first birthday. He was an inveterate liar and an incorrigible thief. After his expulsion he had stolen a large part of his family's collection of valuable paintings and art objects, and gone off to Santa Fe to establish himself as a dealer in fine arts. Now and then he sold an authentic painting or sculpture, but mostly he dealt in stolen works and fakes that he commissioned from an accomplished Romanian forger named Carescu. He later branched out into extortion and other crimes and misdemeanors. His luck ran out in California, and he spent two and one-half years in San Quentin, where he'd met his future partner, the violent Raven Ahriman. Charles was devious and smart, Raven violent; combined, they were the stuff of nightmares.

Charles was a psychopath and, like many intelligent psychopaths, he could be very charming, even lovable, your best friend until he thought of a way to convert your affection into cash. He was not himself violent, but he could probably watch others kill you without suffering more than mild embarrassment.

Now he said, "You *will* stay to lunch, won't you? You must. I'll warm up the food."

"I'll go with you," Petrie said, "to make sure you don't mistake the Drano for salt."

Incense smoke was spreading an acrid haze through the room. It caused instant asthma. I crushed out the fuming pellet, but left the candles burning. The skull leered at the

TV screen where a giddy bleached blonde was gesturing toward a flashing weather map. I picked up the skull. It was big, even without the jawbone, though lighter than I expected, and whiter too, abraded clean by sand and salt water. I tilted it so that I could look into the cranium from below. There were a few grains of sand inside, a patch of mossy substance. The teeth showed the wear you'd expect in a man in his mid-forties. And there were some ugly black fillings in the molars—prison dentistry. I found a hairline fracture on the ridge of bone above the left ear aperture.

Charles paraded back and forth from kitchen to dining alcove, setting the table, bringing in bowls of food, fussing. Petrie came in carrying a bottle of wine. He looked at me. I nodded: it was Raven Ahriman's skull, all right.

In the photograph, Raven Ahriman was leaning back against a ship's railing, grinning, with behind him a tumultuous, foaming sea. The grin was tough, arrogant, a challenge to the world. I derived some satisfaction in comparing the grinning man in the photo with the grinning skull.

Lunch was warmed-over Chinese takeout; sweet and sour ribs, shrimp in a spicy sauce, rice, bean paste, and cereal bowls full of vegetables.

"This is vile wine, Charles," Petrie said.

"It isn't that good," Charles said, "but it's the best that I can afford at present."

But the food wasn't bad, and I was hungry.

"How is Mirium?" Petrie asked.

Mirium had been Ahriman's wife.

"She's as well as can be expected," Charles said. "She sold Raven's trawler, so she isn't quite destitute."

"And how much of the proceeds from the boat sale did you con her out of?"

"She *loaned* me the money to come here from Guyana to petition you to provide her with financial assistance."

"You think we should establish some sort of trust or pension for the widow and her son?"

"Yes, I do. You burned down her house, you killed her husband. Aren't you both morally and ethically obliged to provide for their futures?"

Petrie laughed. "I love to hear you utter words like 'ethically' and 'morally' in your fancy accent. Say 'integrity' for me. Say 'principles.' Say 'compassionate.' "

Petrie picked up a section of tiny ribs and commenced nibbling at them in a rabbity way.

My turn. "It's amazing that you were able to find some of Raven's bones," I said. "Phenomenal luck. But now you've brought the Mackey brothers into our confidential business."

"I told them nothing."

"Nothing?"

"I told them that I was searching for the remains of my dear old father, who drowned in that vicinity when I was a lad. I had, you know, promised Mother that someday I would recover the remains and arrange a proper, a ceremonial, a respectful interment. Et cetera."

"Not smart," I said. "Those Mackeys have spent a large part of their disreputable lives salvaging things from the sea. They know those bones weren't down very long."

Petrie picked up another strip of ribs and, holding them daintily, resumed nibbling.

"Charles," I said, "how the hell did you know where I deep-sixed Ahriman's corpse?"

"He told me," Charles said, nodding toward Petrie. "The oh so brilliant lawyer told me."

Tom slowly lowered the gnawed ribs and stared at Charles. His lips were darkened by sauce and he wore a Hitlerian sauce mustache.

"He told me when he came here in September to threaten me. He said that Raven was dead and now lay on the ocean floor—words to that effect. Well, I knew that Raven had gone out to the lighthouse. That, probably, you had killed him and dumped his body at sea. Where at sea? Not far out. The weather was filthy then, remember? Eureka!"

"You're a bright guy."

"He's a smarmy little turd."

Charles smiled.

Petrie pushed his plate away, wiped his mouth with a paper napkin, and then took a sip of wine which he noisily flushed around his mouth before spitting it back in the glass.

"How much do you want?" Petrie asked.

Charles did not want much; only enough so that he and Mirium might have sufficient resources to recover from the financial reverses consequent on the burning of the house and the "murder." One hundred thousand dollars cash, plus fifty thousand per year for ten years, six hundred thousand dollars total, not excessive for a lawyer of Petrie's income and reputation. Shaw could contribute according to his lesser income. Call it restitution for our crimes, penance for our sins.

"You called this guy bright?" Petrie said to me. "He has the intellectual powers of a mollusk."

Otherwise, Charles said, he would go to the police. There were witnesses to the recovery of the skull, and no doubt other bones down there, other evidence.

He seemed without guile even as he explained the terms of his blackmail and the result—the *"denouément"*—if we failed to comply. Charles, by nature, was so lacking in anything that resembled guilt or shame that his demands sounded almost reasonable.

"Tell him, Dan."

"Tom is now going to rebut your claims."

"Go to the police," Petrie said. "They'll be delighted to see you. You're probably wanted in ten states and three countries. And the Mackey boys, that righteous pair, will make reliable witnesses. You've got some bones. What do they demonstrate? A man is dead. Cause of death? No way to determine that. Identification? No chance of an ID if we walk out of here with that skull. Connection between Ahriman, me, and Shaw. Well, yeah, the Peter Falconer affair. The cops know some of that already. But you, Charles, you scabby entrepreneur, you were complicit in those murders down in the Keys. Go to the cops. I'll drive you there now—a sporty last ride before the iron slams shut."

Charles listened politely to Petrie's torrent of legal logic and personal insult. He raised his eyebrows. He smiled boyishly. Now and then he brushed a floppy wing of hair away from his candid blue eyes. A vague air of ill health lent Charles's boyishness a certain pathos. So young, so charming, so tragic . . .

"Ten thousand dollars," he said. "Enough for me to pay my bill here and leave town."

"Jesus," Petrie said, "I'm really disappointed in you, son. I've always had high regard for your laissez faire larceny, your mythomaniacal lying, your insouciant brand of psychopathy. But you've lost your touch. You reek of doubt. A confidence man who's lost his confidence is just another petty criminal doomed to starvation or spine-warping toil in the prison laundry."

"Five thousand dollars," Charles said. "Two thousand. Don't make me travel by bus."

"But wait," Petrie said. "Inspiration strikes, the Muse whispers. I might, I might just have a job for you. Don't throw up, it isn't anything legitimate. I want you to hang around for a few days. I'll send someone over this afternoon with a little money, enough so you can stay here in roachy poverty or slither out of town. What do you say?"

"The Mackeys know I'm staying in this place. I'm rather afraid of them."

"I'll move you to a different dump."

"I need clothing. Nearly everything I own was lost in the fire."

"You shall be decently shod and attired."

"Very well, then. I am at your service."

Charles dipped his hand into a bowl, removed three fortune cookies, kept one and gave the others to me and Tom.

The cookies were brown-tan, folded like closed flower buds, and had the brittle texture—and probably the taste—of a ceramic material. I cracked mine open with a table knife and unrolled the strip. I read aloud:

"Eastward, your fortune."

Petrie read his: "Rely on your friends."

Charles frowned at his strip, and said, "Both the swan and the swan's reflection are illusions."

"That's so true," Petrie said.

Charles provided a paper shopping bag to contain the skull and bones. He did not appear disturbed to see his evidence, the remains of his good friend and mentor, Raven Ahriman, carried out of the motel unit like garbage. He stood on the walkway, looking down, as Petrie backed the Porsche out of its parking slot. His smile was cryptic; his wave was a languid lift of his right hand, palm out, as if he were swearing an oath.

The traffic had thinned. Petrie accelerated, and ran a traffic light that turned from amber to red as we reached the intersection. Horns blared, a pedestrian leaped back to the curb.

"What's this about a job?" I said.

"I believe in rehabilitation, in salvation. We must do our best to lead errant souls back into the fold. We must forgive, even though we can never forget."

"Tom, you've got the bones, now you dispose of them. It's your turn. Don't expect me to walk off with that shopping bag."

"Not to worry," he said.


I got back to my office at four-thirty and immediately went to the safe where I kept a bottle of scotch. If I didn't lock it away, Candace would now and then come in during my absence and take a nip, which was all right except that she tried to conceal her theft by maintaining the fluid level with water from the bathroom tap. The bottle was inside the safe, along with some documents and the brown paper bag containing Raven Ahriman's skull and bones. Petrie, the son of a bitch, had given me the safe half a year before, and knew the combination, and today he had left the county jail before me. But at least his paralegal had completed my work and delivered it to the bank's lawyers. I packed the skull and bones in a small nylon duffel that I used for an overnight bag.

Usually I stayed in my Bell Harbor apartment during the week, but Martina was upset, preferred to have company, and so at sunset we went out to the lighthouse in her little cabin cruiser, *Puck*.

Cerberus waited up on the landing at the top of the steps that lead onto the reef: he was wet from the afternoon shower, his fur was spikey, and he barked furiously to let us know that he was on the job, and then he raced down the steps and shook all of the water out of his fur, misting the air and wetting both of us, and afterward he lowered his head in fake shame.

Martina was silent as she prepared a light meal. I tried to make conversation, but she was distracted, somewhere else in time, and she replied to my small talk mostly in non sequiturs. She did not eat much. Midway through the meal she got up, said, "Sorry," and walked down the cavelike hallway to her studio.

I cleaned the table, washed the plates and utensils, and then went out onto the reef. Cerberus was waiting for me.

"Where's your ball?"

He was a big dumb brute, but he had learned what a ball was, and he raced off to the south end of the reef, ran in circles, found the tooth-gnawed rubber ball and returned in triumph. I had to wrestle with him before he relaxed his jaws. "You're a dog," I said. "A dawg!" He watched me and the ball with a wall-eyed canine paranoia. "You're a cat!" I threw the ball toward the far end of the reef, and he galloped away. The game was repeated a dozen times. He was too dim for boredom. Each time I had to fight him for the saliva-slimed ball.

Martina was sitting at the table with a glass of wine when I returned to the lighthouse.

"His saliva," I said, washing my hands at the kitchen sink, "congeals into a jellied slime. It's horrible."

Cerberus had found my duffel in the corner and was drooling over it. The bones.

"The dog wants his dinner," I said.

"Well, feed the dog, then."

"Are you all right, Martina?"

"I'm exhausted."

"Do you want to take a quick swim?"

"Not tonight."

"Okay. Then let's go to bed and . . . and . . . what, Martina?"

"Sleep," she said.


I awakened early and, without disturbing Martina, pulled on swimming shorts and went into the central living area. Cerberus, nose on his paws, waited from his rug near the door. "Devil dog," I whispered. Flattered, he thumped his tail against the floor, got up and watched me as I collected the duffel, diving mask, fins and snorkel, and then followed me out onto the reef.

It was a warm, swampy morning, more like July than early June. Light was refracted by the moisture-saturated air, blurring images and doubling the outline of buildings along the town esplanade. A bell buoy at the entrance to the breakwater chimed irregularly in the surging tide, sounding like Morse. I listened, identified a pair of dots, "I"; a pause and then a dot and a dash, "A"; another pause, two dashes, "M"; and then the chiming Morse degenerated into a meaningless alphabetical babble. Cerberus jogged off to hunt for lizards.

I wanted to conceal Ahriman's bones until I had an opportunity to rebury them at sea. There were plenty of hiding places on the reef, niches and angular hollows among the tumbled stone blocks at both the north and south ends; but no place would long remain safe from the dog's snooping. He'd probably drag the bones to the lighthouse door, where he sometimes left tiny lizard carcasses—limp creatures with still a touch of iridescence in their skins—and once he had deposited a bloody seagull that Martina insisted had died of natural causes. She liked to think of Cerberus as nonviolent.

We usually swam at the south end of the island, where a high slab of rock served as a diving platform, and ledges above and beneath the water made egress easy. North, then.

I put on my mask and fins, weighted the duffel with some rocks, tossed it into the water and then followed it down. The water was cool, sharp with salt, and a little murky from the tidal currents. Beards of moss streamed away from the rock wall. The rock itself was black, though speckled with red and yellow accretions, and bright rings of light were reflected off the sandy bottom fifteen feet below. Panicky small fish flashed silver as they darted away. A red snapper—future menu item—slowly finned off into the fringe of weeds farther out. There were many crevices and pockets in the rock, hiding places for small octopuses and eels, but nothing big enough to hold the duffel until I reached the bottom where an overhanging ledge of reef formed little caves. I jammed the duffel deep into the largest of the recesses, turned, and swam back to the surface.

Cerberus, waiting for me, whined and groveled. The sea was no fit place for man or dog. I had brought along a cigarette and butane lighter, and I smoked it slowly, with guilty pleasure.

Martina was awake, cranky, and brewing coffee when I returned to the lighthouse. I explained that I had an appointment and must hurry: tee time was at ten sharp.

"Tea time? You're going to have *tea*?"